SHADOWS

OF THE

MIND

* * * * * *

BOOK ONE

* * * * * *

D.W. Neuman

ALSO BY D.W. NEUMAN

FICTION

Frame of Mind

<u>Shadow Series</u>
Shadows of the Mind – Book One
Shadows of the Soul – Book Two
Shadows of the Service – Book Three
Shadows of the Past – Book Four
Shadows of the Heart – Book Five
Shadows of the Sand – Book Six
Shadows of the Serpent – Book Seven
Shadows of the Future – Book Eight
Shadows of the Children – Book Nine
Shadows of the Ever-After – Book Ten

ISBN (978-0-9839446-0-7)

Lisa, you literally kept this dream alive
for two decades.
Thank you so much for all your
editing and support.

Connie, my new wife and love of my life;
thank you for giving me the opportunity to
shine.

And Brenda, thank you for believing in
me.

The longer I live. The more I realize the impact of attitude on life.

Attitude, to me, is more important than the past, than education, than money, than circumstances, than failure, than successes, than what other people think or say or do.

It is more important than appearance, giftedness or skill.

It will make or break a company…a church…a home.

The remarkable thing is we have a choice every day regarding the attitude we will embrace for that day.

We cannot change our past.

We cannot change the fact that people will act in a certain way.

We cannot change the inevitable.

The only thing we can do is play on the one string we have, and that is attitude.

I am convinced that life is 10% what happens to me and 90% how I react to it."

-Charles Swindoll

All you really have in the end are your stories.

– Paul Anderson

1
Sat June 30, 1990 11:30 a.m.

The day had quickly warmed up as Thomas Clark pulled his 325i BMW into an open parking spot in the small community of Lake Arrowhead, CA. The lake attracted visitors from all over looking for a quick respite from the mundane drudgery of day to day life. Up here, away from the hustle and bustle of the real world, one could easily get lost in the gorgeous atmosphere. Thomas chuckled to himself. *That's why I moved up here.*

Thomas was dressed in denim shorts, a solid white t-shirt and his ever trusty Reebok sneakers. He stopped to admire the lake. It sparkled; and on some days he could swear that it had an almost eerie hold over him, as if a Siren was out there calling his name, beckoning him in to the watery depths. A few motorboats were out in the lake and the gentle sounds of children laughing and splashing could be heard in the distance.

He sloughed off the feeling and walked up the steps to the stores and shops that made Lake Arrowhead feel like a true getaway. Small mom and pop stores bracketed the wooden pier beams that creaked ever so slightly as you walked on them. They definitely reeked of an older, and perhaps even a better time. Maybe that's why people came up here, Thomas thought, to recapture the old days and share that inspiration with their children.

Thomas stopped and pulled open the door of his favorite restaurant, the Waffle House, and took off his sunglasses. He walked inside and looked around.

"Hey, Thomas, good morning."

Thomas finished his scan of the diner. "Good morning Becky. Thanks but my prey is sitting right over there," he said pointing at a man in a business suit sitting at one of the window booths.

"I'll be over in a bit," she replied as Thomas walked away.

Thomas started towards the man who was idly looking out at the lake. Just as Thomas reached him the man turned his gaze towards Thomas and said, "About time you got here. I don't know why you have me drive all the way up here every damn time. Next time we're meeting at the office."

"You always say that Nick," Thomas said while extending his right hand to shake hello.

"You bastard," replied Nick who shook his hand. "I have to say it so I can write this trip off as a business expense."

"Nick, this IS a business expense. Just because you enjoy the scenery just as much as I do doesn't mean you have to pretend you don't." Thomas grinned while he ribbed Nick.

"Yeah, yeah. Love you too. Have a seat. Glad to see you put a lot of effort in to your apparel," commenting on Thomas' extremely casual appearance.

Thomas looked shocked as he gave himself the once over. "You mean you don't like my ensemble?" The start of a grin formed at the edge of his mouth. "I'm hurt, really really hurt Nick."

"Sure you are. In any case, Thomas, save the big words for the children's books."

"Ouch. Will do. But try forgetting about your jacket and tie will ya. Roll up your sleeves a bit. It's summer for crying out loud. You have no idea how out of place you look up here."

Nick was about to retort when his face broke out in to a huge smile. "You got me," he said as he chuckled. Thomas broke into his own half laughter.

2

"It's really good to see you, Nick."

"You too, Thomas. How long has it been?"

"About four and a half months now I guess."

"I agree. So….the big question that you know I have to ask…where are you at with your new book?"

Thomas leaned back in the booth and let out a big sigh. "Right to the point, eh Nick?" Nick picked up on it right away.

"Thomas. Listen to me for a second. We have a contract, my friend, and the deadline is rapidly approaching. I love coming up here, you know that, but in all seriousness you're not making me very comfortable. Give me something; anything."

Thomas was about to answer when Becky approached the table and said, "Can I get either of you something to drink?"

"Ice tea please," Nick replied.

"And for you, Thomas?

"Just a coke please."

"Coming right up," she said as she walked away. Nick caught Thomas' eye.

"I know Nick…I know," he said as he leaned forward.

Nick interrupted. "So what is it, writer's block? After your last book the reviews were out of this world. That was over a year ago, buddy."

Becky returned and delivered their drinks. "Are you ready to order or do you need a few minutes?"

Nick swiveled his head and looked at the waitress.

"I think we need just a couple more minutes. We'll let you know. Thanks."

"No problem whatsoever," Becky replied and departed once again.

Thomas leaned back in the booth. His mood had suddenly switched from playful and energetic to subdued and tired. "Nick, I

3

don't know what to tell you. These past few months I just can't seem to get it together. I'm tired…exhausted almost. I can't concentrate."

Nick took it all in as he sipped on his ice tea. He looked back over the glistening lake water and finally brought his attention back to the table. "Hey Thomas, it's okay. All writer's experience this. Listen. Your last book children's book cleaned house. What was it called again?"

Thomas looked up and said, "The Little Brown Chair."

Nick smiled. "Good. I was just testing you. See, apparently you can concentrate." This brought a slight smile to Thomas' face.

"Bastard," Thomas said.

"What comes around goes around," Nick countered playfully. "So you know I have to ask. What's the next one that has you so brain dead?"

It was Thomas' turn to take a sip from his drink. "The tentative title is 'The Haunted Trees'."

"Jesus, Thomas. It sounds like a children's horror story. Maybe we should market it with some black crayons," Nick added as he gave his friend some shit.

"Ha ha, Nick."

"So what's the story like? Werewolves, vampires, smurfs?"

"Smurfs?"

"Are you fucking kidding me? Those damn blue devils scare the bejesus out of me. Every time my daughter has that show on I want Gargamel, or at least Azrael, to eat one of them. I can't stand them, but my kid seems to love 'em."

Thomas just stared across the table at Nick.

"What?" Nick asked.

"Azrael? You know the cat's name is Azrael?"

4

"What? Me? No. I have no idea what you're talking about. I just can't get to the damn remote when she falls asleep in my arms so the show keeps playing. I swear my daughter is torturing me," he said as he smiled.

"How's your little one doing anyway?" asked Thomas.

"Nice deflection, but I'll let you get away with it," Nick said and waggled his finger at Thomas. "Little Lisa is doing quite well thankyouverymuch. Can you believe she's twelve months old now? And thank you for the card by the way. My wife and I were both surprised you mountain folk know about the U.S. Government mailing system," he said with a tease.

"I like it up here," Thomas retorted bit too defensively.

"Whoa there, buddy. No need to get defensive. Just giving you some shit. You know, trying to keep it light and all."

"Sorry, Nick. I know you mean well. You've been one hell of an agent and a good friend over the years," said Thomas with an apologetic tone.

"Well, Susan and I worry about you Thomas. You've been living up here in the mountains for how long now?"

"Close to nine years now," Thomas answered.

"I'm just saying Thomas. Nine years is a long time. I know you have a birthday sneaking up next month." Thomas shot Nick a 'tread carefully' look. "And I know you don't like talking about it, that's not my point. My point is that you're going to be thirty-three."

"That's your point, Nick?"

"Kind of," replied Nick. "You're young. You're a successful and published writer. Other than that what do you have to show for yourself? People your age are settling down, having kids. If they're not doing that they're at least going out and having fun, if you catch my drift."

Thomas wasn't thrilled with where the conversation had trekked and his face clearly indicated as much. "Where are you going with this?"

"Okay okay, backing off. I don't want to get you totally twittered at me."

Nick leaned back and drank more of his ice tea. Thomas sighed and looked out the window at the water. It was so calming. He knew he wasn't mad at Nick. Nick and Susan had been super to him over the years, trying to coax him out of 'hiding' now and then to make sure he wasn't just a voice on the other end of a phone line every few weeks. The truth was Thomas had fallen in love with the area almost nine years ago when he'd gone skiing in Big Bear. He discovered the little mountain town of Running Springs to be quaint and secluded and had purchased a home there soon afterward.

Nick spoke up. "So talk to me. We've worked together for years on your books. What can I do to help?"

Thomas took a sip of coke and relented. "Listen Nick, I appreciate everything you've done for me. I'm just stuck right now. This past month I just can't get my head straight. It seems that every time I close my eyes..." Thomas said as he trailed off.

"Come on brother...cough it up."

Thomas finally relented and whispered his reply. "I've been having nightmares."

"Nightmares? You're writing a children's book called 'The Haunted Trees' for Christ sake. You're giving me nightmares," Nick joked.

"I'm serious, Nick. I wake up sweaty and exhausted; my sheets are all over the bed. My head's just not in the game."

Nick Raynes looked closely at his client, but more importantly, his friend. He'd met Thomas Clark two years out of college.

6

They'd both gone to USC, at the same time, but their paths had never crossed. Thomas had moved to the LA area to publish his books almost nine years ago. Nick had migrated to a publishing career while Thomas had stayed with his writing. It was blind luck that the two of them met up, but once Nick took a look at Thomas' work he recognized the raw talent. It was just a bonus that they had shared the same alma mater. From day one Thomas and Nick's partnership had had nothing but success. Nick knew that Thomas was one of the good guys, and aside from living on the mountain top away from civilization, he was one of those reliable types. The fact that Thomas hadn't met a deadline was a huge red flag so Nick focused back on Thomas and realized that his friend was actually upset.

"Alright Thomas, I'll talk to my people; let them know you need some more time. You've got plenty of pull since 'The Little Brown Chair' was so successful."

Thomas looked beat. "Thanks Nick, I owe you."

"No worries," Nick replied. "Besides, you've earned some rest. Speaking of, it sounds like you need some."

"Is it that obvious?"

"Far be it from me to say that you look a bit haggard, but you did just tell me you're going through some serious shit. So, with that in mind, what I'm about to tell you doesn't leave this room."

Thomas scrunched his face, puzzled, and looked his friend in the face. "What are you talking about?"

Nick leaned to the right and pulled out his wallet from his back left pocket. He opened it and produced a business card. "I'm giving this to you, but you never got it from me."

Thomas took the card and gave Nick a 'you have to be fucking kidding me' look. Then Thomas scanned it. It had the name of a

'Dr. Bond'. Below that were the words 'Psychiatrist' and a phone number.

"Really Nick? This is your big secret?"

"Shhhh," Nick hushed as he glanced around the room. "Listen. Susan and I had some issues a few years ago. Nothing major mind you, but Dr. Bond helped us through them."

"Rigggghhht," said Thomas.

"Go ahead and mock away Tommy Boy. My job as your agent is to get you to write so I can publish. My job is also to be your friend. As such, I need to watch your back. Call the number. If anything it'll at least get you out of the house and off this mountain," Nick voiced with a tinge of mockery.

Thomas caught the gesture. "Love you too."

Nick knew there was a slight chance that Thomas would call Dr. Bond. *Ah hell, you never knew with Thomas.* He'd had been coming up this mountain for years, meeting Thomas at this very diner time and time again. On occasion Thomas would come to his senses, leave the mountain top, and rejoin society for a night here and there. But as much shit as Nick gave Thomas about living up here Nick was jealous. *It is certainly beautiful and peaceful. Bastard has it good and he knows it.*

Thomas tucked the card away in his back right pocket. Nick took this as his cue. "Miss? Oh Miss? We're ready to order now and we'd love a refill on our drinks please."

2
Sat June 30, 1990 2:45 p.m.

Out in the parking lot Thomas got in to his car and started driving back towards Running Springs. The drive took him south up CA-173, a road that constantly wound back and forth. The sun beat down on his car but Thomas wasn't in a hurry and he thought it seemed a little warm for the time of the year. Regardless July was the next day and traditionally brought mid 80's weather. *Oh how I suffer.*

Coming up to CA-18 Thomas turned left towards Running Springs. CA-18 was called the 'Rim of the World' for a good reason. The horizon stretched on for miles. Sometimes a blanket of clouds would hover just below the mountain ridge and on those particular mornings the mountain community was the only thing that seemed to exist.

Lake Arrowhead was only 8.5 miles from Running Springs but the drive always took Thomas fifteen minutes. On these roads he couldn't drive terribly fast. More to the point, he couldn't drive faster than the posted limits due to the southern facing cliff. To say it was a steep drop was an understatement. Thomas continued driving and soon passed Santa's Village on his left, a popular spot during the winter months. He didn't much care for Santa, not since he'd been a child anyway. Thomas shrugged off the memory and continued home, somewhat lost in thought.

Nick was right, I'm not myself. These dreams are really messing with me.

Once Thomas passed the Village Market the main town of Running Springs was just around the corner. Thomas drove a few more blocks, took a left, a right and pulled into his driveway. *Home sweet home.* The front of his house had a double wide bed

9

of flowers. They were a small hobby Thomas worked on from time to time. They helped him clear his mind, not to mention they also helped him pass the time when he wasn't as his desk writing.

He parked his car in the garage, got out and noticed his Centurion bike hanging from the rafters. His bike taunted him. "Maybe later," he said out loud. Thomas was used to talking to inanimate objects, and even with himself for that matter. He didn't have anyone else to discourse with on a daily basis unless he used his house phone. It was one of the drawbacks of his choice to live in seclusion. As Thomas exited the garage his bike remained silent.

Thomas' two story house had been built in 1985, so it was a fairly new construction. As he walked in through the side door, from the attached garage, he entered his pantry/laundry room. As he opened the door a low tone sounded which indicated he had fifteen seconds to interact with the alarm panel. Thomas punched in his passcode and disabled it. When he bought the house he had a second security pad installed by the front door and a third installed in his upstairs bedroom. Thomas never felt entirely secure and he tried to reduce that anxiety as much as possible by planning ahead.

Thomas turned, left the pantry and walked into his kitchen. It was L-shaped with the stove next to the panty door. It was a somewhat modern kitchen with off-white walls and a green sea foam green trim that ran along the baseboard and ceiling; duplicate colors he shared with his master and guest bathrooms. The stove was gas based which meant that when the power failed, as it tended to with winter storms from time-to-time, he was still able to produce a hot meal. Sometimes he looked forward to those power outages because he could just curl up with a book on the couch, candles all around, and read. Sometimes he spent those moments with pen and paper in hand instead.

Thomas left the kitchen, past the fridge and microwave, and walked into his family room. The soft, leathery brown couch paralleled the kitchen's exit, which also looped around the far side of the family room to a short hallway, which led to his front door and the additional entrance to the kitchen. Adjoining that hallway was a closed door which was his guest room, currently being utilized as a storage room, and hadn't been used in quite some time. Thomas kept the door closed so it wouldn't remind him of what it contained.

The family room was painted an off-white; somewhat softer than the kitchen's color and his couch faced the entertainment center which housed a 19" TV, VCR and cable box. The remote rested on the glass coffee table along with his latest children's book 'The Little Brown Chair', a few Dean Koontz novels and a random magazine or two. The half wall, underneath the stairwell to the second floor, contained two three-foot high shelves which were shock full of VCR movies.

Thomas glided through his family room and took the stairs on the far side two at a time up to his bedroom. His mind remained jittery from the past month's nightmares of which had seemingly come out of nowhere. Over the past few weeks Thomas had woken up exhausted, sweaty and scared; unsure of what was happening. Needless to say he didn't like it.

Thomas reached the top of the stairs and entered his bedroom. A queen sized bed was centered and pushed up against the right wall. A sliding door, which contained a two-sided closet, bracketed the far wall. Both a bureau and a side table found their home in the corner next to his bed, and next to those was Thomas' desk, where most of his writing took place. His IBM PC lay heavily on it, currently off, begging for attention. The left wall of his bedroom contained a huge glass window along with a sliding glass door which led out to a small patio. From time to time he took his creative juices outside and wrote by hand. In the morning the sunlight would slowly creep up his bed and, when it reached his eyes, was a gentle reminder that it was time to start the day. He walked through his spacious bedroom and into his bathroom, which was no exception when it came to size either. It was a good ten feet from the doorway to his Jacuzzi tub. Thomas felt the size of his house was just right as he looked at himself in the bathroom mirror. He turned on the water and splashed his face a few times.

What the hell is wrong with me?

Back at the restaurant, as he and Nick ate, the conversation had turned from Thomas' mental block and nightmares to a more suitable topic, Nick's family. Susan and Nick had met each other during their sophomore year at USC. Their relationship continued after college and they married two years later in '82. Thomas knew he was lucky to have both Susan and Nick looking out for him. He didn't have many friends except Bill and Sam, his two best friends he'd maintained since elementary school.

How many friends will I really have secluding myself up here? Strange that I'm suddenly feeling lonely after nine years.

Thomas headed to the toilet, finished his business, washed up and then sat down on the edge of his bed. He looked over at his desk and let out a sigh.

I should try and write something. Thomas paused. *Oh, who am I kidding?*

He swiveled his head and looked out his huge glass window, the view being neither breath taking nor spectacular. Thomas' house wasn't situated on the edge of a cliff with a million dollar 'top of the world' view. Instead the scenery he gazed at was

12

merely a lot full of trees; lots and lots of trees. Those trees soothed him, for the most part, and formed a protective boundary. Thomas liked them because what lay beyond was dangerous to recall.

Beyond the trees. Wow, I'm tired.

A trill sound emanated throughout the house, startling him. It was the phone on his desk and Thomas thought about letting the answering machine get it, but decided to pick it up instead.

"Hello?"

"Thomas, how the hell are you?" declared the voice on the other end.

Thomas instantly relaxed. "Well shit, look who it is," he shot back as a huge grin appeared on his face. "Sam, how's it hanging?"

"Ha! Always the quick witted one of the group," Sam replied.

"I do what I can. So what do I owe this pleasure?"

"You mean we can't just call to say hi to a friend out of the blue?"

Thomas caught on right away. "Put that other sonofabitch on speaker ya rat bastard!"

"Okay okay…hold on a sec." There was an audible click followed by different voice.

"Luuukkkee, I am your ffaatthher." It was followed by some deep. But low breathing.

Thomas chuckled. "Alright alright, no more. You guys are terrible at this!"

Laughter erupted on the other end.

"Is it William, Will or Bill now?" asked Thomas.

"I think this month I'm going with Bill, but you'd know that already if you actually picked up that contraption of yours and used it once in a while. I believe they call it a telephone. I'll be happy to spell it out for you.

"Shut up already," Thomas playfully jabbed. "I don't know why I put up with either of you after all these years. Hell, I think I'm going to change my number."

"Go ahead," Bill and Sam said in unison.

"It's not like it'll be a challenge," Sam added.

Back in elementary school they had become the closest of friends, the three musketeers, and had been inseparable ever since. They played at recess, sat next to each other in class, and hung out after school and weekends. After elementary they had all attended the same intermediate and high school together. When they graduated high school in 1975 Thomas was the only one of them that had gone on to college while Sam and Bill had decided to join the Army. The sudden departure of his best friends, combined with the relocation to a new area in southern California, hadn't sat well with Thomas. He was used to their comradery, safety and fun. Suddenly Thomas was faced with being on his own and it was unsettling.

Thomas eventually graduated from USC in 1980 and had done a bit of world traveling as a graduation present. By then he'd definitely gotten used to doing things on his own. But after falling in love with the Running Springs area in 1981 all of that had become a distant memory over the years. Bill and Sam, on the other hand had spent eight years serving their country in a variety of locations. Those two had spent those eight years together and, because of that, Thomas felt more like the third wheel than one of the musketeers anymore.

Then, in 1985, Bill and Sam had started a security firm based out of San Francisco where they lived, which catered to the protection of VIP's. Apparently it was a lucrative gig but certainly not Thomas' speed

"So how's security business treating you guys these days?" Thomas inquired.

Bill piped up. "We've been hiring like mad this past year, Thomas. We got lucky with our timing and the location. We never seem to be short on work. You should come up and visit. If you do we'll give you the grand tour and maybe even let you pop off a few rounds at the range. What do you say?"

Thomas paused and looked around his room. He knew his friends meant well and he really missed them. "I don't know guys….it's tempting". *What the hell is going on? What am I so afraid of?*

Sam jumped in. "You know if you don't visit we'll have no choice but to come down there, hogtie you and bring you back up to SF. The wives miss you. But more importantly…," Sam trailed off.

"What?" Thomas asked.

"More importantly our daughters want your books they have autographed." Laughter erupted from the other end as Sam and Bill lost it.

"Fuck you both very much," Thomas responded. The laughter got even worse. He relaxed, smiled and then joined in with his friend's laughter. "You guys suck," he finally said after they died down.

"Seriously though, it's been too long. We miss you, and not in a gay way," Sam informed him.

"Do your wives know you have that fantasy about me?" Thomas poked.

"You sure you weren't in the service, Thomas?" said Bill. "That was straight out of the handbook."

Thomas grinned. "Now, now, who're the grunts and who's the writer?"

"Fair enough," Bill voiced in surrender.

Sam spoke up again. "Fuck you and the chair you write on."

More laugher ensued.

Afterwards Sam asked, "So turnabout is fair play. Seriously, how's the latest book?"

Thomas leaned back in his desk chair. *Here we go again.*

"Hello? Thomas? You still there?"

"Sorry guys. Yeah, I heard you."

"I take it that's a sore subject?" Bill asked.

"No, not really sore….just weird," Thomas replied.

"We've got a few minutes before our new client shows up," Sam said. "Give us the highlights."

Thomas wasn't comfortable talking about his feelings too much and the fact that he had tried expressing them to Nick earlier was uncharacteristic. He acknowledged that his two best friends were concerned and cared enough to ask.

"Here's the deal. You know that shit we went through as a kid?" Thomas asked.

"Of course bro," Bill immediately replied. "We were there too."

"Well…, this is going to sound weird but I've been having nightmares lately and a lot of them have to do with it." Thomas cringed as he pried open that heavily nailed down portion of his history.

Silence emanated from the other end of the line. Finally Bill broke it and said, "Listen Thomas, Sam and I are a little worried about you. Shit, make that very worried. From our perspective you're holed up in the middle of nowhere, alone. It's just not healthy. You have minimal contact with the outside world and when you do it's like we're pulling your teeth."

Sam jumped into the conversation. "We're not saying there's anything wrong with it."

Bill continued. "Yeah, we're not saying its wrong, brother, it's just that it's been way too long since we've seen you. At first we thought it was something you needed, privacy and a place to call your own. But it's been almost nine years."

Sam jumped back in. "And now with the nightmares you're talking about, that can't be good."

Thomas stayed quiet.

"Yo, Thomas," Sam asked. "You still there?"

"Yeah, I'm still here."

"We cut a little too close?" Bill asked.

Thomas exhaled loudly. "No, you guys are correct. Something's not right. Something has to change, and sure I'm a little miffed, but you guys have always had my back." Thomas paused and then said, "I lunch with Nick today."

"Good," said Sam. "How's that suit wearing sonofabitch doing these days?"

"Pretty good actually. He worked me over as well."

"Fucking A, brother," said Bill. "At least someone locally can reach out and smack you for us."

"Does your mother know you talk like that Bill?" Thomas chided.

"What she doesn't know won't kill her. And before you ask, it's no. Around our clients it's always 'yes, sir' 'no, sir". They pay the bills while we keep it professional. However, young Jedi, when on the phone with you I'll fucking swear as much as I fucking want to okay motherfucker?"

Bill and Sam laughed some more.

"Cute gentlemen, very cute. Love you too."

17

"On that note buddy we've got to go to our client meeting and that means money in the bank," Bill said. "Do us a favor and keep us in the loop on what's going on, okay?"

"Will do guys, and thanks for calling."

"Yeah yeah pussy. I'll catch up with you later."

Sam took the phone off the speaker and said, "Hey Thomas, you still there?"

"I'm here, Sam."

"So what's the next step? You know nothing happens without a plan."

"Nick gave me a business card for a shrink."

"Seriously, Thomas?"

"Yeah."

"And…"

"What do you mean?"

"Listen Thomas, you're a bright guy. I'm just a knuckle dragger who makes money doing what I do best. Your best asset is your head and it sounds like it's not on tight at the moment. What's the worst that could happen? Take care of your shit before it takes care of you. Pre-emptive strike and all."

"Thanks Sam. I'll catch up with you guys later."

Thomas hung up the phone and thought about what Sam had just said. It'd been a month now and these nightmares hadn't gone away.

Pre-emptive strike. Hmm. Interesting.

Thomas pulled the business card out of his back pocket and placed it on his desk Afterwards took off his shoes, headed downstairs, retrieved 'Lethal Weapon' from his collection and inserted it into the VCR. He snatched the remote off the coffee table, sat down on the couch, punched the TV's power button and changed the channel to 3. The last thing Thomas heard as he dozed off was, "Jingle Bell, Jingle Bell, Jingle Bell rock….."

* * *

Thomas abruptly awoke. The movie had long since finished and darkened room meant the sun had already set. He shivered and looked around.

Still on the couch I see.

He located the remote in his lap, hit the rewind button and clicked the VCR-to-TV button. Channel 3 lit up the room as he groggily trudged upstairs. Thomas stifled a yawn as he glanced over at the alarm clock on his bedside table. It read 9:57 p.m. in bold, red numbers. Thomas stripped out of his clothes and got ready for bed, now wearing pajamas and some socks.

Thomas returned to the living room, and in doing so he glanced at the TV. Lethal Weapon had finished its rewind process and had ejected and on the television the evening news had just started up.

Must be 10 p.m..

He flipped on the kitchen light and opened the fridge. Nothing inside appealed to him.

Maybe just a bowl of cereal then.

He grabbed the milk carton and closed the fridge. His cereal cabinet contained a few boxes which included Special K, Rice Crispys and Honey Nut Cheerios. He slothfully nabbed the Special K box while the news anchor spoke from the other room.

"…from last month's car explosion, the Army hasn't commented and claims they are still investigating.

"Our leading story this evening takes us back to San Bernardino where the grisly remains of Emmanuelle Rodriguez were found last night. We reported on this story earlier today. This morning Mr. Rodriguez's body was found by neighbors, in his apartment, after they noticed his door was ajar. His body was discovered immediately inside the apartment and was badly mutilated. As we talked with neighbors they said they are extremely frightened and don't recall hearing anything at all."

Thomas extracted a large bowl from the dishwasher, filled it with cereal and then added milk. With the milk back in the fridge he acquired a spoon and made his way back to the couch, the box of Special K still on the counter. He used one of his feet and pushed Lethal Weapon back into the VCR.

The newscast continued as he sat down. "As I said before, this brutal murder took place last night. Investigators have been scouring the scene today looking for clues and have currently been withholding all comments to the medi-"

Thomas clicked the VCR-to-TV button and the screen flickered to his movie.

"Maybe this time I can stay awake for it," he said to no one in particular.

Thomas leaned back and started in on his make shift dinner opening credits started up once again. "Jingle Bell, Jingle Bell, Jingle Bell rock…"

* * *

The movie ended around 11:30 p.m.. Thomas started the rewinding process again, took his empty bowl to the sink and filled it with water.

I'll deal with it in the morning.

He turned off the light in the kitchen, shut off the TV and headed upstairs. Once there he flipped on his bedside lamp and turned off the stairwell light. After brushing his teeth he climbed into bed and pulled his comforter up. Bedtime used to be one of his favorite moments of the day. He could relax, think about his work and drift into any world he wanted. Lately, however, sleeping had been anything but enjoyable.

Let's see what tonight brings.

Outside the trees rustled gently in his quiet neighborhood. Thomas turned off his lamp, got comfortable and closed his eyes.

* * *

The next morning Thomas woke up later than usual, around 9:30 a.m.. The previous night hadn't resulted in any nightmares, but his anxiety had left him fitful.

I'm still tired.

Thomas rolled over and groaned. It was only Sunday.

What am I going to do today?

The sun had squarely invaded his room and his bed was now warm from the sun's rays. Thomas kicked off his covers and slowly sat up.

Well, I might as well try to be productive.

After breakfast he cleaned up the kitchen and then spent a few hours in his garden, toiling in the soil, trying to shrug the bad dreams he'd been having. Happy at his accomplishments and how tidy his garden now was, he put away his tools in the garage and took a shower. Not wanting to sit in front of his computer screen Thomas decided to go for a meandering bike ride on the 'Rim of the World' towards Arrowhead. It had been some time since Thomas had felt relaxed and at ease and he hoped that a leisurely bike ride would bring his mood around. During that time he recalled why he had moved up to Running Springs in the first place and it brought a smile to his face. But he knew that feeling was fleeting.

Take care of your shit before it takes care of you.

Sam's words rung true. Thomas turned around and headed back. "Nothing like a plan to give you direction," he said out loud. The sun warmed his face as he peddled back home.

3
Mon July 2, 1990 10:05 a.m.

"Good morning, Dr. Bond's office, how can I help you?"

"Yes, hello. My name is Thomas Clark. I was referred to Dr. Bond through a friend of mine. I'd like to set up an appointment, the sooner the better."

"Certainly. Let me see Mr. Clark, today is Monday, July second. Dr. Bond has an opening on Wednesday the 4th at 2:30 p.m. for an hour. Will that work for you?"

"You're open on a holiday?" Thomas asked.

"Apparently so," replied the receptionist curtly.

"Thank you. That will be fine. I'll be there Wednesday. Have a nice day."

"You too, Mr. Clark."

Thomas slowly hung up the phone.

That was weird. I can't believe I just made an appointment.

He had no idea what was coming over him. After talking with his friends, and coming to the same conclusion himself, Thomas understood that he should at least talk with a professional.

Thomas imitated Sean Connery. "Bond. James Bond." That made him chuckle. "Until Wednesday then, Dr. Bond."

He went upstairs, turned on his IBM and attempted to make some progress on his latest book for the rest of the day.

<u>4</u>
Fri July 27, 1962 8:03 a.m.

"Get up sleepy head. It's your birthday. Happy birthday, sweetheart!"

Tommy rolled over in his bed and opened his eyes. His mother's was an inch away from his. "Mom! Quit that!" he exclaimed. His mother only smiled and started tickling his sides. "Mom..hehehehe…quit…hehehe….itttt….heehee."

Tommy's mother stopped and stood up. "Happy fifth birthday, sweetheart. Now get up and get ready for school. No presents until this evening, and that's only if you've been good," she teased as she left his room.

Tommy, suddenly recalling what day it actually was, bounded out of bed. He went to his bathroom, at the end of the hallway, and headed back to his room when he was done.

"I didn't hear you washing your hands," he heard his mother call out from the kitchen.

"Aww, Mom."

Tommy trudged back to the bathroom and washed up properly. *She's got good hearing.* He then finished getting dressed for school which was pre-school. With his birthday at the end of July the school planned to hold him back a year to have Tommy start out in kindergarten when he was a bit older. However, he'd shown creative aptitude and his parents had pushed for him to enter kindergarten in September rather than wait another full year. If Tommy did well then he'd be fine, otherwise the plan was to hold him back a year.

When Tommy was fully dressed and his shoe laces tied all by himself, something he was very proud of, he grabbed his small backpack and exited his room. His room was strategically located on the left rearmost side of the house's large deck. It was also connected to the family room and his parent's wing of the house, all of which overlooked the huge backyard, most of it overgrown. Still, there was a lot of space back there and Tommy often looked out of his paned windows and made up scenarios where he had to save the day. Tommy was lucky in the fact that his room had three large windows that gave him a substantial viewing angle to the outside world.

As he walked down the hallway Tommy passed a closed door on his right. Currently his parent's called that the guest room but there had been hushed talk, of which he wasn't supposed to have heard, that it may transform in to a little brother or sister's room. Directly past the guest room was the full bathroom which basically was Tommy's unless his parent's had people staying over, which typically turned out to be his grandparent's on his father's side. He never knew his mother's folks. The hallway opened in to the eating area where the dinner table resided, and was nestled between the large family room and the kitchen. A side room held the combined pantry and laundry room and a few steps up from inside that laundry room was the door to the garage.

A swinging door from the kitchen gave access to the dining room; a room meticulously maintained and rarely utilized unless it was a holiday. The front door bisected the living room, the other big room in the house, where holiday events took place. Across from the front door was a small hallway that branched to both the family room's second entrance and the master suite, the room where his parent's slept.

There was also a basement off the kitchen, but Tommy hardly went down there. Apparently the previous owners of the house had left a child's mannequin and his parent's had both named it and hadn't gotten rid of it. It was named Alice and Tommy didn't

26

like it one bit. Of course, Tommy didn't know that in the room beyond Alice was where his folks conveniently stashed presents. Devious.

Tommy wandered into the kitchen. His mother handed him a banana and his Spiderman lunch pail.

"Did you see what your father made for you?" she asked.

Tommy looked over at the eating area table, he'd passed, and on it was a big poster. He checked it out and, in big letters, were the words 'HAPPY 5th BIRTHDAY TOMMY!' His eyes got huge and an enormous smile appeared on his face.

"Neat," Tommy said.

Tommy's father had already left for work but that didn't mean he didn't want his little man to think he'd forgotten about him.

"This is awesome," said Tommy as he looked over at his mother.

"You'll see him this evening when he gets home from work sweetie," she told her son. "Do you have everything?" Tommy nodded. "Well then, let's go. School's going to start soon."

Tommy raced through the pantry and up the few stairs to the garage. He unlocked the door and stepped in, waiting for his mother to follow. She closed and locked the door behind her. As she hit the button for the garage to mechanically retract she armed the alarm panel. The car parked in the garage was a 1961 Buick LeSabre station wagon. It was a beast of a vehicle with a powerful v8 under the hood and a gas gauge that went from Full to Empty nearly as fast as the Odometer traveled from 0-60. Tommy loved it because the leather seats were comfortable.

Michael, Betsy and Tommy Clark lived in Orinda, CA, located in a small community area off Miner Road. Michael was a consultant and currently had a very lucrative contract for a large company in San Francisco, about 25 miles west of Orinda.

27

Tommy didn't know what a consultant was and at his age didn't really care. His mother stayed at home. As soon as Tommy was born, and started to get older, they decided they needed a bigger house and had moved to Orinda from San Jose, CA about three years prior. Michael's consulting business had really taken off so moving to the somewhat plush town of Orinda was a dream come true for them.

Betsy backed out of the garage and hit the remote to lower the door. She drove off towards Tommy's school, about 3.5 miles away by taking a right on Miner Road. Tommy looked out the window and saw the grass on either side of the road. It looked so organized.

"Mom?" he asked.

"What is it, sweetie?" she replied.

"What's with all the grass?"

"That's for the golfers to play on."

Golfers. Golf. Golf clubs. He broke it down in his head. His father played golf. He'd seen the clubs in the basement, next to Alice. Tommy shuddered.

"Why doesn't dad play here?"

"Maybe someday sweetie. He's on the waiting list to become a member."

"Waiting list?" Tommy asked.

Betsy looked over at his squinted face, something Tommy did while he was trying to figure something out in his head. "Sorry sweetie. He's waiting for his turn so he can play. Like at school, what if there was a toy that someone else was playing with and you wanted it."

"I'd wait my turn," blurted out Tommy, which was followed by a short pause. "Oh, I get it," and a smile came over his face. "Waiting list."

Miner Road ended. Betsy took a right at the signal and merged on to Camino Pablo. Soon afterward they passed the water treatment plant on the right side at the corner of Manzanita Drive. Tommy was always intrigued about what went on in that place. A half mile later the entrance to Wagner Ranch Elementary School appeared and Betsy veered right and headed down the paved slope to the school's turnabout. Wagner Ranch was a K-6 facility but there was also a pre-school portion that ran from 9am to 2 p.m.. Betsy pulled up alongside the curb and Tommy unbuckled his seat belt in preparation to exit.

"Excuse me young man," said his mother.

Tommy had escaped from the seat belt but stopped short at the door handle. He turned back towards his mother who had a serious look on her face. She pointed at her cheek.

"Forgetting something in your old age?" she kidded, and let a smile slip.

"Aww, mom," said Tommy but leaned over to give her a kiss on the cheek.

Her smile grew. "Have a happy birthday little man. Say hello to your teacher for me."

"Okay mom. See you later," he replied and bolted out the door.

"I'll be here at the normal time. By honey, love you."

Tommy had closed the door just as she said that and trotted off to class. *They really do grow up so quickly.* As Betsy pulled away from the curb she started to plan the party that was being held the following day at their house. *I have a ton to do before 2 p.m.. No time to waste.*

Tommy knew exactly where he was going and didn't need any help to get there. He was a big boy now. His mother's 'little man'. He beamed.

He and opened the door to his classroom and strolled inside.

"Good morning, Tommy," said Ms. Ackers, his teacher.

"Good morning, Ms. Ackers," he replied.

He took off his backpack and put it in his cubbyhole, along with his shoes. The giant clock above her desk read 8:57am.

Ms. Ackers continued, "So I hear it's your birthday Tommy. Happy birthday."

He grinned. "Thank you."

More preschoolers strolled in and deposited their belongings in their appropriate cubes just as Tommy had done. In the meantime he found a place on the carpet, towards the back of the room, and sat down. Ms. Ackers was the only teacher here because Mrs. Jones hadn't shown up yet. Once she arrived then the day would get going and all the children would be rounded up for various activities, recess, naps, snack time, etc. His day would soon begin.

* * *

As Betsy left the school she had a mental list of what she needed for Tommy's party the following day. *I need to pick up the cake, candles, balloons, party favors, ice cream, and last minute presents...*

"What else?" she asked out loud. "I feel like I'm missing something. Well, I'll figure it out eventually."

She turned on the radio as she continued to drive around Orinda, with a stop here and there to gather supplies. She needed to complete these tasks and get back to the house to sequester everything before she picked up Tommy at 2 p.m..

John Denver sang in the background, "Leavvving on a jet plane..."

The hands on the clock read 11:31am. Mrs. Jones got the attention of all the boys and girls and announced that it was time for coloring. She was very strict and was a no nonsense teacher. Many children had spent twenty minutes in the time-out chair and weren't looking for a repeat trip anytime soon.

Tommy got up and gathered both crayons and paper from Mrs. Jones. He then returned to his place on the carpet, a spot he could view most of the classroom from. The kids grew quiet in their creative concentration, their tongues darting back and fro as they worked. All the children were thoroughly engrossed with what they were working on. Some had taken pre-printed sheets of animals and were coloring them any which way while others were desperately trying to stay within the lines. Other children had retrieved blank paper and were creating their own designs, generally stick figures she noticed.

Ms. Acker meandered slowly through the group. She was paying special attention to Tommy since it was his birthday. Many of the children would demand to be the center of attention on such a day, but little Tommy Clark just went about this day like it was any other. She had organized the class to sing a round of 'Happy Birthday' earlier that morning to start off his day. No need to have kids pouting later on garnering for negative attention. But she recognized that Tommy never caused any trouble.

Tommy worked away, concentrating very hard on getting it right. He was new at this. Ms. Acker had made her way over him and cocked her head to get a better look at what he was coloring. *He's really intent.* She saw that he was only using one color, forest green, and that he wasn't coloring, he was writing. There were words on his paper.

31

Tommy finished writing and then noticed that Ms. Acker stood over him. He shied away.

"May I see what you have, Tommy?" she asked softly.

Nobody said no to a teacher. The timeout chair, from the stories he'd heard and seen, didn't look like fun. He reluctantly handed his paper up to Ms. Acker.

"Thank you," she said. Show a child respect and it goes a long way was one of her mottos. She examined the paper written in green crayon and read the following:

> See Tom run
> See Tom jump
> See Tom fall

Amazing, she thought. *And he just turned five today. Such potential.*

She handed the paper back to him and said, "I like it Tommy. Good job."

She then slowly continued to observe the progress of the other children while she moved around the room.

* * *

The 2 p.m. bell eventually rang. Tommy, like all the others, collected their items from their cubes, put on their shoes and left. Tommy's new creation was safely tucked away in his backpack and Ms. Acker hadn't scolded him for it.

He made his way to where the parents picked kids up. Tommy's mother was there and eventually she pulled in by him.

"How was the waiting list?" Tommy asked as he buckled his seat belt.

32

Betsy looked puzzled for a second and then realized her son meant the line of cars she'd been in. Chuckling she said, "Fine honey, just fine. How was school on your birthday?"

"It was okay," and left it at that.

Betsy pulled and headed towards home.

* * *

Michael opened the front door, later that evening, around 6:30 p.m.. Some days his father came home earlier, other days he didn't come home until really late. Tommy didn't know what his father did but it must be important to keep him so busy. Tommy greeting him at the front door as it opened.

"How's my birthday boy?" Michael asked as he scooped him up in his arms.

"Hi honey," said Betsy from the kitchen.

"Hey babe."

"I'm good dad. Thanks for the poster. I saw it this morning."

"Hey kiddo, you're welcome. Just wait until tomorrow."

Tommy's eyes widened. "What's happening tomorrow?" he asked with growing excitement.

"Your birthday party of course," his father replied.

"I know that. You're silly, dad."

Michael walked into the kitchen, kissed Betsy and playfully swatted her behind. She gave him an evil look followed by a wink and a smile.

"What's for dinner?" he asked as he lowered Tommy to the floor.

"Tommy's favorite," she said. "Open faced hamburgers, broiled to perfection."

"Yummy!" Tommy cried out.

He loved those. His grandmother, on his mother's side, had made them for Betsy. He had never met his mom's parents, only his grandparent's on his dad's side were still alive.

Michael looked over at his smiling son and back over at his wife. *We are so lucky*, he thought.

"Okay Tommy, go wash up for dinner. I need to talk to your mom for a bit, in private," he added with a wink.

"Is it about my birthday party?"

"Scoot or no presents for you!" Michael threatened knowing he'd never it.

Tommy skipped away to his bathroom and washed up.

* * *

Dinner was about over.

"Thank you, honey," said Michael, "That was delicious." Michael looked over at Tommy's empty plate and said, "So Tommy, it looks like you didn't like the burger."

"I'm stuffed!" Tommy exclaimed, and then a belch slipped out that surprised everyone at the table. "Opps," said Tommy.

Michael was the first to laugh, followed closely by Betsy and then Tommy.

"Well done, son. There's nothing like a nice birthday belch to ring off your new year. Just don't make it a habit," Michael joked.

Betsy started to gather the empty plates and said, "Well, since you boys have earned yet another medal for joining the 'clean your plate club', I'll be right back with some ice cream."

Tommy loved ice cream. The 'clean your plate club' was apparently an old tradition in his mother's house growing up. She kept it going as a reminder to her parents and Tommy didn't mind.

He knew that if he ate everything on his plate then dessert wasn't far behind.

* * *

After dessert had been obliterated, and cleared away to the kitchen, the three of them withdrew to the family room. The room had a leather couch, a small black and white TV, and was the place where game time occurred. Tommy would sometimes watch his parents play card, dice and board games, not entirely understanding the rules but enjoying their interaction nevertheless. This evening no games were brought out.

Michael and Betsy looked over at Tommy on the far end of the couch. Michael spoke up first.

"Okay, Tommy, time to make a decision." Tommy continued to stare at them. "You can either open a couple presents tonight.....OR....wait to open a lot more tomorrow at your party."

Tommy thought about it. Michael and Betsy looked at each other strangely fully expectant that Tommy would want to open something on his actual birthday.

"I'll open them tomorrow," Tommy finally said very confidently.

"Are you sure, honey?" Betsy asked. "We can go get a few right now."

Tommy straightened his back and looked right at both of them in all seriousness and said, "That's okay." His parents were dumbfounded and speechless.

Tommy got up, hugged both of them and said, "Night mom. Night dad."

As Tommy walked back through the eating area into the bathroom his parents could only stare after him.

Michael finally spoke up. "Honey, what did you put in those burgers?"

<u>5</u>
Tues July 3, 1990 2:11 a.m.

BLAM!!

Thomas woke with a start. *What the hell was that!?* He turned on his lamp and inspected his room. The glass window was still intact. *Did a bird strike it?* Thomas got out of bed and examined it closer. His balcony was clear of both birds and broken glass. He turned on the stairwell light and headed down to investigate the first floor.

A minute later Thomas retraced his steps and was back in his bedroom, tired but now awake. He sat down at his desk and turned on his IBM 486. He opened the file he'd been working on and saw the latest lines he'd composed for his next book, 'The Haunted Trees':

> See Tom run.
> See Tom jump.
> See Tom fall.

Thomas pondered before adding more, sure that those words were correct on the glowing screen in front of his sleepy eyes. On occasion he enjoyed to utilize his name when he wrote books. Sometimes he imagined himself as the characters in his books. *A better time.*

He decided not to go back to bed as new words flowed through his head. Thomas typed out another line:

> Tom gets up and calls his dog.

He quickly deleted that line. *Well, that didn't make any sense.*

The clock read 2:25 a.m.. He glanced over at his bed and back at the computer. He really didn't want to go back to sleep anyway, fearful as he was. The past month Thomas had been plagued with nightmares which shattered his perceived escape from reality. He didn't know why he had them, but they were horrible and every night he dreaded to close his eyes. All he knew was that those nightmares had started off gradually and then, within this past week, they had grown even more frightening. Thomas couldn't recall with clarity what those terrifying images were, but all he knew was that he was afraid to experience them again.

He pushed back from his desk and made his way to the mirror in his bathroom. The face that stared back was haggard. I'm wiped out. Thomas straightened up and noticed that his five feet, eleven inch frame had some muscle tone to it. This came from his unregulated weight lifting, due to the fact that he didn't like to be pushed around. He wanted to appear tougher on the outside, but it had been a while since he had used them. The only real exercise he seemed to get these days was biking or working in his garden.

Thomas ran a hand through his blond hair which covered his head but didn't hang down over his eyes or touch his neck. He focused in on his green eyes, which he thought happened to be the most striking feature about his appearance. When someone looked at them from another angle his eyes incorporated a sort of aqua tinge. He had always been hassled about that from his friends over the years. They told Thomas that he would have to list two eye colors on his driver's license application. Thomas didn't mind though; it made him unique.

Ever since he was five years old Thomas knew that he was different. He did what he wanted, not really caring what the other kids thought, but still wanting to connect with them. Over time he had become somewhat of an outcast which affected him as he grew older. If it wasn't for Sam or Bill he might have never had any real friends at all.

Thomas returned to his computer desk as his thoughts drifted back towards his younger years. The computer screen blurred out and his eyes became distant. He knew he had trouble fitting in to the world. Nobody liked him; although that's what his internal demons kept telling him. The fact that he wrote amazing children's books didn't seem to register. He was very reluctant to give himself the proper credit that he deserved. *That's probably another reason why I moved to the middle of nowhere.*

Thomas' mind twisted and turned in the early morning, his eyes never blinked as his thoughts continued to reminisce. Everyone had called him Tom or Tommy; but Tommy had eventually stuck. That is, everyone except this one kid who was in one grade above him. Nigel Clemmings had been his name. Tommy, at age eight or nine, had been in the third grade while Nigel was in the fourth. He couldn't remember exactly was but it didn't really matter because Thomas only recalled what had happened to him during that particular school year. Nigel had called him a loser, and everything else a bully could think up, just to make Tommy feel terrible about himself. Unfortunately Nigel was huge for a kid his age, with jet black hair and thick eyelashes. From Tommy's perspective Nigel seemed to be made out of pure evil and he'd never forget Nigel's name or face. That kid had made his life a living hell.

Coming out of his self-induced trance Thomas blinked his eyes and leaned back in his chair. He attempted to put the awful images out of his mind and concentrate on the computer before him, but he couldn't concentrate. Thomas glanced at the calendar that hung next to his desk and noticed the appointment with Dr. Bond.

Am I ready to talk with a shrin-

He jumped as the phone rang. *Shit, that scared me.* He let it ring a second time before he picked it up.

"Hello?" he asked tentatively. *Who would be calling at this hour?*

There was no answer and the line went dead.

"Whatever," he voiced and replaced the phone in its cradle. The silent reverberation of his words wafted throughout his room. Thomas raised himself out his chair, switched off his IBM, climbed back into bed and looked at the clock yet again. This time it read 2:35 a.m.. As he turned off the lamp the room's darkness washed over him immediately and sweat suddenly appeared on his forehead and the palms of his hands.

"Stop it," he whispered. He was alone and he knew it.

"Stop it," he said again under his breath.

In a desperate attempt to protect himself Thomas squeezed his eyes shut and pulled his covers up over his head like a child. And for whatever reason that helped to alleviate his fears.

Eventually Thomas drifted off to sleep only to toss and turn the rest of the night as if he were trying to escape from something. Garbled words and phrases emanated from his mouth, however, the only one that could be clearly understood was, "Stop it."

Thomas woke up shortly after 7:15a.m.. He managed to get only four hours of sleep and, once again, felt drained and every one of his muscles ached. Reluctantly he opened his eyes and looked around; his demeanor changed immediately.

Something's not right.

Thomas started a mental checklist as he glanced around his room.

Computer on the desk. *Check.*

Phone in its cradle. *Check.*

Calendar on the wall. *Check.*

Something on the window.

Thomas sat up. His eyes fixated on the glass window to his patio. He slid out of bed and slowly walked over to the window. The early morning sun provided just enough light that he could see exactly what was on the glass.

What the hell?

A smudged hand print stared back at him about face high. Thomas raised his right hand to touch it and froze as his hand came in to view. It was covered in something. He slowly positioned his right hand over the hand smudge on the glass window. It appeared to be a perfect match. He lifted his hand to his nose and it bore the sweet stench of copper. Thomas pulled his hand away from his face as fast as he could, but the bile in his throat was already on its way. As he turned towards the bathroom something caught his eye and he barely had time before he projected vomit all over his bathroom tiles.

There, above his bed, on the off white walls two huge words were written in blood. Those words spelled out "Make me!"

Thomas spent nearly ten minutes as he washed and rewashed his hands. The hot water hurt but he barely noticed.

What the fuck. What the fuck. What the fuck.

The water in the sink was crimson pink as it circled the drain.

"Calm down," he commanded himself and turned off the steaming water.

Thomas stripped off his pajamas, threw them in his bathtub and turned around to examine himself. He gave himself the once over and when he couldn't find any cuts he turned to the mirror over the sink.

Nothing, not a goddamn thing.

Thomas, still naked, forced himself to take a deep breath and then let it out. He looked at himself in the mirror. He knew he was tired but he didn't appear to be crazy.

Where the hell did all this blood come from?

Thomas gathered was strength he had left and walked back into his bedroom. He tried to ignore the wall, bee-lined for the stairs and took them two at a time down to the first floor. He briskly walked to the kitchen and snatched the phone off the wall. The yellow sticker on the phone's base displayed the local emergency numbers. He dialed the police and it picked up after the first ring.

"Hello, Running Springs PD. How can I help you?"

Thomas quickly hung up. *What the hell am I going to say? My bedroom wall has blood all over it, it's not mine. Please come on over and take a look?*

"Smart, Thomas," he said as bitched at himself out loud. "That was really good thinking on your part."

The phone rang and Thomas just stared at it. It rang a second time. Thomas backed away. It rang a third time. Thomas took a step closed and reluctantly answered.

"Hello?"

"Yes sir," the voice on the other end said. "This is the Running Springs Police Department. You just called here. Is there a problem?"

Thomas' mind raced. *Fuck.* "You probably get this all the time but I meant to dial 411 and spaced out. When you answered I was totally embarrassed." *Oh God. Oh God.*

There was a long pause on the other end. She finally said, "Okay sir. We might send someone by just to verify that."

"Feel free," Thomas replied as coolly as he could muster. "I'll be here." The call terminated. Thomas slammed the phone back on its cradle. "Fuccckkk."

He looked around quickly.

What the hell have I gotten myself in to?

The downstairs was exactly the same as it'd been the night before. The quickly examined the white walls of his house and didn't see any blood. Compared to the nightmarish crime scene in his room the rest of the house looked picture perfect.

Thomas sat down on the couch. Thomas had been through enough in his life that he knew overreacting would only lead to panic. *I don't have much time.* He raced upstairs.

* * *

His doorbell rang seventeen minutes later. Thomas heard it from the garage, walked back into his house and over to the front door. He turned the knob and swung it inward.

"Mr. Clark?" a uniformed officer asked.

"Sorry about before," Thomas said. "I shouldn't have hung up." He was dressed in his robe and slippers and the officer noticed Thomas' hair was wet.

"It happens more than you know, Mr. Clark. Do you have any ID sir?"

Thomas noticed that the officer's hand was close to his weapon and the restraining strap had already been removed.

"Of course. Please come in, officer." Thomas left the door open and walked into his family room. "It's upstairs in my wallet. I'll be right back."

The officer stared at him. Thomas turned and tried to casually walk up the stairs while he willed himself to relax. Up in his room he grabbed his wallet and retraced his steps. Approaching the officer he slowly held out his wallet and flipped it open to reveal his driver's license. While watching Thomas the officer reached out and took his entire wallet, took two steps back and then glanced at his ID. He immediately relaxed.

"Sorry, Mr. Clark. We can never be too careful."

"I understand. Is there anything else you need?" Thomas asked as he took back his wallet.

"If you don't mind sir I'd like to take a quick look around," the officer said without really asking. "Have a seat on the couch if you wouldn't mind."

Thomas did as he was instructed and sat down. The officer made his way through the kitchen, opened up the guest bedroom and peaked inside, closing it behind him as he made his way to the stairs. He took another look at Thomas to see if there was going to be any issues before he proceeded. He came back down within twenty seconds and joined Thomas in the family room. He then noticed the door to the garage and moved towards it, cautiously opening it. The pantry/laundry room was clear. He took another

44

glance at Thomas and then moved to the actual garage door. The officer came back quicker this time.

"Cleaning up I see, Mr. Clark?"

"What?"

"I noticed your bed was stripped. It must be laundry day. My wife does the same thing every week."

"You caught me," Thomas said as he stood up.

The officer nodded and moved towards the front door.

"Thanks for letting me look around. And next time please watch how you dial."

The officer opened and closed the door behind him leaving Thomas alone.

Thomas exhaled loudly and collapsed back on the couch. His heart beat loudly against his chest. He couldn't believe that he had wiped down his bedroom that rapidly. After he had hung up the phone with the police he had sprinted naked upstairs, grabbed the cleaning bucket from his bathroom and filled it with water from the Jacuzzi facet. He had added some Palmolive to the mixture and dropped a sponge in. The bloody palm print on the glass window was still tacky but cleaned up very nicely. His pillows looked untouched so he moved those to his computer desk. He then stripped his bed and threw it all against the base of the wall. Then he stood on the bed, placed the bucket on his side table and wiped off the bloody words as quickly as he could. In his haste streaks of red drizzled down the wall but were caught up in his sheets and comforter. For ten minutes he labored on that wall, emptying and refilling the bucket three times along the way. Finally Thomas stepped back and gave the wall a once over.

Passable for now.

He emptied the bucket for the fourth time, rinsed it out and put it back under bathroom counter. Thomas raced down to the garage, grabbed two trash bags and flew back upstairs. He divided his pajamas, the sponge and the bedding equally between the two bags. He jumped in the shower to rinse off, exiting thirty seconds later. That towel went in the bag as well. He tied them off, grabbed his robe and slippers from the closet and quickly headed downstairs hoping he hadn't missed anything. Without stopping he tore open the doors leading to the garage just as a vehicle came to a stop in his driveway. Thomas tossed the bags in a corner of the garage and exited just as his doorbell rang.

Thomas was still in shock about what had transpired. He walked to the fridge and pulled out some orange juice. Filling up a glass he downed it in a few gulps. He refilled it and moved to the couch. He leaned back and closed his eyes. He needed to calm himself down.

I'm okay.

He kept his eyes closed for two minutes until his breathing and heartbeat had returned to normal. He opened his eyes again and took another sip of his drink.

What a goddamn mystery. Where the hell did that blood come from if it wasn't mine?

Thomas finished off the second glass, headed to the kitchen, placed the glass in the sink and looked at the clock on the microwave. It read 8:22am.

He silently made his way back to his room. His bed was still stripped clean and his walls were white. However, when Thomas closed his eyes he could clearly see the words "Make me!" still emblazoned on the wall above his head. Thomas shivered and walked into his bathroom. He took off his robe and slippers, turned on the shower and let it warm up. When Thomas saw the steam emanating from behind the frosted glass he opened the shower door. The water was about as hot he could stand and he let

46

the scalding water cascade off his back and down the drain. His mind tried to make sense of the situation he was in. For the next twenty five minutes he stood there letting the water abuse his body in an attempt to wipe away that morning's ghastly memory.

* * *

After the shower Thomas' mind was clearer and a tad more focused. He felt beat up and his brain was still running a mile a minute. His back was also very red and sore. Thomas reentered his bedroom. Nothing had changed. The bed was still stripped and his pillows were on the desk next to his computer. The only good news, Thomas thought, was that the wall above his bed was still white.

"Focus, Thomas," he said. "Take care of your shit before it takes care of you."

The clock read 9:01am. Thomas recalled that he had his appointment with Dr. Bond at 2:30 p.m.. He knew he'd have plenty of time as long as he left the house around 1:45 p.m..

Time to get out of here for a while.

Thomas dressed in shorts, a t-shirt and tennis shoes for the time being.

Plenty of time.

He walked downstairs, into the garage and saw the two garbage bags. He opened up the trunk of his car, placed them inside and closed it.

Out of sight, out of mind.

He pulled his Centurion, 15-gear bicycle from the rafter hook and gave it a once over. The tires, chain and gears looked fine. He was ready to go. Thomas knew that if he stayed in the house his mind would continually focus on the incident and he didn't want

47

that. In fact, he couldn't handle that so he didn't even want to try. At least while out biking he could attempt to keep his mind clear.

He engaged the kickstand, left his bike in the garage and went back inside to obtain a few items that he would need. He found his helmet, filled his water bottle and grabbed two bananas.

When's this day going to be over?

Thomas closed the door to the laundry room, armed the alarm and pushed the button for the garage door. Pocketing his keys in his hip bag he climbed onto his bike seat, snapped the kickstand up and rode down his driveway in a flash. Bicycle riding was an activity Thomas looked forward to each time he planted his feet on those pedals. He enjoyed it so much because he was able to get away from everything and anything that plagued him. He associated it to the freedom of motorcycle riding, just at a slower pace.

Riding west on CA-18, towards Arrowhead, Thomas shifted to third gear. After many years of living in the San Bernardino Mountains Thomas knew how demanding the roads were both to him and his bike. He didn't know where he was going after this morning's 'incident' and he didn't really care. The only thing he did know was that if he kept riding he would end up in Arrowhead. Passing a mileage sign Thomas saw that he was correct.

Only five more miles.

Riding in silence, and trying not to think about anything, Thomas noticed that the weather hadn't changed much since earlier that morning. The air was still warm and the hottest part of the day was still to come. Soft, feathery clouds drifted throughout the blue sky like lost pets not knowing where their home was. He reached down for his water bottle and drank deeply.

48

Coasting around one of the numerous mountain curves, Thomas looked down at his bicycle. He was shocked to realize that he was riding a motorcycle.

What?

He looked up at the road.

No way!

Thomas looked down again. The motorcycle had disappeared altogether and Thomas was now riding nothing but air currents at about 25 mph.

This can't be happening!

"Impossible!" he screamed in to the wind.

The plants and trees around him started to laugh and call him a fool. Tree branches reached for him as he sped by. Voices surrounded him. Everything mocked him!

"Tommy, Tommmmy. Come on, Tommy. What are you gonna do, cry for me? Cry Tommy, cry. Cry you little shit! When I say cry, you cry! I control you, Tommy, remember that."

* * *

Birds whistled in the trees above; all around. *Something hurts.* Blue sky. Dry earth.

"Ouch!"

Thomas opened his eyes and slowly sat up. Trees and ferns surrounded him.

"Ouch!" he cried out again.

Thomas gently caressed his left arm as pain shot through it. Thomas moved it around a little, wincing against the pain, until he was sure it wasn't broken.

"Lucky me," he said sarcastically. "What the fuck else are you going to throw at me today?"

49

Thomas slowly stood up and looked around. Still dazed he tried to grasp what had happened. His Centurion was fifteen feet behind him, tangled in all kinds of plant debris along with his helmet, so he made his way towards them. All he could remember was the strange sensation that he had floated.

That was too weird. I was riding my bike and then I wake up here.

Thomas suddenly felt wetness along his lower back. *Oh crap.* He gingerly reached behind him with his right arm and discovered that his bananas had not been as lucky. *Whew.* Thomas pulled them out and discarded them in the foliage. He retrieved his bike from the branches and winced a bit when he used his left arm to help yank it clear. He picked up his helmet and clipped it to his bike.

Realization spread across Thomas' face.

I blacked out. I blacked out while riding and went off the side of the road.

Thomas took a long look at where he had landed and silently breathed a sigh of relief. Cliffs are indigenous to the San Bernardino Mountains and he had been extremely fortunate because he'd landed on a narrow strip of land which jettisoned out from the main body of the road. Any further left or the right would have left him singing in the clouds rather than looking up at them.

Hefting his bruised body, along with his bike, Thomas climbed over a fallen log to get back to the highway that was about twenty feet away. Cars cruised by him and he could see the faces of the people who gave him curious glances. On the side of the road Thomas examined his bicycle and concluded that it would need a trip to the repair shop. The front wheel had definitely come in to contact with something solid. Thomas looked back at the log.

Explains why I got tossed so far.

He squinted at his wristwatch. It was 9:53am. He was only a few miles from home and walking with his broken bike would only take an hour or so. He straightened his rumpled hair and started in, his bike balanced on its back wheel, as Thomas held on to the handle bars and pushed the bike in front of him. The fact that his left arm throbbed slowed his progress down as he had to rest it every few minutes.

Shit. This is going to take longer than I thought.

Beep beep!

Thomas jumped a little and looked back. A gentleman in a '87 sky-blue Ford pickup truck had stopped and tapped his horn twice to get Thomas' attention. The passenger window was already down as Thomas approached.

"Everything alright, son?" the man asked.

"My bike chain must have slipped off its gears and tangled my foot up. Instead of braking to go around a corner I panicked and sped through it. I got tossed in to a grove of ferns, and hurt my arm, but I think it's only a big bruise. I must have landed on it."

Thomas found it easy to lie to this man. How could he tell him the truth? *Well I had this dream about riding on air and then I woke up in the ferns.* The guy would give him an oddball look and speed away thinking he was a nutcase.

"Sounds like you were very fortunate."

"Yeah, real lucky," Thomas replied.

"Put it in the back, son."

Thomas lifted his damaged bike in to the back of the truck, climbed in the passenger seat and closed the door. The man had his hand extended and Thomas shook it.

"George Miles."

"Thomas Clark."

"Very nice to meet you, Tom."

51

Thomas noticed right away that this man was very sure of himself. George appeared to be in his late fifties and had a nice round belly that extended over his waistline. He made Thomas feel very welcome and at ease from the moment he stepped in to the truck. Thomas let go of his hand.

"I just live a few blocks past the center of Running Springs," Thomas informed him.

"No problem, son. I'll have you home in no time."

"Thanks for stopping. That was really kind of you."

George looked over at Thomas and their eyes locked for just a second. Thomas looked away. George said, "You're welcome."

Driving into Running Springs Thomas asked George to drop him off the corner where the Fire Station was. George pulled over to the side of the road and let Thomas out, who then extracted his bike from the back of the truck before he closed the passenger door. George leaned over towards Thomas.

"Take care of yourself, Tom. You're a bright man with a future ahead of you. Deal with whatever's eating you before it's too late."

George drove off and left Thomas with his mouth hanging open. He watched as George's truck disappeared around a curve.

Will this day get any weirder? What did George see? How does he know anything?

Without the answers to any of those questions Tom slowly pushed his bike back to his house.

7

Sat July 28, 1962 8:15 a.m.

Tommy woke up to the morning sun that shined through his slatted window shades and brightened up his room. He stretched and kicked his covers down towards the bottom of his bed. Typically on a Saturday Tommy would sleep in but he had woken up much too excited.

Today is my birthday party!

Tommy climbed out of bed, put on a pair of socks and headed to his bathroom. When he was finished he made sure to wash his hands just in case his mother was up and about.

"Tommy, is that you sweetie?" she asked from the kitchen.

Instead of answering Tommy raced to her and purposely slid the last six feet on the wood floor with his socks. He misjudged and the momentum plunged him into the back of his mother's legs.

"Whoa there, tiger," she cautioned.

"Sorry, mom."

"So, how's my birthday boy?"

"Excited!" Tommy instantly replied.

"Well you should be. Your friends will be here in a few hours honey."

"Moommmm," he said. "They're not my friends, they're just kids from school," Tommy insisted very specifically.

Betsy knew that once Tommy started kindergarten he'd figure relationships out. He was too young and didn't have a brother or sister to challenge the attention he currently received. Tommy had never spoken badly about the preschoolers in his class, or had any problems with them, but he hadn't talked about any of them either. When Betsy had asked who he had wanted at his first real birthday party, with his previous years' parties consisting of family, he just shrugged his shoulders. So Betsy took it upon herself to invite his entire class. She figured it'll be overkill but you only turn five once.

"In any case sweetie, they'll be here after lunchtime. Why don't you go see what your father is up to?"

Tommy scurried off through the dining room, down the hall by the front door and into his parent's bedroom. His father was still in bed sleeping. Tommy carefully climbed on the bed, careful to not disturb his father, and then pounced on top of him!

"Oooof!"

Tommy started to giggle uncontrollably. His father grabbed him tightly and said, "I guess you're my blanket now," as he pretended to go back asleep as he held tightly to his son. Tommy struggled and struggled to get away. He managed to free one arm and he started to tickle his father, who had little choice but to release him.

"No fair!"

"Ha ha. I got away!"

Michael rolled over and reached out to grab Tommy again. "ROOAARR!" he growled. Tommy had scooted away but his father had snatched his right arm. "Got you now! Rawwrrr!"

"Eeeeeeeekk!" Tommy shrieked.

"What is going on in here?" his mother announced from the doorway.

Tommy and his father stopped playing and both looked up. Betsy had her hands on her hips in a mock attempt to be serious.

"Rawr?" his father questioned.

There was a brief silence and then all three broke into hysterics.

"Happy birthday, son," said his father as he pulled Tommy close and gave him a real hug.

"Thanks, dad."

"Honey. We need to prep for the P-A-R-T-Y," as she spelled it out to her husband.

"PARTY!" Tommy cried out.

"Well, well, looks like Mr. Smarty Pants knows what we're talking about," Michael said as he ruffled his son's hair. "In that case you can help me out."

"Sure dad."

Michael looked over at his wife and she gave him a wink. Michael continued talking to Tommy. "I think I saw some presents earlier for you but I can't remember where they were."

Tommy squinted and said, "Come on, dad, don't mess with me."

After that comment coming from their five year old son they couldn't hold back their laughter.

"Hehehehehe. Okay okay. Let's go see if we can find them," said his father. "Where do you want to start?"

Tommy led his parent's to the living room and peered behind, under and around every conceivable hiding spot. Nothing. He then moved on to the dining room, but here weren't too many places to hide a present, he thought, other than china cabinet. Tommy still came up empty. Tommy pushed through the swinging door to the kitchen and started to open the cupboards.

Behind him his mother said, "Colder".

He walked towards the laundry room.

"Warmer," his father informed him.

He walked into the laundry room.

"Colder."

Tommy backtracked, turned and took two steps towards the family room.

"Colder."

Tommy turned and walked towards the hallway that led to his room.

"Warmer."

He skipped the bathroom and headed towards the guest room. *They have to be in here.*

"Colder."

Puzzled Tommy took a few tentative steps towards his own bedroom and looked back over his shoulder at his parents.

"Warmer."

He took another step.

"Waarrrmmerr."

One more step and he was at his bedroom door.

"Hot!"

Tommy gave them more look as if to say 'you have to be shitting me' and entered his bedroom. His parents followed and there, stacked against his little brown chair, were a few wrapped gifts. Tommy's eyes opened wide and ran over to them. They hadn't been there when he'd woken up.

"Nicely done, sweetie," Michael said to his wife who had enough time to grab Tommy's presents from the basement while Michael kept him distracted.

Excited, as any young boy would be, Tommy didn't waste any time to rip and tear open his packages. Shredded wrappings surrounded him as parents looked at each other and smiled. Not hiding his utter joy, Tommy examined each present he had received.

First he looked at the red dump truck. It had a yellow payload and a hydraulic lift that dumped everything on the ground when a lever was depressed. It had four huge wheels and the entire passenger zone was surrounded by glass. He had wanted one ever since he saw it in the Sandpiper toy store window a few months ago.

Tommy put the truck to his left and picked up the baseball mitt, bat and softball he'd unwrapped. He knew his father had been telling him that baseball was the sport of a lifetime. He'd started to show interest in the sport so Michael had picked up this set. Tommy tried on the mitt and slammed the ball in to it a few times as he grinned at his father. Afterwards he picked up the bat and discovered that letters had been burned in to the side of it. Those brown letters spelled out 'Tommy'.

"That's cool, dad," he said when he saw his name.

He then took a few practice swings of the bat. Wrapping paper was strewn everywhere around him.

"Thanks, mom. Thanks, dad," Tommy told them and gave them each a big hug.

"You're welcome, son," said Michael.

Being an only child Tommy was given lots of attention, but his parents made sure not to overly spoil him. They didn't want him to grow up expecting everything to be handed to him. Of course, they thought, he's only five, which is why they wanted him to have a big birthday party.

Tommy looked up and saw his parents' eyes. A special bond was there between them and they made Tommy feel loved. He hugged them fiercely. His parents embraced him as well. They were definitely a happy family.

Being the big boy that he felt he was now, Tommy said," If you don't mind I'd like some privacy please."

Controlling their laughter Betsy and Michael retreated to the kitchen for some breakfast. Tommy took a look at his dump truck, bat, mitt and ball again before he headed to his bathroom. He stripped out of his blue pajamas and started up the shower.

Betsy popped her head in the door. "Do you need any help, sweetie?"

"No, I got this."

Tommy had watched his father go through the motions of turning on each facet and testing the water to make sure it was the right temperature. *Done.* After that he was supposed to pull up on the lever, that was on the nozzle, to make the water come out up top. *Done.* Tommy concentrated hard while Betsy watched him complete each step just fine. Tommy stepped in to the shower and pulled the curtain closed. Because he was so small the water didn't directly hit him. *Feels like I'm out in the rain.* His mother smiled and left her son alone. Showers were new to Tommy because up to this point his parents had only given him baths. He was growing up and this is what grown-ups do, he had told himself and Tommy was determined to take showers from now on; but a bath every now and then definitely wasn't out of the question.

After finishing his shower, and successfully not getting any shampoo in his eyes, Tommy dried off and went back to his bedroom. He dressed in the clothes his mother had laid out for him. They consisted of a white pair of dress shorts and a blue button down shirt. If this day was any other day than his birthday then he wouldn't have wanted to wear these clothes. However, so far his birthday had started out great so why not wear the special clothes his mother wanted him to.

* * *

The doorbell started to ring around 2 p.m. that afternoon as the kids from school began to arrive. Some of the parents stayed and were ushered in to the kitchen area to congregate with the other adults. The children gathered in the living room and the packages they brought started to pile up in the room's corner, which had been thoroughly transformed. Balloons and streamers were all over the place and the dining room table's extensions had been added. The paper table cloth that covered it was adorned with bright birthday colors, letters and images of cake.

As more and more kids showed up Tommy felt more out of place. He knew he was in his own house but there were a lot of strangers around, and that made him feel uncomfortable. Part of him wanted them to leave but his mother had told him that people are what life is all about. Friendships make you happy and loved, she had said, and Tommy had tried to understand what she meant. He shrugged off his discomfort and started to enjoy himself.

At 2:14 p.m. the last guest arrived. Betsy gathered all the children together and started to some games. First there was pin-the-tail on the donkey. Once all the kids had their turn at being spun around the donkey looked utterly dead and prizes were handed out to the winners. Soon after the clown arrived; an extra treat by his parents. The entire living room was soon in an uncontrollably uproar as the clown discovered, much to the children's delight, endless amounts of money behind their ears and noses. He also made balloon animals for a bunch of the kids before he departed.

Before more festivities could commence a chorus of adult voices started to sing "Happy Birthday". Everyone stopped talking and joined in as Tommy turned crimson with some embarrassment. Everyone moved to the dining room as Tommy sat down at the head of the table. As the singing continued his mother brought the cake forward and placed it in front of him. There were five candles planted in the white frosting and the words "Happy 5th Birthday Tommy" decorated the top.

The song ended. Tommy wished for a bicycle, inhaled deeply and then blew out all five candles. Cheers rose as all five candles went dark. Betsy moved in closer and handed Tommy a cake knife. This was his first birthday where he had been allowed to cut the cake. Betsy looked around for the decorated paper plates, for the cake, but couldn't find them. She went back to the kitchen and looked through the shopping bags, but they weren't there either. Betsy realized she must have forgotten to pick them up and scolded herself.

She beckoned to Michael and he came over. "I spaced on the plates. I'll be right back. Start getting people back in the living room for presents and we'll save the cake until afterward."

Tommy still held the cake knife as Michael came over and took it out of his hand.

"Present time!" he announced.

Tommy scooted out of his chair as all the kids headed back to the living room. Betsy grabbed her purse and headed to the garage. After she backed out of the driveway she saw Tommy waving to her amidst his friends. Betsy waved back and continued down the street to town. Tommy watched her depart and then headed back inside. He was definitely was ready for presents.

Tommy's classmates made a semi-circle around him while he sat in front of the gift pile. They all begged him to open their present first. Tommy didn't know what to do so he randomly grabbed a box and tore in to it. That present happened to be larger than the rest and a little boy named Charlie grinned because it was his. It turned out to be a foot tall G.I.Joe doll with all the accessories. A number of the other boys let out soft groans of displeasure because they had wanted it for themselves.

Tommy thanked Charlie for the gift and grabbed another, its wrapping paper decorative and shiny. This time Tommy discovered a model kite that needed to be assembled. He had never had a kite before and he couldn't wait to test it out. The joy on his face was enough to please the young boy who had given it to him. At age five it's very difficult to handle someone not liking what you've given them. It hurts.

The phone started to ring in the kitchen. Michael went to answer it.

Tommy picked out another gift and started ripping at it.

A huge CRASH emanated from the kitchen and some of the adults cried out.

The children drew quiet as everyone's attention turned to the disturbance in the kitchen. Tommy almost had the package open.

The sounds of breaking glass.

His package now open.

Loud shouts filled the empty air.

Tommy gazed down at the matchbox car in front of him.

"NO! NO! NO! NOOOOOOOOO!!!"

Michael burst through the swinging kitchen door. Tommy looked up from his matchbox car, never seen his father like this before and became terribly frightened.

The matchbox car slipped from his fingers and fell to the floor.

His guests scattered in all directions as Michael bee-lined towards Tommy.

Tommy saw the fallen matchbox car and reached for it.

His father, tears streaming down his face rushed to his son.

Tommy couldn't see the matchbox car anymore; his father has picked him up and now held him tight. He could see the matchbox car now; his father had stepped on it. It was no longer fresh and new; it was bent, broken and destroyed. As the image of the matchbox car burned in his mind Tommy wondered where his mother was.

8
March 19, 1987

Two men waited in a square room, both dressed in suits. The wall across from the double doors contained an obvious two-way mirror. The larger of the two men, a muscled giant at six feet three stood in front, closer to the doors while the shorter, more athletically built male stood closer to the mirror. A stainless steel medical table, affixed with leather restraints, was bolted to the floor. Equipment, around the table, patiently waited to be utilized. A very bright overhead light spotlighted the table. Video cameras, pointed towards the table, were in each of the four corners.

The double doors burst open and an enraged young Caucasian man, in his early twenties, was wheeled in. He was strapped down on a gurney and dressed in a typical hospital gown. The muscled giant moved to intercept the gurney.

"What the fuck is happening?" the prisoner cried out.

"Restrain him," ordered the shorter man.

"Don't you fucking touch me motherfucker!" the prisoner yelled.

The giant grabbed the flailing man's throat with his left hand and gripped tightly. The prisoner's eyes widened as his air supply was cut off. With his right hand the giant worked the gurney's straps and freed the victim. Immediately the prisoner, with both hands, grabbed the giant's left arm and attempted to release the powerful grip.

"Mr. Peterson, will you please hurry up. I don't pay you for incompetence."

The giant replied, "Yes sir. Sorry, Mr. Glib."

Mr. Peterson, who seemed to dominate the room merely by his sheer size, moved the flailing prisoner to the room's metal table

63

and secured multiple straps. Mr. Peterson finally released his grip on the man's throat. As the prisoner started to suck in huge gulps of air Mr. Peterson attached a heartbeat sensor pad to his chest. The sensor was attached to an EKG machine and a very rapid pulse appeared the machine's screen.

"Thank you, Mr. Peterson," said Mr. Glib. "You can go now. If I need you I will ring."

Straightening his suit out Mr. Peterson said, "Yes, of course, sir," and exited the room through the double doors.

The young man's eyes were full of fear as his eyes darted around the room. He didn't like where he was, didn't know what the hell was going on and certainly didn't want to be any part of it. The prisoner looked up into the eyes of the man Mr. Peterson had addressed as 'sir'.

"Who the fuck are you?" the man challenged. "What the fuck is this place?"

Without missing a beat Mr. Glib walked over to the table and gave the man a long onceover.

What a fine specimen. Well built, young and healthy. This one is full of energy too. Perfect. "It is unfortunate that fate brings you here today. Granted, you were scheduled for execution in the next few years, so maybe we'll just save the taxpayers some money and get it over with today."

Mr. Glib looked directly in to the man's eyes and got the exact reaction he was looking for, absolute fear and panic.

"Let me out of here you fucking psycho!" as he violently struggled against his restraints.

"Then again, someone had to be in the same place as you are now. It might as well be you since you are the filth of society," sneered Mr. Glib. "Have a nice day."

64

Mr. Glib exited the room and was replaced by another man that was covered from head to toe in protective gear and a reflective facemask. In the individual's hand was a rather large needle that contained a large amount of black liquid.

The prisoner struggled even harder and couldn't take his eyes off the needle.

"Get the fuck away from me you asshole!!"

The man grabbed the prisoner's forehead, forced the head back to expose the neck and waited. From the speaker in the ceiling came Mr. Glib's voice, now stationed behind the two way mirror.

"Proceed."

"Cut it out man! I've going to kil-"

The prisoner's shout was abruptly cut off as the large needle pierced his throat and the EKG machine spiked as the man's heartbeat sharply elevated. All that could be heard was a distant gurgling noise in the back of his mouth and the cameras captured everything. Bubbles formed between his clenched teeth and spilled down the side of his face. His eyes flipped back, farther in to his brain and his body sadistically convulsed, stopped short by the leather restraints.

Nineteen seconds had passed. The thrashing stopped and the EKG flat lined.

"Check him," the voice boomed over the speaker.

The suited attendant placed two fingers on the man's throat and waited. Nothing.

"I think the dosage was off, sir," he ascertained.

The loud speaker crackled, "Thank you for your brilliant observation you idiot. Dispose of the body and then come to my office."

"Yes, sir."

9
Wed July 4, 1990 10:31 a.m.

By the time Thomas wheeled his damaged bicycle home it was just after 10:30 a.m.. His mind still reeled a bit over what George had said to him. *Take care of yourself, Tom. You're a bright man with a future ahead of you. Deal with whatever's eating you before it's too late.* George was a complete stranger and the third person, in as many days, to notice that something was wrong.

Thomas walked up his driveway with his damaged bike and, after opening his garage, hung it on its rafter hook. He unlocked his house door and pressed the garage door button. As it closed he entered and turned off the alarm. Thomas stripped down and left his clothes in a pile on the floor. The dirt he's land in, the walk back as well as the squished bananas, had left a rather unsavory smell about his person.

He walked through his house, up the stairs, to the bathroom and started up the shower for the third time that morning. Once the water was warm up Thomas stepped in and started to nurse his sore body and muscles.

Afterward the shower Thomas examined his body in the foggy bathroom mirror. A bruise had already formed on his upper left arm. It didn't hurt too much but he certainly didn't want to aggravate the injury. He stepped out of his bathroom and paused by his closet.

What to do.

Thomas knew he had to keep busy or else he'd over think everything he'd been through today.

My bed looks bare.

He had a couple hours before the appointment with Dr. Bond so he dressed in some denim shorts before he extracted some new sheets from the his closet's top shelf. Luckily he still had an old comforter and removed that as well. Thomas quickly made the bed, but couldn't help but glance at the scrubbed down wall, every now and then.

Stop looking at it.

The fresh aqua sheets, he'd chosen, complimented the dark blue comforter. He changed out the two pillow cases and tossed them where they belonged.

It almost looks normal.

Thomas took the old pillow covers, and the used towels from the bathroom, and headed to the laundry room. He started a load on cold, put the towels and pillow coverings inside, then added his dirty bike clothes from the floor. He closed the lid and let it run.

I'm hungry.

Thomas wandered to the kitchen and fixed himself some lunch. A few minutes later he walked out of the kitchen with a two baloney cheese sandwiches and a coke. He picked up the remote, sat down, thumbed the on button took a bite. He kept changing the channel, not really paying attention, as he ate his sandwich and mindlessly drifted off.

What did I do? Where did that blood come from? I'm so confused. What the hell is going on?

As Thomas ate, surfed and thought about the day's events, a voice from the TV brought him out of his daze. His thumbed stopped from proceeding to the next channel.

"…was found dead in his Redlands house this morning after neighbors called police complaining of very loud noises. When the police arrived they discovered his front door open and, upon entering, found the victim face down in a pool of blood. The apparent cause of death was a hand axe which was found embedded in the back of his skull. Investigators are unwilling to discuss any more details until they've had a chance to comb through the crime scene. The police have confirmed that a struggle ensued prior to the victim's death. Once again, Mr. Rupert Jones, age fifty-one, was found dead early this morning in his Redlands home. We'll have more on this story as details are made available.

"In World News, Iraq has…"

Thomas turned off the TV and realized he hadn't moved a muscle.

The axe. Did I wear gloves?

"Wait. What?" Thomas said as answered himself out loud.

What do I mean, did I wear gloves? I don't remember anything from last night. Stop it. Stop thinking like this.

Thomas started to tremble, like a light shiver but he couldn't stop. Thomas put his sandwich down and wiped his now perspiring brow. He didn't like what he had just heard. Not only had a murder occurred at the base of the mountain he called home, but he'd literally woken up with blood on his hands.

I'm not a killer. I don't want to hurt anyone.

The coincidence was compelling and he couldn't stop dwelling on it.

"What the hell have I done?"

* * *

Wed July 4, 1990 1:27 p.m.

The next two hours for Thomas dragged by and now he didn't want to have anything to do that meant leaving his house. Part of him feared he would black out and come to with an axe in his hands, so instead he'd sat on his couch for two hours as his appointment drew nearer. During that time Thomas had gone back and forth, in his head, on what the newscast had reported and remained fixated on where the blood in his room had come from. It troubled him deeply.

Thomas went upstairs and changed in to a blue striped Oxford, a pair of acid-washed jeans and a new pair of Reeboks. On the back he took his lunch dishes and dumped them in the sink. On his way to the garage he noticed that the laundry had finished, transferred the load to the dryer and started up a cycle.

His watch read 1:35 p.m.. *Here we go.*

Thomas set the alarm, locked the door and got into his car. He had purchased a new 325i BMW a few years back and he loved it. He enjoyed how the wheels gripped the road. But, he knew if he thought about it, driving was just another form of distraction for him. He opened the garage door, back out and closed it behind him.

As he headed through Running Springs Thomas marveled at how such a small town could survive because it felt like winter was about the only time the town was full of people. Today was an exception to those rules because it was July 4th.

Turning left at the junction he drove his BMW down 330. The first ten or twenty times he traversed this mountain highway he thought it would never end. In reality the drive was only fifteen miles long and now, since he'd driven it so much, he didn't particularly notice how long it took. It was as if all the twists and turns in the road were one in the same.

As he materialized out of the mountains 330 merged into the 30. His BMW seemed to know where it was going and Thomas soon found himself in the heart of San Bernardino. Twelve minutes later he parked at Dr. Bond's office building. He found the elevator, took it to the second floor and located office 232 right down the hall. He entered and found himself in a typical waiting room, but no one else was there. Untold numbers of psychological journals, pamphlets and magazines lined the room next to the empty chairs. Thomas felt uneasy.

"You're early, Mr. Clark," said a young female voice.

He recognized the voice. Thomas turned and saw the woman he had conversed with a few days prior. He looked at his watch and saw that it read 2:21 p.m..

"The last appointment was cancelled so Dr. Bond is available, Mr. Clark."

"Thank you," Thomas said with a little uncertainty.

"Please step right through that door."

Thomas meandered down the hallway to Dr. Bond's office. He rapped lightly on the outer door but didn't receive a reply. He turned the doorknob, found it unlocked and entered.

"Hello, Mr. Clark. I'm Dr. Bond."

Startled by this introduction Thomas stopped in mid stride with the door handle still in his grasp. He looked over to his right and saw stunning blond who stood by a desk. Not understanding where Dr. Bond was Thomas was unsure how to proceed. The young woman stepped forward with her hand extended.

"Mr. Clark, I'm Dr. Bond. Dr. Laura Bond."

Thomas just there with his mouth open, stunned.

"You… you're a woman," he said as he shook her hand.

"Apparently my best impersonation of James Bond went right over your head." She smiled at him. "Won't you please come in and sit down."

He closed the door and took a seat. He glanced around the room and noticed Dr. Bond had apparently decorated the office in her personal taste. Clinging to one side of her spacious office were her diplomas and degrees that designated, as well as proved, that she was a professional psychiatrist.

Harvard. Interesting.

An imposing bookshelf took up another wall of the room. As he leaned closer he saw that it contained both psychological books and fictional novels. The titles of the books were hard to read where he was sitting but he could make out a few words on some which classified them in the genre of killings, murders and deaths.

"You're not the first person, Mr. Clark," she told him. "Other clients of mine have been just as surprised when they see me for the first time. Do you have any issues discussing your issues with a woman?"

"No, no, of course not. It's just that I'm not used to sharing anything with women ever since my mother was killed."

Thomas was surprised that he'd actually just said that.

"And yet, Mr. Clark, you've just shared your first insight with me."

He averted his eyes away from the bookshelf and to Dr. Bond. He realized that he was extremely nervous and she picked up on this right away.

"Please relax, Mr. Clark. I'm not going to hurt you."

Thomas cleared his throat and tried to recompose himself.

"First off, please call me Thomas. When I hear Mr. Clark I can't help but think my grandfather is in the room. Secondly, I am a bit uncomfortable. This," he said as he swept his arm around the room, "is completely new to me, and to top it off I've had one hell of a day already."

"You can call me Laura if that makes you any more comfortable," she replied. "So you've never talked with a professional before then Thomas?" she asked as she jotted something down.

Thomas shook his head no. "Well, on second thought, not since I was a kid."

"I see." She made another notation.

"Any reason you have so many books on death?" Thomas asked while as he pointed to her extensive collection.

Dr. Bond smiled. "Do they disturb you Thomas?"

"No," he quickly replied. "No, they don't disturb me. It's just that it seems weird for a psychiatrist to have those types of books."

"Perhaps. It's a hobby of mine. I like to read when I have free time. What do you do for fun, Thomas?"

He returned his gaze back to her. Dr. Laura Bond was just over five feet-six inches tall and had the body of a Miss America Queen. Thomas' gaze started down at her feet as he moved up her legs.

Amazing.

His eyes traversed northward. Her breasts, very well defined under her white blouse, were perfect.

"Thomas?"

"Huh?"

"Earth to Thomas."

"Oh. Sorry."

"What were you thinking of?"

"Nothing," Thomas said. He crossed his legs.

"I see." Dr. Bond said, but not really taking his answer at face value. "So what brings you here today, Thomas?"

Thomas squirmed in his seat and Dr. Bond tried a different tact.

"Let's start with something easy then, Thomas. Who referred you to my office?"

"I'm not sure I should say," Thomas answered. "He didn't want me to talk about it."

"Well, let me assure you that whatever we talk about is kept in the strictest confidence. If your friend recommended me then perhaps that speaks for itself."

Thomas thought about it. "Alright, it was Nick, Nick Raynes who gave me your card. He's an old college buddy of mine. Apparently you helped him and his wife Susan out with something. He was vague."

"Oh yes, Mr. and Mrs. Raynes. And you knew him from college?"

"We both went to USC. We didn't really know each other at the time. We met up later when I was looking for representation with my first book. He's been my agent ever since."

"Very interesting. And what do you write about? Fiction, non-fiction?" Dr. Bond asked.

"I write children's books, Dr. Bond…, I mean Laura."

"And how long have you been writing, Thomas?" she inquired as she made a note on her paper.

Thomas felt more at ease now. Clearly answering questions within his comfort zone was very easy and Dr. Bond was just trying to get any overview of who he was.

"Technically I've been writing since I was a kid, but professionally I started after college. Although, after graduating I traveled for a while."

"Anywhere in particular?"

"I kind of did the 'backpack across Europe' routine you hear about all the time."

"All by yourself?" she asked.

"Yeah. I've been kind of a loner for a long time now. When college finished up I realized I hadn't gotten out and seen the world yet. I'd been hiding away just doing what society expected from me."

"What society expected of you? What do you mean?"

"Well, it's complicated," he said. "There were some issues I had to go through when I was younger, the kind of issues that can really mess with your head. Anyway, I guess I got through all that and finished school, then headed off to college. I don't know. I think I was just carrying on like everything was fine."

"Sounds like you weren't okay with that."

"I felt trapped maybe; definitely different than everyone else."

"How so?" she probed.

Thomas shifted in the chair. "Abandoned," he told her softly.

Having said that word Thomas suddenly doubled over in his seat while holding his head in his hands. His body started trembling.

"Thomas, what is it?" Laura asked with genuine concern.

Thomas didn't respond. He started to sob and his trembling continued.

"Please Thomas. Talk to me. You've got to let it out or it will consume you."

Those words immediately made Thomas think of George Miles. *Take care of whatever's eating you before it's too late.* Thomas took a really deep breath, exhaled and sat up. Laura handed him a couple of tissues. Thomas blew his nose and dabbed his tears away.

"I think I really need to talk," Thomas said.

Laura was clearly moved by Thomas. He seemed like an intriguing man. She liked his blond hair and she guessed he was about five inches taller than she was. He had strolled in to her office defensive and unsure of the situation. And apparently he had been expecting a man. But she had done her job, casually talking with him while leading the conversation. Now a minor chink in his armor had just been breached.

75

"I've got all day, Thomas. Just take your time and elaborate. I'm here to help."

The time on her desk clock read 2:53 p.m.. He leaned back in his chair.

Laura leaned forward and said, "Let's start with the abandonment you feel. Did it have anything to do with your mother passing away?"

Thomas froze. "How do you know about my mother?"

"I listened to you, Thomas. One of the first things you said to me was that you hadn't really talked to a woman about you mother's death."

"I really said that? Wow, I really must be losing it. I don't remember that. I'm not sure I want to talk about that."

"Okay, let's build up to it. Where were you born and what was your childhood like?" Laura crossed her legs and prepped her pen for additional notes. "Whatever you want to tell me is okay. I want to get to know who you are, and granted that will take a number of sessions, so why don't you start at the beginning."

Oh she's good.

He knew it was in his best interest to unburden himself but that didn't make it any easier to open his mouth. Thomas leaned back in his chair and began.

"I was born on July 27, 1957 in San Jose, CA. When I was two my parents, Michael and Betsy, moved to Orinda which is about fifty-five miles away from San Jose. My dad was a consultant, and to this day I don't know what he did nor did my parents ever talk about it with me. My mother stayed at home and from what I can recall my childhood was the epitome of perfection. I was happy and life was good. My folks were the kind of parents that every child should have growing up. They

loved me dearly. But that all changed when I turned five."
Thomas paused.

"What happened when you were five?" Laura looked up from
her notes.

"I don't really like to talk about it." Thomas squirmed again.
"I don't even like to think about it."

"Trust me, Thomas. I know you don't know me but you can
trust me. Whatever happened is part of who you are and it affects
you. I'm here to help you. Talk to me."

Thomas stole a glance at Laura. She looked like she was
clearly engaged and wasn't bullshitting him.

Fuck, this rabbit hole is going to be deep.

Thomas took a deep breath and let it out. "Well, on my fifth
birthday I had this birthday party. You know, games, a clown,
everything. The day started out great. The party was going along
as planned and happy birthday had just been sung. My mother let
me cut my cake, by myself, for the very first time." Thomas
smiled as he thought about the memory. "After it was cut I
distinctly remember my mother looking for paper plates. She
couldn't find any so she left my party to buy some in town. I saw
her leave, waved to her and she waved back. Anyway, my dad
focused the party away from cake eating to opening presents until
she returned. I was in heaven. I think I was opening my fourth
gift when our phone rang. My father got up to answer it and the
next thing I know it felt like time had slowed waaay down."

Laura looked at Thomas and saw a man clearly in pain as he
wrestled with his past. "It's okay, Thomas. Take your time."

He took another deep breath. "Anyway, I was opening a
present when a loud crash emanated from our kitchen. My father
comes storming out and he's screaming, but it's like I can't hear
him. Parents and kids are scattering to get out of his way. I had

never seen my father like this before and it scared me shitless. The gift I had just opened was a matchbox car and as he startled me it fell out of my hand. He came over and started hugging me and stepped on it by accident. That's when I started crying. I was so scared of what was happening that I wet my pants and started to bawl. Other kids were crying and the parents that were there had ushered the other kids out of the living room and into the kitchen, away from us. I had never seen my father cry before in his life."

Thomas's watery eyes brimmed, spilled over and ran down his face. Laura gently presented the tissue box. Thomas took a few and covered his face.

"He stopped hugging me. He knelt down next to me and looked straight in my eyes. My father could barely get the words from his lips as he told me what had happened. He said that another car had slammed into ours and that mommy wasn't coming home, but I didn't understand him. He looked down on the floor and saw the gift that he had stepped on; the matchbox car. He had to have been in shock because he told me exactly what happened to her. He said that the matchbox car was how mommy's car looked now and that mommy was inside. I took the car from him and stared at it because it was crushed and destroyed. I dropped to the floor and started banging my hands and feet as I pleaded for my mother. My father tried to comfort me as best as he could but he was in too much pain of his own to help me." He paused. "I forgot what happened after that."

Thomas bent over and sobbed. He hadn't told anyone, in that specific detail, about his mother's death before. He took a few more tissues and attempted to compose himself, but his body shook and great sobs rippled through him as he finished telling Laura what had transpired so many years ago. He had never felt so much pain in his life before, but he also felt better. It was an odd feeling. Thomas wished he had shared what had happened to him with someone earlier in his life but he had been too scared to even bring it up. He just didn't want to relive it.

"Thomas, I'm so sorry for your loss. You should be proud though. That was a fantastic step you just took. Thank you."

Dr. Bond sat back in her chair and waited until Thomas was finished. She had never met a patient share the way he had ever before in her career as a psychiatrist. But she knew his pain and desperately wanted to help him through it, and because of that felt closer to Thomas than any other person who'd walked through her door before. Since was certain he would share more.

Laura wrote down a few more observations and looked up from her writings as she wondered about the amount of pain Thomas had been in as a little boy; but more importantly how he survived. From the age of five his mother died and he was left only with his father to raise him. Any child would have tremendous trauma brought on by this horrific event. Laura wanted to ask questions about what happened but she was afraid he would turtle up on her. Besides, she thought, there is plenty of time to heal him; he's made it this far.

Thomas became quiet. Never before had he trusted anyone as much as he trusted the woman sitting in front of him. Somewhere deep inside of him he was glad he had talked about his mother's death. He was young and it had been so unfair. Why did she have to leave him? All he wanted was a mommy to love him and care for him. All the other kids in the school got that. Why couldn't he? At that age Thomas had wanted to be with his mommy. After she died, and in turn, for the rest of his life, he had isolated himself away from other people, especially women. He was tired of feeling the way he did and he wanted something different. At least some part of him surrendered to the intense feelings that had been

79

bottled up for so long. His friends knew, he thought. *Hell, even George knew.*

Wiping away the tears that had streamed down his face, Thomas lifted his head and looked in to Laura's emerald green eyes.

"Thomas, I…I'm so sorry. You were such a small boy. Have you kept this inside of you all this time?"

"Yes. I turned away from everyone's help. Not having my mother there for me anymore left me numb for the longest time. Kindergarten started about five weeks later and the kids kept their distance from me, because of what happened at my party. It was heart wrenching."

"I can only imagine," Laura said. "All I can say, Thomas, is that I'm really glad that you opened up. You've kept this inside of you too long and it's affected who you are. But this is just the beginning for you. I want you to go home now and relax. You've earned it. I'd like to see you again on the 6th. Does 4:30 p.m. work for you?"

"That's fine. Thank you, Dr. Bond. I mean, thank you, Laura."

Thomas rose out of his chair and headed towards the door.

"You're welcome, Thomas. I'll see you then."

Thomas walked to her office door, opened and then closed it behind him. He hadn't felt both this shitty and good since he could remember. He'd obviously been scared to confront his past, but now that he had started to it made him feel more confident about himself.

As he departed the office building, Thomas made his way back to his BMW and slowly drove home. He had a lot to think about, and now that his Pandora's box has been cracked open, his mind started to flood with memories.

* * *

Laura watched Thomas rise from his chair and vanish down the corridor. She wondered about who Thomas thought he might be. *Traumatic events change people.* She knew there was a lot more to Thomas Clark and she was particularly interested in peeling back the layers to help him find out. *I can't wait.*

10

October 16, 1967 8:55 a.m.

"Hey, Tommy!"

Tommy Clark entered the school grounds. Ever since his fifth birthday party the majority of his classmates, and others, had maintained their distance while he continued to dwell on that tragic day. When his sixth birthday came around the next year Tommy refused a birthday party, and on the actual day itself he stayed in his room and didn't come out. The following year he repeated the same thing. At school he still liked to play and seemed to be handling the loss of his mother just fine but the teachers now noticed a darker side to Tommy. He didn't talk a lot and kept to himself, and the other kids sensed it too.

"Hey, Tommy!" cried the other boy once again.

Tommy turned his head towards the shout, saw Sammy, and smiled. Sammy was actually Tommy's only true friend since kindergarten, and had been at Tommy's fifth birthday party. Sammy Paige was his name, average height for a third grader with a full head of black hair. Sammy's parents were divorced and he lived with his father. Sammy never saw his mother so he could relate. Since that point they became best friends and had stayed that way ever since. The other kids didn't know what to think about them. Sammy and Thomas needed each other for support because at times it was hard to deal with not having any female figures around to love them.

They ran towards each other and met halfway at the swings. Tommy was ten and Sammy was nine years old. Sammy's birthday was coming up in a month on November 15.

"Tommy, guess what?"

"Hey Sammy, what's up?"

"You know my birthday is coming up and I'm going to have a party," Sammy said with excitement. "I wanted to let you know."

"Awesome," Tommy answered, but without any real energy behind it.

Sammy caught on. "Oh, hey Tommy. I'm sorry. I didn't mean anything by it. What'ya got there?"

Tommy showed him his baseball bat and glove. Everything in his room had become a disaster zone since his mother died. Her passing had been just over five years and yet it still lay heavily on Tommy's mind.

God how I miss her.

Recently his father had asked him to clean out his closet and Tommy had discovered a few lost treasures. In that process he also found his red dump truck which he had loved so much. He had forgotten about the presents that he had received on that birthday, since he'd thrown everything into his closet. He denied himself a childhood and leapt into his own world of fantasy to cope with that particular loss in his life.

Sammy looked at the bat and his eyes glowed. "Let me see it," he said.

Tommy let Sammy hold his bat while he hit his glove with his right hand.

"Wow! It even has your name on it!" Sammy finally gave it back. "We should hit some balls after school."

"Well, I don't have a ball and I don't know where to get one."

"I guess we could borrow one from the sports equipment in the classroom?" Sammy suggested.

"Yeah. Good idea. Let's do that."

The bell rang and the entire playground moved towards their respective classroom. The two boys both ran to class and squeezed through the door just in time. Their teacher, Ms. Murray, couldn't stand tardiness; but as a teacher she was gentle, patient, kind and understanding. Tommy liked Ms. Murray so he made sure to get to class on time. No need to get on her bad side.

"Good morning class," announced Ms. Murray.

"Good morning, Ms. Murray," they replied in unison.

Next up was the pledge of allegiance. She did this every morning just to make sure that her students were paying attention to what she was saying. She also did it to pick out any of the potential trouble makers of the day. Ms. Murray taught in such a way that allowed learning to be fun, not a burden, and she always taught them with a smile on her face. That pleased Tommy. However, when you goofed off she would be on your case in a minute and had told the class that if you respect me I'll respect you; save your goofing off for recess and lunch. After that speech only a few kids tested her and, once they had, rarely tried again.

Class droned on. Tommy usually paid attention because he liked to learn but something bothered him. He had found a way to deal with his mother's death by making up imaginary stories and then lived in them. Today was just like any other day but he still didn't feel good; something was definitely wrong. He started to draw on his paper while Ms. Murray taught and was lucky that she didn't notice him. On his paper he drew a dump truck. If only he had his crayons; he would color it red.

Tomorrow I'll bring it to school so Sammy and I can play with it at recess.

With a smile across his face Tommy looked up from his paper and began listening to what Ms. Murray had to say.

Ms. Murray looked out over her class, as she talked about addition and subtraction, and noticed little Tommy Clark. He wasn't smiling again and she wondered if he ever would. She'd heard about his mother's accident and had tried her best to give

85

him the extra time he needed in class. Her eyes moved to other children in the room as she continued her lesson. Eventually she settled back on Tommy she saw that his attention was focused on her again; and he had a smile on his face.

* * *

School let out at 2:20 that afternoon. Sammy and Tommy left their classroom and headed towards the field. Earlier they had managed to swipe a baseball from the classroom's P.E. equi p.m.ent and were pretty pleased with themselves. They laughed and had a good time as they caught the ball for each other. Time passed and the school had emptied out. The older kid's school day had ended and they were getting on buses on the other side of the campus; which meant no one else was around.

Ten minutes later they got interrupted.

"Hey, momma's boy!"

Sammy and Tommy stopped their game of baseball and looked over to the entrance to the field. There stood Nigel Clemmings. Nigel was in the fifth grade and had transferred to Wagner Ranch this year. The rumor was that he had been held back in the second grade so he was already twelve years old. What made him so different was that he was quite large for his age. He must have been at least 5'5" with dark, black hair. All the other kids in his grade didn't come close to how large Nigel was. But what seemed to make him so menacing was that his eyebrows were extremely thick, which made him appear somewhat like a Neanderthal man.

Nigel started to walk towards them. By this time, though, Sammy and Tommy had subconsciously moved closer to each other. Security in numbers was the only thing they knew. They two looked around again and didn't see anyone.

86

This is bad.

"Hey, buttheads."

Nigel drew closer. He was a monster. He terrorized dozens of kids at school to make himself feel better. The rumor was that his family was really screwed up and that his father beat him. In turn, Nigel just did the same thing to everyone else.

"Hey, Tommy. Let me see that bat." It wasn't a question.

By this time Nigel was only ten feet away and they silently considered running.

"You move and you die," Nigel commanded as if he read their minds.

Petrified with fear neither Sammy nor Tommy sprinted away. Even if they both ran in the opposite directions he would chase one of them down and that person would regret having lived. Besides, they both knew he would be at school the following day.

"I said," he screamed at them, "give me that bat!"

Still frozen in fear, Nigel leapt and grabbed the bat from Tommy's clenched hands. The only thing Tommy could do was utter a low groan.

"Thanks, you little shit. Nice, Tommy, it even has your name on it," he mocked.

Nigel took a few swings of Tommy's bat and smile grew and grew. Every couple of swings he would take a step towards Sammy and Tommy; who still hadn't moved. Finally one of the swings barely missed the top of Sammy's head and that snapped them out of it.

"Run Sammy!" Tommy shouted.

The two sprinted away and headed for the school buildings. Nigel stood his ground for a second until he realized his prey had vanished. He turned and ran after them.

"Hurry Sammy, we can lose him by the dumpsters!"

When he looked over his shoulder Tommy saw that Nigel was about forty feet behind them. When they sprinted around a corner Tommy slipped on some loose gravel and tumbled to the hard concrete. Nigel was on him in a second.

"You're dead Tommy," Nigel growled.

Sammy had stopped when Tommy fell and now he just stood there unsure of what he could do to help his friend.

Nigel raised the bat over his head. "Get back here or I'll crack his head open!" he bellowed at Sammy.

"Run Sammy!" Tommy cried. "Get some help!"

Sammy hesitated only for a moment before he ran off to find someone, which left Tommy all alone with Nigel.

Nigel snickered. "Bad move. Now I'm going to teach you a lesson. You will worship the ground I walk on, won't you, Tommy?"

Tommy looked up at Nigel and his tormenter's sinister smile filled him with horror. This wasn't your normal bullying, Nigel was out for blood. Feeling the pain from the gravel in his cut hands, Tommy slowly stood up and backed up against the school wall. Nigel eyed his prey the entire time, a huge grin on his face. Tommy was scared and on the verge of crying, but he tried to hold them back the best he could and not look frightened. He knew it was only a matter of time before his tears would slip out of their own volition.

"I'm going to do to you what my father does to me, only worse," Nigel promised as he raised the bat over his head in preparation.

Nigel suddenly fell to the ground and screamed, "OOUUUCCHHH!"

A large rock lay next to him and blood oozed from his head. Tommy looked around and saw Sammy with a second rock in his hand, just in case the first one he threw missed or hadn't hurt Nigel. Tommy hesitated and then retrieved his fallen bat off the ground. Nigel was still writhing and howling as the two boys ran practically the entire way back to Sammy's house, nearly two miles away, without stopping. Neither of them wanted to think about what would occur at school the next day when Nigel caught up to them again.

"Holy crap. Holy crap. Holy crap," Tommy repeated. "You totally saved me, Sammy. Thanks!"

They had never fought back before. They had struck a blow to Nigel and they let their egos go crazy with the knowledge that they had won this battle.

In Sammy's kitchen they stopped to get a snack. Sammy's father, much like Tommy's, worked so they were both latch key kids. From Sammy's backyard Tommy could see his house, which was about three hundred yards away. If there wasn't any wind they could yell to each other, much to the chagrin of their neighbors.

While they ate all they talked about was how they had finally beaten Nigel. Neither of them enjoyed being bullied and on numerous occasions Nigel had physically assaulted them. Thankfully they typically got away with minor cuts and bruises. As they finished their snacks Tommy told Sammy about his red dump truck that he had recently excavated out of his closet. His love for the truck hadn't diminished over the years but the memories that went with it were still remained with him.

"I can't wait to see it, Tommy."

"I've got to go, Sammy. I'll see you tomorrow."

"Bye, Tommy."

The day was over for now and Tommy had to go. Sammy closed the door behind him as Tommy walked down the road and around a few twists and turns. Luckily his house was close enough to Sammy's that it wasn't a huge trek. When Tommy did get home he let himself in, turned off the alarm, as his father had instructed him to do, and headed to his room. The house was empty and he knew his father wouldn't be home for at least a couple of hours. The silence was deafening but that didn't seem to affect Tommy. He had become a fighter of life. His father told him that he must be strong and that he needed to go on with his life. Tommy hadn't quite understood those words at the time. All he knew was that his mother had died and he had lived. That didn't mean he didn't miss her every single day.

In his room Tommy lay down on his bed and started to softly cry. He usually cried when his father wasn't home because he didn't want his father to see him as anything but a strong young man. The tears flowed endlessly, fueled by the pain that resided in his heart. Some wounds heal, but never completely.

He also felt lost and confused, and with extra problems like Nigel didn't help at all. It was just another predicament that made Tommy resentful and he didn't know what to do about it.

Looking around his room Tommy finally laid his eyes on his red dump truck. It was parked, in the corner of his room, next to his little brown chair. Tommy's eyes cleared up and eventually a small smile started to form that lifted away some of his sadness.

11

Thursday July 5, 1990 11:31 a.m.

Thomas woke to a sharp sound and rolled over in bed. There it was again.

Stupid phone.

"Shit," he mumbled as he made himself get out of his warm surroundings. He picked up the phone on the fourth ring.

"Hello?"

Silence. Shortly thereafter a dial tone emanated from the receiver. Thomas hung up the phone in disgust.

His room was somewhat darkened even though his clock clearly displayed 11:31am. The curtains he had pulled over the windows had done their job. He had wanted to sleep in today, as yesterday had been somewhat brutal, for a variety of reasons. Some days he loved to sleep in. He didn't have a job to commute to unless he counted the six feet it took to get from his bed to his computer. Thomas enjoyed writing and was his own boss. He also knew that some days it was hard to stay motivated, and Nick stayed on his case about his next book. Naturally, Thomas didn't like to disappoint and adhered to the fact that his word was his bond.

Thomas swished open the curtains and the sun stung his eyes. He left the sunlight behind, marched into his bathroom and prepared his shower. Once it was ready he stepped in and the hot water helped to clear his mind. As he washed his hair, and the rest of his body, Thomas started to think about the previous day at Dr. Bond's office. He had clearly overcome some of his fear and let out a great deal of pain that had held him back since his mother's death. Thomas felt relieved that he could trust someone enough to share his intimate secrets with, although truth be told, he hadn't planned on talking about his mother. He had chickened out on telling Laura about his blackouts and the strange wall art, so now the only thing he had to do was go back and do just that, even though he still didn't have a clue what was really going on.

It's too fucking weird.

Thomas opened his eyes and noticed that his skin was bright red. He'd lost track of time and reduced the water's temperature.

It was like I was a different person.

Not only was he surprised by his openness, he was also overcome by the beauty and quality of Dr. Laura Bond. She was someone that he wanted to get to know because he felt comfortable and safe with her. That was definitely something new.

Thomas turned off the water, stepped out and dripped water all over the tiled floor. He wasn't sure what he was going to do today and that's why he paused.

Well, I could work more on my book or I could go outside and work in my garden.

He pulled a towel from the rack and dried himself off. As he was doing so he decided to dress in gardening attire so he could spend some time outside in the sun. Thomas dug some old clothes out his closet and dressed in a pair of cutoff jeans, some old tennis shoes and a tie dyed t-shirt that he'd bought at Venice Beach a long time ago. His ratty outfit gave him the appearance that he actually lived on Venice Beach itself.

Thomas went downstairs, disarmed the alarm, and entered the garage. He located the proper gardening tools, pressed the garage door button and proceeded to his garden. When he got there he surveyed the work that needed to be accomplished. He had two huge beds of flowers that needed to be weeded, and the earth around the flowers need to be turned up, to allow the water to

92

properly soak into the ground. He estimated that it would probably take two or three hours.

Thomas started on the far left side of his house where he had originally planted some flowers, which continued along the front of his house and ended on the right side. He had planted them for two reasons. First was that they would add character and beauty. The second, and probably the most important, was that Thomas planted them to escape from the world as well as what was trapped inside of him.

Thomas spotted weeds between his blooming blossoms and e knelt down on his knees. He grabbed the weeding tool from his collection, poked the ground right in front of a weed and gently lifted it and its roots out. He put the weed aside and went on to the next one he could find. He continued this process until his garden was halfway completed. He paused and wiped his brow.

It was the middle of the day and Thomas was hot and tired. He lay back on the lawn and closed his eyes, exhausted. Deciding that he needed and deserved a rest he got up and walked inside. He took off his shoes before he went inside, not to track any dirt, and made himself a pitcher of orange juice. Outside he poured himself a glass and downed it in a couple of gulps. He remained thirsty so he poured himself another one. This one he took his time with.

Afterward he lay down on the grass and rested for another ten minutes before he continued. He was pretty thorough with his work because he hadn't missed one weed, but he enjoyed being thorough on whatever job he worked at.

As he continued to dig and remove weeds, Thomas came to an area in his garden that had been freshly dug up.

"Damn dog," he cursed.

Once in a while the next door neighbor's dog came over and used his garden to bury its 'presents'. Sometimes Thomas found a buried bone, while other times the dog has contributed its own fertilizer. What upset Thomas was that the digging and burying damaged his flowers.

At least the dog is only a Chihuahua.

Thomas looked closer at the mess the dog made this time and saw something else buried just beneath the surface.

"Back to bones this time little fella. Well, that's just great."

Thomas pulled at the exposed end of the bone, but it didn't budge. Thomas pulled harder.

"What the hell..."

Just then the bone came free and dirt exploded everywhere as Thomas held the prize firmly in his hand. But he had to look away because sun light, which reflected off the bone, hurt Thomas' eyes. He shifted his arm to different angle to get a look at what he held in his hand. It was an axe.

* * *

Thursday July 5, 1990 7:18 p.m.

Redlands, located at the base of the San Bernardino Mountains, contained pockets of upper class housing. Victor Salva had found the right house years ago in this area and lived comfortably.

Victor's day had been long and he was beat. He'd just driven home from Los Angeles after spending the day there in meeting after meeting with potential business clients. He preferred to do his business over the phone but there were days when face-to-face meetings were the only way to close deals. He smiled. Victor knew he had made great progress on his current project and within the next two weeks he was positive that he'd have it nailed down. Of course, securing in large insurance prospects took time, but with the proper amount of wining and dining his potential clients typically signed on the dotted line.

Victor entered his house, having parked in the garage, took off his sports coat and laid it on the back of his couch. He was a bigger man, rounder than most. He opened his fridge, grabbed a Heineken and made his way over to his lounge chair where he proceeded to kick off his shoes. His feet ached. He used to remote to turn on the television, changed it to channel 2 and the news popped on. He sat down, leaned back and took a hefty swig of the beer.

Oh, that's good.

He switched back and forth between the channel 2 and 7 news. Five minutes later something scratched the screen door on his porch, located at the back of his house.

Just as I get comfortable the cat wants in. He'd better not want to be let out afterwards.

He got up slowly and walked to the back door as he heard the cat scratch at it again.

"Coming, PussPuss. Give it a rest already, I've had a long day."

When he opened screen door, the cat burst through and shot into the house. His cat exploded across the room in a blur.

"What's wrong PussPu-"

The first blow caught Victor in the back of the head and he collapsed to the floor, dead. His attacker pried the axe from his skull as his body spasmed then came to a rest. Blood oozed profusely from the open head wound. His attacker lifted the axe and brought it down over and over into Victor's inert body. By the

95

time he was done the body had been gutted and blood splatter was covered every conceivable surface.

After the finished, the assailant made sure that he hadn't left any footprints in the spreading pool of blood. Satisfied that the job was complete, and in relative silence, he left through the front door, but left it ajar. As he crossed the threshold a soft meow was heard from inside the house.

12

Friday October 20, 1967 10:30 a.m.

Recess, the time when children run amuck and use up their limitless energy. Recess, the time when teachers get a quick respite. Ms. Murray let her class outside for a twenty-five minute recess. Sammy and Tommy made sure they were the last ones who left the classroom. They had been watching their backs for the past four days but Nigel hadn't attended since the incident. They speculated that he was recuperating from the nasty, but necessary blow to his head. They also wondered how his father had dealt with him.

After they looked around they raced to an available 6'x6' sandbox. Sammy and Tommy then proceeded to mark out territory amongst each other in the confines of the sandbox. Tommy had brought his red dump truck to school again while Sammy had brought some matchbox cars, a scooper and some army men. Their standard plan was to build a city, have the army guys invade and then everything would be destroyed. Whenever they played they always liked to destroy their creations for a couple of reasons. One, they were boys and that's what boys do. Secondly, if they left their sandbox city built then the myriad of other kids in the school would end up destroying it anyway. Therefore, Sammy and Tommy made sure they annihilated everything before recess was over.

They quickly molded buildings and roads with their hands as they laughed among themselves and talked about Halloween that was rapidly approaching. Sammy wanted to be a Cowboy who dazzled people by showing off his marksmanship skills. Tommy, on the other hand, wanted to be a clown because his father had taken him to see a circus during the summer. He'd seen all the clowns and most of them appeared to be very happy. He hoped, more on a subconscious level than on a conscious one, that he too would be happy if he dressed that way.

Ten minutes in and their sandbox city was nearly complete. A few minutes later, and a couple of finishing touches, and the sandbox had been transformed.

"Hey. Can I play?" asked a redheaded boy from their class.

Sammy and Tommy looked up and saw the boy next to their sandbox. He didn't seem to have many friends and they had noticed he typically hung out by himself on the swings.

"This sandbox is locked," Sammy informed him. "You can't play because we won't let you,"

"Oh," came the dejected reply.

Turning to Sammy, Tommy said, "Come on. Let's let him play."

"But he doesn't have anything to play with," Sammy insisted.

"So we'll let him play on Monday if he brings some stuff, okay?"

Sammy considered it and then agreed. "Yeah! More stuff to use to destroy the city!"

Tommy looked up at the kid and said, "We'll let you play if you bring some toys next week."

The kid's face turned from a look of utter rejection to a brightening smile. "Thanks guys! Can I watch you play?"

Tommy and Sammy let the kid watch. He wasn't very big and obviously didn't have too many friends. They allowed him to join in because they were the same way, but of course they didn't acknowledge that.

"What's your name?" Tommy asked.

"I'm Bill."

"If you're going to hang around with us you can't have a name like Bill," Tommy told him. Tommy pointed at Sammy and said, "His name is Sammy and I'm Tommy. If you're going to be playing with us then we'll have to change your name. I think a cool name is Billy."

Sammy nodded and Billy smiled. He had never been accepted by the other kids and now he had found some friends.

"So what are you going to bring on Monday Billy?" Sammy asked.

"Well, I just had my tenth birthday this last weekend."

"Happy Birthday," Tommy and Sammy said in stereo.

Billy smiled again. "Thanks. Anyway, let me surprise you on Monday with a few things." Billy motioned towards the sandbox city and said, "It looks like the city is going to be attacked at any time."

A wicked smile came across his face. Sammy and Tommy started so smile as well.

"Why don't we destroy it now?!" cried Tommy and all three proceeded to jump, raining destruction down over the buildings.

Their work was done in seconds and they all started to laugh. After they were done they collectively took a moment to notice noticed that they were all different. Sammy had black hair, Tommy had blond hair and Billy had red hair.

"What now?" Bill asked.

"I dunno," Tommy replied. "Swings?"

"Yeah," Sammy nodded, "that sounds fun."

Tommy retrieved his red dump truck as Sammy collected his cars and army men. The three then walked over to the swings. While they swung back and forth they started to brain storm about all the things they could do together. But then the recess bell rang and they jumped off to head back. Somehow, within a matter of the past fifteen minutes, they had all become closer. For them, and without really knowing it, that's exactly what they needed in their lives.

Thomas knocked on the office door, entered and closed it behind him.

"Hello again, Thomas. Please have a seat."

"Thanks."

"It's been two days and I've been going over my notes of what you talked about. If you don't mind, I'd like to have you take a test."

"What kind of test? I'm fine," Thomas asked a hint of defensiveness.

"Relax. I assure you this test will only help you," Laura said calmly. "After taking it I'll be able to understand you a little bit more, that's all."

"I'm a little confused. I thought if we just talked that would be enough for you to get to know me?"

"You're absolutely right, Thomas. What I'm hoping is to get an overview of who you think you are. There are patterns in life we obtain when we're children. We don't always realize that some of these patterns are destructive and are actually harming us even though we believe they are helping us. I want you to see some of your patterns that you don't consciously recognize."

Thomas leaned back in his chair and thought. *If I really want help then I'll need to change. I can only change if I realize the things that I'm doing wrong.*

"Is this the kind of test where you show me an inkblot with an image of a bat?"

Laura smiled. "I could definitely pull those out if you'd like, Thomas, but I'd like to probe deeper. What I'm proposing is the

MMPI. It's a personality test with several hundred yes and no questions."

Thomas relaxed. "Okay, I'll do it."

"Excellent." Laura opened up a file cabinet and pulled out a blank MMPI. Afterwards she sharpened a pencil and handed both to him. "You'll need to answer all of the questions. Use the pencil to fill in the ovals. It'll take some time to complete but don't worry about that."

He took the test from her hands, got up and exchanged places so he could use her desk. Thomas began to think about what had been happening to him.

Why can't I just tell her what's going on with me? Why don't I just let her in? Because she'll use it against me. I'll be hurt and I don't want to ever feel that type of pain again. You're being ridiculous. She's not going to hurt you, she's here to help you. Maybe she'll understand? No. She'll stay away from you. But why? That's the way it is.

He tried hard to get a grip on his internal debate as he opened the test and started to read.

In the statements listed below answer yes or no.
Example questions:
Once in a while I think of things too bad to talk about.
I think I would like the work of a librarian.
I have nightmares every few nights.

Thomas read through the example and the instructions. *Who am I?*

Laura looked over towards him and asked, "Any questions, Thomas?"

"No. It seems pretty straightforward."

102

"It is. Just answer the questions with your first instinct. It's usually the correct one.

"Thanks."

Thomas let out a deep breath, turned the page and began.

* * *

Monday October 23, 1967 10:39 a.m.

Their sandbox city was nearly complete. The three of them had rushed out to one of the playground's sandboxes to construct and then destroy their city. Tommy, Sammy and Billy enjoyed their time together and had become fast friends. Since the previous Friday the three of them had told each other about their families and what each of their homes lives entailed. Coincidentally Billy's parents were still together, but now in the process of a divorce, and that weighed heavily on his shoulders and Billy was glad that his new friends could relate to his impending situation. The fact that their families were a mess allowed only strengthened their bond.

Their city was now complete and Tommy's huge red dump truck rolled down the main street. Sammy's army guys were positioned at the other end of the street and opened fire on the truck. The seemingly small matchbox cars were pushed down into the sand as the truck slowly rolled over them. The scooper, that Sammy operated, bore down on the huge truck. It was a face off; scooper against truck. Sammy and Tommy made engine noises like they were gunning their vehicles. They pushed them together and the fight was on!

Out of nowhere Billy's huge Godzilla appeared and flipped the scooper over with a tremendous roar! It was out of commission. It was Truck against Godzilla now. A huge part of the town, that still stood, is where the battle now migrated to. Sammy moved some more army guys into firing range but they were soon crushed under Godzilla's heels. The battle raged on and neither side made any headway.

All three of them were so thoroughly engrossed in the battle that they jumped when a huge foot came out of nowhere and stomped on Tommy's red dump truck. The impact cracked the truck's windows, both fenders twisted and two wheels popped off. It had happened so quickly and in the aftermath the entire sandbox was quiet. A few seconds later the three boys looked up and saw Nigel. He stood over them, his head wrapped in gauze. He had returned.

They got up quickly and immediately looked around for a teacher. Fortunately one was stood about fifty feet away and was within yelling distance. They knew were safe for now.

"When I get you shitheads alone I'm going to make you all suffer. I don't know who your new wimpy friend is," Nigel threatened as he pointed at Billy, "but he's dead too."

All three of them stood there fixated on their nemesis who loved the sound of his own voice.

"My dad punished me in ways you've never dreamed of. Because you did this to me," as he motioned to his bandaged head, "my father decided to teach me a lesson on how to be tough. I'm going to show you three little shits that very same lesson."

Tommy, Sammy and Billy remained frozen in place as Nigel stood in the sandbox. Recess was almost over and they needed to retrieve their toys from amidst the ruined city. If they didn't then the other kids who came out to play after them would take them. Nigel knew that the bell was going to ring and that a teacher was

104

only a short distance away, so he turned around and picked up the dump truck he had stomped on.

The teacher started to walk back towards her classroom.

Thirty seconds till the bell rang.

All of them just stood there.

The teacher walked away. Tommy, Sammy and Billy didn't move.

Twenty-one seconds till the bell rang.

The teacher walks around the side of the building.

Fifteen seconds.

Nigel smiles and raises the truck high above his head.

Nine seconds.

Tommy's eyes open wide in shock and disbelief.

Five seconds.

Tommy makes a moved for his truck but is unable to grab it.

Three seconds.

"Noooooooo! Doooonnnnnn't!"

The bell rings.

Nigel hurls the truck downward into the cement, which surrounds the sandbox, and it smashes into multiple pieces. The dumper flies off and the other two wheels skitter away. It's completely destroyed.

"Bye Tommy. Thanks for letting me play with your truck. It was really fun."

As Nigel walks away, laughing, Tommy knelt down by the remains of his beloved toy and cried.

14
Saturday April 16, 1988

"Sir. We're almost ready."

"Very well," Mr. Glib replied over the PA system. "Is the patient ready?"

"Yes, sir."

Mr. Glib stood back from the one-way mirror and observed that his plans were slowly coming together. He had spent a lifetime working on this idea and now it was now becoming a reality. This was to be his sixteenth test subject in the past year. The previous subjects had met with similar fates as the first one, but his scientists assured him that their recent modifications would yield a positive outcome.

With the help of the penal system, and the United States Government, Mr. Glib had access to an endless supply of death row inmates to perform these tests on. Nobody would miss them, not that it mattered. All that he cared about were results and until these subjects stopped dying he had to press forward. A new 'volunteer' had recently been chosen to be injected with his formula. However, this young man was actually a volunteer and had only been told that he would be a testing out a new drug. The risks were high but he'd been told the rewards of both freedom and money would be his. Joe, the twenty two year old Caucasian death row inmate, immediately jumped at the chance.

The double doors to the testing chamber opened and Joe confidently walked inside. He was followed by an assistant and an armed guard. The guard posted himself inside the room; his right hand poised on his sidearm, and kept his eyes on Joe.

"Please get up on the table and lie down," instructed the assistant. "I'm going to strap you down now."

"Fine. Just hurry it up," Joe retorted. "I want to get this over with."

The assistant started with his legs restraints. After those were secured he firmly immobilized Joe's arms. The process was completed as Joe's body and head were restrained. Joe smiled throughout the entire process as he dreamt of his freedom.

The assistant attached the EKG wires and announced, "We're completely ready now, sir."

The guard and the assistant turned and left the room. A man, wearing protective gear and a reflective facemask, entered the room. Joe heard someone come in but wasn't able to turn his head.

"Proceed," Mr. Glib's voice barked through the speaker system.

Joe lay relaxed on the steel table, held tight by the leather straps. Joe had killed two police officers in a botched robbery three years prior. They had been in his way and he had shot them without a second thought. Fourteen hours later he was captured in a standoff at his apartment. His trial, and subsequent conviction, imprisoned him on death row courtesy of a maximum security facility.

After he accepted the offer to be become a guinea pig, a decision he'd easily made rather than being electrocuted, he'd found recognized he has started to daydream more. He had been transferred from an out of state facility to this location, but he had no idea where 'here' actually was, and had been instructed to follow the rules. If he did he'd be treated with respect and his deal would remain. Joe had weighed this new opportunity and had done everything they'd asked of him. He had his own room, TV, three meals a day and he no longer was subjected to the never-ending and consistent prison noise.

Out of the corner of his eyes Joe focused on a wicked looking needle.

His smile vanished. "You're joking, right?"

The EKG feedback rose sharply. The man in the protective gear closed in, the black liquid now clearly visible.

"You're not going to stick that huge thing in me, are you?" Joe struggled but the restraints held him fast.

The man grabbed Joe's head and shoved it backward to expose his throat.

"Don't do it man!" Joe started to buck.

Apparently when he volunteered for this experiment he hadn't asked any questions. He knew he was going to be injected, but that was it.

"Stop! I quit! I don't want to do this anym-"

The needle sank deep into Joe's throat. His eyes rolled back into his head as the needle was removed, a spot of blood remained where it had punctured. Joe gurgled and thrashed about as the EKG monitor spiked for fifteen seconds before it dropped sharply. Joe lay still on the table, no longer fighting. His eyes were closed and the monitor barely registered any life signs.

"Is he alive?" Mr. Glib demanded from the observation room.

The assistant checked Joe's pulse and eventually discovered it.

"Yes, sir. However, it's only ten beats a minute."

"Just keep him stable. This is the closest I've come to success and I will not have it taken away from me. When he comes around let me know. In the meantime, keep that faceplate on, ss that understood?"

"Yes, sir."

15
Friday July 6, 1990 6:01 p.m.

"I'm finished," Thomas stated.

"I'll score it this weekend and we can meet again on Monday." Laura moved over to her desk, retrieved her day planner and flipped over to Monday. "How does 1:30 p.m. sound?"

Thomas sat up in her desk chair and leaned forward. "Have you ever done something you didn't want to do but you had no control over your actions?"

Laura, a little puzzled said, "I can't say that I have, why?"

Thomas sighed. "I've been having a lot of weird 'things'," he said as he mimicked air quotes "happen to me lately yet I don't remember doing them. It's almost like there's another person who lives in my body that I can't see or hear. Do you understand?"

"I don't follow you, Thomas." Laura said a bit concerned. "What are you trying to say?"

"Nothing. Forget it. I'll see you on Monday at 1:30, okay?" Thomas got up and headed towards the door.

"Are you sure you're okay, Thomas?"

Thomas turned and looked back. "I'm fine," he said as he put on a fake smile. Afterwards he turned and left her office.

Laura watched him leave. *FINE. Fucked-up, Insecure, Neurotic and Emotional. He was trying to tell me something and I didn't get it. I'll have to ask him about that on Monday. I hope he's okay.* She caught herself. *What's happening to me? I'm paying so much attention to him that I'm ignoring what's going on in my life. Why do I care so much about what happens to Thomas Clark? I've had my own share of problems in the past that I'm not sure I can allow myself to get close to anyone again. I can't get hurt that way. I've got to remember that I'm the doctor and that I'm helping him.*

"Guess I'm fine too," she announced out loud.

She took Thomas' MMPI and placed it her briefcase, paused and almost pulled it back out. Somehow she stopped herself as her inner monologue continued to nag her. *Why do I care so much?*

*   *   *

AS Thomas left Dr. Bond's office he didn't felt slightly out of control, unsure and definitely afraid of himself. He didn't know how to get back in control, especially since he wasn't aware of when he'd even lost it.

There was still plenty of sunlight out when he got back to his car. He got in and just sat in it for a while. Thomas wasn't sure of what he wanted to do or what he should do.

Why didn't I just tell her? Because, you moron, she'll push you away and leave you alone.

Dr. Bond. Laura. Thomas felt an attraction towards her that he tried to push away but the wanting desire kept circling back to remind him. If he let her into his life, and she judged him for it, then she would leave him and he might feel the pain, just as he had when mother his mother died. He couldn't risk that until he was sure that she wouldn't judge him. Even then it would be difficult to open up and be completely honest with these complications in his life.

He started up his BMW and drove, mostly on autopilot, while his brain continued to mull things over.

What is going on with me?

He started to think about what had happened the day before he had dug up the axe. He was convinced there was dried blood on it and he'd become paralyzed with fear on the spot; his worst fears. He didn't want to admit that he was responsible for the death of a stranger and questioned if he'd really had done anything, mostly because he didn't have any memories of it.

"Shit. Who am I kidding? I woke up with blood on my walls and on my hands. I found the axe in my garden. To top it all off there was a news report on television about a guy who was axed to death."

Thomas started to hyperventilate and nearly sideswiped the vehicle next to him.

Get a grip! I don't want to be a killer. I'm not a killer. Am I? Killing can't be a part of my life. I won't accept it. I'm a puppet.

Thomas' internal battle raged on as he hit CA-30, turned in to CA-330, and up up the mountain to Running Springs.

Get a fucking grip Thomas.

"What did I do?" he asked aloud. "What's happening to me?"

Thomas' emotions caught up with him and he quickly pulled the car over in a turnout. In seconds his emotions overtook him and he started to cry. But his tears weren't from sadness; they flowed down his face from the sheer panic he now experienced.

"I am so scared of who I am. I can't control anything in my life. This is just like grade school where someone else is pushing my buttons and I can't escape. But now the person who is pushing the buttons is me. I don't understand what is happening."

Thomas slammed his fists on his steering wheel and peeled out of the turnout. He pushed his car a little faster than it should around one of the sharper turns on 330 and his wheels screeched. He snapped out of his trance.

What am I trying to do, kill myself? That thought lingered in his consciousness. *What if the other side of me is so powerful that I have to die to escape from it? What the hell is going on with me?*

113

The remainder of the mountain drive flew by until Thomas reached the top. He'd never driven up the mountain so reckless before and he felt shaky. Running Springs lay just around the bend and he told himself that he'd try and relax when he got home, currently overwhelmed with feelings of self-doubt.

What about that test I just took? I wonder if Laura will come to the conclusion that I'm apparently some kind of maniac in my spare time?

He took a right at the exit and drove towards his house and wondered if he would ever be or feel normal. He was scared shitless. He had to assume that there was another side of him that he wasn't aware of due to the mountain of evidence that he's seen. He had to be the killer; what other explanation could there be?

What do I do? Do I turn myself in?

AS he pulled up into his garage, and turned of his motor, Thomas slunk down into his seat. He was ashamed of who he was and what he had become. He hoped things could be different for him and wished life shouldn't be so difficult or detrimental to his wellbeing. If only grade school hadn't been so hurtful. If only his mother hadn't died. If only Nigel hadn't…

* * *

Friday July 6, 1990 7:01 p.m.

Laura packed up her things and headed home a few minutes after Thomas left. Her receptionist had already left for home around 5 p.m.. These past few days with Thomas had been really interesting and her interest was piqued. In fact she had moved some other patient's appointments just to make room for him. Clearly, she thought, something was eating away at him and hoped

114

that the hundreds of questions he'd answered would somehow paint a clearer picture.

Laura had left the office and gone straight home. Her house wasn't too far from her San Bernardino office. She pulled her Volvo into her Redlands garage and secured the garage door behind her with her remote.

You never know who's out there.

She exited, punched in her house alarm, unlocked her door and entered. Laura placed both her briefcase her purse on the counter and began to search her house as she turned on one light after another. She knew she was a little jumpy and had every right to be. Her old boyfriend, Rick, had stalked her a few years back after she'd broken up with him. He hadn't taken the blow to his ego well and refused to let her go.

She had beaten herself up many times over the fact that she hadn't seen Rick's dark side, especially since she was a trained professional. *Love is blind.* She had processed her feelings about his actions over the years and, now because of him, tried not to let her guard down when it came to her personal safety.

Laura owned a two bedroom single story house in a very decent part of Redlands. When she moved in she had made a point of introducing herself to her neighbors. They all liked her, especially her somewhat noisy older lady neighbor from across the street, Mrs. Bedderman, who would occasionally stop to ask when she was getting married. Every time Laura would put on a fake smile and explain about how she hadn't found Mr. Right yet. Mrs. Bedderman would pat Laura's hand and say something typical like, "Time is short dear. You'll find your prince." Course, she had never met Mr. Bedderman, joking in her head that Mrs. Bedderman had killed him and then buried him in their basement.

115

But Laura knew that was just her fascination with the crime and forensic books she tended to read.

Laura picked up the scattered mail from the floor that had been deposited through her front door slot. She didn't even glance at it as she piled on the counter. Instead she headed for her bedroom to change into something more comfortable. She emerged wearing black sweatpants and a white t-shirt.

It's definitely time for a beer.

On her way to the kitchen she located her TV remote and turned clicked the power button. She then opened the fridge, pulled out a Corona, popped it open with the magnetic fridge bottle opener and took a swallow. She snatched her briefcase off the counter, took a seat on her couch and put her beer down. She removed Thomas's MMPI and placed it on the table as well. She took another swig of her Corona to further relax her from her week's work load.

Laura thoroughly enjoyed being a psychiatrist. Helping others was second nature to her and was very fulfilling. She came highly recommended for her no nonsense approach and extremely likeable demeanor. The only disparaging she'd ever heard had been from a couple she'd counseled after they had abruptly stopped attending their sessions. When she followed up the wife had replied, "I thought my husband was in to the counseling because he couldn't wait to go and I thought we were making progress. What I didn't realize was that he couldn't wait to go so he could check you out." Laura didn't have much to say, had politely wished the woman well and hung up.

When Thomas had informed her that Nick Raynes was the one that had referred him, Laura had nearly smiled, nearly misplacing her poker face. They hadn't been the couple that divorced, but they were a couple that had some very interesting fetishes.

Oh Nick and Susan.

Laura took another sip of her beer as she thought back to when those two had visited her office, their marriage on somewhat rocky grounds. As it turned out Susan was cheating on Nick with another woman. At first Nick was devastated, but wanted to work it out. Over the course of a half dozen more sessions they were happily managing their needs though a number of compromises. First, they promised never to lie to each other no matter what the issue was. Secondly, and as a huge ego boost to Nick, it turned out Susan wanted to share her friends with Nick, but didn't know how to express her needs to him. So, a few times a month now Nick and Susan had a ménage a trois, and Nick couldn't have been happier with the outcome. She doubted Thomas knew the details and she wouldn't have shared them with him anyway.

"…last night in Redlands there was a brutal murder."

The words *Redlands* and *murder* caught her attention.

The female anchor continued. "Sometime Thursday night the body of Victor Salva was discovered. Sources say that a next door neighbor discovered the gruesome scene when the victim's cat wouldn't leave her front door. She took it back over to the victim's house only to discover the front door ajar. Inside she discovered a horrific, bloody scene. She fled and immediately dialed 911 from the safety of her own house.

"Let's go live to the scene. Ken?"

The scene changed to a live shot outside the victims' Redlands house and police tape encircled the house. Laura recognized the house immediately because it was less than a mile away from where she lived. She had been interested in buying a house near there before she'd settled on her current one.

"Thanks Lisa," said Ken who was live at the scene. "I'm here at the victim's house, a Mr. Victor Salva. Last night this was the scene of a horrific act of violence."

The scene changed to previously recorded video.

Ken continued his report, "This is footage taken last night as the M.E. removed the victim's body from inside the house."

A large black body bag was being wheeled out the front door on a gurney.

"We talked to the residents of this quiet community and they are shocked."

An elderly woman was in front of the microphone. "This is absolutely appalling. I don't feel safe anymore. What kind of world do we live in where this is acceptable behavior?"

Ken came back on the screen with a live shot. "Police aren't speculating at this time but this would appear to be at least the second murder in the Redlands area in the past few days. So far the police aren't sharing much about this latest murder.

"Back to you, Lisa."

"Thanks, Ken. In World News tonight the buildup of forces in Iraq has prompted the United States to…."

Laura muted the television, got up and starred out her front window. She didn't feel safe anymore.

16
Saturday, November 18, 1967 2:30 p.m.

Tommy stepped out of his father's vehicle.

"Don't forget the present, son," Michael told him.

Tommy turned back and picked up the gift wrapped package. "Thanks. dad."

Tommy closed the door as his side window rolled down. He looked at his father who sat in the driver's seat.

"What time do I need to pick you up?"

"Sammy said his dad will drop me off after the party's over."

"Okay, Tommy. Have a good time. Love you." Michael backed out of Sammy's driveway and headed home.

* * *

To say that Michael worried about Tommy, ever since Betsy's accident, would be a vast understatement. Hell, he even worried about himself from time to time. It hadn't been easy for either, losing both a wife and a mother. Their house seemed so empty and most of the time, when Michael got home, he found Tommy in his room engaged imaginative gameplay with his toys or at his desk, pencil in hand feverishly at work. There were times, over the past years, when he'd walked in and seen his son's tear soaked face. The only thing Michael could do was would hold onto his son tightly. They didn't talk about the accident; they just endured it as best as they could. But Michael was concerned because he'd noticed Tommy was more withdrawn that usual in the past few months. He'd also observed his son's cuts and scrapes, but had assumed they were from roughhousing at school since Tommy hadn't mentioned anything about them.

Michael made a mental note to talk with Tommy and see if everything was okay as he pulled into his driveway and cut the engine. He was thrilled that Sammy lived so close and Tommy had a friend he would hang out with. Tommy had said, one night about a month ago, that he and Sammy met a new kid at school by the name of Billy. During those four weeks the three had spent most weekends playing at Sammy's house. Tommy had also mentioned, and not too slyly, that Sammy and Billy had bicycles and that he'd like one as well. He'd been using theirs to practice on when they were playing. Michael told Tommy that he'd think about it, but secretly wanted to wait until Christmas to surprise Tommy with one. He knew it was about time Tommy had a bike, and Michael knew he had to start letting go of his over protective nature. He didn't want any harm to come to Tommy and not buying him a bike until he was ten years old seemed like another way of keeping him from being out on the street. Aside from the traumatic event that had taken place five years previously, kids are kids, and you can only protect them for so long and for the right reasons.

Michael got out of his car, locked it and headed for the front door. Once inside he went to the kitchen and cleaned up this morning's breakfast dishes. Both he and his son had slept in this particular Saturday so breakfast had started later than usual. On the weekends Michael enjoyed cooking pancakes, waffles, eggs or even a mean bowl of cereal for his son. He knew that he didn't get to spend nearly enough time with Tommy, mainly because of the long hours he worked, and he wasn't thrilled that day after day Tommy came home to an empty house. Thankfully Michael called on his folks, Ed and Claire, to drop by now and then to check in. They were in their early sixties and had retired already. After Betsy's death they had moved to Orinda to be closer to their son and grandson. They knew Michael was putting on a brave front for Tommy and attempted to alleviate the pressure, as much as they could, while their son coped.

Ed and Claire loved Tommy and, aside from being withdrawn, they knew their grandson was extremely bright and resilient. Tommy had dazzled them with stories of pirates, treasure, dragons and voyages to the far reaches of the Earth. There had been times when Ed started up a bed time story with Tommy, each taken turns perpetuating the story until twists and turns continued to evolve it right before their eyes. More often than not Tommy was fully awake and alert, after his grandfather had left his room, as he recollected the tale they had just created together. Ed loved to see Tommy smile as their narrative wove, his excitement growing as the story took a nasty curve. Ed and Claire both knew that the last five years had been very trying on Michael and, equally if not worse, on Tommy. Any smile they could get from him was a sign of hope.

After Michael cleaned up he headed back to his master bedroom. Annexed directly off of that room was a small sunroom, now converted into his study. The room had a generous view of the deck and the rear of the house. During the day the sun shined through its windows and easily warmed it. Michael's desk was pushed up against the far wall so when he sat he was able to enjoy the view rather than keep his back to it. Behind him, in the opposite corner was a large safe. It was about five feet tall and three feet wide and was securely bolted in to the floor. Above the safe, high up on the wall, were two hooks and cradled in them was a pump action 12 gauge shotgun. His father had instructed Tommy never to touch either the safe or the gun. Tommy had asked why not? His father, as he looked him directly in the eyes said, "Promise me that you'll never touch the gun or the safe.

Remember, your word is your bond." Tommy had promised his father. Tommy, as curious as ever, had spent a lot of time in his father's study and started at both the safe and the shotgun; but had never touched them.

Michael sat down in his leather chair, swiveled in it one-hundred-eighty degrees and dialed in the combination to his safe. He opened it and extracted a folder that contained some documents. He turned back around, placed the folder on his desk and slowly opened it.

Time to work.

* * *

Tommy watched his father back out of the driveway, then turned and walked to Sammy's front door. Just as he was about to ring the doorbell Sammy sprang out from behind the bush near him and screamed, "RRRAAARRRR!!"

Tommy jumped and nearly dropped the present. "You jerk!"

Sammy laughed. "Hahahahaha. I totally got you," he giggled as he pointed at his friend.

Tommy put the present down and took off after Sammy into the backyard. Sammy was still laughing.

"I'm going to get you!" cried Tommy and tackled Sammy on the grass.

They wrestled for a few seconds and then they both started stopped and laughed. Sammy stood and pulled Tommy up to his feet.

"Happy Birthday, jerk face," Tommy said.

"Thanks, Tommy."

They both turned their heads towards the front of the house as they heard a vehicle pull up.

Tommy turned to Sammy and said, "Let's do the same thing to Billy."

"Oh yeah!" Sammy nodded as they scrambled to hide behind the bush. "Shhh….Shhh."

From the driveway the car was moved off and Billy appeared down the pathway. He paused when he saw the wrapped present which sat near the front door. *Weird.* He continued up to the front door and paused again when he heard a rustle behind him. He turned to his right and caught sight of his friends just as they leapt out at him.

"RAarrr…" Tommy and Sammy cried out together but then stopped short. The gig was up.

"Nice try guys," said Billy as he smiled.

"Yeah, yeah. We tried," Sammy said as he gave Billy a high five. "Good to see you, Billy!"

"You too. Long time, no see," Billy replied. They all started to snicker over that statement they'd all been together just the previous day at school.

The front door opened and Sammy's father poked his head out. "Are you boys ready to head out?"

"Hell yeah!" Sammy boomed.

"Excuse me?" his father cautioned.

"I mean, heck yeah, dad!"

"Better," his father said as he let out a slight grin. "Come on inside boys so we can get this party started."

Tommy picked up the gift he'd brought and all three of them tromped inside, clearly excited about the upcoming birthday festivities because it was time to head to the batting cages. They were going to hit balls and eat pizza and had already decided it was going to be the best day ever. They couldn't wait!

In the distance a lone car turned left onto a street a few hundred yards away down the hill, and then turned right into an empty driveway. Michael Clark got out of his vehicle and walked towards his house.

17
Friday December 8, 1967 2:09 p.m.

Tommy, Billy and Sammy all looked at the clock mounted above Ms. Murray's desk and noticed it read 2:09 p.m.. School would be getting out soon and they had planned to go to the Orinda Community Center Park afterwards. The new Jungle Gym tower had just been built and they had been dying to play on it. It was cold out but that didn't stop them from having as much fun as they could together. Besides, Nigel wouldn't be at the park and that was the primary reason they wanted to leave school as soon as the bell rang.

Nigel had continued to bully and harass the three of them, non-stop, since the red dump truck incident in October in which Nigel had crushed not only Tommy's truck, but his heart as well. It was a game for Nigel to see if he could make them cry or lose control and he would try anything to get the rise he wanted. Nigel had returned to the sandbox a few days later and destroyed the newly built city that the three of them had built during that particular recess. A teacher had been patrolling the school yard and had seen the incident. She had sent Nigel off to the Principal's office, but that didn't cure how the boys felt. Why did he have to bully them? What had they ever done to him? They had no choice but to deal with Nigel's harassment because he made a point, every day, to make sure they acknowledged his presence, one way or another

The three boys had successfully avoided Nigel for the past month, after school, because Nigel was in the grade above them, which meant he was educated in a completely different classroom. So when the bell rang the three of them rushed to take the back way out of school rather than migrate to the buses which were lined up at the front of the school. So far they had been able to ditch Nigel very successfully by crossing the soccer field and scaling the chain-link fence. That fence bordered the woods commonly known to the students as the 'Nature Area'. A main residential road intersected the woods about five hundred yards away from where they scrambled over the fence. They'd then follow a trail through the Nature Area which would come out by the E.B.M.U.D. (East Bay Municipal Utility District) water treatment plant. Tommy always thought that name was funny. *Mud.* A small bridge allowed two-way traffic over the small creek that ran by E.B.M.U.D. and eventually made its way behind Wagner Ranch School. From there they would walk home. Billy's house was closest and Sammy's was as the top of the hill. Tommy's, on the other hand, was the furthest away.

AS they walked through the woods like they normally did, Tommy, Billy and Sammy joked about how fun the jungle gym was going to be. All around them were huge oak trees and the ground crunched under their pint-sized feet. They were almost to the road.

"Nice to see you again wimps," said a shadowy figure that emerged from behind an oak tree.

The three of them stopped dead in their tracks. Panic set in and time seemed to slow down.

"I don't remember the last time I really beat the living shit out of you guys. You know, what goes around comes around."

Nigel stepped out farther with a tree branch in his hands. He was about fifteen feet away.

Sammy spoke up first. "Leave us alone. What have we ever done to you?"

Nigel took a step towards Sammy and pointed the branch at him. "You are low life. You don't deserve to go without

126

punishment. You'll take what you deserve!" he screamed. His rage was unheard of.

Nigel elevated the branch over his head and started towards them, who were still huddled together. They scattered and Nigel chose Billy to run after.

Billy yelled, "HEEEEELLLLPPPP!!"

Hopefully somebody would hear him and come to his rescue. The wind kicked up and leaves fluttered down from the trees above as Nigel caught up to him. Billy looked over his shoulder just in time to see the branch descend towards his head and tripped over an exposed root. As he sprawled to the ground Nigel tripped over him and fell down as well.

"Sonofabitch!"

Billy popped up and ran for his life. Nigel picked himself up, retrieved his branch, looked around and spied Tommy about forty feet away. His eyes narrowed and he bee-lined right for his new target. He couldn't wait to beat the crap out of Tommy with his stick just like his father had done. Tommy saw Nigel come at him and signaled Sammy to get ready as Nigel ran.

Tommy didn't move.

I almost have him now.

Trees everywhere.

Tommy smiled.

I'm going to get him.

Nigel pulled the make shift club behind him like a bat. "FFUUUUCCCKKKKKERRRR!!" he screamed.

But then came the sound of a whip and Nigel landed hard on the forest floor, the wind knocked out of him. Unbeknownst, Sammy had bent back one of the larger saplings from the tree next to Tommy, and had released it with perfect timing. The branch had struck Nigel high in the chest. The momentum from the branch, as well as Nigel's speed, propelled his body to the ground.

Nigel didn't get up.

"All right!" Sammy yelled.

"We got him!" cried Billy.

"Is he dead?" asked Tommy.

Sammy motioned for them to leave. "I don't know. Who cares? Let's get out of here. The road is right here and we should get home."

"Sammy's right, Tommy," Billy added. "We should go home now."

"Okay. Just let me see if he's dead."

Tommy walked up to Nigel's body and bent down. His two friends crowded around and pulled on Tommy's shirt. The sound of cars on the road was audible as Tommy looked at Nigel and saw that there wasn't any visible damage. In fact, Nigel wasn't even bleeding. Out of nowhere Nigel's right hand shot up and grabbed Tommy by the throat. Billy and Sammy screamed and tried to pry the hand off but Nigel's left hand curled into a fist and punched Sammy in the face. He went down hard and started to bawl.

Tommy couldn't breath and began to choke.

"I've got you now you little shit. I've waited for this moment. No teachers, nobody to see what happens to you."

Tommy's face turned red. Nigel made his way to his feet and maintained a firm grip as Tommy gasped and attempted to beat on Nigel's arm. Nigel, now fully upright, released his grip and grabbed Tommy by the back of his neck and pants. Billy seized the moment and launched himself at Nigel, but the massive bully kicked Billy away with his left foot. Billy went down next to Sammy, who still cradled his face in his hands.

Nigel made his way towards the road and held Tommy off the ground in front of his as he walked.

"Do you like to play in the road Tommy? Huh, answer me!"

Tommy coughed and gagged, not able to resist in the condition he was in.

"Well, like it or not I'm going to turn you into road pizza."

The street, with the bridge on their left, came into view. It banked sharply upwards to the right and disappeared over the horizon. Anyone coming from that direction wouldn't have time to register if anything was in the road. Nigel held on to Tommy tightly as another car cruised by.

Tommy had regained some of his senses and now attempted to fight back against, although there wasn't much he could do being held like a sack of potatoes off the ground. Cars continued to pass them but nobody stopped.

Nigel grinned from ear to ear.

"Stop it! Stop it!" Tommy screamed.

"Make me!"

And with that Nigel tossed Tommy out onto the road.

* * *

Friday August 3, 1962 1:35 p.m.

Oakmont Cemetery was very peaceful. Tommy was curious about it but uncomfortable at the same time. As far as he could see graves and head stones lined the green grass. Trees poked out from the ground here and there and a warm breeze wafted through his hair. A large awning had been constructed, lined with rows of chairs, which all pointed towards a raised platform.

What's that?

Tommy saw a large hole next to a mound of covered dirt. His young hand held pretty tightly by his father. Around the edge of the cemetery cars continued to park and dispense people, most of them not entirely sure they wanted to be here today.

Michael looked around at everyone and recognized some of them from work, while others were friends and neighbors. Everyone came up to him and told them how sorry they were.

Who are you? Must be Betsy's friends.

Michael thanked each and everyone one of them for honoring Betsy with their presence. He bit down his quivering lip more times than he could count.

"Hello son," Ed said behind Michael. "I'd ask how you're doing but that would be the dumbest question of the day."

"Grandma! Grandpa!" cried Tommy and wiggled free of his father's death grip.

"Hey there champ," said his grandfather. "I'd pick you up but I might hurt my back."

Instead Ed kneeled down and gave Tommy a hug.

"Be careful, Ed," Claire warned. She turned and hugged Michael. "I'm so sorry. If there's anything we can do you let us know."

Michael let a tear slip down his face and his mother gently wiped it away for him.

"Thanks, Mom."

Tommy held on to his grandfather's hand and continued to look around at all the people. He didn't know who they all were.

Ed bent down to Tommy's level. "You look good, champ."

Tommy's father had dressed him up in Church clothes today for some reason. Just then, from around the bend a strange car pulled up. It was longer than usual and Tommy had never seen a vehicle like it before. Ed stood up and watched it approach.

"Grandpa? What's that?"

Ed looked down at Tommy and followed his finger towards the car. "That's a hearse."

"A hurts?" Tommy asked.

"A hearse, Tommy. Why don't we walk over here and check out the flowers," his grandfather said as he led Tommy away. Tommy looked back over his shoulder again and saw a long container being removed from the rear of the vehicle.

Michael's mother saw the coffin just as Michael saw it.

"Oh God," he whispered as another tear streamed down his face.

"It's okay, sweetie. It's okay."

"I miss her so much, mom."

"I know, sweetie. I know."

The attendants picked up his wife's casket and respectfully carried it to the awaiting platform.

"I don't think I can do this, mom. I can't..." Michael got weak in the knees.

"Ed." Claire got Ed's attention immediately and motioned for him to come over. Ed left Tommy, who was interested in some flowers, and went over to help his wife.

Tommy sniffed a flower. It was okay, he thought. What he liked was the different colors. Then he looked over his shoulder and watched as his grandfather made his way to his father and whispered something in his ear. Michael straightened up immediately and glanced over at Tommy who, by now, had wandered over to the rows of chairs and up the middle aisle. The long box was on the pedestal and he made his way up to it. Tommy raised his right hand and felt the exterior of the box. It was smooth.

"What're you up to Tommy?" his father asked behind him.

"What's this box for, Dad?"

Michael knelt down and turned his son towards him. They looked at each other eye to eye.

"This box is called a coffin, Tommy."

"A coffin," Tommy repeated.

"Mommy's inside it."

"Why can't I see mommy?" Tommy asked.

The coffin's lid was closed and secured. Michael swallowed hard and tried not to think about the car wreck.

"Listen to me, Tommy. We can't see mommy right now."

"Why not?"

Michael searched for an easy answer to his son's tough question. There was no way he could explain that, in the accident, Betsy had been horribly disfigured. There was no way he could begin to explain how he had to go down the Coroner's and identify the love of his life. There was absolutely no way he would paint a picture like that for his son.

"Mommy's on the waiting list for Heaven, Tommy."

Tommy's eyes opened as he processed what his father had just said. "Mommy's in line to get in to Heaven?" he asked.

"That's right, son."

Tommy turned back towards the coffin and leaned his head against it. "Dad, I miss mommy," and started to cry.

Michael joined in.

18
Mon July 9, 1990 1:37 p.m.

"So why don't you tell me what's going on, Thomas?" Laura asked.

The two of them had shared idle chitchat since he'd arrived, but now she felt it was time to focus.

This is my third visit and I don't have anything to lose.

Thomas relented and his demeanor illustrated as much. "I don't know what to say anymore. I'm unsure of who I think I am. It's possible I may be two different people because I just never see the other side of me."

"Alright. Why do you think you have different personalities?"

Thomas stiffened because it meant that he either had to tell her or never come back.

"You wouldn't believe me if I told you."

Laura tried to remain as professional as possible. She knew Thomas definitely had his share of personal problems and they seemed legitimate. She knew childhood trauma both changes and affects people in different ways.

"Try me. I've been helping people for a long time now and I've heard my share of stories."

Thomas was now in unknown territory. He had opened up his heart to Laura already, but this took it to a completely new level. If he confided in her she could very easily turn her back on him forever. The air in the room thickened as Thomas ventured forward.

"I had this accident was I was ten years old. Well, I wouldn't exactly call it an accident."

Thomas paused. Laura's full concentration was on him.

"There was this bully named Nigel Clemmings, who was in the fifth grade, while I was in fourth. He had transferred to the school that year. He was a huge kid with one hell of a chip on his shoulder and he used to always bully me; well us. I had two friends at school that garnered his attention as well. Their names were Billy Nicholson and Sammy Paige. They're still my best friends to this day."

Laura smiled at Thomas. "Go ahead."

"Nigel used to harass us most days and sometimes after school. After a while we smartened up and started to take other routes home, and in doing so we managed to avoid him for a long period of time. But one day he figured it out and waited for us to come to him. Long story short, he hit Sammy in the face and broke his nose. He practically snapped Billy's leg in two and he nearly killed me. That's where the accident comes into play."

She leaned forward. "What happened?" she asked with genuine interest.

Thomas paused and his face contorted. He tried to hold back the rush of hot tears but they spilled out anyway. He didn't want to feel this pain.

"To start with Nigel practically chocked me to death. When Sammy and Billy tried to stop him that's when he broke Sammy's nose. I almost passed out, but he let go of my throat and propelled me forwards. I was so out of it I didn't know what was happening, but I do remember the road."

"What else do you remember?" Laura probed.

He grabbed a tissue from a nearby box and wiped away his tears.

"I screamed at him. I screamed at him to stop but he wouldn't listen. He laughed. He laughed that horrible laugh as he tossed me out into the street. Tires screeched and horns blared. The next thing I recall is when I woke up in the hospital. My father was there by my side and he smiled at me."

A new wave of tears flooded his eyes. Laura handed over a new set of tissues.

"Thomas, that's absolutely horrible. I just don't understand how this ties to your thought process about split personalities?"

"The doctors performed a myriad of tests because I had landed on my head, full force, and had blacked. I found out later I was lucky I hadn't been hit by any passing vehicles, but apparently it had been close. Their tests seemed to revolve around my cognitive ability. There was some fear that I had sustained some brain damage."

"Understandable," Laura commented. "What did these tests conclude?"

"They actually never told me. They spoke to my father about it at length though. And from the look on his face it was clear he was very concerned." Thomas leaned back in his chair and said, "Are you sure you want me to keep going?"

Laura wanted to know everything. She was amazed at how serious Thomas was willing to take his therapy. *Maybe he'll want to take it even further.* Laura stayed as professional as she could even though she desperately wanted to hear more. "It's up to you Thomas but you're doing great."

Thomas took a breath. "For a while I told the doctors, and my father, that Mom had been in the room with me. As it turns out, while they observed me, I did have full length conversations with my mother, but I don't recall that I ever did. Maybe I made these things up. They were real....or seemed real."

"What did you two talk about, Thomas?"

"I can't remember. I really wish I could. My father never said whether they recorded them, but it didn't seem to matter because

135

in a few days she stopped appearing altogether. I didn't have any more conversations after that. The doctors concluded that any damage I sustained was temporary. Some days later on December 22, 1967 I was released and my father took me home. I learned later that I had been in the hospital for nearly two weeks."

"Do you think that because you talked with your mother in the hospital that you think you have a split personality?"

"I don't know. Maybe. But there's more to it than that."

"What do you mean?" she asked.

Laura noticed that Thomas was very nervous now, almost agitated. *Bingo.*

"I never had a problem with something like that again, well, not until a few days ago."

Laura didn't say a word and waited for Thomas to resume.

Here we go. "Last week I woke up and there was blood on my hands and my bedroom walls."

Laura hadn't expected this twist. "Blood? How had you hurt yourself?"

"I thought the same thing at first, but there wasn't a scratch on me."

"Do you have a pet?" Laura asked as her concern rose.

"No, I don't have any pets," Thomas countered.

"I don't understand then. Where did it all come from?"

"I didn't know until I caught the news later that day. Some guy named Rupert Jones was killed. Hacked to death. I think that was me."

Thomas looked directly in to Laura's eyes.

"Wait. What?"

Laura didn't like where this conversation had turned. Had she read Thomas completely wrong?

"Where else does that much blood come from? Midair?"

Laura played along as her eyes darted around her office. "I don't know. Aren't you jumping to conclusions?"

I can scream and I can run. Laura didn't think she'd find herself smack dab in the middle of the books she thoroughly enjoyed. *This is not happening.*

"I don't think so. I didn't know what to believe until I outside in my garden."

"Your…your garden?" she asked nervously.

From the bag he'd brought Thomas withdrew the axe he'd unearthed. Laura saw that it was encrusted with particles of dirt and an underlying layer of blood. He picked up on her horrified expression as she sprang to her feet.

"Where did you get that thing?" she demanded as she edge towards her door. "If this is a joke it's in very poor taste."

Thomas placed the axe back in his bag and softly said, "I'm sorry."

He kicked the bag away from him. Laura had nearly screamed but now stopped herself abruptly.

"Go ahead and scream. It's not like I have anyone else to confide in."

This situation as a first for her and she reminded herself that she was a professional. On top of that Thomas' vibe she interpreted as non-threatening. Laura moved back to her chair and sat down.

"I'm sorry too, Thomas. From my point of view that was pretty intense."

"I understand, but I just don't know what to do. I think it's the axe that was used to kill that man. Like I told you, I found it in my garden. What other proof do you need? I've got to be batshit crazy or something."

Laura leaned back and thought. There were many explanations for what had happened to Thomas but who knew what the correct one happened to be.

"Were you aware of any of your actions?"

"No, I don't remember a thing and that's what scares me the most. What am I supposed to do? Am I in control of myself or am I a raving lunatic?"

Thomas started to cry again and this time he couldn't seem to stop as his entire body wracked and shook. Laura was at a loss of what to do. She had never experienced anything like this before but knew that he was desperately reaching out to her. Somehow she ascertained that he was telling the truth and was confused about his personal identity. She wanted to help. *Where to begin?*

Thomas eventually calmed down and used tissues littered the floor.

"Why does this have to happen to me? I don't want to hurt anyone. I couldn't live with the knowledge that I've hurt somebody. Maybe I should just kill myself. If I did that then I wouldn't be able to hurt anyone else."

Laura took Thomas' threat seriously but deflected it. "You won't be doing anything stupid like killing yourself Thomas. Do you understand me? When you think about it there is no concrete proof that you've done anything. I believe that you didn't kill anyone."

"How can you be so sure?" he asked as he looked directly at her.

Laura opened her desk and extracted a folder. "This your MMPI profile. Overall it classifies you as a peaceful person. You tend to avoid any type of violent confrontations. You are kind, gentle and compassionate." Laura closed the folder and regarded Thomas. "What more do you want to hear?"

"Wouldn't I have to take two tests since I am two different people?"

"Seriously, Thomas, I don't think you had anything to do with that murder."

"What's happening to me? What do I need to do?"

"Thomas," she said as she placed a hand on his knee, "are you willing to take a chance?"

Thomas was confused. "I thought that's what I've been doing."

"You have, Thomas, you really have. That's why I'm a little reluctant to bring it up, but maybe it's worth a try."

"What are you talking about?"

"I'm talking about hypnotic regression therapy. If you want to give it a try you'll need to come in for some extended sessions."

"Hypnosis? I don't know. What would regression therapy accomplish?"

"Well, for starters, we can definitely clear your name in that man's death."

Thomas looked relieved. "Really?"

"Really, Thomas. Regression hypnosis, in layman's terms, will allow me to delve in to your mind and locate your hidden memories. What you can't remember is still in your head, I just need to find it."

"Will I remember anything from the process?"

"At first the only thing I'll want you to recall is that you have been hypnotized."

"Why?"

"Typically speaking, Thomas, and I don't mean any offense, an individual with serious childhood traumas has more repressed memories than they're aware of. But let me put it another way. At the beginning of your first session you knew exactly what you've told me now and nothing more."

"Okay."

"Then let's say that after that session you suddenly had twenty other traumas, or serious repressed events, now rattling around in your brain. You'd go crazy. If I probe little by little then we can talk about what I've discovered in a controlled environment."

"I understand now. Good idea."

Thomas thought for a minute or so. *Damn this is scary. I wonder what the hell I can't remember I'm not aware of. Either way I have nothing to lose at this point.*

"Okay, I'll do it. When should I come in?"

Laura looked at her schedule. "Well, we can start at 6 p.m. on Wednesday evening. How does that sound?"

"I just hope it works, Laura. I'll be here."

"Let's give it a try, Thomas. You should be very proud of the work you've done here today. I'm sorry again for reacting the way I did."

"Trust me. You're not the only one."

He got up, said his goodbyes and left. He wanted everything to be okay because he hated his nightmares. As he go into his car he said something out loud.

"If only she knew."

* * *

As soon as Thomas left Laura realized he'd left his bag, and the axe protruded from it. She knew she had an obligation to call the police but Laura didn't believe that Thomas had killed anyone. She picked up the bag, opened her large desk drawer and dropped it inside.

140

I'll just put this away for the time being.

19

"He's coming around, sir."

Everyone else left the room as Mr. Glib walked around the table and looked down at Joe.

What a wonderful specimen. He's full of life and so ready to give it up for my greater good. What an idiot.

"What's your name?" he asked.

Joe's eyes fluttered. The light from the ceiling was exceptionally bright and he squinted. Above him he made out the outline of a man, who had gray, combed back hair who was dressed in a suit.

"What's your name?" Mr. Glib repeated.

Where am I? Who am I? "I know who I am. I know who I am. I know who I am."

"Yes, of course you do."

Joe felt like everything was in slow motion, as if his environment wasn't real. He felt tired.

"Where am I?" Joe mumbled.

"You're in my house now, Joe," Mr. Glib declared with authority.

"I'm in prison?"

Mr. Glib laughed. "Hahaha. Not exactly, Joe. How do you feel?"

Joe half-heartedly tried to get up. "Groggy. I can't get up." He tried again but the restraints held him down.

"You're my first success, Joe." Mr. Glib shot his arms up in victory. "Revel in that with me!"

"I don't understand," Joe replied, his eyes half open.

Mr. Glib placed his face very close to his guinea pig. "It doesn't matter. You're the first of many. Welcome to my future."

Joe passed out.

"Someday you may appreciate all the effort I've put in to getting to this moment." He straightened up. "Gentlemen, please make sure that his young man is properly taken care of. Commence with phase three."

"Yes sir," a voice from speaker system pledged.

Mr. Glib paused and spoke again. "And gentlemen, if there are ANY problems, come see me immediately. If he dies now it's on your heads. Do I make myself clear?"

"Extremely clear, sir."

20
Tuesday July 10, 1990 9:30 a.m.

Thomas begrudgingly woke up. He'd left the curtain open and the morning sunlight now poured through his large window. The previous night he'd driven straight home from the session with Dr. Bond. *Laura.* He'd made a quick meal and thought about hypnosis. It intrigued him.

I wonder what's in my head that I don't know about.

The entire time he'd driven home, up until he finished dinner, Thomas had dwelled on everything he'd experienced in the past week. It was overwhelming but he was strangely okay with the problems at hand. Instead of running and hoping they'd go away, he was now in the process of facing his demons. Thomas smiled a bit and gave himself some credit.

After dinner he decided he needed to relax so he cleaned up in the kitchen and then found one of his favorite books, 'Watchers', by Dean Koontz. After he prepped for bed he read it until midnight, and then dozed off.

With the current state of things Thomas didn't have a plan for what he wanted to accomplish today. The standard list of things to do crossed his mind. There was writing, gardening, biking and cleaning. Then there were the new options in his life that included crying, screaming, cursing, fear and disbelief. *Lucky me.*

"Well shit," Thomas said as he sat up in bed. "Gardening, biking and cleaning are out for the time being. I'm definitely full on crying and screaming so I might as well be productive and write."

He looked over at his computer and it only stared back, mocking him.

Who am I kidding? I can't concentrate right now.

145

Thomas lay back down over and put a pillow over his head to block out the bright light.

Hypnosis.

The thought of it still lingered. Thomas wondered if it'll be like a dream. Growing up he'd seen magicians on TV who swung a stopwatch back and forth in front of their volunteer. Once under the magician would plant a suggestion so whenever he snapped his fingers that person would cluck like a chicken. Thomas had thought it was ridiculous. Course, when the magician would wake the person out of the trance that individual would asked, "So when are you going to hypnotize me?" and the audience would get a good laugh. Naturally, afterwards, each time the magician would snap his fingers the poor volunteer would indeed cluck, prompting the audience to roar each and every time.

Thomas only hoped that it all had been staged. *The last thing I want is to give up control.*

But there was nothing he could do about it. He'd already agreed to give the regression therapy a try and, quite honestly, he had nothing else to lose. His mind had been eating away at him for years and apparently in the past month he'd unknowingly reached his breaking point. Thomas desperately needed answers so attempting something like hypnosis didn't seem too farfetched. Hell, he'd completely let his guard down with Laura and that had surprised him. He kept his defenses up most of the time so people couldn't hurt him; an unfortunate side effect of his childhood trauma. Unfortunately those same defenses kept people at an arm's length. But he knew Sam and Bill would always be there for him even though their relationship had never been the same between them again, at least for Thomas. He'd withdrawn from society as he'd grown older. Sure, he had Sam and Bill throughout the rest of elementary, junior and high school to lean on, but after that Thomas had been surrounded by strangers in college. The shock value was akin to jumping in to a frozen lake. Thomas' senses had skyrocketed as he panicked and thrashed around at first. Eventually Thomas had found his rhythm at USC, smiling and doing what everyone else did. But Thomas still feared life and the dangers it could contain, and had, as he continued to grow older.

Thomas looked around his room. He wasn't looking at anything in particular, just a quick survey and inventory of his life.

What am I doing?

Thomas came close to an epiphany. For a split second his entire life nearly aligned around what he needed to do. He felt elated and hopeful, but then it slipped away.

I hate when that happens. It's so frustrating!

He groaned and slipped out of bed.

* * *

Thomas puttered around the house for a while after breakfast. His bike needed to be repaired; he didn't know what else he'd find in his garden; and he couldn't psyche himself up to write. Eventually he decided to clean up a bit and spent hours washing and rewashing the floors, counters and walls in each room. Psychologically it was very detoxing because Thomas put a lot of time and effort in to it.

That evening, many hours later and with his house smelling of Pine-Sol, Thomas collapsed on the couch with a beer in hand. He felt like he really accomplished something and mentally patted himself on the back. During the process he'd even made a discovery. In the guest bedroom he had a number of boxes stacked up in the corner. During his cleaning frenzy he'd gone through each box in an effort to reduce clutter and in the process had discovered dozens of stories, drawings and pictures he'd created as a kid. Thomas had immediately stopped and transported the collection up to his room. He placed the full box on his computer desk and resumed cleaning. Within the confines of that box lay untold treasures and memories waiting to be rediscovered.

21
Wednesday, July 11, 1990 6:09 p.m.

"Good evening, Thomas. How are you feeling tonight?"

When Thomas had walked in to Laura's office he didn't know what to expect. He had figured maybe the entire room would have been replaced with a new look for the regression.

Silly me.

The only new addition was a video camera mounted on a tripod which pointed at the chair he typically sat in.

"Hi Laura. To be honest I'm a bit apprehensive, but nevertheless here I am."

Laura smiled. "You'll be just fine. We'll start off slow tonight and see what happens."

Thomas nodded and sat down in his normal spot. "I'm assuming you want me here?" he said as he motioned towards the video camera.

"Don't worry about the camera. It's there so I can review our session later. A lot of information will come my way during your regression and I won't be able to make notes at the same time. You understand."

"Of course, of course," he said with a half-smile. "You're the doctor."

Laura let Thomas finish getting situated. "Do you mind taking your shoes off, Thomas? It'll help you get more comfortable."

"No problem," he acknowledged and took them off.

Laura said, as she fiddled with the video camera, "So what have you been up to for the past two days?"

"Well, as you can imagine, my mind has been absolutely racing. Of course, I have no idea why."

Laura looked up and saw that Thomas was joking. He was nervous but seemed in relatively good spirits.

"My mind's a blank too," she retorted.

Thomas smiled. "Seriously though, you won't find a cleaner house in Running Springs. I literally spent all day Tuesday cleaning and scrubbing it from top to bottom."

"Some nervous energy perhaps?" Laura probed.

"You could say that. Nervous and trying to shut off my brain more like it. I collapsed that night on the couch and woke up there the next morning."

"Good for you," Laura said as she grabbed her chair and scooted it closer to Thomas. "And what about this morning?"

"Well, after waking up and having my senses assaulted from the lingering cleaning products, I took my damaged bike down to Marcus' shop. He worked the bent wheel back in to shape while I waited. It was also good to get out of the house for a bit."

Laura sat down and looked straight at Thomas. "How about now? How're you doing?"

"More relaxed, I guess."

"Okay, let me tell you how this works, Thomas. I'm merely going to talk to you. I'll ask you to close your eyes first and then I'm going to softly talk to you. I'll verbally lead you down a path and by the time you arrive at the end of it you'll be under hypnosis."

"It's that easy?" Thomas asked.

"It's only as easy as you want it to be, Thomas. I can't force this on you. You have to be a willing participant which means I'm going to ask you one simple question right now and you need to answer it honestly."

"Okay."

"Thomas, do you trust me?"

Thomas hated that question. Trusting someone meant they had a master key and any defenses you had could be nullified because they could hurt you whenever they wanted. Thomas only trusted a few people in his life and could count them on one hand. However, in the same breath, he knew he had no choice but to move forward and deal with his current circumstances. He knew Laura had done nothing but help him from the get go and he hadn't gotten any weird vibes from her.

Thomas nodded. "I trust you."

"Good," she said. "All I'm going to do this evening is evaluate how you react to my process. Nothing crazy or over the top. Sound fair enough?"

"No, that sounds perfect. Thanks Laura."

She smiled at Thomas and he returned it. He was now in her hands. She knew when he verbalized his trust that it was a major hurdle. *Progress.*

Laura began. "Okay. Sit back and relax. Close your eyes and try to clear your mind."

Thomas shifted around in his chair and followed her directions.

"With your mind free of cluttered thoughts your body begins to float. You only hear my voice talking as your body gently glides. You are weightless and don't have a care in the world. Off in the distance you see a bright light. The light is warm and inviting. You are drawn to it. Your body drifts towards it."

* * *

Thomas sat peacefully in the chair. Laura had just finished the regression process which had taken about five minutes of softly walking him through her process. He seemed to take to it very well.

"Thomas. Can you hear me?"

"I hear you," he replied.

"What do you see?"

"A bright light and it's warm," he said dreamily.

"Good Thomas. How do you feel?"

"Safe. Relaxed."

Perfect. "Thomas, I'd like to ask you a few questions."

"Okay."

"When were you born?"

"July twenty-seventh, nineteen-figty-seven in San Jose, California."

"How old are you now?"

"I'm thirty-two."

"Thomas. Do you trust me?"

Thomas hesitated for a second before he replied. "Yes, I trust you."

"Good, Thomas. I'm here to help you. I won't hurt you."

Thomas didn't reply.

"I'd like to teach you a phrase, Thomas."

"A phrase?"

"That's right. I'd like you to remember a specific phrase for me. This phrase will be very powerful and it will protect you. Listen to my voice, Thomas. Listen carefully. The phrase you need to remember is…"

* * *

"Three. The bright light is fading in the distance."

"Two. Your body is getting heavier."

"One. You are relaxed and awake."

Thomas slowly opened his eyes and blinked as he looked around. "I'm sorry. I didn't mean to fall asleep." He sat up in his chair and Laura smiled. He looked over at the clock. It read 6:43 p.m.. "Wait. Really?"

"You were fantastic, Thomas. You did a great job."

"So it worked? I didn't feel a thing. I swear I just closed my eyes."

"Pretty neat, eh?"

Thomas sat up straighter. "So what happened?"

"Tonight was just a test run. You were relaxed. I asked a few basic questions, like when and where you were born. After that I brought you back out."

"So what happens when it's for real?"

"The same exact thing, Thomas. You'll wake up normally like you just did. I'll start with things we've talked about and go from there. I won't know more until you're regressed to various moments in your life. We'll have to try it and see what happens."

"Kind of like shooting in the dark a bit, isn't it?"

"Initially it will be. Once I start asking about specific details I'll have a baseline of questioning I can tangent off of from there." She looked right at Thomas and said, "It'll be fine. Trust me."

22
Thursday July 12, 1990 6:07 p.m.

"Sorry I'm late," Thomas said.

"Don't worry about it." He came in and sat down in his chair.

"Nervous?" Laura asked.

"A bit." Thomas took off his shoes. "Yesterday's regression didn't bother me so let's do this again."

Thomas tried to relax as much as he could in the chair. *Today is the big day.*

"How are you feeling?"

He opened his eyes and melted as he looked at Laura. She was gorgeous. "No time like the present," Thomas informed her.

"I need you to look at me and concentrate on my voice. Don't talk to me unless I ask you a question."

Her voice was soft and charismatic and he was so comfortable in the chair. Her voice...so beautiful, so sweet. He thought he was dreaming. Thomas floated through a meadow. He liked the meadow. He felt safe within the meadow. He didn't want to leave. Around the edges of the meadow were darker trees, menacing and evil. The meadow where he was at was bright and the trees couldn't get him. Thomas shivered. He was suddenly afraid.

A whisper blew by him like the wind. It was a friendly breeze that didn't want to hurt him like those trees did. The voice passed by him again. He looked for the voice but couldn't find it. It danced just out of his sight. It brushed by him again. He sat down on the meadow and looked up into the sky. Clouds filled the sky. One in particular looked like...no, it couldn't be. Thomas blinked his eyes and the cloud dissipated. A new image filled the space. No, not that either. He started to panic. He looked up to the clouds again and saw a huge sandbox. People were playing in it. Was that him? Billy. Sammy. They were there too. He smiled. He forgot about the other images. They waved at him and then they were gone also. He yawned and closed his eyes. It had been a busy day and he relaxed. Everything was going to be okay.

* * *

Laura was concerned. She had anticipated how Thomas might react but he had gone beyond her safety zone. Thomas had pulled his legs up in the chair and now sat in an upright fetal position. His head thrashed back and forth. The only thing she had asked Thomas was about his relationship with his father, and that's when he started to panic. It took Laura almost two minutes to calm him down.

Relieved to be back in control Laura continued.

"Thomas. Do you like the meadow?"

"It's beautiful. What are all these scary trees doing here?"

"What trees, Thomas? Describe them to me."

"They're surrounding me. I can't leave the meadow unless I go through them. Why do they surround me?"

"What do they look like, Thomas?"

"They are black with huge trunks. The tree branches look like arms that want to reach out and get me. I'm safe in the meadow. I can't ever leave."

"Just stay where you are, Thomas. Don't go towards the trees. I'll protect you. Trust me."

Thomas tried to curl up tighter on the chair.

Laura noticed, "What are you greatest fears?"

He started to shake again.

"Relax Thomas. Calm down. Nothing's going to happen to you."

He calmed down faster this time.

"What are you fears?"

"I don't want to be alone."

"Who left you alone, Thomas?"

"Where are you, Mommy? I need you Mommy. Please come back. Mommmmmy!!"

His painful scream filled her office and his cries hurt her ears. Thomas was in real pain.

"Easy Thomas. Slow down. Breath. You'll be okay. I'm right here for you."

He continued to tremble from his repressed feelings about his mother and her death. Tears streaked down his face. Laura waited for them to subside before continuing. She knew she was making progress.

"Now listen to me, Thomas. You're back at school when you were a child. Billy and Sammy are there. You're in the sandbox."

"Is Nigel there? I'm scared."

"No, Nigel is nowhere around," Laura assured him. "He can't get you."

"I know he can't."

"What do you mean that he can't get you?"

"He can't get me. He's not around."

"That's right, he's not around." Thomas' voice had lowered and he had a devilish grin on his face.

"What do you see, Thomas?"

"I see Billy. I see Sammy. I don't see Nigel. He can't get me. I don't want him to."

* * *

"Three. Two. One."

Laura looked at Thomas and smiled. Curled up in the chair, Thomas looked like an innocent little child. *Too bad he had to go through so much pain. How the heck did he survive?*

Thomas stirred in his seat. His eyes fluttered and then opened.

"That was a great sleep. This chair is so comfortable. Did it work again?"

Laura got up, turned off the video camera and sat back down. "I asked about your mother, father, Billy, Sammy and Nigel. I got mixed reactions across the board. You have some really scary issues to deal with. It's going to take some time but we'll get through it."

"My life isn't my own right now. I need it back, Laura. If these memories are holding me back then we need to keep pressing forward."

"I'll do my best, Thomas. These walls that you have built up inside you, your defenses, are substantial. It's going to take some time to break through them."

"I'm aware of my normal defenses. Are you saying that I have some I'm not even aware of? Would that explain my memory loss?"

"You bet it would. There are different explanations, but in a nutshell you've blocked out whatever those events were because your mind was unable to cope with the reality. Your conscious mind does not remember them but your subconscious certainly does. As I continue to dig through your subconscious I'll eventually locate the trigger. However, once that happens you might consciously remember whatever they were. The plan is to lead you up to that point and not trigger a surprise recall.

Thomas sat back in his chair. *What the hell could I have forgotten?*

"That's actually pretty scary and upsetting to think about, Laura. Waking up with blood on my hands wasn't exactly my best day. And, like you said, I don't remember it. The real issue is what else in my life don't I remember?" Thomas suddenly wanted to go home. "Is it wrong to say that I'm afraid to remember?"

"No, Thomas, it's okay. You're also not alone. We'll get through this together."

23

Monday December 25, 1967 8:21 a.m.

Tommy slowly woke up and looked around. He hadn't liked the hospital and was happy to see that he was now in his own bed. *Whew.*

But then he realized what day it was. Christmas had finally arrived in the Clark household. He had waited for this moment for an entire year and loved it. He had noticed that his father hadn't been in the best of moods lately, but Tommy surmised that nearly getting killed would put a damper on anyone's spirits.

In the hospital Michael had asked Tommy what had happened out in the woods that day, but Tommy couldn't remember. Michael had talked with Billy and Sammy's fathers and had found out more details. He discovered that a fifth grader named Nigel Clemmings had been bullying the three of them since the beginning of the school year. Michael had been surprised because Tommy hadn't mentioned any of it. The police had investigated the incident and had placed Nigel in juvenile detention, then released to his father's custody. Billy and Sammy's parents had filed charges against Mr. Clemmings, and Michael had joined in on the lawsuit.

Tommy got up, put his slippers and robe on, and ran into his father's room. He jumped on the bed and pounced on his father who took him in his arms and gave him tons of kisses. Apparently he was in much better spirits.

"Aww dad…quit it." Michael only smiled and held on to him even tighter.

When Michael had received the call that his son had been admitted to John Muir Hospital he had dropped everything to be by his son's side. The first week had been a roller coaster of emotions as the doctors were unsure of Tommy's condition. Michael had even witnessed his son talking with his dead mother, which had been eerie enough. On top of that he was informed that his son had been the target of a school bully, and that bit of information had taxed Michael's psyche because he thought he knew everything about his son.

So the times when Michael wasn't at the hospital he spent decorating the house in holiday attire, and his obsession was noticeable to Tommy when he was released from the hospital. It seemed that every conceivable location in the house had been adorned with something Christmassy.

Michael knew his son was going to be okay physically. What he wasn't so sure about was how Tommy was mentally handling everything, but so far he seemed to be acting like a normal ten year old.

"Did Santa come last night, Dad? Did he? Did he?" he said as he pestered his father to get his lazy butt out of bed.

Tommy knew that the living room, where the tree and all the presents awaited them, was off limits until his father gave him permission. Michael always enjoyed this ritual.

"I don't know, son," he asked while attempting to hold back a fatherly grin. "Have you been a good boy this year?"

"Well geez, dad. I think I've been. Can we go out there now?"

"Sure we can, Tommy. Wait for me while I get my slippers and robe on."

Instead of waiting for his father, to take his time and walk to the closet, Tommy raced and retrieved them instead.

"You're sure in a hurry aren't you?" his father inquired.

"You know I am. I want to see if Santa ate the cookies and milk I left out for him last night. I bet he gets hungry flying

162

around in that sled of his and having to climb down all those chimneys. He needs to be cared for and looked after so he'll remember us and come back next year."

Michael stared at his son. *Still so innocent.*

They left the master bedroom and walked towards the living room. Tommy couldn't contain his desire to see what the man in red had brought to the Clark's household. AS they rounded the corner Tommy had to stop to take in all the sights that were before him.

"Wow," he breathed out as his jaw hit the floor.

There in the midst of the blinking tree, the multicolored packages, the half drunken glass of milk and all the decorations, stood a dirt bike. It was dark green. It had off road tires and was fully decked out. On the front of the bike was a license plate with the word 'Tommy's' emblazed upon it.

Tommy took a step towards it, then another, and another, his eyes fixated on the bike and nothing else in the room. It was beautiful. Tommy had continued to drop obvious hints about wanting a bicycle, and somehow his father had picked up on them. He whirled around as Michael stood in the archway and observed the way his son had reacted. A smile had instantly formed when he saw happy he'd made his son. Tears of joy formed in the corner of Michael's eyes but he willed them away because he didn't want to upset Tommy into thinking that anything was wrong. This Christmas was to be extra special. Tommy looked at his father and saw a smile on his face.

"Thanks, dad! Thankyouthankyouthankyou!" Tommy ran over and hugged his father.

"You're welcome, son." Michael responded.

Tommy then went back to examining his new found treasure. It was amazing. He couldn't wait to take it outside and test it out. He also couldn't wait to show it to Sammy and Billy.

Michael went over to his son and put his hand on his shoulder. Tommy glanced up and they locked eyes.

"This is from your mother and me. We knew that one day you'd need one."

"I wish Mom were here," Tommy said.

"So do I son, so do I."

The two left his sparkling new bike in the middle of the living room and slowly sauntered off to the kitchen to make a delicious Christmas breakfast. The day had just begun and it was already filled with heartwarming memories.

24
Tuesday April 19, 1988

"Sir, we're ready."

Mr. Glib rose out of his chair, looked through the observation window and enjoyed his Scotch on the rocks. He had finally accomplished his lifelong dream of controlling other human beings. He reveled in his success and all that was left now was a preliminary test run.

Mr. Glib pushed a button and said, "I'll be right down. Make sure that Joe is properly prepped."

"Yes, sir," came the reply.

He pushed another button on his control panel and a secret door slid open along his office wall. Mr. Glib put down his drink, walked into the small box and the door closed behind him. In seconds his private elevator descended to the testing level. Below that was another layer of hell that only a few people at RHP knew about. Years of failure after failure were stored there. All those deaths and it was still sealed up tightly, unbeknownst to his current staff. Failure was not a part of his overall plan. If failure was a part of what was going on it was always someone else's fault. He would never accept it.

Never again will I feel the pain of humiliation.

The elevator door opened and Mr. Glib walked into the lab area and saw that Joe sat on the table dressed in a lab coat. With a motion of his hand the guard and the assistant left the two of them alone. Joe looked at the man who approached him.

"How are you feeling today?" he asked Joe.

Joe was visibly uncomfortable. "I still don't know your name and I don't know why I'm here. What is this place?"

Good, he doesn't remember a thing. "I offered you a job and you accepted it. Don't you remember?"

"I don't remember," Joe replied. "What job are you talking about?"

"The job is easy. You wanted to be my lab assistant."

"I did?" Joe paused. "Oh, I remember now. I did."

The intercom buzzed overhead. "Sir, you're needed in the observation area."

"I'll be right back," he told Joe and left the room.

Joe got up off the table and gazed around the room. He was tired and his mind felt a little fuzzy. He didn't remember how he had gotten here exactly but he was dressed as a lab assistant, so it had to be true.

The phone in the lab started to ring. Joe looked over at it.

I work here.

On the fifth ring Joe picked it up. "Hello?" Joe's body immediately stiffened.

From the observation room above Mr. Glib smiled.

25
Monday December 25, 1967 9:09 a.m.

Breakfast consisted of scrambled eggs with cheese, white toast, three strips of bacon and orange juice. Michael prepared the breakfast while Tommy tidied up after him. They had learned to clean up after themselves diligently after his mother had died because there was no one else at home that would do it for them. Since that point they had to take care of the house as well as each other.

Laundry had become a problem, but Tommy typically took care of it. Michael usually worked all day which left Tommy home alone after school to care for himself, so Tommy did a lot of the chores and looked after the house. Michael knew that his son didn't have much of a choice to grow up so quickly, and any normal child his age would have put up a fuss to help around the house, but Tommy hadn't complained once in the past five years.

Dishing up their portions onto separate plates, they both headed into the dining room to enjoy their food. However, they ate in virtual silence. If an outsider peered through the window and saw them there, they would swear that the father and son each appeared to be in deep thought; and indeed they were.

Michael was proud of his son and individually they had learned to cope with the tragedy they couldn't escape from. But Tommy still longed to fully understand why his mother was gone. *Why did it have to be her?* For years he blamed God for making a mistake and he hated God for that. Likewise, Michael hadn't been able to fully come to grips that Betsy was no longer a part of their lives. It wasn't fair. Five years later he still missed and thought about her every day. He wished he could forget the memory of her from that horrific day, the image of his battered wife as her eyes

167

stared through him as she lay on that cold morgue table. That image continued to haunt him. She never blinked, nodded her head or even acknowledged his presence as he stood over her. *Those eyes, oh those eyes.* Michael sat and tried to think about the good times he had with his wife, but his rage still boiled inside him. He couldn't forgive the drunk driver that had taken his loved one away. He had wanted so desperately to kill that son of a bitch but that man had died at the scene as well.

Tommy sat quietly and dwelled on his Nigel situation and what he was going to do about it. He was scared of him because Nigel had actually tried to kill him. Tommy wasn't sure how far he would go next time, that is, if there was a next time. He could do something to Nigel before Nigel did something to him, but Tommy had heard that Nigel was on house arrest, whatever that meant, and knew Nigel would always be home. He had to solve the problem. *It always seemed to work in the movies, why not now?* Tommy started to plan.

As they finished breakfast Michael cleared off the table. Tommy followed him to the kitchen so that he could wash them.

"Forget about them for now, Tommy. There are other things that we should be doing instead."

Tommy understood immediately what his father implied and raced to the living room to examine his bicycle and the numerous other presents that littered the base of the tree. Michael followed his son and once again a smile broadened his face.

At least one of us is happy. The smile left his face.

Santa had come through. This was definitely the best Christmas ever. Never had Tommy seen so many packages at one time and wondered why there were so many, but that thought drifted once he started tearing into them. It was fabulous. He enjoyed every second of every rip and tear. Occasionally he noticed his father behind him. He started to wonder why his father wasn't opening anything, but then he focused on what he'd just opened and froze. Inside was a gift that brought tears to his eyes. It contained a miniaturized replica of a mechanical scooper. Michael realized a change in his son and joined him.

"It's to go with your dump truck, son."

Tommy started to shake and his floodgates burst open. Tears poured down his face.

Michael didn't understand. "What's wrong, son?"

Tommy looked his father in the eyes and started to explain. Everything that he held inside sprouted forth like a geyser because the pressure was just too much to hold back anymore. He told his father everything that had happened between his friends, himself and Nigel. His father listened intently and asked questions when he needed clarification.

After Tommy had finished spewing forth the incidences with Nigel, along with Sammy and Billy, Michael hugged his son. He had had his doubts about whether or not Tommy was having problems at school but he had no idea it had been this severe. Tommy's stories seemed to come across like they were straight out of a horror book. This personal vendetta this Nigel kid had against Tommy was unreal.

So much emotional and physical torture that damages and affects people for the rest of their lives. It had to be stopped. I'm surprised that my Tommy is still alive and functioning like a regular person. He must have so much hatred inside of him. I'm just glad that he released part of it to me. He's too young to handle a kid like this.

Tommy's tears had subsided by now but he kept staring at the scooper in front of him. His mouth formed words but nothing was audible to Michael's ears. Unbeknownst Tommy was swearing

169

that he was going to make Nigel pay for everything he'd done and he already knew what he was going to do. An evil grin appeared on his face, just for a moment, before he hid it from his father. He didn't want any suspicion to be raised or any questions asked about what he was suddenly so happy about. All he knew was that Nigel would pay.

Eventually Michael left Tommy alone in the living room and went back to the kitchen. He had too many of his own thoughts in his head. What was he going to do about Nigel? *Obviously this kid's home life was horrible, but that's no excuse to try and kill my son.* Michael had wanted this Christmas to be special and yet he was now depressed.

*   *   *

Tommy watched his father leave the room. Afterwards he got up and went to his room. The gifts that he had received sat right where he left them because now he had a desire to fulfill and that's what he intended to work on. He opened the door to his room and then closed it behind him. He glanced around his room but didn't see what he was looking for.

It must be in the closet.

Tommy rummaged through his closet until he finally emerged with the prize he had been so diligently searching for. He had found his bat.

*   *   *

It was Christmas, and the spirit was still there, but somehow the two of them just couldn't get back into the swing of the day. Tommy cleaned up the mess he'd created and made several trips back to his own bedroom with his presents. Then he asked his father if he could ride his bike down the street. Michael let him go.

Tommy could ride a bike with ease. He was glad to have his own now because he was tired of borrowing Sammy or Billy's at school to practice with. He loved to ride because that gave him the freedom he always wanted and now he could be in control and have fun at the same time.

He pushed his bike out the front door. As he made it to the driveway Tommy contemplated which way he should go. If he went left then he would have to bike uphill to get back to the house. If he went right he could go downhill first and then bike back to the house on a relatively flat incline. He decided to go left. Why not try and do the hardest thing first? If he did that then he could do anything else.

He expertly pushed off and swung his leg over the bike seat. He tried to let the cool breeze relax him but his thoughts of Nigel continued to plague his thoughts. He was surprised that he had told his father everything that had gone on, because he didn't want to seem like some sort of momma's boy who couldn't take care of his own problems. Yes, he wanted to take care of it himself, and that's exactly what he planned on doing.

As he turned the corner Tommy started to contemplate what he was going to do to Nigel and when he was going to do it. He had retrieved the bat earlier and now decided that using it on Nigel would be the most convenient way of dealing with his problem. As Tommy continued to ride another grin appeared on his face again. If anyone had peered had seen it they would have sworn that the Devil himself had ridden by.

It would work. It has to.

Michael watched his ride away from the dining room window. He let the drape close and sauntered back to the kitchen to tidy up the last couple of items. But Michael's confusion masked his inability to effectively clean, and he had to rewash them again due to his lack of concentration. All he worried about was his son and that asshole bully. It just wasn't fair. Tommy was just a young boy and he certainly didn't deserve such abuse.

With the kitchen clean, Michael went to his study and started to write a letter. Minutes flew by. Once he finished he sealed it in an envelope and put it on his desk.

I'll deliver it tomorrow.

He picked up his desk phone and dialed a familiar number.

"Hello."

"Hey, dad. Merry Christmas."

"Honey, its Michael," he heard his father say through a cupped hand. "Merry Christmas, son. How's Tommy?"

Michael paused. "He finally told me everything that happened dad. I don't know how he survived."

Michael took a few minutes and filled his father in.

"I understand. We'll be over tonight for dinner and we can talk then. Your mother wants to say something to you."

Michael heard the phone being passed off.

"Merry Christmas dear," his mother Claire said. "I love you."

"I love you too, mom. I'll see you both this evening."

After he hung up Michael stripped down and took a long, hot shower in an effort to wash off the horrors that Tommy had entrusted him with. He wasn't convinced it would work.

* * *

Tommy returned home forty minutes later and let himself inside, his breathing a bit labored. As he parked his new bike by the Christmas tree he heard the shower. The water suddenly turned off and he could hear his father toweling off.

What is this house arrest they were talking about? Why hasn't someone done anything about Nigel?

Tommy wondered if anything was actually going to be done. But Tommy was pleased his father hadn't said much because it would make Tommy's job a lot easier. Nigel wasn't going to be a problem for much longer.

* * *

The doorbell rang around 6:30 p.m.. "Tommy, would you please get that?" his father asked.

"Okay, dad."

Tommy went to the front door and opened it. His grandparents stood there.

"Merry Christmas, Tommy!" they both said in unison.

Tommy smiled and hugged them both. His grandparents were fun to be around. They had been born in 1904 and always had plenty of stories to tell their grandson. The Great Depression, the automobile, the World Wars, etc. His grandfather, Ed, had kept him up late at night, on many occasions, to tell Tommy about one thing or another. Quite often Michael, Betsy or Claire would find Ed passed out in bed next to Tommy, both snoring away.

"Merry Christmas Grandma and Grandpa."

They came inside and Tommy closed the door behind them.

"Hi Mom. Hi Dad," Michael said as he exited the kitchen. A delicious wafted in from behind him.

Claire hugged her son. "Merry Christmas."

"Merry Christmas, Mom."

He turned to his father, and extended his hand, "Merry Christmas Dad."

Ed took his hand and said, "You too, son."

Tommy's grandmother turned back to him. "So what did Santa bring you?"

Tommy led his grandmother off to his room while Michael motioned towards the dining room table. His father took a seat and so did Michael.

"He seems okay," Ed said.

"I know. That's what scares me. From a complete breakdown he transformed into a happy go lucky kid. It's pretty extreme."

"Kids are resilient. I can't remember being that age any more, and maybe you can't either, but he'll survive. He's stronger than you think."

"I don't know, dad." Michael stared at the painting on the wall; a table with fruit on it. "Maybe."

* * *

Dinner was delicious and the conversation had remained neutral. Afterwards the table was cleared and, courtesy of Claire, slices of homemade pumpkin pie were served. During dessert Michael's parents talked about their recent travels abroad. At age sixty-three they still had quite a few destinations on their list to cross off. Their latest trip had been to England. But Michael found his own thoughts wandered as he listened to his mother go on about this place or that place. At some point during the conversation even Tommy had started to yawn. Soon afterwards

Tommy said his goodnights to his grandparents, was excused him from the table and headed off to bed.

"That's our cue," Ed said as he got up from the table. Dishes were gathered and brought in to the kitchen.

"Don't worry about the dishes. I'll take care of them."

"Are you sure sweetie?" asked his mother.

"Absolutely, mom. Thanks for the wonderful dessert."

Michael turned to his father. "Dad, do you have a second?"

Michael led the way back to his study as Ed followed behind him, picked up the envelope off his desk and presented it to his father.

"What's this?" asked Ed.

"Tuck this away at home. It's a power of attorney and a few other things."

"I don't understand."

"Just tuck it away someplace safe, dad. Can you do that please?"

Ed looked at his son closely and then tucked the envelope away in his jacket pocket.

*   *   *

Later on, after he watched some television, Michael crept into Tommy's room and sat down on his bed. Tommy had crawled into it just a few minutes prior and opened a book. He wasn't much of a reader but he sure got a lot of ideas from the books he did read. He liked to write out little fairy tales about castles and princesses and how they get rescued; about goblins and dragons and werewolves. When he got into his imagination he soared. It was like an open invitation to escape everything and anything around him. Nobody could affect him or take away his happiness. Well, only one person could, but that would soon be over.

"Tommy," his father asked, "are you going to do anything?"

"What do you mean, dad?"

"About Nigel."

"No," Tommy lied.

"Your friend's parents and I are suing Nigel's father. I want you to know that we're doing everything we can to make this right. Nigel won't be coming to school anymore. He's on house arrest."

"What exactly is house arrest?"

"Basically it means he can't leave his house. We believe he really should be in jail for what he did to the three of you. I just want you to know that you or your friends shouldn't worry about him anymore."

"Okay, dad."

"I love you, Tommy Clark, I really love you."

"I love you too, dad."

"Goodnight, son."

"Goodnight, dad."

As Michael closed the door to Tommy's room, Tommy looked over to the other side of his room. His bat was still there.

* * *

Tommy woke up with a start. Noise. Loud noises were all around him. He was confused. It was like he hadn't woke up completely yet and things were happening all around him that frightened him.

What's going on?

"Get the kid out of here!"

"Someone grab the kid."

Tommy's eyes had just begun to focus when two strong hands came down and plucked him out of his bed. He was carried through his house and out the door into an awaiting police car. The door was slammed behind him and it started to pull away from the curb. Tommy saw an ambulance parked in his driveway along with a couple of other police cruisers. He didn't know what to do. All the excitement caught up with him and he started to cry.

26
Saturday July 14, 1990 2:13 p.m.

"Why are you doing this to me? Stop it! Get off!"

Nigel crushed Tommy with his large body as Tommy fought to breath.

"Get off," he squeaked and choked on his last few seconds of oxygen.

"I'm going to kill you, Tommy Clark!" Nigel screamed as Tommy squirmed underneath him.

"I can't breathhh, get offff..." Tommy tried to say as he blacked out.

* * *

"Three. Two. One."

Thomas awoke from his journey, one that had led him down many different paths that afternoon.

Laura hovered close by. "How do you feel?" she asked him.

Thomas sat up and rubbed his head. "Drained. I feel like my body's here but my brain has been running a marathon. Is that normal?"

"For what you were just going through it certainly is. You're certainly racking up the frequent flier trauma miles, Thomas," she joked.

"Ha ha. Very funny," but he smiled nevertheless.

Laura got up from her chair, went to her desk and poured a cup of coffee.

"Do you want a cup?"

Her late night sessions with Thomas had left her reviewing her notes after he left so she finally decided to bring in a coffee maker. Coffee, while she worked, helped her focus.

"No, thank you."

Laura had been spending an enormous amount of time with Thomas. They'd only met ten days prior but she already found herself attracted to him. She knew that intense situations drew people together; maybe that's what's going on here.

Maybe, maybe not.

She wondered why she made all these special plans just so she could help out Thomas. What if they did get involved? What if he hurt her and left?

I'm not sure I'm ready to take that chance.

Laura had been involved with a man named Rick Surge whom she had loved him very much. He had won her heart five years previously and their relationship lasted two and half years. Rick was the kind of guy that everyone was drawn to, being naturally charismatic, caring and funny. As soon as anyone met him they couldn't help but to like him. Unfortunately his personality led him where it shouldn't have.

Laura had been away from their apartment and Rick knew she'd be gone all day. He took advantage of her absence to invite another woman over and Laura walked in on them having sex in their bed. Rick didn't even try to explain. In fact, he told her to close the door on the way out. He never said he was sorry and never explained his actions. From that day she vowed to never let herself be in a position where she could be devastated like that ever again.

Noticing her feelings for Thomas only confused and upset her because she didn't want to compromise herself. Becoming a psychiatrist was what she had wanted to do ever since she was a little girl. When she and Rick got together she was almost out of med school. She began her own practice right before he humiliated her. All she wanted to do from that point was to help other people out with their issues. Laura spent long and hard hours with her patients. Perhaps if she ever stopped and acknowledged her own pain she might have to deal with it. Instead she just worked harder. Over the past three years she had done a good job of burying her feelings.

Laura turned away from her desk, took her cup of coffee and sat back down next to Thomas. As she did this their eyes met and they briefly ogled each other. Laura eventually broke their gaze as she recalled her painful feelings. She took a sip of coffee and realized she was tired. It had been a long session of hypnosis today and they had much to discuss.

Thomas had been thinking along the same lines as well. He found Laura extremely attractive but was puzzled on what prompted him to want her. Maybe it was because of the intense bond they had developed in the past ten days. Perhaps it was the fact that she clearly wanted to help him through his deepest fears. Or perhaps it was just as simple as Thomas man; Laura woman. In any case Thomas' fear of rejection would rear its ugly head if he tried to ask her out anyway. *Nothing like mother issues to soil a relationship.* Thomas struggled with his inner turmoil. Not only was he confused, he was denying himself the right to have a life that could include someone to actually love. If he took a chance then maybe he would be happier.

Why can't I let him in on my feelings? I work on everyone else's issues but my own. Thomas wouldn't hurt me, so why am I afraid? Even if we were to get together I'd probably be stuck in the roll of his mother. What type of relationship would it be? I wonder what he's thinking. What do I do?

Thomas kept glancing over towards Laura and noticed that she was lost in her own thoughts as she sipped her coffee.

I wonder if I should take a risk. Besides, it's only dinner and it's the least I can do to thank her for all the help. It wouldn't really be a date, you know, more of a get together.

Thomas continued to rationalize his thoughts. He was unaccustomed to feeling soft and sensitive towards a woman.

While his conscious mind battled with his subconscious, Laura asked, "Thomas, what are you thinking about?"

Thomas jerked his head up with a start.

"Oh, I was um, thinking about, um, dinner."

"Dinner? What do you mean?"

"Well I was thinking that dinner would be nice."

"You're still confusing me, Thomas."

Here we go. "Christ. This is tough for me."

Here it comes she thought.

"Would you'd like to go out to dinner with me?" Thomas asked.

He was nervous. As soon as the words left his mouth he lowered his eyes. He knew the price of failure but he had risked it anyway.

"Thomas," she said. "Thomas, please look at me."

Thomas looked up and caught Laura's gaze. "I would love to go out to dinner with you. We still have a lot to talk about that doesn't have anything to do with you."

"What do you mean?" he asked.

"We both know that you are afraid of having people that you love leave you. What you don't know is that I am very much afraid of having people I love hurt me as well. I help people get through their pain and fears everyday yet I continue to ignore my own feelings. I just want you to know that about me right now so

182

that we don't go around hurting each other. As long as we know what our fears are then we're being honest."

Thomas let his gaze drop.

"What's wrong, Thomas?" she inquired.

"The first day I saw you I wanted to be with you. You seemed to have this aura about you that allowed me to share all the pain that I kept inside. I don't think you know how much of a difference you make in people's lives Laura; you've certainly made a huge transformation in mine. I want to be with you every moment of everyday. However, there still remains a problem because I don't know what the hell is going on with me. I don't know if I did all those terrible things. If I did, and we can prove that, then I'm going to jail. If I'm not guilty then we can make the best use out of the free time we'll have together. I don't want to lose you. If we start something here and now, and then we have to split apart later, I don't want to feel that pain and neither do you."

"I don't think you understand, Thomas. Today's hypnosis session was quite different from your previous ones."

Thomas hadn't expected that response. He straightened up in his chair and said, "What do you mean?"

"Instead of the consistent meadow scene, you voluntarily walked into the woods."

"You mean I wasn't scared of those huge trees with those tangled branches for hands?"

"Apparently not, Thomas. However, when you did walk into the trees you started to sweat. You also screamed out about Nigel not allowing you to breath. To be honest, it scared the hell out of me. I brought you out of it as quickly as I could."

"What else happened when I walked in to the woods?" Thomas asked as he got increasingly more excited over this apparent breakthrough.

"You kept mumbling every now and then about how it wasn't fair. You also kept shouting 'Stop it'. What do you think?"

"When I was in grade school, with Billy and Sammy, Nigel used to bully us. I would yell 'Stop it'. Not only would it surprise him but it would call the attention of the school yard monitor. I got used to saying it all the time.

"The other phrase, about it not being fair, I'm not sure about. It could be about any number of things, from Nigel or my mother dying. What do you think?"

"It's plausible. Actually I'm not sure about a lot of what you said today. They were weird."

"Listen, Laura. Getting back to our other discussion, and I know it sounds forward, but I want to hear about your pain too. I want to help you like you're helping me."

Instinctively they both stood and Laura embraced Thomas. She hung on like she didn't want to ever let him go and Thomas embraced Laura just as tightly. The anticipation of what their future could bring was felt both hopeful and inspiring. Their new budding love was just enough to block out the darkness of the world.

* * *

The night had long since fallen and the moon cast sinister shadows across the roads as automobiles prowled the empty streets of San Bernardino. Nobody wanted to be caught out in this gloominess.

A dark figure merged with the icky blackness. A few seconds later a vehicle engine spurted to life and sped off into the night. The owner of that car would surely be surprised to find it missing the next morning.

Somewhere close by to Laura's office a voice whispered into the night and only one other person could hear him.

"He's getting closer, sir."

*   *   *

Saturday July 14, 1990 11:27 p.m.

Knock knock.

No lights came on and no one stirred in the house. He waited five minutes just to make sure. Still nothing. He made his way to the back of the house. A children's swing set was here and some toys were scattered on the back porch. He carefully proceeded up the porch stairs and edged his way over to the back door. Still nothing. From beneath the folds of his black jacket a crowbar emerged and he shoved it in to the door jam. As for was applied the lock popped open. The door swung inwards very quickly, hit the counter behind it and shattered one of the glass panes with a crash. Seconds later an upstairs light illuminated the stairway.

I don't have much time.

Without a need to conceal his noise any longer the intruder dropped the crowbar and pulled a hand axe from his jacket.

"Who's there?" asked a shaky female voice from the top of the stairs.

He rushed to the bottom of the stairs and caught her eyes. She froze in terror but then started to scream when she saw the axe.

"AAAAAHHHHHHHHHHHHHHHHH!!!"

The intruder rushed up the stairs just as she turned to run back to her room and grabbed her hair with his left hand. He violently pulled back, which toppled her off her feet and she hung by her long as she tried to get her feet under her.

185

"AAAAHHHHHHHHHHHHHH!!!"

From a side bedroom a young boy peered out into the hallway, his eyes wide with fear.

"Mama?"

"Police, let her go!" came the shout from the bottom of the stairs.

The intruder turned as a large officer took his first steps up the stairs towards him. She still screamed and struggled as her son was stared at her from his bedroom doorway.

The officer advanced. "Drop the axe! Do it now!"

The attacker brought the axe down.

The police officer cried out, "NOOOOOO!!!"

Blood gushed in a crimson arc as the axe blade found an exposed artery.

Her young son screamed and fainted.

The officer was halfway up the stairs now.

The intruder dropped the axe, grabbed the dying woman's hips and tossed her down the stairs towards the oncoming policeman. Blood sprayed the walls as she sailed through the air. The officer was caught off balance and the two bodies tumbled to the landing below. They crashed into the table next to the front door as unread mail went flew everywhere.

The assailant rushed down the stairs and kicked the officer in the face as sirens were heard close by, no more than two blocks away. The intruder bolted through the front door and escaped.

Before additional police arrived the woman bled out all over her entryway. Her blood pooled around the unconscious police officer and Silvia Platt's mail was scattered everywhere, all of it now a dark red.

27
Thursday November 23, 1989 5:15 p.m.
Thanksgiving

"Thank you, Mr. Peterson. That will be all."

Mr. Peterson left Mr. Glib's office. Since the successful results of his most recent test run Mr. Glib had pushed his timetable ahead as rapidly as he could. Numerous tests had been completed, in the months that followed the miraculous breakthrough, and he had eagerly looked forward to this day. Tonight would be the ultimate test to see if his mind controlling chemicals worked seamlessly. Tonight his patient was going out to hunt.

The intercom interrupted his thoughts. "Sir, they're ready for you."

He used to his private elevator and met his entire staff in the main laboratory. All eighteen lived in fear of their boss and put on fake smiles as he entered the room.

"Thank you all for joining me here. I know its Thanksgiving and you want to be with your family, so I'll make this quick. Congratulations are in order. The last few years have been very demanding on all of us. You all have put in a tremendous amount of time and energy into this project. Without each and every one of you we would not have the successful results that we now have."

They all looked around at each other in mild confusion. Mr. Glib had never praised any of them before.

"You have all earned a well-deserved break. So, in preparation for such an occasion, I have taken the liberty of making reservations for all of you."

One of his staff piped up. "Reservations, sir?"

"That's right. When you were brought on to work at RHP one of the questions you were asked about your dream vacation. I have personally reviewed your answers and on the table behind me are packets with your names on them. They're all expense paid trips for you and your family, plus spending money." Mr. Glib motioned towards the table. "Go ahead and find yours. Only the best for such a hard working team of brilliant scientists."

Mr. Glib moved to the side of the room and watched as his staff found their packet and opened them.

"Holy crap, I'm going to Scotland!" said one scientist.

"I'm off to Asia!"

"New Zealand, here I come!" exclaimed another.

The reality hit each of them pretty hard. For years they had toiled under his leadership, which was more a dictatorship. Rarely had they been allowed to see or visit their families, and now they were going on two month paid vacations. The project they had signed on to had been heavily classified and the NDA's they had each signed had been thick. As employees of Rising Hope Pharmaceuticals (RHP) they still knew that the project they were associated with was heavily funded by the U.S. Government, especially with guards who patrolled the subterranean facility. It would have been foolish for any of them to believe they worked on a regular assignment.

Everyone seemed very relaxed and started to share where they were going with each other.

"Mr. Peterson, my office in five minutes."

"Yes, sir."

Mr. Glib left them all behind, with their broad smiles and stupid faces.

What a bunch of idiots. I am the only one responsible for this project's success.

188

He took his private elevator back up to this office and Mr. Peterson walked in a few minutes later.

"Mr. Peterson."

"Sir?"

"How are we with plan Tango Oscar?"

"Details are still being finalized sir."

"Thank you, Mr. Peterson. That will be all."

As Mr. Peterson left Mr. Glib rose out of his padded executive chair. He walked over to the glass window that separated him from the main laboratory down below and observed his latest creation. It struggled on the table below against the bonds that held him.

Talking to no one in particular Mr. Glib said, "Soon my army will be ready. People will pay and I will be the one to deliver that punishment. I will negotiate all deals with my currency of pain. I will destroy all those who dare stand in my way and crush them like insects beneath my feet."

He stepped back from the glass and slowly circled his office. "They will die. They will all die. I will command those deaths. The government will be taken out of the loop." Mr. Glib stopped suddenly as if remembering something important. "And him, that little bastard, he's the one I'll crush. I will make him pay for all the crimes he's committed. I won't destroy him though; instead I will make him suffer!"

Mr. Glib sat down at his desk and started to map out his new plan just as Mr. Peterson barged in.

"Sir."

Mr. Glib pulled a .38 caliber snub nosed gun from his right drawer and pointed it Mr. Peterson's face. He slowly pulled the hammer back.

Mr. Peterson pulled up short, froze and cautiously backed up towards the door.

"You really should knock next time," as he lowered the gun and placed it back in his drawer.

"Tango Oscar will be ready in three days, sir."

"And our newest member of the family….how's Frank doing?

"He's in containment now but can be made ready with fifteen minutes."

"Very well. Dismissed."

"Yes, sir."

"Oh, and one more thing Mr. Peterson."

"Sir?"

"Happy Thanksgiving."

"You too, sir. Thank you, sir."

Mr. Peterson left the office with a slight sheen of sweat upon his forehead.

"Now, where was I? Oh, yes…"

* * *

Thursday November 23, 1989 8:33 p.m.
Thanksgiving

For Ben and Nancy Kilpatrick it had been a wonderful Thanksgiving. They had been married for two years and their third anniversary was only months away in February. They lived in Los Angeles, close to Universal City, in a two bedroom apartment that overlooked downtown. They had just returned from a Thanksgiving lunch with some friends in Orange County, and the time had gotten away from them. Evening had arrived before anyone at the party knew it.

Ben drove at night since Nancy had a problem with halo's from the oncoming traffic. On the way home she reminded herself she needed to make an appointment to her eyes examined. Ben pulled into their carport and turned off the motor.

Nancy giggled as she recalled some of the conversations they'd had with their friends. Ben smiled at his wife's amusement, opened the door and stepped out. A gloved hand shot out of nowhere, struck him in the throat and he silently collapsed in a heap on the ground. Nancy fiddled with her seat belt release as the man took Ben's place in the driver's seat.

Why would Ben get back in the car?

Nancy turned to look at her husband, but instead came into contact with the barrel of a 9mm Berretta. It was the last thing she saw. The blast took her in the right eye and the hollow point didn't exit out the back of her head. She slumped in her seat as blood gushed from her wound.

The large man positioned Ben back in the driver's seat and then placed the weapon in Ben's right hand. The man pointed the weapon under Ben's chin and pulled the trigger for a second time. Teeth and pieces of Ben's jaw flew as he slumped over next to his dead wife.

The man, satisfied with the scene he'd created, left.

28
Tuesday July 12, 1990 7:02 a.m.

Since the previous days progress at Laura's office, Thomas
was pleased with himself. He was surprised that he had jumped in
with both feet and asked Laura out. It was such a giant step
compared to how he typically acted around women. Although still
very afraid of rejection, he at least had looked fear in its face and
confronted it. Besides, she had said yes. This brought another
smile to his face. By God, he had taken a huge risk. But the
rewards could be amazing! What if he would have been rejected?
What is she had flatly said no? What if...

Oh, stop it Thomas. You'll drive yourself nuts. She said yes
and that's all that matters now.

He pulled his bed covers up further to ward off the cold.
Thomas had woken up early and was a bit antsy, due to little sleep
due and the fact that he still rode his emotional high over his newly
found courage.

He propped up his pillows, stared at the ceiling and reflected
on what had transpired over the past couple of weeks. He still
wasn't sure what the hell was actually going on. Would he
ruthlessly kill for no reason, and more importantly, not remember
it? This particular notion puzzled him the most. *Why can't I*
remember what I've done? Why is it that I only recall bits and
pieces from my past?

Thomas looked at the clock, saw that it was 7:08am, rolled out
of bed and trotted off to the bathroom. He wasn't very happy
about reliving his past again, especially fourth grade, with Nigel,
because it was the worst. *Thank God for Sammy and Billy.*
Having both of them as friends helped ease the pain. Too bad
Nigel had hurt them as well. As Thomas thought more and more

about Nigel he soon realized that he hasn't asked himself the most important question of all. He looked in the mirror and his unblinking reflection stared right back at him.

"Where is Nigel now?"

The last thing Thomas remembered was that Nigel's father moved away during the lawsuit. He had just upped and disappeared and no one had heard from them again. Thomas let that realization sink in a little, and then wondered if Nigel even remembered who he was, or if he even cared. *It was a long time ago.*

Thomas considered this. *I wonder.* He walked back in to his bedroom, picked up the phone on his desk, started to dial Laura's number but a knock on his front door interrupted him. Thomas didn't move. The knock came at the door again, this time with urgency.

Thomas crept down the stairs. He snuck over to the front door and hesitated.

Who comes around at seven o'clock in the morning?

Thomas didn't ask who it was or make any noise whatsoever. Instead he silently looked through the peephole. Outside on his front porch were two men dressed in business suits, who wore dark glasses and carried what appeared to be suitcases. One of them raised his arm and knocked again, forcefully.

"Come on Mr. Clark, we know you're in there. Open up and make this easier on yourself. There is nowhere to run and you can't escape."

Thomas stood rooted to the floor. He couldn't believe what he had just heard.

Who are these men and what do they want?

He didn't move. The knocking stopped. Without any warning the door burst open, hit Thomas in the head and propelled him across the floor. His head was filled with start as he writhed around. Two hands gripped him under his arms, pulled him up violently and then shoved him against the wall. Thomas' head cracked against the wall and he nearly passed out. He slumped in the man's arms.

"Bring him in to the living room and put him on the couch. He's not going anywhere," said the smaller man.

The giant picked Thomas up and carried him to the couch. From his physical appearance he looked like he could take on two Raider football players with ease. This guy was a giant.

"Let him recover so that he can answer our questions. You've roughed him up enough. Go check out the rest of the house while I try and talk with him. If I need help, I'll yell."

Without s reply his huge partner walked off to inspect the rest of Thomas' residence. Thomas lay sideways on his couch. He had been tossed on it just a few moments before. His partner sat next to him, removed his dark glasses and opened his briefcase.

The living room, from Thomas' point of view, seemed to twist and spin simultaneously. His head throbbed and he felt like he was going to throw up. He remained still as he tried to focus and collect his thoughts.

Who are these assholes?

If he could only find out what was going.

"Don't worry, Mr. Clark. We're here to find out what you know. And believe me, you'll tell us everything. You really have no choice."

As he finished his little speech his partner reappeared and said, "It's clear." He pointed at Thomas and said, "What's wrong with him?"

"Other than feeling like shit he's fine. He's pretending to be unconscious. That's okay though. If he thinks we're going to fall for it then he won't mind this needle I'm about to plunge into his arm."

With that Thomas painfully shifted his position to an upward one. Arrows of pain pierced his head and he fell off the couch and onto the floor.

"Grab him and prop him back up will you. I'd rather have him sitting when I inject him."

Thomas once again felt strong hands. He tried to resist by flailing out with his arms but was cut short with a swift punch to his gut. There was no way for him to resist.

"Hurry up and give him the shot," urged the larger one.

"Then hold him still so it doesn't break. We have to be extremely careful with how we deal with him."

No longer able to hold onto reality, Thomas let himself relax. He kept hearing bits and pieces of conversation between his two assailants and wasn't even sure that the needle that they stuck into his arm was real or some type of delusion. Thomas stayed with the idea that it was a delusion only because his mind wasn't his to control, at least not for the time being.

After receiving the quick punch to the stomach, and nearly losing consciousness, Thomas was injected with a needle in his right arm. Any remaining resistance ceased a few seconds after the drug circulated within his bloodstream. The larger of the two intruders helped Thomas gently lay back on the couch. Thomas would give them no more trouble until the drug wore off.

"Good work. After we're finished we can scrub this place. When he returns to this world he'll either think it was a dream or he won't remember a thing. In either case he won't be making any trouble."

"Let's hurry up and get this over with, I'm hungry."

"Relax, will you. This takes time. I have to make sure I gave him the right amount of Sodium Pentothal. If you're so hungry go and make yourself something to eat in his kitchen, but clean up any mess you make."

Thomas didn't feel good all of a sudden. He felt as if his entire body was starting to burn up, especially his right arm which felt on fire. He hurt. Thomas tried to call out but couldn't. His throat; what was wrong with his throat?

Why do I taste garlic? I've got to move. I've got to get myself out of danger.

Thomas tried to push himself up and soon realized that his body wouldn't respond to his mental commands. This can't be happening. Thomas started to panic.

No! No! Cut it out! Stop it, you're hurting me!

Thomas awoke with a start and noticed his sheets were drenched in sweat. He quickly sat up.

Ouch!

His head hurt. He scanned his room for the two men. Nothing. What the hell was happening to him?

Have I completely lost it?

He sat up in bed further and let the sheets fall across his legs.

My arm!

Thomas inspected his right arm. Nothing. He checked his left arm. Nothing. Thomas then spent the next several minutes inspecting his entire body both visually and with his hands. He couldn't locate a single needle mark.

Thomas climbed out of bed, headed into his bathroom and checked his body in the mirror. Nothing. He stared intently at the reflection before him.

Wait, what?

He didn't recognize his reflection. Some stranger, trapped within the frame of the mirror, stared back at him. Thomas recoiled in fear and horror. The right half of the man's face was practically torn away and an empty eye socket gazed back at Thomas. The left half of the face attempted a smile. Pieces of flesh fell off the face along with some bloody brain matter. Thomas couldn't move. He could only anticipate what was going to happen next. He knew that face only too well. It reached for him with a hand that stretched out from behind the mirror and grasped for Thomas. The hand brushed his throat.

"Poor some sugar on meeeee."

Wait, what?

Thomas opened his eyes. From his night stand he heard his clock radio playing Def Leppard. Thomas slapped himself in the face really hard.

Fuck, that hurt! Apparently I must really be awake this time. A dream within a dream, now that's weird.

That face though, he thought he knew that face. The men though...he didn't know who they were. Thomas tried to shrug off the dream and readjust to the real world.

Getting out of bed he glanced at his clock. It read 7:12am. With his reddened cheek Thomas headed into his bathroom and took a shower. The water was refreshing and really seemed to revitalize him. As the water pounded down over his back he wondered if his dreams were somehow related to his struggle with his memory.

Why can't I remember?

He tried to reconstruct more of his childhood memories but Thomas only succeeded in eliciting quick images. They appeared and disappeared in his head too quickly to really tell what they were. He could remember Sammy and Billy as clear as if they were standing in the room with him. What was more concerning was that as hard as Thomas tried he couldn't pick a time in his childhood to relive. It was as if most of his childhood memories were now absent.

He pondered everything at once and lost track of time. Eventually he noticed his hands had pruned so he turned off the shower and toweled himself dry.

Why am I so different?

He walked in to his bedroom and got dressed. The clock read 7:43am. He took in a deep breath, held it and then let it out.

Nothing I can do about it right now. Time for a quick bike ride and then I need to tidy up the house again.

29
Tuesday December 26, 1967 7:30 a.m.

Tommy awoke slowly. He was still groggy from the previous night's mysterious adventure and still wasn't sure what was going on. He was in bed but it felt weird; different. It wasn't his bed.

"It's okay, son. You'll be all right now."

"Dad. Dad, is that you?" Tommy hugged the man and said, "I was so scared that you weren't coming to get me. These men came and…"

Tommy let his arms fall from around the shoulders of this man who was definitely not his father. The hug had been returned but it hadn't felt like his father. Tommy drew back into his sheets and looked up at the face that now peered at him.

"Hello, Tom," his grandfather said.

"Hi…grandpa…?" Tommy replied, unsure of his words.

"How are you this morning?"

Instead of answering his grandfather's question Tommy surveyed the room they were in. Everything around him was white. He didn't feel safe. He didn't like this place. He didn't know why he was here. He wanted his father. He wanted to go home.

Tommy started to breath heavily. His grandfather leaned over and pulled Tommy close. At first Tommy resisted but he had nowhere else to go. He couldn't run, he didn't even know where he was or what was going on. Tommy hugged his grandfather back.

"I want to see my dad. Where's my dad? Where's my dad?"

A tear rolled down Ed's cheek. "I want to see him too, Tom. I want to see him too."

Tommy looked up at his grandfather's face. Tommy had never seen him cry before and it frightened him.

"Where's my dad, grandpa?" he asked again.

Wiping away the tear his grandfather stoically told his grandson, "Your father is with your mother now."

"What? Why?"

"I wish I knew, Tom. I don't know what I can say to you. You lost your father and I lost my son. It isn't right."

Tommy was in shock; numb. "My father's...dead?"

"Your father died in his sleep last night."

"Then what was that loud sound I heard?"

His grandfather looked at Tommy and asked, "What sound was that?"

"I don't know. I woke up when I heard it. Dad didn't come into my room so I went back to sleep. Do you think it was a dream, grandpa?"

He paused and then said, "Perhaps it was, Tom."

A nurse came in an interrupted them. "How are you this morning young man?" she asked.

Tommy didn't understand why he was in a hospital. Only nurses worked in hospitals.

"I'm okay, I guess."

Without missing a beat she said, "Well that's good to hear. I'll see you later."

Tommy trailed her with his eyes as she departed. He turned back to his grandfather.

"Grandpa?" he asked. "Why am I in the hospital?"

His grandfather hesitated. "Well Tom, the police officers didn't have a safe place for you last night. They didn't get in touch with us until later so we could come pick you up. Do you understand?"

"I guess," Tommy answered.

Ed looked closer at Tommy. His grandson seemed numb.

"Grandpa?"

"Yes, Tom."

"Where am I going to live? When my mom died I stayed at home with my dad. But now that he's gone there's nobody left at home but me."

Tommy bent over and placed his face in his hands. He cried and cried and cried. When he had lost his mother the shock was too intense. His father had always been there to help and support him. The last thing Tommy wanted to admit was that his father was gone. There was nobody left to love him. His family was gone, taken away from him and he hated the world for it. All he wanted was his family back.

As Tommy continued to sob his grandfather soon joined in. It was a moment that would not be forgotten. Between the two of them it was one of the closest moments they would share with each other for the rest of their lives.

30
Sunday July 15, 1990 3:30 p.m.

Thomas returned to his house by 2:15 p.m. that afternoon. The dreams he'd endured that morning continued to plague him so he biked over to Arrowhead for breakfast. Thomas was still unsure of his present state of mind and wasn't convinced that a bike ride would be safe. However, he didn't want to just sit in his house all day either. He seriously needed to clear his head.

* * *

In Arrowhead there are numerous nooks and crannies which have shops and little stores tucked away in them. Amidst them was his favorite destination, the 'Waffle House'. The delicious aromas that wafted from this establishment were enticing and Thomas enjoyed coming here to think and eat; it was peaceful. He hadn't been back here since his last meeting with Nick.

Thomas took a booth by the window that overlooked the lake and attempted to relax. For whatever reason he felt safe here, by the water, and relished in its peace and tranquility it offered him. When Thomas would let his imagination go he could almost feel as if he was one of the birds, flying low over the water; low enough that he could see his reflection perfectly, but high enough that when his wings beat down they would skim the water. It was exhilarating.

"Sir?"

Thomas opened his eyes.

"Sir, would you care to order now?"

Thomas's gaze shifted from the water to the young man in front of him.

He's new. "Sure. I'll have the deluxe with a large orange juice please."

"As you wish, sir." The server departed.

Thomas looked back over the lake. It was early and a little chilly, but it was warming as the sunlight had recently reached the mountain top. Living on the mountain was one of the things that Thomas felt grateful for because he didn't subscribe to the fast paced rhythm of the city that lay miles away. The mountain provided security, freedom, fresh air and nature in all forms. Thomas didn't know how anyone could stand living, or for that matter, breathing the smog infested air that suffocated the valley every day. Years ago he had decided to hide away from the world so he wouldn't get hurt, and it wasn't until recently that Thomas felt safe in his mountain retreat.

Lot of good that did.

Someone approached and Thomas turned his head.

"Here's your large orange juice. Your order will be right out."

Thomas wondered why he was so on edge.

Why shouldn't I be? Look at everything that's been happening. Why aren't I insane?

Thomas took a gulp of orange juice as he mind continued to grind away. He was glad that he had taken the advice of his friends because his problems weren't going away. If would have tried to run from them they would have only followed, but more importantly, he wouldn't have met Laura. Meeting her had been a blessing in disguise and Thomas felt privileged to be in her presence. He had fallen for her from the beginning. His problems did seem to melt away when he was around her. *And so what if she's my psychiatrist, I don't care.* Thomas just wanted everything to work out so they could live happily ever after.

"Right," he said out loud in his booth. "Just like a fairy tale."

Thomas took another sip of his orange juice. He just wasn't sure that everything would be okay. Progress was being made on his issues but he wasn't convinced that he didn't have some sort of maniac locked up inside him.

The server reappeared and dropped off his steaming plate of waffles, topped with whip cream and strawberries. Typically Thomas ordered the same dish every time and forgot about his self-criticizing as he refocused his energies towards devouring the delicious food. Seven minutes later Thomas had renewed his membership in the 'clean your plate club'. Nothing remained; even the extra syrup was gone.

Thomas sat back in the booth and let out a small belch. *Ahhhh.* A few minutes later the check was placed on his table. Thomas got up, paid the bill and left a tip as he headed out the front door. He decided not to go straight home, at least not on a full stomach, and went window shopping instead. More accurately, he actually enjoyed watching all the people who visited Arrowhead. Some groups were the average family types; wife, husband, two kids that were either well behaved or screamed for this or that. Other individuals seemed to avoid people and just go about their own business. Then there were a few that Thomas couldn't stand; the people that were only out for themselves. They stepped on anyone to get what they wanted.

While Thomas silently judged these individuals a nagging feeling formed in the back of his mind.

I dislike these people because they remind me of Nigel.

Thomas turned away and continued to walk around. He drifted towards the lake and was rewarded to find a few people that were already water skiing and a small crowd had gathered at the shoreline railing to watch their performance. Thomas shared in the crowd's enthusiasm for a bit and then wandered away. The rising temperature meant it was going to be a hot day and Thomas knew he still needed to get back home. He made his way back to where he had chained up his bicycle.

Thomas made it back home at 2:15 p.m.. He hadn't realized he had spent so much time in Arrowhead.

Guess that's what happens when you lose yourself in thought. He knew had just over an hour to tidy up.

* * *

His house didn't need much, especially since his deep scrubbing a few days prior. Afterwards he jumped in the shower, dressed and waited on the couch. He was just about to turn on the television when a knock came at his front door. His mind immediately wandered back to his morning's dreams. Thomas tried to clear his head as the knock came again. He got up, tip-toed to the door and peered out the peephole. Thomas didn't see two men in suits this time. He did, however, see Laura who stood there with the sun shining behind her. Thomas opened the door and greeted her.

"Please, come in," he said as he stepped back.

Laura was dressed in a white sun dress accompanied by an equally white sun hat. To Thomas she seemed to glow. His eyes must have given him away since she took the compliment and said thank you with a smile. Laura eyes danced around the room as she took everything in. She liked what she saw but decided not to let on.

Thomas had been shocked. Laura's appearance was completely different than what he was used to. He stood in the front hall, door wide open, as she sauntered inside and into his living room. He finally shut the door and joined her.

"Do you like it? Thomas inquired.

"Like what?" she responded coyly.

"My house."

Laura let Thomas watch her as she looked around the room some more. "It's got potential but it's lacking something though."

"And what might that be?" Thomas asked as he drew closer.

"That's why I'm here. I'm the woman and I have the magic touch." Laura stood only inches away from Thomas and her heart seemed to beat in her throat. "If you don't hurry up and touch me I don't know what I might do to this place."

Thomas' breath caught in his throat. His hands slid down to her waist and he pulled her close. Their bodies seemed to melt together, forming a single entity. He looked down at her and she started to meet his eyes when the brim of her hat battled his forehead.

"Sorry," she breathed and tossed her hat away.

Laura barely had enough time to draw in a new breath before his mouth was upon hers. She let herself relax and opened herself up to him. The kiss was hot and full of passion. Her own feverishness was only too apparent and she couldn't seem to get enough of him. Laura broke the kiss, took Thomas' hand and led him upstairs. They smiled at each other, giddy.

As they climbed the stairs Thomas was glad she led the way. He very much enjoyed watching her rear sway beneath the thin material of her dress. They made it to the bed when she slowly turned to face him again.

"Get a good look?" she asked with a grin on her face.

Thomas started to search for an answer but was interrupted as she put a finger to his lips.

"Just leave everything up to me, Thomas. Remember, I'm still the doctor and you're my patient," she said obviously enjoying herself.

He longed for her touch and had dreamed of this moment with her. Thomas had never felt so drawn to another human being in his entire life. Words darted to and fro inside his already confused brain as he attempted to comprehend what was about to happen.

Sounds and expressions took the place of unneeded words as they embraced once more. Their eyes met and their instincts took over. Laura's eyes sparkled, seemingly generated from within her own soul; her look mesmerized Thomas and he couldn't look away. Her want brought such hope and confidence back in to his damaged heart. He knew the look and hadn't seen it for a very long time. All Thomas saw was love.

Laura broke the spell as she kissed him softly upon the lips. At first Thomas didn't respond, but as she kissed him again his need began to pour forth in a wave that swept them both up. Thomas pulled Laura as close as he could and she melted against him. Thomas's right hand slid down and gently caressed her right breast. The fabric of her dress was thin and as he encircled her nipple; it hardened and pressed against the palm of his hand. Laura breathed hard in his ear.

Laura guided him towards the outstretched bed in an attempt to lie down so that she wouldn't collapse first. She pushed Thomas down on the bed. He landed on his back and looked up at her. He reached for her but her look rooted him in place. Laura lifted her arms up and crossed them behind her. Her nipples stuck out even more wanting to break through the fabric barrier that held them. All this time Laura kept a close watch on Thomas and got the reaction she had sought. His eyes grew huge and she felt him undress her. That's exactly what she wanted.

Thomas didn't know what to do. He wanted her over here, not over there.

Why is she teasing me?

Suddenly he understood. He couldn't believe what he was seeing.

Those breasts. God, I've got to have them.

They were straining against her dress. He realized he stared at them. He caught her grin. Laura had lured him into another one of her traps. However, in this case, Thomas loved what he saw and what she was doing.

As she let the dress slip from her shoulders, and float to the floor, she was rewarded with an unmistakable bulge in Thomas' pants and quickly closed the distance between them. She wanted him as badly as he apparently wanted her.

As she sauntered towards him Thomas knew it was only seconds before she would be in his arms again. Her body was like he had fantasized; perfection. Her nipples were darkened and drew the majority of his attention. His gaze traveled southward. She wore white panties that revealed a deeper part of her that he wanted to desperately explore. He looked up at her with a stupid grin on his face. She lowered herself onto the bed and breathed a few words.

"Take off your clothes," she purred.

Thomas was beyond the point of rational thought. Her voice hit him like a ton of bricks and there was no need for her to repeat her request.

Laura's eyes widened as the last of Thomas' clothes were removed; she couldn't resist anymore. She removed the last of her remaining barriers and stood up to meet her new lover. They let their eyes play over each other's bodies. Their eyes met and they both drew closer together, pursuing what they both desired.

Laura's hand grabbed hold of him. Thomas' eyes widened. She let a single fingernail meander around him and Thomas let out an uncontrollable moan. It was his turn to lead her to bed before he crumpled to the floor from weak knees.

* * *

"So much for going out and having a bite to eat first," Thomas joked.

They both still lay in bed, totally spent. The bedding was strewn everywhere, save for a single sheet they had draped over themselves. Laura had laid her head on his chest and he softly stroked her hair. The time had flown by while they had explored and devoured each other's bodies.

"Sorry about that, Thomas," Laura softly countered. "I couldn't help myself."

"Not that I minded," he replied with a smile.

"Oh yeah. I needed that just as much as you did."

Laura moved to get up.

"Where are you going?"

She turned and gave him a kiss. "As much as I want to stay in bed for the rest of the evening with you, I've worked up a large appetite. Can you blame me?" Laura winked at Thomas, got out of bed and headed towards the bathroom. "Anything I shouldn't be touching in there?"

"Ha ha. Very funny."

He heard the shower water turn on. "Fresh towels are in the side closet."

"Thanks. You know, I could use some company in here."

A huge smile appeared on his face. "Are you trying to kill me or something?"

212

"You're on to me," Laura retorted and stepped in the shower.

Thomas was drained and his muscles ached. Course, he didn't want to remember how long it had been since he'd been with a woman. He recalled the time in Amsterdam while he had traveled abroad; that had been interesting. Over the past decade he could count the amount of partners he'd had on one hand, with a few fingers left over, but those moments had been just been about sex. He hadn't had to let his guard down and be vulnerable because he didn't fear he was going to lose any of them. It had just been out of his human need for a connection. Laura was different. Very different.

"Are you going to join me in here or not?" she cooed.

Thomas felt his loins stir and chuckled. He walked into the bathroom to join her.

"Oh my," she said as the shower door opened. "We can't let that go to waste, now can we?"

* * *

Laura stepped out of the shower and left the hot water wash over Thomas' sore back muscles. She toweled off and walked into the bedroom. She had surprised herself by being so forward with Thomas.

Forward, I was slutty as hell.

Laura giggled. She and Thomas had just spent the past few hours in an exhaustive romp. They had acted like teenagers as they explored each other's bodies. The first time they had rushed, not being able to hold back. The second time they had slowly worked each other up to such a frenzy that by the time they released they couldn't hold back. It had been absolutely amazing. The third time in the shower had been icing on the cake.

213

Laura knew Thomas had his dark side but she trusted him nonetheless. She was helping him through it all and he had put his entire life and hope in her hands. She knew that was a near impossibility for Thomas, but he had done it anyway.

The phone rang on his computer desk. She looked at it. It rang again.

"Thomas?"

"What's up, Laura?" Thomas replied from the shower.

Ring ring.

"Your phone is ringing."

"Would you mind answering it?"

Rin-

Laura picked up the phone. "Hello?"

"Eye, Tommy."

"Hello?"

The line went dead. Laura looked at the receiver, shrugged and replaced it on the cradle.

The shower turned off as Laura reentered the bathroom.

"Who was it?" Thomas asked.

"I thought someone said 'Hi Tommy', but then the line went dead."

"Well, it sounds like it was Bill or Sam. They must not have been expecting a female voice when they called. They'll call back if they're not busy." Thomas smiled.

"Well that's good to hear. It appears I don't have any competition."

"Har har Laura. You're on a roll today."

Laura smiled and got out of the way just as Thomas tried to playfully swat her butt.

* * *

Having dressed, finally, they headed downstairs. It was well in to the seven o'clock hour.

"Can I get you something to drink before we head out?"

"Absolutely. Water for the time being please."

Thomas headed in to the kitchen as Laura sat down on the couch. She picked up the remote.

"Do you mind if I turn on the television?"

"Me casa es su casa."

"Gracias."

The television came to life as she pressed the power button and she tuned in to CBS. '60 Minutes' was on. Thomas walked in with a glass of water and handed it over.

"Thank you."

He sat down next to her while she drank half of it straight away. "You said you were thirsty but I had no idea."

Laura cocked an eye at him and playfully teased, "Well, it's your fault."

"I bet it is." They both chuckled as new lovers tended to.

The television changed over to a live news bulletin. "Once again the peace was shattered last night in the Redlands community. A woman, Ms. Silvia Platt, was brutally murdered in front of her four year old son. The officer who responded told us that he will never forget what happened. He heard the sound of breaking glass coming from his neighbor's backyard around 11:30 p.m.. He immediately investigated, located the back door window broken in and called for backup. Upon entering the house the officer heard screaming coming from the top of the stairs. He rushed to the bottom and looked up. A man had Ms. Platt by the hair so the office identified himself as police. Before the officer could get to her the assailant sliced open her throat, with an axe, and had tossed her down the stairs. In the ensuing escape the officer was knocked unconscious. Police arrived within two minutes but no suspects have been arrested. Ms. Platt's four year old son, Danny, was taken to a local hospital for observation. Currently there is no update on the boy's status."

Laura muted the television and looked over at Thomas. He was staring at her.

31
Wednesday January 3, 1968 1:30 p.m.

Tommy had been here before. The grass; the trees; the tombstones. Nothing much had changed during the past five years as he took in the vast playground of the dead. Everything was impeccably manicured just like before. In fact the tent and the chairs lined up underneath it, were setup in the exact same location.

* * *

The previous week had been an absolute blur and Tommy was still numb to all the changes. His grandfather had taken him from the hospital to their house. His grandparents had moved to Orinda after Betsy had been killed because they wanted to be closer to both their son and grandson. Having Michael's parents close by had been a godsend to both Tommy and Michael. A few nights a week Tommy and his father would have dinner with his grandparents, switching off hosting duties as Michael's work hours allowed. Michael thought it was important to have some sort of mother figure in his son's life.

Ed and Claire had moved to Orinda Woods and had a two-story, three bedroom house decorated with numerous mementos from around the world. They both enjoyed traveling and, as always, obtained knick-knacks from wherever they went. Tommy enjoyed visiting them because there was so much to take in; his imagination was boundless with the potential adventures from all the trinkets.

When Ed brought Tommy home, the day after Christmas, Claire had already prepped the guest bedroom for him.

"This is my room?" Tommy asked.

"You bet it is, sweetie," Claire replied.

Tommy slowly walked around his new 16x16 room and took it all in. He'd been in here many times over the years. A double sized bed was in the far corner parallel to the window. Previously it had been in the center of the room but Claire had decided to push it against the wall to give her grandson more open space. A door opened in to an L shaped walk-in closet. Next to it was the door to the bathroom with a shower tub.

"Do you like it?"

Tommy stopped and turned his head towards his grandmother and tears streamed down his face. Claire rushed over and pulled him close to her, rocking him as they both huddled on the carpet. This same scene repeated itself many times over in the days that followed.

Ed made many trips to his son's house to gather Tommy's belongings. Clothes, toys, books, you name it. Everything that had been in Tommy's room he retrieved. Tommy hadn't wanted to go back there yet. Ed knew that at some point he'd start to ask, but until that time he had wanted to make Tommy's transition to his new home as comfortable as possible.

Tommy had lost his mother, and now his father. Ed and Claire had just lost their son and they were also having a hard time dealing with that. During the day they put on a brave front for Tommy as he got readjusted, but at night soft sobs emanated from their upstairs master bedroom.

It had been just over a week since the tragic death of this father and Tommy was alone now. He knew his grandparents meant well and loved him very much, but somehow that didn't matter all that much at the moment. He felt numb, both inside and out. Minutes turned in to hours which turned into days. It was all the same. For a ten year old Tommy had experienced more than his fair share of suffering already and it had taken its toll.

On top of that he'd heard his grandparents crying. He'd also overheard them in the kitchen, or their bedroom, talking in hushed whispers. Tommy had to assume it was about him.

* * *

The same hearse drove up, as far as Tommy could tell. Similar looking men, wearing suits, took his father's coffin and positioned it on the raised pedestal. The same pile of dirt was covered by the same green cloth. Everything was the same and Tommy felt nothing.

A strong hand grasped his shoulder. Tommy looked up at his grandfather and then back at the coffin. No words were spoken. Things would never be the same again.

I'll never be the same.

The news report, from the night before, had taken the wind out of their sails. Laura knew Thomas wasn't responsible for that particular murder but that didn't quiet her inner voice.

What if he is the killer? He had the axe. He had the blood on his hands.

She fought off her doubts and concentrated on Thomas. She believed he was a kind and gentle person, especially how he looked at her; the way he had touched her. She was drawn to him so fiercely it both scared and exhilarated her.

After Laura had muted the television Thomas turned to look at Laura.

She thinks I'm the killer. I don't think I am, but maybe it's true.

He told her about the strange dreams he'd had about the men who'd come into his house; who stuck him with a needle. He also mentioned how he saw a horrific face in the mirror.

Time slipped away as they talked and, at some point, they ended up eating and eventually headed up to bed. They fell asleep cuddled together.

The alarm woke them up at 7:30 a.m.. Thomas leaned over and turned it off.

"What time is it?" Laura asked.

"Seven thirty."

They lay there, in each other's arms for a while and gazed up at the ceiling. Laura broke the silence first.

"Thomas, I need you to know something."

They turned to face each other.

"What is it?"

Laura paused. "What we did last night was amazing."
Thomas smiled and started to speak but Laura cut him off. "But it was also very unprofessional. I'm torn between my personal and professional feelings towards you. I'm supposed to be helping you, yet I slept with you instead."

Thomas smiled at Laura, who clearly was at odds with herself, and made a comment.

"I really do appreciate the house call, doc."

She looked him straight in the eyes for a second, and then started to laugh really hard.

"Okay. I deserved that. That was a good one."

"Listen, Laura, what we did happened because we wanted it to happen. I don't know the rules but I do know that you have been selflessly helping me. Look at all the time you've invested in me. Its working and you're the reason. So whatever you think you need to do about us, don't. I want us to keep working on the issues. More importantly, I need and trust you, Laura. If you want to cut out the physical aspect, because it interferes, then I understand and we can take it slow. But if you think you can handle being professional and intimate with me at the same time, I'd like that very much."

She took it all in and chewed it over.

"I'd like that too."

They kissed deeply but suddenly stopped.

"Wow," they both exclaimed at the same time.

"Yeah, no more early morning French kissing without brushing our teeth," Thomas stated.

They both giggled as Laura glanced over at the clock.

"Shit. I've got to get home so I can get ready for work." She rolled out of bed and put on her sundress.

"Too bad. I love the view from here."

"You're bad mister," Laura said and playfully waggled her butt for him. "Sorry to run off like this. Why don't you come in tomorrow afternoon for another session? Say around 3:30 p.m.?"

"I'll have to look at my calendar." Thomas pantomimed looking at his scheduler. "Yup, looks like I'm free." He smiled.

"Any more smiling out of you and you'll be hopeless." Laura walked over to Thomas' side of the bed, leaned down and gave him a quick peck on the lips. "I'm out of here. See you tomorrow."

At the doorway she stopped, looked back and saw him stare after her. With her left hand she slowly caressed her body. She started at her thighs and moved upwards. She stopped as she reached her left breast, gave it a slight squeeze and smiled at him.

Thomas could only lay there and watch as she toyed with him. *Sooooo unfair.* "Tease!"

He picked up a pillow and threw it at her. She giggled, headed downstairs and Thomas heard the front door open and close.

* * *

Thomas could still smell her scent lingering in the bed sheets. He hadn't wanted her to leave, but such is life and he got up shortly thereafter.

After a leisurely shower, and a quick cereal breakfast, Thomas drove his car down the mountain towards San Bernardino. He felt like going for a ride, plus he needed to resupply.

Maybe there'll be time later.

The drive down 330 was uneventful. He eventually arrived at the grocery store, parked and headed inside. He retrieved a cart and started over in the vegetable section on the far right. While he meandered he couldn't help but relive the previous day's

223

encounter. She was so beautiful and enticing. Her curves had tantalized him while her dress clung tightly to her body; so tempting and teasing. When they kissed the pure, unbridled passion they both had bottled up, surged through them. They clawed at each other, digging in and wanting more. It was as if-

CRASH!

Thomas was so lost in thought he had run into another shopping cart.

"I'm sorry," Thomas said to the man in front of him.

The man turned around, looked at Thomas and said, "Well, if it isn't Tom Clark. Fancy running in to you here but I guess you ran into me." The man chuckled.

It took Thomas a second to recognize who the man was. "George? George Miles?"

George put his hands up mockingly as if under arrest and jokingly replied, "Guilty as charged."

"I didn't know you shopped here, George." Thomas saw George's cart was empty. "I guess you just got here."

"Oh every once in a while when the shelves get too low I venture down the mountain. What about you?" he asked looking in to Thomas' cart. "Looks like you're stocking up."

From behind Thomas a woman's voice asked, "Excuse me?"

Thomas turned around and noticed that the woman had her arms full. She continued and asked, "Are you using that cart? I came in only needing two things and, you know how it gets, one thing led to another."

"I'm sorry miss. My friend is using that cart."

"Who?"

Thomas turned around and George was nowhere to be seen. His empty cart was still where Thomas had run in to it. Thomas looked around, a bit confused, and then back at the lady.

"Sure," he said hesitantly, "Go ahead."

"Thank you so much. Have a nice day," the woman said as she deposited her arm load of items into the cart and headed off.

Thomas headed down the aisle and took a right peering down the row of registers. He didn't see George.

Strange.

Thomas shrugged and continued to shop.

* * *

With his shopping cart now full Thomas made his way to a register to check out. He had purchased a couple of steaks that he hoped Laura would enjoy the next time she was over.

I hope that's sooner than later.

Along with the standard milk, cereal, vegetables and various snack items he loved, Thomas had also purchased a Hallmark card for Laura. He thought it was a little sappy but he wanted to surprise her.

Outside the store Thomas wheeled his bagged purchases over to his car, unlocked his trunk and popped it open. He grabbed the first bag of groceries from the cart, went to place them in the trunk and realized that his trunk was full already. He had forgotten about the two black hefty bags he had placed there nearly two weeks prior.

Aww fuck.

33
January, 1990

Travis and Tammy Jones had arrived in Edinburgh, Scotland the previous day off a magnificent airline experience. It had been the first time they had flown first class and the eleven hour flight from LAX had made the start of their trip even more pleasant. When they landed they were whisked away to a luxurious five star hotel in the heart of Edinburgh. After they were dropped their driver handed off rental keys to their own vehicle and told them it was at their disposal for their entire visit. The two checked in and were escorted to a penthouse suite. Once the bellhop had been tipped the excited couple took in the breathtaking and panoramic views. Tammy hollered and screeched as she rushed around and checked out the suite. At twenty-nine she had never been abroad. They had married two years prior and had never been able to take a proper honeymoon due to the fact that Travis had immediately taken the research position at RHP. He worked long hours and wasn't home as much as the company had promised he would be. That absence had started to affect their marriage.

Travis was blown away by the penthouse suite. He kept expecting to wake up from the royal service they had been receiving but his long hours at work had finally paid off. He walked up to one of the full length windows, stared out at the beautiful scenery and saw Edinburgh castle off in the near distance. He felt like he was on top of the world.

"Trav," his wife cooed, "come into the bathroom."

Tammy had finished checking out through every nook and cranny that their suite had to offer.

Travis pulled his gaze away and followed her voice into the master bath. The steam, from the shower stood in, had started to build up.

"There you are," she said playfully. "Get your dirty ass in here mister!"

Travis didn't need any additional convincing. He stripped down in record time as he watched the hot water pool off his wife's breasts and down her legs. She opened the door and beckoned, with one finger, for him to join her.

* * *

Auckland, New Zealand.

I'm finally here.

Robert Hind had waited to explore New Zealand for the past decade and couldn't believe that he'd finally arrived. At forty-one he had begun to notice some grey in his hair; that had been a wakeup call. He didn't feel terribly old but he knew that realistically half his life was now in the rear view mirror. He had pledged his past three years to RHP, and aside from the nice salary, the only thing he'd gotten in return was his grey hair.

Robert stretched his legs as the plane pulled in to the international terminal; the first class cabin on the second floor of the 747 had been a delight. During Robert's twelve hour flight from LAX he'd been in the best of hands and he hoped that his return flight was just as enjoyable.

After he debarked he retrieved his luggage and headed through customs. He was in and out in no time. On his way out he noticed a gentleman, dressed in a suit, who held up a sign with his name on it. Robert stopped and soon discovered that a limo waited to take him to his hotel. He surrendered his bags and started to enjoy his well-deserved vacation.

Throughout the ride his driver briefed Robert on the area's history. He was informed that Auckland was known as 'the maiden with a hundred suitors' due to the fact that many, many tribes wanted the area as their own. Aside from that the driver chatted about a number of things but Robert had hardly listened. Instead he watched, looked and strained his neck as he took in the surrounding sites.

The driver had phoned ahead so as they arrived at the five-star establishment all that was required was a quick signature from Robert. A private elevator took him up to the penthouse, and when he opened the door he discovered his luggage and belongings had already been brought up.

I could get used to this.

Robert yawned. Even though the flight had been comfortable he'd been unable to sleep. In an effort to acclimate he called room service and then took a soothing shower. Afterwards, his meal had been delivered and set up on the outside patio which overlooked the ocean.

Amazing.

He finished off his filet mignon, which had been perfectly prepared, and prepared for bed. Robert was ready to explore Auckland but he knew he had to recharge first. As soon as he slipped into bed his head hit the pillow, and he was out.

* * *

January. What a perfect time to visit Honolulu.

Fredrick Rickman, thirty-six, sat out on his penthouse balcony and drank deeply from the chilled Corona he held in his hand. He smiled.

Damn, that's good.

He soaked in the sun's rays as they bore down on him. Fredrick had arrived that morning on a flight out of LAX. The five hour flight had seemed shorter, but that was due to the numerous vodka tonics he'd ordered.

Fredrick, although he preferred Freddy, took his vacation in stride. He knew he deserved it and was damn well going to make the most out of it, especially since RHP hadn't spared any expense. From the moment he had been picked up from his house, and all the way to Hawaii, he'd been treated like royalty. He loved every second of it and planned to take it further, having been very specific personally when talked with the Concierge. The man on the phone assured him he would not be disappointed.

Freddy finished up his beer on the patio and headed inside. In the two hours since he'd arrived all he'd done was unpack.

And drink three beers.

He didn't care though, he was on vacation. The time was 1:25 p.m. and he was hungry. Freddy left the penthouse suite behind and ventured outside to find someplace to eat.

* * *

Travis and Tammy took the first day to settle in. Minor jet lag, combined with new adventures just steps outside their hotel, made them both giddy and exhausted. After the shower they'd fallen into bed and slept until the morning. When they eventually opened their eyes it was just after 11am local time. They stretched and looked over at each other, smiles on their faces.

230

"Dare I ask what got in to you?" Travis asked.

"I have no idea what you're talking about my dear. Can't a wife say thank you?"

"If that's how you want to do it from now then sign me up," he replied with a chuckle. "Besides Tam, you deserve this trip just as much as I do."

"You don't have to say it sweetie."

Travis looked right at his wife. "Thank you for being there for me. I know my job has kept us apart. The project I'm on should be finished in six months. After that I'm all yours and we can start our life together."

"I've missed you," Tammy said.

"I've missed you, too."

"Okay," Tammy said as she dabbed at her wet eyes, "enough of that. We have a city to explore!"

It's going to be a good day.

They got ready and headed downstairs, since they knew Edinburgh Castle was in walking distance. They wanted to explore the city so they took off on foot rather than drive their rental. Tourism wouldn't take off again until spring so the streets weren't packed. It was a little chilly outside but they didn't mind. It was all an adventure.

Along the way they popped their heads into various shops and started to unwind. They were together, on vacation, and not in a rush. A pub was on the corner and they decided to get some food. After treating themselves to some Tempura appetizers they both decided on a nice 8oz fillet. The bartender was curious about LA and had asked them a variety of questions about it. Travis and Tammy took it all in stride, as they ate everything. It was so delicious. Just as they thought they couldn't eat another bite the proprietor topped off their experience with a slice of Chocolate

Velvet Cream pie. It tasted heavenly. They finally said their goodbyes and headed out the front door.

The weather had changed, as it does in Scotland, and they felt a slight drizzle. They thought about waiting it out, but they saw they were definitely closer to the castle. As the pressed on they arrived at a crosswalk and waited for the light to change.

"Love you sweetie," said Travis.

"Love you, too," Tammy replied and gave her husband a big hug. They both smiled.

The light changed and Tammy and Travis commenced across the street. The young couple never saw the bus that hit them.

* * *

Robert woke up in a strange room, but then quickly remembered he was in New Zealand. It was 9:53am local time. Since his ride in the limo the day before, and everything that whizzed by so quickly, he came up with an idea. He picked up the phone and had reservations made for him. Afterwards he took a shower, dressed and headed downstairs where he enjoyed a leisurely breakfast in one of the hotel's restaurants. A town car picked him up at 11:15 a.m..

Robert was headed back to the airport because he had booked a helicopter tour of the area. He'd brought along a camera and couldn't wait until he was high above the ground to enjoy New Zealand's landscape and all its beauty. When he arrived he signed a few release forms and watched a safety video. Finally he was taken outside and climbed into the front left seat. The pilot took over the right seat and motioned for Robert to put a set of headphones on.

"First time in a helicopter?" asked the pilot.

"Yes. I've always wanted to try one out."

"I know what you mean," the pilot replied. "The views are definitely worth it. My name's Jim."

"Robert. Nice to meet you, Jim."

Jim flipped a variety toggles and switches and the helicopter came to life. The rotors spun up and eventually they were at lift speed.

"Here we go, Robert."

The pilot throttled, pulled up on the collective a hair and spun them around to face the opposite direction. The tower cleared them and instead of a vertical liftoff, like Robert thought would happen, Jim took the helicopter a few feet off the deck and punched the throttle. The runway flew by them just a few feet below Robert.

Exhilarating!

"That was awesome."

"I thought you might enjoy that," Jim announced.

By this time Jim had taken them up a few thousand feet and flown them out over the water. The views were spectacular and Robert rapidly clicked off shots.

"Make sure you have some film left, you'll need it where we're going."

"Where's that?" Robert asked.

"It's one of our hidden treasures. Trust me, you won't be disappointed."

They were over the water, headed north, when loud noises filled the cockpit. Robert and Jim both jumped.

BANG. POP.

"What the fuck!?" cried Robert.

"Oh crap oh crap oh crap!" Jim yelled as his controls turned sluggish.

The helicopter suddenly yawed to the left and Robert was thrown against the left window. The craft started to violently shake.

"Mayday mayday. This is-"

Before Jim could transmit any further the helicopter experienced a complete power loss and shut down. The pilot tried in vain to control their rapid descent, to no avail. Robert screamed as loud as he could but without power there wasn't anything Jim could do. He had been in some close calls over the years but never something this catastrophic. As the ocean rushed up at them Jim thought of his wife and two small boys.

They hit the water with brutal speed and the force of the impact shattered most of their bones. They drowned after the craft sunk beneath the water's horizon.

* * *

After lunch Freddy had spent the day walking around Waikiki. The weather was perfect and the beaches were lined with scantily clad women, whom he couldn't take his eyes off. This was quite the change from the lab he'd been locked up in for weeks on end, without the ability to touch a woman, or himself for that matter. Everyone had discovered that cameras were everywhere; even in their rooms. Everyone that worked on the project at RHP had signed on to that type of strict surveillance, including Freddy, and now that he was on vacation he had some catching up to do.

Freddy was openly selfish. He wanted what he wanted when he wanted it, period. At his job he had to curtail his desires or risk losing out on the massive payday that would come in a few months. Still, there were times at work where his urges had almost taken over and gotten him in trouble.

Mind over matter.

Freddy had spent the day in the sun and wasn't used to it. It had drained him. He was hot, a little sunburned and he needed to cool off. He was right around the corner from his hotel so he headed back. Upon entering his suite he stripped out of his clothes and took a shower. The cold water splashed over his body and sent chills up and down his spine.

Oh, that's good.

After thirty seconds he adjusted the water and relaxed as it warmed up.

He eventually left the shower and made a call to room service to order dinner along with a bottle of scotch and some ice. While Freddy waited he dressed in Dockers and a short sleeve buttoned down shirt. He was barefoot and walked outside to his balcony again. Evening had fallen and the sun had set, although the orange hue on the horizon was beautiful. He popped open another Corona and looked out over his domain. Freddy was on top of the world and he felt like a king.

Twenty minutes later there was a knock on his door. He opened it and ushered in his dinner; steak with all the trimmings. Once the server had departed Freddy poured himself a double and sat down. The clock read 6:59 p.m..

He'd taken his time with his meal and savored each bite. He'd also refilled his glass a few times and had started to feel no pain.

Time to dial that back a little.

He headed back out to the balcony and let the wind brush over him as his empty dishes had been cleared away.

Time is close. She'll be here soon.

He nursed a Corona while the time slipped by. At 10 p.m. the doorbell to his suite chimed and Freddy smiled.

Right on time.

He put down his beer and sauntered over to the door. He opened it slowly and was met with a stunning Asian beauty, no older than twenty-three. She was dressed elegantly and carried herself with presence.

It's good to be the king.

A few hours later she departed and Freddy eagerly refilled his Scotch, now only in his boxers. He couldn't remember where the rest of his clothes had ended up as he ventured back out to the balcony. Waikiki was still bustling with energy and the waves rhythmically crashed on the beach below him. He gulped down his drink and scanned the horizon.

I could seriously get used to this.

The night was gorgeous, clear and only slightly chilly. A few goose bumps had formed on his arms but that didn't bother him.

Two more weeks of this and I'll never want to go back.

He grabbed his bottle of scotch, topped himself off and gulped down half of it. The weather seemed to have gotten colder. More goose bumps formed on his arms, but now they started to itch and Freddy couldn't think straight. He leaned against the balconies railing for support.

What's going on?

He felt thirsty. He saw the glass in his hand and downed what remained in it. Freddy teetered on his feet and the glass slipped from his hand. The waves called to him. Freddy reached for them and felt weightless as his knees gave way.

What nobody witnessed was that Freddy had convulsed to death, on his balcony, from an apparent allergic reaction.

34
Monday January 8, 1968 8:15 a.m.

"Have a good day, sweetie."

Tommy half-heartedly waved goodbye to his grandmother as she pulled away from the school curb. Christmas vacation was officially over. Tommy slowly turned and made his way towards his classroom. His entire life had been turned upside down once again, and he knew his grandparents were there for him, but it just wasn't the same. He'd never feel the warmth of his mother's embrace or eat his father's famous weekend breakfast ever again. It had been heart wrenching for Tommy to deal with that realization and the wound was still extremely fresh.

The days that followed his father's funeral Tommy hadn't left his room, other than to have a bite to eat now and then. He'd spent his time drawing pictures, and some of them unsettled his grandparents. They had been drawn with crayon in heavy black lines. A black sun shined down on a black car. Black grass sprang up next to a black tree. Black stick figures stood around the black car. More black stick figures were under the ground with X's for eyes. The only item in the drawings that wasn't black was a short stick figure. That was always drawn in red. Ed and Claire had been concerned and had discussed that maybe a child psychologist should take a look at him, but they quickly dismissed that idea. Potentially putting Tommy through anything else, at the present time they determined, wouldn't be helpful. Instead they concluded that his environment needed to remain stable. They knew their grandson hadn't seen his friends since the start of the holiday break and hoped it would do him some good to finally reunite with them.

Tommy, with his head down, didn't walk with any kind of purpose when they spotted him.

"Hey Tommy!" they both yelled together. Billy and Sammy started to run towards their friend.

Tommy paused and looked up as his two best friends raced up to him.

"Hey Tommy. Long time no see!"

They were both clearly excited to see Tommy, but he didn't say a word. Instead he just looked right at them.

"Tommy?"

Tears started to stream down his face as he blurted, "My dad died."

He fell to his knees. His tears were endless.

* * *

Ms. Murray had been informed of Tommy's situation and kept a close watch on him throughout the day. She also noticed that Sammy and Billy had moved their desks closer to Tommy as if protecting him. She was happy to see that.

He needs his friends right now.

* * *

Recess. Freedom. A few other classes were already out on the playground as they headed over to the swings.

"What'd you want to do, Tommy?" Sammy asked.

"I'm sorry guys," Tommy said. "I'm not in the best of moods."

Sammy and Billy looked at each other and then back at Tommy.

"It's okay," Billy said. "We stick together no matter what."

A minute passed as they swung back and forth.

"It's horrible. I have this emptiness inside of me."

"Listen Tommy," Sammy interjected. "This might not be the best time to tell you this but I think it'll cheer you up."

Tommy cocked his head towards Sammy and saw his friend smile.

"What? What is it?" asked Tommy.

They all stopped their swings.

Sammy continued, "Well, I overheard my dad on the phone last week. I think he was talking to his lawyer or something. Anyway, my dad got really upset. Apparently Nigel's..."

Tommy flinched when he heard the name.

"...family suddenly moved out of town and they don't know where. One day they were there and the next morning they were gone....vanished. Everything's gone. They don't know where they are."

"So?"

Billy jumped in. "So Tommy, that means no more Nigel here at school!"

Tommy's brain had to decipher the information Billy has just imparted.

No more Nigel at school. No more Nigel. No more Nigel!

Tommy smiled for the first time since his father's death and they gave each other high fives. They were all ecstatic. For Tommy Clark it was turning in to a good day. He had a long way to go but this was as good of a start as ever.

35
Tuesday July 17, 1990 3:30 p.m.

Thomas knocked lightly.

"Come on in."

Thomas walked into Laura's office. She looked radiant.

"I hope I'm not early Laura," he said and went to kiss her. Laura stopped him.

"As much as I want to, Thomas, and believe me I want to, we have to draw the line in the sand when you're here."

Thomas took a step back. "You're absolutely right. It's just that I couldn't seem to help myself. I mean, look at you," he said as he motioned his hand up and down her body.

"Stop it, Thomas, you're embarrassing me," she said while mildly blushing.

He grinned, sat down and took his shoes off. "So, what do you have in store for me today?"

"Well, I've been reviewing your other regression sessions. I'm interested in pursuing a specific avenue of memories now."

"Which ones?"

"Well, I can't say they're enjoyable, but I'm specifically interested in your memories of you being bullied by Nigel."

"Bullied or beaten Laura?" Thomas looked right at her and she shuffled in her chair.

"You're right, Thomas, I'm sorry. I didn't mean to sugarcoat it. I want to take you back to various times when Nigel beat you. Today would be your fourth time being regressed and I'm starting to see a pattern."

"There's a pattern?"

"Potentially, Thomas. It's too soon to tell."

Thomas mulled it over. "What would it mean?"

"Exactly, Thomas, exactly."

* * *

"THE CHICKEN SAYS CLUCK!"

The first thing Thomas noticed was he was exhausted. The second thing was he felt something crawling on his forehead so he wiped at it. His hand came back wet with perspiration. Then he noticed his breath was ragged.

"Are you okay, Thomas?"

Laura stood over him, clearly concerned.

"I...I don't know." *What the hell?*

Laura handed him a bottle of water and he immediately emptied it.

"Thanks," he said.

"Take your time."

Thomas worked to control the need to gasp for air. He would take a deep breath, pause, and then exhale. He wiped his forehead again.

Laura sat down. "What do you remember?"

Thomas thought about it. "Not a damn thing actually. When the other sessions ended I never felt like this."

"And what is that feeling, Thomas?"

"I don't know exactly. I'm tired, sweating and apparently out of breath." He looked over at Laura and said, "And since we're both still fully clothed it's not what I was hoping for." He attempted a smile.

"Cute, Thomas," she said and returned his smile. "But seriously, is there anything else that you can put your finger on?"

"Well, this might sound strange, but I feel like I've been wrestling."

"Struggling perhaps," Laura offered.

"That's it! Perfect. Wait. What?"

She leaned forward. "Remember when I said I wanted to explore the beatings you received?" Thomas nodded. "Well I found one all right."

"I'm not following you."

"Listen, Thomas, I have something to tell you." Laura sat back. "During the first regression session I implanted a phrase in your head."

Thomas suddenly felt uncomfortable. "What do you mean you planted something?"

"Implanted. Basically I had your subconscious learn a phrase that would give me a quick way of bringing you out of a regressed state. It was for your protection."

"So let me get this straight. You put something in my head without telling me? More importantly, you didn't ask. What the fuck Laura."

Thomas started to get up but she stopped him.

"Thomas, the reason you feel like shit is because I had to use it."

He froze.

"That's right. You were fighting for your life today. I was really frightened and you had all but blocked me out. My ability to guide you, your safety line so to speak, was nearly obliterated. You didn't acknowledge me anymore, Thomas. You were thrashing and screaming. I didn't have a choice!"

"Okay okay. You just took me by surprise," he proclaimed and sat back down.

"Thomas. I was going to talk to you about it but there wasn't any reason to upset you." Laura took a breath. "I'm not happy I had to use it but I'm glad the option was available. Sorry."

243

Thomas had taken it all in. He understood his initial reaction. It violated the trust he had placed in her hands, but as he calmed down he started to realize how bad the regression must have been."

"I'm sorry, Laura. I should have trusted you. My knee jerk reaction was clouded by the fact that I felt like I had just been run over by a train."

"You should have seen it from my point of view." Laura shuddered a little.

"Okay, so we're both sorry. Is there anything else I should know about?"

"There's nothing else I haven't told you. I swear."

"Good enough for me," he said with relief. "So where do we go from here? What's the next step?"

"Well, I need to go over today's session and make some more notes. Do you want to have lunch tomorrow?"

"Sounds good."

Thomas put on his shoes and got up to leave. He wanted to hold her but rules were rules. The last thing they needed was being caught canoodling on her desk. That thought brought a smile to his face.

"One more thing, Laura."

"Yes?"

"What's the phrase you implanted?"

"You're probably going to hate me."

"Uh oh."

"Well. The phrase is 'the chicken says cluck'".

Thomas stared at her with disbelief. "Really? You really had to use something like that?" He started to laugh. "At least I didn't start to actually cluck when you said that."

Laura smiled. "Don't be too sure," she said with a wink.

Thomas opened his mouth in shock.

"Kidding. I'm kidding," Laura joked. "Now get out of here before we both cross the proverbial line."

"I'll see you tomorrow. Bye, Laura."

"See you tomorrow, Thomas."

He closed the door behind him and headed down the hall.

The chicken says cluck. She's hilarious. No wonder we get along so well.

* * *

That evening Laura finished dinner, then cleaned up her dishes and then looked around for something else to do.

Maybe I'll do laundry.

She sighed. She knew she was delaying the inevitable. The tape. Today's session. She wasn't sure she wanted to watch it. She had experienced it already once today.

Get a hold of yourself. You're a professional dammit.

But Laura knew it was more than that. Her strong feelings for Thomas were getting in the way of her job and she didn't want to experience Thomas' pain again. She just wanted to take it all away from him. Laura loved it when they teased and lightly flirted with each other, but Thomas' smile she couldn't get enough of.

Enough day dreaming...get to work.

Laura pulled the session's tape from her work bag and inserted it into the VCR. She pulled out her notepad and powered everything up. The television flickered to life and after a few seconds of snow the camera focused on Thomas as he sat in her office chair.

"Go ahead and close your eyes, Thomas," she heard herself tell him from off camera.

245

"With your mind free of cluttered thoughts your body starts to float. You only hear my voice talking whil-"

Laura fast forwarded the tape past the initial portion. She slowed it down when she saw his relaxed demeanor and pressed play.

"Where are you now, Thomas?"

"I think I'm at school."

"Look around. What do you see?"

Thomas craned his head in the chair. "Nothing."

Laura tried a different tact. "Look down at your feet. What are you standing on?"

Thomas lowered his head in the chair. "White cement. Polished."

"Now where are you?"

"Nowhere," he replied.

Thomas perked his head up.

"What is it, Thomas?"

"He's here. I know it! I've got to hide. There's nowhere to hide!" Thomas' voice started to rise.

"It's okay, Thomas. He can't hurt you."

Thomas relaxed back in his chair.

"Look around again Thomas. Where are you?"

On the television Laura watched for the second time today as Thomas stood straight up and screamed, "HE'S HERE!! OH MY GOD HE FOUND ME!!"

Laura heard herself on the tape saying, "You're okay, Thomas. He can't hur-" Thomas cut her off.

"CRY TOMMY!!"

The voice came from Thomas but it wasn't his voice. It was a nasty, demeaning and egotistical voice. It sent chills down her

246

spine and Laura shuddered for the second time as she heard it again.

"CRY TOMMY!!" he screamed again as he put his arms up to protect himself. "NOOO! GET OFF!!" cried Thomas, clearly switching in to his role as Tommy.

He fell back into the chair and violently thrashed about fighting for his life against some invisible foe that was on top of him. Thomas's eyes were wide open in fright, well past the panic stage. He fought with all four of his limbs.

"STOP IT!!" he bellowed on screen. Thomas' hands went to his throat and started to squeeze.

"Thomas! Thomas! Calm down. He can't hurt you!"

Laura was partially on screen now. She was as close to Thomas as she could without one of his wild limbs being able to connect with her.

"I caann't bre...athhh."

"Oh fuck."

Laura closed her eyes as she heard herself say those words as she relived what Thomas' had going through. She knew she had lost control of the session and she wasn't proud of that. The fact that she had feelings for Thomas only intensified everything.

"Stoooop iitt," Thomas whispered out as he choked himself.

"THE CHICKEN SAYS CLUCK!" Laura screamed off camera.

Thomas froze and his demeanor immediately changed. He loosened up. His hands fell from his throat into his lap and he breathed heavily. Sweat trickled down the sides of his face.

"Are you okay, Thomas?" Laura, on screen, now stood over Thomas.

"I...I don't know."

Laura turned off the tape, got up off her couch and headed into the kitchen. She needed some coffee. When she had experienced Thomas' memory earlier today she didn't have a lot of time to process it. Everything had happened so quickly that her primary concern was that he was okay. She had gotten lucky.

What if the phrase hadn't worked?

Laura stood in her kitchen and started to softly cry.

36

Friday May 26, 1990 7:44 p.m.

"Yes, General. I'll see you shortly."

Mr. Glib hung up his private line, stood up from his desk and gazed down into the observation area level below. He pressed a button and, shortly thereafter, Mr. Peterson entered through his office doors.

"Sir?"

Mr. Glib turned around. "Mr. Peterson. General Michaels, and his entourage, will be arriving shortly. What's our current status?"

"Sir. We're ready for the meet and greet."

"And Operation Bravo Charlie?"

"Bravo Charlie is prepped and ready to deploy if required, sir."

"Very good, Mr. Peterson. Please make sure the staff knows our guests are inbound."

Mr. Peterson turned and departed.

* * *

RHP, or Rising Hope Pharmaceuticals, was a biotech research facility located on the outskirts of south San Bernardino. It had been built in a small industrial park eight years previously, was four floors high and housed approximately 25000sq/f. A large parking lot had been built around the entire building which extended out for seventy five yards in every direction. A high security fence, topped with razor wire, had been constructed around the perimeter. Having so much open space between the perimeter and the facility allowed the security cameras a better chance to spot any intruders. Security at RHP was minimal, visibly at least. Two cameras were mounted on each corner of the building. At the front of the building was a gated fence with a guard shack, who verified the identity of everyone that entered the facility. The closest neighbors were a quarter of a mile away.

Once past the perimeter gate the main entrance contained a secondary checkpoint. Here employees would gain access to the facility by swiping their ID badge, and then a guard would visually confirm their face against a computer database. On the way out employees belongings were meticulously searched. Once past the main entrance employees would take an elevator to either the second, third or fourth floors. However, the eighteen or so that worked on the 'special project' would take a special elevator. Once inside that elevator there weren't any visible buttons so the employee would scan their ID again to make the elevator descend. When the doors opened four levels below the the employee would find themselves in a square, glassed off room, guarded by two armed guards housed behind thick glass. Here they'd find a third ID verification. Past that their belongings would be x-rayed before they'd be allowed admittance.

It was an arduous process for the 'project' employees, but they rarely got to leave RHP, as each of them signed up for extended research duty that obligated them to remain on site.

* * *

Fifteen minutes later the four-star general arrived with three other men; his aide and two bodyguards. They were quickly cleared through security and met with Mr. Glib and Mr. Peterson.

"General, good morning," Mr. Glib offered as he extended his hand.

"Morning," General Michaels replied gruffly and shook it.

His aide and one bodyguard flanked the General while the other hung back about ten feet. Mr. Glib noticed they were both armed with Glock 18 fully automatic 9mm hand guns.

"Ready for war I see," Mr. Glib commented.

"Let's get this dog and pony show over with," the General replied.

"Very well. This way gentlemen."

Mr. Glib led them over to the private elevator and they road in the four levels down in silence. Once there they exited, walked in to the glass security zone and Mr. Glib scanned his ID. The doors opened.

"What would you like to see first, General?"

The underground facility was impressive the General had to admit, as he looked around.

The taxpayers would have a shit if they knew about this place.

Throughout the guided tour he learned that there were a total of three floors below ground. The observation area alone combined two full floors of open space. All the research and training areas were located in the combined second and third floor zones. A complete kitchen, exercise/lounge/library area, and private individual bedrooms made up the bottom floor. The General didn't breathe a word nor had he met or seen any staff.

They must all be in their rooms.

Afterwards Mr. Glib led them to his private office.

"General, may I speak with you privately?"

General Michaels motioned to his staff to wait outside, along with Mr. Peterson who closed the door after him.

"Something to drink, General?"

"Scotch on the rocks." He sat down in a chair in front of Mr. Glib's desk. "Quite a place you have here, Eternal."

Mr. Glib stiffened for a second and then relaxed. It'd been awhile since he'd heard his first name, and as it turned out, it typically was General Michaels who enjoyed reminding him about it. He poured the scotch and handed it over.

"Jim," Mr. Glib began. "I thought you didn't want to get your hands dirty?" He sat down in the chair behind his desk.

General Jim Michaels drank. "I see you like the good stuff. This scotch must be twenty years old."

"Cut the crap, Jim. What are you doing here?"

General Michaels looked squarely into Mr. Glib's eyes. "How long has it been now Eternal; five, six years? The money to build this facility came from me. The money to run this facility came from me. The men you've used as lab rats came from me." The General's voice got louder after each statement. "What I'm doing here, Eternal, is checking in on my investment."

Mr. Glib sat behind his desk un-phased by the General's power trip. "The monthly reports I send are very detailed. They also give you plausible deniability. Try again, Jim."

General Michaels continued. "From what I understand the drug is a success, and has been working for over a year now. Correct?"

"Correct."

The General shifted in his chair and took another drink. "So what's the problem?"

"There isn't a problem, Jim. Aside from the initial side effects, we discovered in our earlier candidates, the current test cases have been very favorable."

"How reliable?" The General leaned forward, now very interested.

It was Mr. Glib's turn to smile. "Jim. Let's just say that my dream, combined with your taxpayer money, have finally come to fruition."

"Not good enough. You've been running this project without any oversight far too long now. I'm here to remind you who's in charge. I want a demonstration."

Mr. Glib took it all in and didn't bat an eye. He'd anticipated the General's request.

"I understand, General." Mr. Glib punched a button and Mr. Peterson stepped back in.

"Sir?"

"Mr. Peterson. Please send Joe to the training area and 'Be Careful'," he emphasized.

Mr. Peterson nodded. "Right away, sir."

"You certainly have him jump like a good little soldier, don't you Eternal?" The General chuckled.

Putz. Who did he think he was? Mr. Glib turned towards the glass behind him. Below, in the training area a floor down, Joe had just entered the large room and wore a lab coat.

"General, he's ready."

General Michaels got up from his seat, walked over to the large observation window and saw a young male lab assistant all alone.

"This is your demonstration?"

"Give me a moment, General."

Mr. Glib picked up his phone and dialed a number. In the training area below the phone on the wall rang. Joe looked over at it, looked around for anyone else, and then walked over and picked it up.

"Hello?"

As he stood next to the General Mr. Glib said a few words in to the phone and then hung up. From his vantage point the General witnessed Joe stiffen.

"Great demonstration, Eternal," he mocked. "This is what my money is being used for?"

"Wait for it, General."

"Wait for what? He's a stat-"

Just then Joe dropped the phone, immediately hit himself in the face and break his nose. Blood spewed everywhere. The sound was clearly audible through the glass.

"What the fuck?" stated the General. Mr. Glib only smiled as he watched the demonstration continue.

Joe didn't make any sounds as he calmly walked over to the opposite wall and removed a Bo Staff. He whipped it around quickly struck himself on the right knee, breaking it. He fell to the floor on his left knee, still as silent as ever.

"What the hell is he doing?" exclaimed the General.

Joe broke the staff in half over his left thigh and, with the broken end facing towards his face, plunged it deep into his throat. The crimson spray was far more obvious from their observation point. Blood ran freely down Joe's throat and pooled on the ground around him. Seconds later, unable to control his actions, Joe collapsed, spasmed a few times, and then lay still.

"Satisfied, Jim?"

After the initial shock wore off the General said, "That was amazing. One question though, why did you have him kill himself?"

The General retook his chair and picked up his scotch glass.

Mr. Glib sat down as well. "That was Joe. He was my first 'candidate' to survive. That was two years ago. The issue we discovered, back then, was that a person's will is directly related to the success of the drug. If they resist the drug then they'll eventually go insane, like Joe had."

"So why did Joe respond to your directions today?"

"He'd been injected with a number of booster shots, over the past two years, as the drug become more perfected. It doesn't change the fact that he had lost his value to me. Mr. Peterson had just given him a booster so the chances of Joe resisting were next to none."

"Very impressive, Eternal. What's the current status?"

"A finalized product is projected to be ready in two months."

"Excellent," replied the General. "This is what's going to happen. We're moving this operation to Washington. I will oversee the final stretch of the project."

Mr. Glib bristled. "I'm not aware of you having a location where this project can be moved to."

"Don't worry about that. You've done a good job here but now I'm taking it over. You and your staff will be well compensated. Let them know that, by contract, they will be displaced to Washington for the foreseeable future. Do you understand?"

"Yes, of course, General."

"Damn right you do. Pack up and I'll see you in a week."

With that General Michaels turned and left Mr. Glib's office. Mr. Peterson escorted them upstairs, through security and back outside.

* * *

General Michael's town car pulled out of RHP's parking lot, through the security gate, and headed back towards Norton Air Force Base. The General loved busting Eternal's balls and had thoroughly enjoyed taking the project away from him at the last minute. For years he had been secretly funneling money to Eternal Glib.

What a fucked up name is Eternal anyway?

The concept of 'human control without realization' was a military's wet dream. Throughout the decades brain washing had achieved some small accomplishments here and there. When Mr. Glib had proposed his idea General Michael's had seen the ramifications that could come from it and had taken the financial gamble. A billion dollars had been easy to hide. He knew that if the project was successful the military payday from it would be priceless.

Soon it'll all be mine. America's enemies won't know what hit them.

Norton AFB was only a few miles from the project's base of operations, which made it easy to fly in to check on Mr. Glib's progress. But General Marshall didn't have a chance to continue with his thought process as an explosion blew his vehicle ten feet in the air and shredded everyone inside it.

* * *

Mr. Glib picked up his buzzing phone line.

"Sir. Operation Bravo Charlie has been executed successfully."

"Excellent, Mr. Peterson."

General Marshall had indeed been Bad Company.

37

Wednesday July 18, 1990 12:01 p.m.

Thomas met Laura in a small café, close to her office, for lunch. The sun was hot on her skin as she waved him over to a secluded table on the café's patio. Thomas made his way over and sat down.

"Hey," he said. "How are you?"

"Hi, Thomas. I see you didn't have any problems finding my favorite home away from home."

The waiter noticed Thomas and advanced towards them. "Dr. Bond, it's very nice to see you again. What can I get you both to drink?"

"Ice tea, Patrick, thank you," Laura replied.

"And for you, sir?"

"A coke."

"Excellent. I'll give you a few more minutes." The waiter departed.

"I guess you're a regular," Thomas said with a smile.

Laura loved Thomas' smile and had wanted to see it again after she rewatched the regression tape the previous night. It had disturbed her and she'd gone to bed quite upset.

"So, Thomas. How're you feeling after yesterday?"

"I headed home and basically collapsed in to bed."

The waiter delivered their drinks. "Are you ready to order?"

Thomas hadn't had a chance to look at the menu.

"I'll have the cobb salad," Laura decided. "You should try the club, it's really good."

"The club it is then," said Thomas.

The waiter disappeared.

"Anyway, I just wanted to apologize again. I lost control of the session. It really scared me." She turned her head away.

Thomas looked at Laura. "Hey, look at me," he said quietly. Laura brought her eyes up to look at his. "It's okay. Trust me. With absolutely everything that has happened to me in my life, you're one of the rare good things. You told me it's a process. We're going to run in to some bumps along the way."

Where do you come from? You're amazing.

"I know. And thanks. The fact that I'm emotionally involved with you only compounded my scare factor. I love what I do, Thomas. The fact that I want to help you hasn't changed. Unfortunately wanting to jump your bones when I do see you is definitely a distraction."

It was her turn to smile as Thomas' face turned red.

"Are you blushing?"

"I don't know what you're talking about."

"Oh my God, you are." She chuckled and smacked his hand that rested close to hers.

Thomas laughed with her and then asked, "So what's the plan for this week?"

"I was thinking about that before you arrived. Tomorrow's no good. Do you want to plan for Friday afternoon? If that works then we can go out to dinner afterwards, my treat." She added as an afterthought. "No hypnosis on Friday; just conversation."

"Deal," Thomas said. "What time?"

Laura opened her scheduler. "Three-thirty would be perfect."

"I'll be there."

Thomas took a sip of coke as the restaurant filled up with the lunch crowd. Laura wanted to know more about Thomas but this wasn't the place to play psychiatrist. Sometimes it was hard for her to shut off that part of her brain off.

"What?" Thomas asked.

"Huh?"

"For a second there it looked like you were going to ask something, that's all."

"I totally was and you caught me."

"What were you going to say?"

Laura paused for a second. "Honestly, I want to know more about you, Thomas. But I stopped myself because it sounded so clinical in my head. Dumb, huh?"

"Not at all. I mean, I have seen you naked," he joked as they grinned at each other.

"Fair enough, fair enough. So does that mean I can ask about you outside of our sessions without sounding like a doctor?"

"Fire away, Laura."

The waiter came back over to the table. "Cobb salad for the doctor, and the club sandwich for the gentleman. Anything else?"

"Thank you, Patrick. I think we're all set."

The waiter left.

"You were about to say something....doctor?" Thomas chuckled.

"Talk about perfect timing," Laura said and dug in to her salad.

Thomas took a bite of his sandwich. "Mmm. You were right. Delicious."

"Told you so." She paused and then said, "Okay. Since you gave me the green light, do you mind if I ask about your experiences you had as you grew up?"

"Not at all. What part are you interested in?

"Well, honestly, all of it. Just an overview of how you grew up I guess."

Thomas took another bite of his sandwich and followed it with a sip of coke.

Where to begin? "Well, I guess I should start with something you don't know. My father passed away on Christmas Day when I was ten."

"Thomas, I'm so sorry," Laura interjected.

Thomas gave her a weak reassuring smile and continued. "From that point on I lived with my grandparents, Ed and Claire. They're my dad's folks. Anyway, when I headed back to school Sammy and Billy informed me that Nigel, and his family, had moved away. From that point on things got a lot easier for all of us. Fifth and Sixth grade at Wagner Ranch came and went and we graduated to OIS."

"OIS?" Laura asked while eating.

"Right, sorry. It stands for Orinda Intermediate School." Thomas took another bite. "Seventh and eighth grade weren't too bad. After we graduated from middle school we went to Miramonte High School. There were some new bullies at Miramonte, but nothing we hadn't experienced before. They didn't bother us for very long."

"Why's that?"

"The three of us were older and bigger. Sammy and Billy were athletic while I just did my writing thing. Anyway, aside from being my best friends they also had my back. It didn't take a genius to figure out that when you messed with one of us you'd have to deal with all three of us." Thomas smiled. "Those four years weren't too bad either."

"So no talk of a girlfriend yet I see," Laura prodded.

"No, you're right. The bottom line, when I really look back to those days, is that I was afraid of everything. The two people that loved me had left me. It's not that I wasn't interested in girls, I was just closed off. I figured if I didn't start something then I would never get hurt. The guys would bust my chops about it too from time to time. They knew what I was doing, even if I didn't, and they always meant well."

"I understand."

"So I did really well in high school and had applied to a few colleges. I ended up being accepted in to USC." Thomas paused. "The issue was that this was going to be the first time I was going to be away from everything and everyone I knew, but it only gets more interesting."

Laura had nearly finished her salad and continued to listen intently. "Go on."

Thomas downed the rest of his coke and said, "Sammy and Billy decided to enlist in the Army together. My grandparents, who were seventy-one at this point, decided that since I was leaving for college that they would sell their house and move to Rossmoor."

"Rossmoor?"

"It's an adult community for retirees in Walnut Creek. It's gated and has golf courses, tennis, etc. They had become interested in it while I was in OIS and had planned to move there for years. They purchased a house there by the time I graduated high school. Anyway, aside from the fact that my two best friends would be gone, that I was about to move to an entirely different city, that my grandparents were about to move; there was one huge bomb that I wasn't prepared for."

"What was it?"

"My grandfather took me down to the local ice cream shop after I graduated, a little place called Loard's. I figured he wanted to celebrate. So after we get our ice cream and sit down, he drops the first bomb, which is their move to Rossmoor. I took that in

261

stride; I mean, they were seventy-one years old and had been raising their grandchild. They definitely needed a break."

"What was the other shocker?"

Just then Patrick came back to the table. "So how are you two doing?"

Laura had to pry her eyes off Thomas to look up at the waiter. "Could we get our drinks refilled please? Other than that I'm finished. Thomas?"

Thomas's plate was nearly cleaned but he was full. "Go ahead. I'm done. Thanks."

Patrick cleared off the table. "I'll be back with your drinks."

Laura quickly refocused on Thomas and said, "So what was the second bomb?"

Thomas smiled and said, "I don't know. Maybe I should keep that carrot out there for another time."

"Don't you dare!" she joked and pretended to throw her napkin at him.

"Okay, okay. I give up." They both smiled as Patrick came back and dropped off their drinks.

"Thanks, Patrick," said Laura. He turned and headed off.

"So back to the story," said Thomas. "So we're sitting there eating our ice cream and he pulls out this very official looking envelope. I looked at my grandfather, as he handed it to me, and had asked what it was. He told me to open it."

"And?"

Thomas looked down at his watch and said, "Whoops. Look at the time. Gotta go." Thomas pretended to get up.

"Don't you dare, Mister!" Laura played. "Spill it."

Thomas grinned and sat back down. "When I opened the envelope I quickly realized that my father had left me a trust fund.

262

I wasn't supposed to know about or have access to it until I graduated high school."

Laura's eyes widened. "You're right, that is quite a shock."

Thomas looked closely at Laura. "You're really not going to ask?"

Laura took it in stride. "Listen Thomas, that's your business. I just want to know about you."

Thomas sat back in his chair and drank some coke. *Interesting.* "Well, I'll tell you anyway." He leaned back forward towards Laura. "The trust fund contained twenty-two point seven million dollars."

"What!? But how?" Laura stopped and her mind started to deliberate. "What did your father do for a living?"

"Exactly the same question I asked my grandfather. He told me he didn't know."

"Did you believe him?"

"What else could I do? I think I sat there dumbfounded, trying to wrap my head around it, as my ice cream melted."

"Wow. Twenty-two million dollars. That's insane."

"Tell me about it. I'm eighteen years old and suddenly a millionaire."

"What happened next? I mean, I would never have known you had money like that." Laura drank some of her ice tea.

"I keep that close to the vest. Aside from Sam, Bill and of course my grandparents, you're the only other person that knows."

The realization hit Laura like a ton of bricks. *He really trusts me.* "I...I don't know what to say."

"You don't have to say anything, Laura. It's just part of the story; it doesn't define who I am."

"So what'd you do then?"

"Long story short, I basically helped my grandparents pack up and move, then headed down to Los Angeles and found a place to live while I attended USC. Bill and Sam headed off for Army training at Fort Benning, Georgia."

"How you'd deal with the change?"

"At first I was scared of everything, quite frankly. It's hard to explain. Everything was new. No friends, new environment, you know the drill. But after no one tried to kill me I settled in. The routine was school mostly."

"Mostly?"

"Well, I took classes in pursuit of my Creative Writing major. I spent a lot of time in the library reading, writing and studying. The mostly part comes from the fact that during my second year there I met Samantha."

"Here we go. Finally, a woman."

"Haha. But yes, finally a woman, thankyouverymuch."

"So what was she like?"

"She was kind actually." Thomas' eyes grew soft as memories kicked in. "She became my world."

"So what ever happened to you two, if you don't mind me asking?"

Thomas refocused. "She was my first and I loved her. I didn't think I had that in me but apparently I did. She made me smile and laugh. Life was really good." Thomas's smile faded. "After eight months of pure bliss I came home to find her in my bed with another couple. She had assumed that I would join in and the four of us would have a great time that evening. What she hadn't figured out was that I didn't want to see her getting fucked by a stranger while I watched."

"I'm sorry, Thomas."

"I don't know, Laura. Maybe I was too naïve or too blind. We broke up. Later on I learned that Samantha and that guy were going out. He had left his girlfriend to be with her. Just another one of my life experiences I had to deal with."

"I'm guessing you steered clear of women from that point?"

"You guessed it. When they keep leaving you why bother even trying, right?"

"I didn't mean to get you down. I'm sorry."

Thomas shook his head lightly as if trying to rid himself of the memory. "I'm okay. Where were we?"

"Well, what about college?"

"I graduated in eighty. My grandparents had been catching up on their world travels, ever since I had moved out, and had recommended that I give it a shot."

"And?"

"So that's what I did. I put everything in storage and took off. I only had a backpack, some clothes and my journals to write in."

"Wow. That must have been amazing. You went alone?"

"Yeah, all by myself. And before you ask the answer is yes, I was totally scared shitless."

"But you went anyway."

"There were many reasons I did, but it all boiled down to this; I didn't know what I was going to do with my life. The direction and routine I had with school was suddenly gone. I also hadn't been anywhere. I was pretty secure in the fact that I could rely on myself to handle being alone since it wouldn't be any different than college. So I took my grandparent's advice and headed to England first."

Laura was transfixed. She had forgotten about her ice tea. "Where else did you visit?"

"There's still plenty for me to see, but off the top of my head, hmm…let's see. England, Ireland, Scotland, France, Spain, Portugal. Then I flew to Greece. From there I headed up Italy to a variety of cities. A bit of Switzerland and in to West Germany. Belgium and the Netherlands finished up Europe for me."

"There's more?"

"Yeah, I was hooked at this point."

"And you were still by yourself?"

"I had gotten used to it. Granted I wanted to talk to someone about the experiences from time to time so I wrote a ton in my journals. Although, when I did visit Amsterdam I was a little naughty."

"You didn't?"

"Well, by this time I felt I'd earned a break. I had wandered in to the Red Light District. I was so shy it was embarrassing, but apparently my libido did the talking for me. I was young, alone and horny. During the five days I stayed in Amsterdam I visited the RLD a few times and we'll leave it at that."

"Say no more," Laura joked. "So that was Europe you said. Did you go someplace else?"

"I flew and spent a little time on India's east coast. From there I dabbled in the Philippines, Taiwan, South Korea and Japan. After that it was Australia and New Zealand, then back to CA."

Laura just stared at Thomas. "That sounds absolutely amazing. What a trip. How long did it all take?"

"In total I think it took about nine months."

"Nine months. Holy crap. That must have been grueling."

"Actually, at first it was stressful and I wasn't having a lot of fun. I contemplated quite a number of times to pack it in and head back to Los Angeles. But each day brought a new adventure. On top of that I didn't want to let myself down. As the weeks passed

266

it became easier to be out in the world on my own. Some days I was lonely and other days it didn't bother me at all. When I got tired I just took some extra time where I was and relaxed before I moved on."

"Well, I'm officially jealous," Laura announced.

"After I got back to Los Angeles my mind was a lot clearer and I wrote feverishly day after day. Sometimes I wrote stories, other times I just drew pictures. As it turned out I ended up having a knack for children's stories. Pretty weird, right?"

"Not necessarily, Thomas," Laura said. "Think about it. Maybe writing children's books has been a way for you to go back and capture the innocent times when you were young. You were robbed of your innocence. You've been through more than anyone should have. I can understand. But what about where you live now? Why Running Springs?"

"After meeting Nick, and getting my publishing off the ground, I took some time off. I went skiing in Big Bear. The mountains seemed very peaceful and private. I thought I needed to be alone, and was used to it, so I bought a house."

"But you don't live or act like you have money. How come?"

"Why should I? It's nobody's business. I don't need a lot to get by in this life. I can write in peace and quiet. Nobody bothers me. Besides, why make myself a target."

There it is. "What people don't know they can't use against you, is that it?" asked Laura.

"Pretty much. I've been in Running Springs ever since."

It was Laura's turn to sit back. Thomas had just run her through his entire life. The fact that he had trusted her with all this information was astounding, but she knew he had needed to talk to someone and it had turned out to be her. *His life has been filled with drama. I don't blame him for wanting to escape it.*

267

The waiter made his way back over to their table. I'm sorry to bother you Dr. Bond. Is there anything else you'd like?"

"Just the check, Patrick, thank you."

Laura looked over at Thomas. She could see the young child he once was inside him, fighting for its chance to get out. She could also clearly see the high, defensive walls he'd built around himself. *Something's changing in him and he knows it.*

"So that's my story," said Thomas.

Laura reached over and grabbed his hand with hers. "Thanks for sharing. You have no idea what this means to me."

Patrick came back with the check. Laura squeezed Thomas's hand and then pulled out money for lunch. Thomas began to protest.

"No, I invited you," said Laura. "Besides, we'll get to fight over the check when we have dinner on Friday." She smiled.

"I can't wait," he said.

They both got up from their chairs, walked through the restaurant and headed outside. They paused as they reached her Volvo.

"Thanks for lunch, Laura, and for listening."

"No, thank you. It was very educational. Maybe one of these days I can see the photos from your world tour?"

"You're not trying to get back inside my house now, are you? I remember the last time you came by." Thomas grinned.

"You wish. But I'll leave you with this to think about." She leaned in and kissed Thomas deeply on the lips and the abruptly pulled away. "I'll see you at three-thirty Friday."

"Tease!" he said as he watched her get in her Volvo and drive away.

38
Thursday July 19, 1990 12:17 p.m.

"Hello?"

"Hey, Nick."

"Thomas. You always seem to call while I'm eating lunch."

"Oh shit, sorry."

"I'm just kidding. What can I do you for?"

"Listen, Nick, I took your advice."

"Whoa. Stop the presses," Nick teased. "Did my ears deceive me? You did what?"

"Yeah, yeah. Cut me some slack."

"So which advice did you take this time? Wait, let me guess. You moved off that god forsaken mountain? No, that's not it. You're calling to tell me your latest book is finished?"

"Eat shit and die brother." Thomas heard Nick laugh at his expense.

"Okay, Thomas. What's going on?"

"I called Dr. Bond and we've been having regular sessions."

"Really? That's fantastic. How're they going?"

"They've been pretty intense. We're working the issues through. Speaking of issues, she told me all about why you went to see her."

"Wait. What? No she didn't. She did?" Nick voiced with a hint of panic.

It was Thomas' turn to laugh. "Just kidding, buddy."

"You fucking asshole. I just about spilled my drink all over me. The next time I see you....why I oughta..." Nick chuckled. "Good one, Thomas. You almost had me."

"I couldn't help myself, Nick. Heh heh. Anyway, the reason I'm calling is to let you know that I'm not going to be able to make the deadline."

"I knew you were behind Thomas but I had no idea it was that bad. Writer's block or what?"

"It's hard to explain. The issues I'm going through are complicated. The bottom line is that there's a lot of weird shit going on at the moment and it's taken priority over my career. I just wanted to let you know that the book will be delayed until I can clear my head."

"I understand, Thomas. I'll run some interference for you on this end. The powers that be will be disappointed but oh well. The company has been backing a winner for years so I'm sure they'll cut you some slack. Don't worry about it."

"Thanks, Nick, I appreciate it. Now finish your lunch and say hello to Susan for me, will ya?"

"You got it, Thomas. Hang in there. If there's anything you need just let me know."

"Will do. Later."

Thomas hung up the phone.

* * *

After Laura had driven away, the day before, Thomas had gone to see a movie. With so many emotions, events and memories he needed a mental break. Thomas merged on to the I-10 west and then turned north on to I-215. He exited at Island Center and curved around until he found a parking spot close to the theater. He walked up to Pacific Theater and checked out what was playing.

"Awesome," he said under his breath and walked up to the ticket counter.

"Can I help you?" asked the attendant.

"One for Die Hard 2, please."

"That'll be four dollars and twenty-five cents."

Thomas handed over the money and received his ticket, haven forgotten that the sequel to Die Hard had come out two weeks prior. He had another forty minutes before it started so Thomas wandered into the arcade and killed time.

* * *

"Good afternoon, Sandbox Enterprises. How can I direct your call?"

"Thomas Clark for Sam Paige."

"One moment, Mr. Clark, I'll see if he's available."

Thomas heard the sound of his call being transferred and then picked up on the first ring. "Thomas, what's up?" said Sam. "It's been a few weeks."

"Hey Sam, I know. Are you guys busy? Can I bend your ear for a few minutes?"

"We're not tasked currently. Let me run down Billy." Thomas heard the phone put down. "Hey Billy!....Yeah!?....Tommy's on line two!" Sam picked the phone back up. "He's getting on."

"Thanks, Sam."

The line clicked and Bill jumped on. "Hey Tommy. How's our major stockholder these days?"

"Hey guys. Listen, sorry to interrupt."

"Don't sweat it bro," Bill said. "We have a gig coming up tomorrow that we need to prep for, but other than that we have some time. What's up?"

"I started seeing that psychiatrist that Nick recommended."

"And?" Sam asked.

"Those nightmares I told you guys about, from our childhood, well, they've been coming up a lot in my sessions."

"How're holding up bro?" asked Bill.

"Laura has me doing hypnotic regression."

"Wait a second," Bill interjected. "Did you just call your shrink by her first name?"

Oh shit. "Yeah," Thomas replied.

"Well dip my balls in hot fudge, I do believe we have a winner," Bill mocked. "There's a joke about her being a head doctor in there someplace, but I just can't put my finger on it."

"Billy, shut the fuck up," said Sam. "Can you believe I have to work with this guy, Thomas?"

"I heard that," Bill countered. "Don't make me come down the hall and kick your ass!"

"You and what army," Sam pushed back, clearly smiling on his end of the phone. "But seriously, Thomas, Bill's just kidding. How're the sessions going?"

"Thanks, Bill."

"I'm just playing, Thomas," Bill told his friend. "Back to what Sam just asked..., how're the sessions?"

"They're intense guys. She has me talking about my mother's accident, my father dying and our best buddy Nigel."

"Christ. Nigel," Bill said with loathing. "I hated that kid."

"You and me both," said Sam. "Is she helping you out, Thomas?"

"Yeah. In fact, aside from Bill's natural obnoxiousness, he's right. Dr. Bond…, Laura, and I have gotten close."

"Way to go," Sam said.

"Insert gratuitous statement here," Bill added, "but seriously, all the best to you both brother. Sam and I know that you and the ladies have never gotten a fair shake."

"Thanks guys."

"Speaking of tough subjects, Thomas," said Sam, "what are your plans this year for your birthday? We were hoping maybe we could all get together or something. Maybe introduce us to Laura?"

Thomas had forgotten all about his birthday that was right around the corner on the 27th. Then again, he'd been intentionally forgetting about it for the past twenty two years as it was.

"Good question. I've been feeling different lately. I'll keep you guys in the loop. Maybe we can get together."

"Awesome," said Bill.

"So what's the gig you have going on tomorrow?" Thomas asked as he changed the topic.

Back in 1984, after getting out of the military, Sam and Bill had the idea of opening a VIP protection service based in San Francisco. They had both seen their share of action as Rangers and, with their very specific set of skills they had acquired, hadn't wanted to transition to police officers. By 1985 they had come up with an actionable plan and had found a location in Marin, just north of San Francisco, where they could build their office and training area. Their goal was to create a private security business for high paying clientele. The mission of the company, otherwise known as Sandbox Enterprises, was to protect dignitaries while they were visiting the Bay Area.

They had talked to Thomas about their idea from the get go. When Sam and Bill had finalized the specifics, almost a year later, Thomas had surprised them with his millionaire status and they had no idea he had money. They knew writing books paid the bills but they didn't know about the trust fund. Thomas had filled them in about it and then offered them fifteen million dollars to help them get started. Immediately his friend had become ecstatic. The land purchase, and building out the structures, took a significant amount of the money. They had started out with just the two of them running the business and their excellent reputation in the spec-ops community awarded them with multiple references. Within two years of SANDBOX's launch they had sixteen ex-military personnel working for them and the jobs hadn't slowed down.

"So what's SANDBOX stand for again?" Thomas asked.

"Listen to this fucking guy," said Bill. "He throws a little money around and wants us to dance like monkeys." He laughed.

"Translation," Sam replied, "is that Billy loves you for letting us do what we do best Thomas."

"Okay okay. Sue me. It stands for **S**ituations **A**lways **N**ecessitate **D**ecisive **B**lueprints or **O**peration e**X**tremes," Billy quoted.

"Thanks monkey," kidded Thomas.

"OOOooooAAAhhhaaahh."

Sammy interrupted. "If you two primates would stop throwing shit at each other I believe there's a question on the floor." They all chuckled. "Thomas, there's a Saudi Prince coming in to town who wants to see the sights and has a small security group for his primary layer. Sandbox has been hired for layer two because we know the terrain. It should be a no brainer but Bill and I have been working with the rest of the operators to go over the routes and destinations looking for potential ambush sites, etc."

"And there's a shitload of potential places, Thomas," Bill added, "but the prince will be in good hands. We have it covered."

"I meant to ask how the earthquake cleanup is coming?" Thomas inquired.

On Oct 17, 1989 the Bay Area was hit by a major earthquake. Freeways had collapsed, a section of the upper deck of the Oakland/Bay Bridge had broken loose, and there was excessive damage all over the Bay Area.

Sam answered. "The bridge was back up in a month, which was good. They're still demolishing Interstate eight-eighty where the freeway completely collapsed in on itself."

"I remember reading about that," Thomas commented. "There were a lot of casualties from what I recall."

"Yeah, pretty grim," said Bill.

"Sounds like you guys are at home in your element. I'll let you get back to it and I'll be in touch with any birthday plans."

"You got it, Thomas," said Sam.

"Later brother," said Bill.

* * *

Thomas hung up the phone slowly. He really missed his best friends and had been more than happy, five years ago, to finance their operation. The potential to make money was definitely there but it had been more than that for all of them. To protect people was what it was all about, plain and simple. It had been that way when Bill and Sam decided to enlist in the Army, and decidedly so when they'd created their business. Thomas was proud of what they'd accomplished and knew they were very good at their job.

Thomas looked around his bedroom. His computer sat there, taunting him. For years he hadn't had a problem with writing. Endless stories flooded through him and he would mold them in to something special. He had written, by hand, for years. Eventually he'd tried using a typewriter, but he hated it. He'd bought the computer recently and it had taken some getting used to. Still, it sat there, taunting him and he didn't like it.

Screw it.

Thomas changed into biking clothes and headed downstairs. It was early afternoon and maybe a quick spin around the town would loosen both his brain and body up a bit. He opened the door to the garage, closed it and then armed the alarm. He pushed the button for the garage door and it swung upwards and let the sunlight in. He pulled his bike from the rafter hooks, did a quick inspection, jumped on and rode off.

A few blocks away from his house was downtown Running Springs. It was kind of the running joke anyway. Running Springs's version of a downtown was a couple blocks of commercial shops off of Highway 18. It had the basics; a market, coffee shop, post office, ski rentals, a couple of inns, a realtor and a liquor store. If you blinked you'd practically passed it already. There was a 7-11 style store about a mile west from Running Springs called the Village Market and Thomas decided to head there. It was too late in the day to ride to Arrowhead and back.

On the way over Thomas had a few minutes to reflect on the changes that were happening to him. He'd been feeling an urge to reconnect with the people he loved. He wasn't happy living alone anymore and he knew his friends were correct; he had been hiding out in the mountains all these years. What had that achieved?

And what about my birthday? Maybe it's time to get out of hiding?

276

Within a few minutes he reached Village Market and turned right into the parking lot. As Thomas engaged his kickstand a familiar voice spoke up behind him.

"We have to stop meeting like this." Thomas turned around and George Miles stood there. "Tom, what brings you out on a day like this?"

Thomas was puzzled. "What do you mean? It's really nice out."

"I don't mean the weather, son. It's just that you have that look about you like your brain is chewing on something."

Who is this guy?

Thomas didn't have a response for George and just stood there, rooted to the ground by his bicycle. George smiled, took a couple steps towards Thomas and got within a few feet of him. He took his time and looked Thomas up and down.

"Yup," George said, "you're definitely thinking about doing something different with your life. I have a nose for it." George backed off.

Thomas finally spoke up. "Who are you? How could you possibly know anything about me?"

"Don't you worry about that, Tom. I've known you for a long time. What's bothered me is that for nine years you've been living up here, alone, trying to control everything in your life. But lately you've actually, and finally, gotten a taste of what life is all about. You're taking control and not hiding from what's been holding you back all these years."

Thomas' face scrunched up in confusion. *What the fuck?* "George," Thomas began, "thanks for your concern but I'm going to go inside the market now."

As Thomas turned to open the doors George said behind him, "You're on the right path, son."

Thomas paused, the door halfway open, and slowly turned his head back and looked back. The parking lot was empty.

39
Tuesday September 7, 1971 9:05 a.m.

Tommy, Sammy and Billy disembarked the school bus and paused, taking in the large campus that spread out before them for the first time. Miramonte High School. The years had flown by since they had been at Wagner Ranch Elementary, and then at OIS for 7th and 8th grade. It was the first day and their excitement and apprehension were evident.

"Freshmen orientation is in the gym," a voice boomed over the loudspeakers. "All freshmen please proceed to the gym for orientation at nine-o-five."

"I guess that's us," said Billy.

They all nodded and merged with the crowd heading towards a large building. As they neared it they saw the double doors were open and it was indeed the gym. Bleachers lined each side of the basketball courts as they found seats.

The introduction by the school Principal was fairly standard. The trio had heard a similar greeting when they'd started 7th grade. Class schedules, a map of the campus and locker combinations were to be picked up directly following his 'welcome to high school" speech. The Principal spoke for ten minutes and then excused one bleacher section at a time to retrieve their packets.

After they each got their schedules they compared what classes they had together. As it turned out they each shared English, Science and History. Then a series a series of bells rang. It was 9:30 and the first day of high school started. Consulting their maps, and class schedules, they headed off in different directions for 1st period.

* * *

By Thursday they had the routine down. Class, class, class, lunch, class, class, class, PE. The junior and seniors had already made their presence known that this was their campus. Tommy, Billy and Sammy pretty much kept to themselves but were friendly to everyone. Making new friends would come naturally, but it was only the third day of school and everyone was still speculating the cliques.

It was lunchtime. Tommy, Sammy and Billy had already scoped out a place they could meet on the athletic field bleachers. Tommy was the first to arrive. He opened up his bag lunch, pulled out a red apple and took a bite. He'd started to read a lot after he moved in with his grandparents. 'Creativity is the key to success' his grandfather used to tell him. He pulled out a book from his backpack entitled 'The Wild Boys: A Book of the Dead' by William S. Burroughs. This novel had interested Tommy because it had to do with the struggle with society.

A shadow fell over the page Tommy was reading.

"Hey, Orphan."

Tommy looked up and saw a face he didn't recognize. The kid was older, bigger and wore a varsity jacket. His buddy stood next to him and they were both grinning.

"You heard what I said," he sneered. "Orphan."

"Yeah yeah...Orphan Annie," his buddy added.

Tommy was transfixed. He stopped chewing and time slowed down. *Not again.* The varsity player snagged the book out of Tommy's hands.

"What's this shit? You a fag or something?"

His buddy added on, "Faggotty orphan."

"Can I please have my book back?" Tommy asked.

"Can I pweese have my book back?" the jock mocked.

"Hahahahaha" laughed his friend.

The varsity player smacked Tommy' head with the book. Tommy winced as the apple flew out of his hand.

"How do you like that shit faggot?"

Two more shadows suddenly flew in. The two juniors, who were taunting and standing in front of Tommy a second ago, were now on the ground. They had been tackled.

"WHAT THE FUCK?!" the jock cried out. His buddy was struggling with someone else close to him. "YOU'RE DE…" he yelled but was cut short with a hard right knee to his groan.

The varsity wearing junior instantly turned pale, went fetal and started to whimper as he held his damaged testicles in his hands. Tommy saw Sammy get off him and jump over to help Billy. Billy had taken down the sidekick so hard that the wind had been knocked out of his opponent. The fight was over before it even got started.

Sammy looked at both of the fallen bullies to make sure there wasn't an immediate threat. He then turned to Tommy and said, "Hey Tommy, you okay?"

Tommy was still processing what had just happened in a matter of seconds. He knew that his friends had been taking Judo classes together at the Community Center but he'd never seen them in action.

Tommy got up from the bleachers and picked up his fallen book. He looked down at the two bullies. The varsity jock and his sidekick were out of the fight.

"Thanks guys."

"Are you kidding," said Billy. "We've got your back."

"Definitely," Sammy added.

Tommy put his book back in his backpack and then slung it over his right shoulder. "Guess we'll find another place to eat lunch today," he joked.

They smiled and walked back towards the school campus. They never looked back.

40
Friday July 20, 1990 3:29 p.m.

Thomas strolled in to Laura's office and sat down. He noticed the video camera wasn't setup.

"Hi, Thomas."

"Hi, Laura. No video camera today?"

She glanced over to where it was usually set up and then looked back at him. "No. Today I thought we'd just talk. Maybe we could chat about anything that's on your mind?"

"Well, you've been on my mind," he said with a grin.

Laura smiled. She didn't mind the attention one bit.

"Sorry, I couldn't help myself."

"We can get in to that later." She winked at Thomas. "I've been thinking a lot about your life story." Laura paused.

"I'm assuming that's a good thing?"

She sidestepped his comment. "I don't want to downplay your life, Thomas. You've had some very traumatic experiences and they've made you who you are today. In some case you're stronger, and in other cases you're weaker because of them. My point is you should give yourself the credit for taking a stand. You made the decision to make a change in your life."

Thomas remained quiet.

"What I'm trying to say Thomas is that I'm thankful."

"Thankful? I don't understand."

"I know it sounds weird, and I'm totally crossing the professional line here, but yes thankful. I'm thankful that you walked in to my office two weeks ago; thankful that you're facing your demons; and thankful that we've started to connect. We're very similar, Thomas. We hide behind our defenses so we can't get hurt. What we failed to realize is that we were just hurting

283

ourselves the entire time." Laura shifted in her chair uncomfortably.

"It's okay, Laura. To be frank about all this, you've been my saving grace. I've just been hiding and it's been eating away at me for years. It's just recently that I've started to believe it's not healthy. You've helped me out more than I can thank you for. The more I think about it I feel like we've known each other for a lot longer than two weeks."

"I feel the same way, Thomas."

The each took a breath and just gazed at each other, not saying a word.

Laura eventually broke the silence. "Speaking of hiding, and I don't mean to hurt your feelings, but your birthday is coming up in a week. Do you have any plans?"

Thomas squirmed a little. *Hell, even Sam and Bill asked me about my birthday.* He had thought about it while biking yesterday. "I'm in new territory here, Laura."

"Explain."

"Typically on my birthday, and like it's a huge surprise, I have holed up in my house. I wallowing all day, not answering the phone, and feeling sorry for myself. Other birthdays I have flown to San Francisco and have visited my parent's graves without telling anyone I was in town."

"And now?"

"Exactly. Now I feel like I want to do something different. If I revert back to my normal routine of hiding away in the mountains then what have I really learned or accomplished about myself?"

Laura took this all in and was nodding. "I like where your head's at. Any conclusions?"

284

"Maybe we could get away next weekend? Palm Springs? Bill and Sam want me to visit but I didn't want to be presumptuous and assume you'd want to meet them so soon."

Laura smiled. "You've spoken so highly of them. At some point I'd definitely love to meet them."

"I'd like that too. I think we should save that for another time though."

"Oh," she said.

"I think we need a break actually. Getting away, just the two of us, for the weekend isn't a bad idea. At least we'd know right away whether we can stand each other for extended periods of time." Thomas chuckled.

"Very funny, mister. But is does sound nice. Some massages and pampering. You really know how to get to a woman's heart, Thomas." It was his turn to smile. "So about dinner this evening."

"What's the plan?" he asked.

"Why don't you meet me at my place around eight-fifteen."

"Dress code?"

"Slacks, button down and a sport coat would be perfect."

"Consider it done."

Laura wrote down her address and handed it to him.

"I think I can find your house."

"Good. I'd hate for you to get lost and some other lucky woman get her hands on you."

Thomas paused and cocked his head at her. "You're breaking your own rules again."

Laura grinned and said, "And what rule is that, Mr. Clark?"

"You're a big tease." He had a huge smirk on his face.

"Once again, I have no idea what you're talking about. Now get out of here and I'll see you in a few hours."

Laura shooed Thomas out of her office and closed the door behind him. *He's going to be the death of me yet.* She was giddy.

* * *

Thomas rushed up the mountain and got home as quickly as he could. His face hurt from how much he'd been smiling. He couldn't wait to see Laura again. Once he arrived he headed upstairs and took a nice hot shower and allowed the water to work over his back muscles. When he finally stepped out of the shower his bathroom was full of steam. Thomas looked like a cooked lobster but he felt more alive than ever.

Love how anticipation changes my mood.

He shaved and then got dressed in a nice dark blue button down shirt and khakis. Before he left he packed a few things away in an overnight bag. He felt a little presumptuous for doing so.

You never know.

Thomas headed down to the garage and set the alarm behind him. He opened the trunk of this BMW and paused.

There's nothing to fear. I didn't do it. I'm a good person.

Thomas reached in and pulled out both black trash bags that had been sitting in there for the past few weeks. He placed them in the corner of his garage, walked back and deposited his overnight bag in their stead. Driving out of his garage Thomas felt rejuvenated. He was stepping up to his fears and dealing with them.

Who am I?

* * *

Thomas wasn't the only one that had rushed home. Laura parked her Volvo in her garage and entered the house. She always had fun teasing Thomas. The reactions she got from him only spurred her on.

Poor bastard.

She put her briefcase down and headed to her bedroom.

Time to make myself presentable.

* * *

Laura heard a car pull up to her house a little after 8 p.m.. She looked out the front window and saw Thomas emerge from his car. The doorbell rang. Laura took her time as she walked over and opened it.

"Sorry I'm earl…Wow, you look great!" Thomas said as he cut himself off.

Laura had decided to wear a long, flowing gown. It was held up by thin straps of fabric over her shoulders. She had her hair tied up on the back of her head.

Laura smiled. "You're early, Thomas, but your reaction wipes the slate clean. Please, come in."

She stepped back and allowed him to walk in, closing the door behind him. "You clean up pretty good yourself."

"Thanks," he breathed in her ear.

Laura turned around and Thomas was right there. He gently put his right hand behind her neck and pulled her to him. He kissed her lightly and drew back. They locked eyes but their breath had become ragged. They kissed again and it was deep and passionate. Thomas broke it off.

"Why did you stop?" Laura asked wanting more.

"I believe turnabout is fair play," he said as a smile crept over his face.

Laura felt like she either had to hit Thomas or jump him. Instead she started to laugh. "So that's what it feels like to be teased. I'll have to be careful in the future."

"Come here," he said softly.

Laura seemed to glide the short distance to him and they embraced; their lips hungrily found each other. Their tongues darted; probing; exploring; loving every second. Thomas reached down and gently squeezed Laura's behind. She let out a little sigh. It was her turn to break it off.

"Oh my God, you're killing me here," she said, a bit out of breath. "I'm tempted to cancel our dinner reservation now." He caught the twinkle in her eye.

"You and I both, but something tells me we might need all the energy we can get for later."

"You're bad, Thomas, but I like that." She looked in the hallway mirror and checked her hair. "It doesn't look like I got mauled too badly."

"I'll do a better job later," Thomas said with a smile.

"Promise?"

As they walked out of her house they were both grinning and having a great time. The night had just begun.

"Why don't you drive," Laura proposed.

"My chariot awaits." Thomas opened his passenger for her.

"Shouldn't there be a towel for me to sit?"

"A towel?" Thomas asked?

Laura looked right in Thomas' eyes and said, "Yes, a towel to sit on. You got me so very wet."

She watched his reaction of total shock as she said it. He stuttered and could only watch as Laura got in to his car with a huge smirk on her face.

* * *

They tried not to rush through dinner. During that time they traded stories back and forth as they tried to ignore their hunger, which wasn't being sated by the food they were eating.

"So how many books have you written?" Laura asked.

"I've actually lost count. I started writing when I was young. In fact, just the other day I found a box in the guest room that was filled with my work. Anyway, they've all blended together over the years, intertwining with each other in one aspect or another."

"What about published books?"

"The children's books? Maybe a dozen over the years."

"Anything I'd know?"

"Well," said Thomas, "unless you're hanging out in the children's section of the library, or your local book store, I doubt you've read anything of mine."

Laura was interested. "Tell me about them."

Thomas finished chewing a piece of steak and then dabbed his mouth with his napkin. "I have my favorite. It was the last one that was published."

"What's the title?"

"The Little Brown Chair."

"What's it about?"

"I tell you what. I don't want to spoil it for you so I'll let you read it on your own one of these days." Thomas smiled. "Trust me, Bill and Sam's daughters love it, or so they tell me."

"It's a deal," she said. "Talk to me about another one."

"Well, there's 'The Sandbox' and 'The World to Tom' that aren't too bad."

"The Sandbox. Interesting. What's it about?" She took a sip of wine.

"I'm sure this will come as a huge shock to you but it's about some kids who build, create and destroy things in their sandbox. One day, while playing in it, they are transported to a huge sandbox far away. It becomes their world. They find out that they can build anything that they can think of. Their dreams become reality. They end up fighting off a big sand monster that has attacked their sand town. At the end of the story the school bell rings and wakes them up from their fantasy world. They can't wait till tomorrow to play in the sandbox again."

"I like it, Thomas. Imagination and the underlying tone that dreams can come true."

Thomas raised his wine glass and saluted Laura with it. "Pretty good deduction there, doctor."

"And what was the other one called. Tom's World or something?"

"A World to Tom," he said. "That book is really a quick overview of what the world had to offer from a child's perspective."

"How so?"

"It's a pop-up book. The main character is a boy named Tom. Yeah, I know, big stretch on the name." Laura grinned. "But basically it tells a story, from his point of view, of traveling all over the world and experiencing its wonders." Thomas was starting to get animated. "So for example, when Tom visits Rome that page has a huge coliseum pop-up. Below it the narrative talks about gladiators, tigers and lions. Then when he visits Paris the pop-up is the Eifel Tower. You get the drift."

Laura loved it. Thomas was clearly in his element and could talk about his passions for days. She really enjoyed seeing him smile. The typical weight he carried around on his shoulders didn't seem to faze him this evening. *I can't believe I fell for him this quickly.*

Someone walked up to the table. "Did you save any room for dessert this evening?"

Thomas and Laura stole a glance at each other before she said, "I think we're going to have dessert at home this evening."

"As you wish." Thomas produced a credit card and handed it off. The waiter retreated.

"So," Thomas said, "what do you propose we nibble on for dessert?"

"Whatever you'd like," Laura replied.

The waiter couldn't get back to the table fast enough.

* * *

Thomas pulled into Laura's driveway for the second time that evening and as soon as they parked they couldn't keep their hands off each other. The windows quickly fogged up.

"Yip yip yip," came the sound of a dog right outside the car.

"Laura dear? Are you alright?"

Laura and Thomas suddenly stopped and froze.

Laura opened the passenger door and got out, straightening her dress. "Yes, Mrs. Simpson, I'm just fine. Why don't you head on home."

Mrs. Simpson peered through the driver's side door and Thomas opened it. She stepped back and glared at him when she noticed that his shirt was slightly pulled out of his pants.

"Well I never," she said. "Yip yip yip yip" cried her Pomeranian dog.

Laura came around Thomas's side and said, "Mrs. Simpson, why don't you take Benji home now?"

Mrs. Simpson stomped off, clearly unhappy that she caught Laura frolicking in the car. Benji yapped the entire way across the street.

Laura and Thomas looked at each other and started to laugh. "Well that slowed us down a bit," he joked.

"Only for the moment," Laura countered.

Thomas got out of his car and opened the trunk.

"Forget something?" she asked.

"Just an overnight bag."

"I see, "she said. "Presumptuous are we?" Laura was trying her best to sound serious.

Thomas caught Laura holding back and said, "You haven't seen anything yet."

They both busted up laughing again. Laura took Thomas' free hand and led him back to her house. She opened the door, let him inside, and locked it behind them. Her kiss came out of nowhere and melted Thomas to the core. Laura pushed him away and turned her back on him. Thomas was about to protest when she slowly walked towards her bedroom. One shoulder strand slowly fell off her right shoulder and slid down her arm. She paused and looked down her right arm, first at the strand, and then back at Thomas.

"Oops," she said and continued walking.

Thomas immediately dropped his bag and bolted after her.

41
Friday June 6, 1975 1:30 p.m.

"Hey, Tom! Tom!"

Tom looked across the quad and saw Bill coming towards him. When he approached he asked, "Hey, have you seen Sam yet?"

"He said to meet us right here. He knows we only have thirty minutes until the ceremony starts," Tom said.

Sam snuck up behind them both and tapped them on the shoulders. They all wore graduation caps and gowns. Bill and Tom turned around. "Way to know your surroundings Bill. They're going to murder you at Basic," Sam said.

"What the hell are you guys talking about?" Tom asked.

Bill looked at Sam and said, "Do you wanna tell him or should I?"

"I don't know, he might faint," said Sam. They both chuckled.

"Fuck you both very much. What's going on?" Tom asked.

Sam put his arm around his friends's shoulder and said, "Well my friend, it's like this. While you're headed off to college to become smarter, we're heading off to the Army to protect that right."

"Aww man, Sam," Bill complained, "you fucked up the delivery."

"No I didn't. Shut up." Bill and Sam started to mock fight as Thomas smiled.

"Quit it you guys, you might hurt each other's pussies."

Sam and Bill stopped and looked at Thomas. Bill piped up and said, "At least I know what one is." Sam and Bill started to laugh all over again. Thomas didn't find it nearly as hilarious.

"Ha ha," Tom mocked.

"Hey, I'm just kidding buddy," said Bill as eh slapped Thomas on the back. "We're all friends here. You're just not a lady's man. Give it some time. No sweat brother."

"You're wrong, Bill," said Sam.

"I am?"

"Tom has had two steady girlfriends for a while now." Sam held up both his hands and made fists, then pumped them up and down in the air. They were practically rolling on the ground now.

"God how I hate you both," Tom said, but he was smiling. Only people that you trusted could cut you so deep. "But seriously, I didn't think you guys were going to go through with it."

"Why not?" they asked in unison.

"Well, I guess because the war ended two years ago," Tom said.

"Tom," started Bill, "It's not all about going to war in some other country."

"No?"

"No. It's more than that, and this is going to sound cheesy, but we want to help people. There are a lot of bad guys out there and we want a crack at them."

Sam jumped in. "Remember back when we were freshmen and we had that altercation on the field?"

"Altercation. Nice big word for you, Sam," Tom poked.

"Fuck you too. My point is this; we didn't get fucked with from that day forward." Sam looked at Bill and then back at Tom. "We're just going to take the ass kicking from local to global." Sam and Bill grinned.

"You guys are hilarious but I wish you both well. Don't quote me on this but I'll fucking miss you both."

"You'll be fine, Kemosabe," Bill said.

"High School is about to be behind us and the world is our oyster," Sam added. "Speaking of, how's the USC process? We know you got in but when are you taking off to find a place to live?"

"I don't know. I need to talk to my grandparent's about that. The paperwork from school says the sooner the better or I could get stuck farther away from campus."

"So can I ask a favor?"

"Sure Bill," Tom replied.

"Can I pwease have a bedtime story?" Sam and Bill died laughing again.

Tom grabbed Bill's graduation cap, tossed it away and Bill ran after it still chuckling.

"Listen Tom, you're the smart one out of our trio."

"What? Shut up." Bill returned with his cap.

"No seriously, listen. Go out in the world and kick its ass. Leave the other shit behind you. We're going to be friends forever and you know we'll always have your back. Just make us proud, okay?"

"What he said," Bill added and then turned serious. "I may give you a ton of shit brother but it's only because I love you. That day, at the sandbox, you guys could have turned me away, but you didn't. We've been through more shit than I want to remember, and if it wasn't for you two I don't know if I would have survived."

Tom was speechless. They all looked at each other, and without speaking hugged each other.

* * *

Tom found his grandparents while they were walking to the field's bleachers.

"Hey grandma. Grandpa."

"Hi, Tom."

"Hi sweetie," said his grandmother.

"So where are we sitting for this shindig?"

"Over here, grandpa." Tom led them to a specific section and seated them. "I'll be over there with my class," Tom said as he pointed to the chairs below the raised podium.

He then joined his class and waited for the ceremony to begin.

* * *

"Congratulations to the class of nineteen-seventy-five! May all your dreams come true!" announced the Principal over the speaker system.

A myriad of hats flew in to the air. Everyone screamed and hugged each other. High school was now behind them and college was on the horizon.

"Congrats," Sam said.

"Yeah, congrats you guys," Bill said.

"Congrats," Tom heard himself saying.

"We'll catch up with you later tonight, Tom," Sam told him. "Drop by the house around seven."

"You got it."

Thomas wasn't feeling like himself. He knew that he'd be heading off alone on his own adventure soon. He didn't know when he'd see his best friends, who were joining the Army. *So many changes.*

A strong hand landed on Tom's right shoulder. He turned and saw his grandparent's.

"Congratulations, honey," Claire said.

His grandfather said, "Tom, let's go to Loard's for some ice cream."

42
Saturday July 21, 1990 8:35 a.m.

"Morning."

Thomas rolled over, opened his eyes and saw that Laura was looking at him. "Morning cutie."

They gave each other a quick peck on the lips. Laura smiled and snuggled in close, putting her head on his shoulder. He put his arm around her and held her tight.

"Last night was wonderful," she said.

"You don't have to tell me, I was there," Thomas joked. "I didn't know you were going to pull out the puppet though."

She pinched his sides playfully and said, "Stoppp."

Thomas smiled. It had been a wonderful night. The teasing; the playing; the fondling; the screaming; oh my.

"What'cha thinking?

"Quite the loaded question my dear," Thomas replied. "Last night I was focused on you specifically."

"Don't I know it," she purred. "Thank you."

"This morning I've got a lot swimming around in my head apparently."

"Such as?"

"Us, for one thing. My birthday. My grandparents. My repressed memories and what they mean. Whether I'm a murderer or not."

"So just a few things."

"Yeah, just a few things."

They cuddled quietly for a few minutes, each lost in their own thoughts. Laura eventually broke the silence. "Did you have any plans for this weekend? Did you maybe want to spend some time together?"

Thomas didn't take long to answer her. "Laura, that sounds like a fantastic idea."

"Oh good." She squeezed him and climbed out of bed.

"Where are you going?"

"Do you still have a million things on your mind?" she asked.

"Yup."

"Well then, maybe I can fix that." Laura turned and walked slowly towards the bathroom accentuating her moves. "Care to join me in the shower?"

Thomas didn't need to be asked twice.

* * *

Afterwards they had gotten ready and made breakfast together. It was simple meal of toast, bacon and some scrambled eggs. Thomas added some cheese in the eggs while they were cooking. They quickly devoured it and decided to make it a low stress day. Their first stop was the mall. It had opened at 10 a.m. and was quickly filling up. Thomas and Laura strolled from end to end, holding hands, and took their time enjoying not only what the shops had to offer but each other. They stopped at an ice cream shop. Laura chose a sugar cone with a single scoop of coffee. Thomas decided on a scoop of rocky road in a regular cone. They walked over to the benches nearby and sat down.

"How is it?" Laura asked.

"Delicious," Thomas said as he caught a drip running down the side of his cone. "Yours?"

"Yummy."

They sat there taking in the surrounding atmosphere and people watched. Neither of them rushed to finish their ice cream. It was perfect.

"I'm having a great time."

"So am I, Laura."

They both smiled at each other and finished off their cones.

"What now?" Laura asked.

"Do you want to see what's playing at the theater? Maybe afterwards we can get some lunch and go from there?"

"I like it."

They got up and headed towards the theater. There were a number of titles playing. Laura saw that Ghost was one of them. She had heard about the movie and apparently its popularity was rising since its release the week before. She persuaded Thomas to see it, so he bought tickets and they headed inside. They had gotten lucky as it was just about to start.

Just over two hours later they exited and immediately covered their eyes as the sun hit them.

"Okay, I'll admit it, that was a good movie," Thomas said.

"Thanks for letting me talk you in to seeing it." Laura smiled.

"It's definitely different than the typical movies I go to but that doesn't mean I can't try new things."

"Maybe I'll take up pottery." Laura giggled.

"Very funny. Are you hungry?"

"I could definitely go for some food now. That popcorn aroma has my mouth watering."

"Me too. There's an IN-N-OUT Burger close by."

"You can't take me there," Laura said.

"Why?"

"Because I'll order way too much and eat it all, without sharing. I love IN-N-OUT."

Thomas started to laugh. "You should have seen your face when you said that. That was awesome."

"Quiet you! Now take me to get my food before I gnaw something else off." Laura winked.

They walked over to the IN-N-OUT, that was right by the mall, and they each ordered a Double-Double, fries and a shake. When the meal came they practically ate in silence as they scarfed the delicious food. They were in heaven.

"Damn that's good," Laura said. "If I had a vice, this food would be it."

Thomas only smiled at her.

"What?" she asked when she noticed him staring.

"Nothing." He paused and then said, "This," motioning in the air between them, "is just really nice. I'm having a great day. Thanks."

"Me too, Thomas. I haven't hung out with someone like this in forever."

"It's been a long time for me as well."

They sat there, working on their milk shakes, as the sun beat down on them. It felt wonderful. It was definitely a good day.

* * *

That afternoon they decided to go play some miniature golf. They goofed off the entire time and carried on as if the weight of the world didn't matter. Back at Laura's house they started drinking beer as they worked on dinner. During the meal they switched over to wine. During the next four hours, while they chatted, the third bottle was finished. Laura and Thomas eventually stumbled to bed, promptly fell asleep draped in each other's arms, very happy their day had turned out so well.

302

43
Sunday July 22 1990 10:15 a.m.

A knock came on the door.

"Come in."

Mr. Peterson opened the door, stepped in with two men dressed in lab coats behind him. Mr. Glib looked up from his desk at them. They both looked very nervous.

"Sitrep?"

"We have final confirmation, sir," Mr. Peterson said. "It's ready."

"Is this true, gentlemen?" Mr. Glib asked the two scientists.

Jack Thompson and Steve Hodgson were the two senior scientists that had signed on to the project years ago. They were the last two scientists that had been retained, and quite coincidently, the last two that were alive. They were beyond nervous; paranoia had set in. The other sixteen scientists had never returned from their vacations. Steve and Jack didn't know whether to think their colleges were dead or alive. However, between the two of them they knew better.

Jack stepped forward. "Yes, sir. The final test phase has been completed. We're done."

Mr. Glib slowly stood up. "We're done? Did you just say that we're done?"

Jack stood frozen in place. He'd experienced this before.

"I've finally completed my dream and you want to take credit for it?"

"No, sir. Of course not, sir," stammered Jack. Steve stood next to him, perspiring.

"Mr. Peterson," Mr. Glib snapped.

"Sir?"

"Get these two out of my sight."

"Sir!"

Mr. Peterson put a hand on each of their shoulders and physically twisted them around to face the door. He pushed them out and closed the door behind him.

* * *

"What the fuck are we going to do?" Jack whispered. He and Steve were huddled in one of the empty bedrooms. Jack was visibly shaking.

"No shit, Jack. Keep it together man," Steve said. "We have to get out of here."

"They didn't come back, Steve. They didn't come back."

"It's okay. Just relax and let me think this out." Jack started to cry. "We need a distraction." Steve thought some more. "Stay here, I'm going to the lab."

* * *

"Mr. Peterson."

"Sir?"

"What's the status of operation Charlie Whiskey?"

"A few more days of observation sir and it'll be primed."

"Perfect."

* * *

"Are you up for this?"

"Like I have a fucking option, Steve!"

"We either do this or we're dead anyway, Jack."

304

"Fuck."

"Ready?" Steve asked.

"No, not really."

Steve and Jack left the common area and headed up stairs to the lab. The place was empty and deserted. It was an eerie feeling as they walked up another flight of stairs towards the main elevator area. It was the only way out. The two armed guards that were typically stationed there had been reduced to one in the past two days. They could sense the myriad of surveillance cameras tracking them as they progressed. Steve glanced over to Mr. Glib's office. The desk behind the glass wall was empty.

Weird.

As they approached the glassed off elevator the guard stepped out in to the hallway and blocked their advance.

"Gentlemen, you know the rules. This area is restricted."

The guard wasn't worried about a couple of dweebs and placed his hand on his holstered weapon. Steve and Jack came to an abrupt halt a few feet away. The guard noticed that one of the dweebs had his fists clenched. Jack and Steve looked at each other and then suddenly rushed the guard, knocking him down. They stepped back and pulled damp hand towels out of their lab coats. The guard had recovered and un-holstered his weapon but Steve raised his right hand and threw a small vial to the ground. It exploded and the immediate area filled with smoke. They could hear the guard cough and gag. The wet towels were tough to breathe through as they worked their way around the downed guard and in to the glassed elevator room.

"Fuck. My eyes hurt," Jack cried.

Steve was hardly paying attention. He had to get out of here, the titanium tetrachloride diversion wouldn't last long and who knows what army waited for them in the lobby above. Steve had quickly made up a batch in the lab after coming up with the plan to escape. He pulled out his keycard and swiped. Thankfully the elevator was ready and the doors opened right away. Steve entered, swiped again and pressed the lobby button.

"Get your ass in here, Jack! Move goddammit!!"

Jack stumbled to the elevator door. His eyes were red and tears streamed down his face. Steve pulled Jack into the elevator as the doors started closing. Three rapid shots rang out and hit Jack in the back. The momentum carried him to the rear of the elevator where he slammed into the wall. He crumpled to the elevator floor in a heap, dead. The doors closed and Steve felt the elevator start to rise.

"Fuckfuckfuckfuck!"

Steve dropped his wet towel and breathed in the fresh elevator air as the lobby rapidly approached. The elevator stopped and the doors slid open. Steve waited a few seconds and then peaked out. It was empty.

Guess they didn't get a chance to sound the alarm yet.

Steve exited and walked as casually as he could, breathing deeply, to the security station in the lobby. Two security personnel were on duty and didn't look twice at him. He swiped his card and then exited the building. He knew his car was parked in the back parking lot but he didn't want to waste any time. For all he knew the battery was long dead after sitting there for the past year.

Steve tried to control his breathing and walked over to the perimeter fence guard shack.

"Can I help you, sir?" asked the security guard inside.

"No, thank you. Just heading out to get a bite to eat around the corner," Steve said.

"The closest food is half a mile away, sir."

"I've got a large appetite tonight."

Very good, sir. Have a good evening."

The guard popped the security gate and it swung open. Steve walked through it and never looked back.

* * *

A number of blocks later Steve hailed a cab. He had ditched his coat as soon as he was out of sight of RHP. He wasn't going to be able to sleep for a long time.

Everything will be fine if I just keep to the plan.

The cab lumbered on into the night.

44
Saturday July 5, 1986 3:30 p.m.

The Continental flight landed on time at 1:45 p.m. at San Francisco International. Dressed in jeans and a polo shirt Thomas wasted no time in retrieving his carry-on and exiting the plane. He knew he didn't have a lot of time before the wedding started as he headed to obtain a rental car. Twenty minutes later Thomas left the airport, drove north on 101, Cut west over 380 and then north on 280 towards San Francisco. 280 became CA-1 and Thomas followed the signs along 19th Ave towards the Golden Gate Bridge. Traffic was lighter than Thomas remembered, but then again, it had been years since Thomas had driven through San Francisco. He was glad he took 19th rather than taking Van Ness through the city. He knew he'd saved time.

The weather was absolutely beautiful, and the view equally stunning, as Thomas crossed the Golden Gate bridge. He drove through the tunnel at the top of the hill and eventually exited at Spencer Ave. He made his way down to the water and found a parking spot close to the Spinnaker. The time was 2:57 p.m.. He got out, grabbed his carry-on and headed towards the restaurant. At the door he identified himself and was shown where Bill and Sam were waiting.

"Holy shit, Thomas, we didn't think you were going to make it," said Bill who came up and gave his friend a hug.

"Good to see you too, bro," Thomas replied.

"Well, well, well, look who decided to show up." Thomas turned around and saw Sam with a huge grin on his face. "Come here." Sam bear hugged Thomas. "Really good to see you."

"Wouldn't miss it for the world," Thomas barely managed to breathe out. Sam let go.

"We missed you last night, Thomas," Bill said. "A few us of visited the Hustler club for our last free night. As the best man you should have been there, bro."

"Sorry about that. I got hung up."

"Leave the man alone, Bill, he has a right to squat up on that mountain of his, all alone, and miss out on all the grinding that took place last night," Sam said. "Of course if you mention a word of that to our future wives I'm afraid no one will find your body." Sam smiled.

"Speaking of women," Bill interjected, "I don't believe you've met ours. We'd introduce you but the ceremony is starting soon, and with the bad luck and all. Hurry up and change."

Thomas changed in to his suit that he'd brought and was ready to go in a few minutes. The guests were gathering so Bill and Sam headed out to greet them. Thomas went looking for the brides. After a little investigating Thomas found what room they were in and politely knocked on their door.

"Yes?"

"Hi. My name is Thomas Clark. I'm the best man. May I come in?" Thomas said through the door. The door cracked open and a myriad of women, of various ages, were inside.

"Please come in, Thomas. My name is Kim Roads," she said as she let him in and closed the door behind him. "My sister Julie is the other bride to be."

"Pleased to meet you both."

"We've heard a lot about the mysterious Thomas Clark," Julie said. "Let us get a good look at you."

Both of them were in their wedding gowns. The final touches to their primping were taking place around them.

"Go ahead and do a spin for us," Kim said.

"A spin?" he asked.

"You know, a spin," Kim repeated as she twirled her finger in the air to illustrate. Thomas blushed.

"How cute," Julie said. "No wonder the boys love him so much."

"We're just kidding, Thomas," Kim said smiling. "Bill asked us to mess with you a bit. It's very nice to meet you too."

I'm going to kill him. Thomas relaxed. "So you're sisters?"

"Guilty as charged," Julie replied. "Twin sisters to be exact."

"This is quite a production then."

"A double wedding, you mean?" Kim inquired. Thomas nodded. "Actually, it's what we've wanted since we were little girls. The only hard part was meeting the right men. I think we got really lucky there."

"Bill and Sam are two of the nicest guys I know. But I'm a bit biased since I grew up with them."

"How long are you in town Thomas?" Julie asked.

"I leave tomorrow."

"Oh, that's no good. You'll need to change that. Bill and Sam haven't seen you in a long time. You can't skip out that quickly. We'll talk about it later tonight. Sorry to chat and run but we're about to head down the aisle."

"That we are," Kim confirmed. "Thanks for coming by, Thomas." Kim opened the door and Thomas walked out.

Wow, those two are a handful.

Thomas made his way back to the main area and the view hit him. The entire room contained floor to ceiling windows. Angel Island, Alcatraz, the Bay Bridge and San Francisco were all visible within this room.

Nice location guys.

"Hey, Thomas." Bill walked up to him. "Sam's still schmoozing the guests. Did you meet our ladies?"

"Remind me to kill you later," Thomas replied.

"Heh heh. Sorry about that, I couldn't resist."

"They're great, Bill. Congratulations."

"Thanks, Thomas. We're really glad you're here. It's been too long." Bill paused. "Anyway, the ceremony is beginning soon. We'll talk later, bro." Bill took off to collect Sam.

* * *

The wedding was amazing. The sunlight was perfect and backlit the ceremony. Both Kim and Julie glowed.

"I now pronounce you man and wife. You may kiss the bride."

Sam and Bill did just that.

45

Sunday July 22, 1990 10:30 a.m.

When Thomas and Laura finally woke around 8:30 a.m. they were still tired. Laura rolled on her side and Thomas spooned her. They fell back to sleep in no time. Two hours later they woke up again.

"Good morning," Laura whispered.

"We have to stop meeting like this," Thomas kidded.

"I know. It's downright sinful," said Laura as she played along.

"What would people think?"

"Totally. We have to stop," Laura said.

"What was your name again?"

"I don't remember yours either. Just take me already."

And with that their morning stretched even closer to noon.

* * *

Thomas left her house shortly after 12 p.m.. Their frolicking in bed soon turned into them frolicking in the shower.

Nothing like a morning romp to get the day started.

Thomas drove though Running Springs; he was almost home. As he turned into his driveway he noticed, once again, that a specific area of his garden was out of place. He'd been reluctant to fix it but he was feeling better about himself and the recent events in his life.

Time to play in the garden.

After changing he headed back to the garage and grabbed his gardening supplies. It was hot out but he only planned on tidying up the garden and not spending the entire day on it. He walked closer to the hole that had contained the axe, paused and stared at it. It had been two weeks since he'd found that axe and convinced himself he was a murderer; two weeks since his entire life had changed dramatically; two weeks since he'd started the painful process of taking control of his life; two weeks since he'd met Laura and fallen in love.

Love? Did I just admit to myself that I love Laura?

As Thomas started to work on the gaping hole he found himself smiling. Laura was fantastic. She made him laugh and cry. He wanted to be around her and missed her when they were apart. Life was definitely taking a turn for the better.

As he dug in the soil, filling in the hole and reordering his flowers, his mind continued to meander. His birthday was five days away. Every year he did his best to ignore that hateful day. He typically disregarded everyone and hid away, not wanting to remember. However, this year's birthday started to look hopeful. Laura wanted to spend it with Thomas, out of town, and with all the progress he felt he'd made the trip sounded like a great idea. He knew he had a long way to go before his life would feel normal, but he was hopeful for the future.

As he finished up he started to think about his mother and the brief time he'd had with her in his life. It was the same feeling he'd had for his father.

I wonder what my grandparents are up to?

Thomas cleaned up and took all the tools back to the garage and stored them. He headed upstairs and took a quick shower to rinse off the dirt and the slight sheen he'd acquired while being out in the sun. Afterwards he dressed, picked up the phone on his desk, and dialed.

"Clark residence," his grandmother answered.

"Hi, grandma."

314

"Thomas! How are you? We were just talking about you." Thomas could hear his grandmother cup the phone and talk loudly. "Ed. Ed, it's Thomas." She came back on the line. "Thomas, let me get your grandfather." She put the phone down and then heard it being picked back up.

"Thomas?"

"Hey, grandpa."

"We were just talking about you."

"That's what grandma was just saying. Good things I hope."

"Always the kidder," Ed said and then added, "What're your plans next week?"

"I have a few things going on. Is there a problem?"

"No. Nothing like that. Your grandmother and I would like to have you visit sooner than later is all. We have some paperwork for you to sign and, well, your birthday is next Friday."

Thomas paused for a second. His typical reaction would have been to avoid seeing them around this time of year. However, Thomas caught himself and said, "I'd love to see you both. I'll make the reservation as soon as I get off the phone. I can arrive on Tuesday if that will work?"

"Claire, Thomas says he can be here Tuesday." He heard his grandmother in the background saying something but he couldn't hear it. "She says that'll be fine and she can't wait to see you."

"I can't wait to see you two either. Love you, grandpa."

"Love you too, son."

Thomas hung up the phone. *Paperwork? I wonder what that's all about?*

Thomas looked up United's number in the phone book and made the plane reservation to SFO for Tuesday morning. Afterwards he called Hertz for a rental reservation.

It's going to be a busy week.

315

46

Monday July 23, 1990 2:30 p.m.

"Hi, Laura," Thomas said as he entered her office. He wanted to go over and give her a big hug but knew this wasn't the time or place for it.

"Hello, Thomas." Laura had to resist the urge to kiss him. It was distracting.

Thomas noticed that the video camera was setup. As he sat down he pointed to it and commented, "So, another session?"

Laura sat down in her chair. "We need to keep delving in to your mind, Thomas. I'll steer away from Nigel this time around and work a different angle."

"Okay. Oh, before I forget, I talked with my grandparents yesterday. They wanted me to visit right away. There's something to do with signing paperwork or something like that. They weren't really clear. Anyway, I'm flying out tomorrow morning for a couple of days."

"Has it been awhile since you've seen them?"

"Unfortunately. I haven't been on the ball with keeping in touch with friends and family." Thomas paused and then smiled. "But that's changing."

Laura liked it when Thomas smiled. "So we're still on for your birthday weekend?"

"Definitely. It's going to be a busy week, that's for sure. I'll be back in town Thursday. We can leave town Friday afternoon, if your schedule permits."

Laura had pulled out her daily planner. "I think that'll work. I have two appointments on Friday but the last one should be finished by two. Sounds like we're set." Laura smiled.

"I can't wait," Thomas said.

"Neither can I." Laura sat there and just stared at Thomas. *I'm really lucky.* "Shall we begin Thomas?"

He took his time before answering. "Time to get this party started."

* * *

Everything around him was blurry. Tommy drifted from one person to another. *Where am I? Who are these people? What are they saying to me?* He heard whispering all around him. Someone grabbed his hand. Tommy looked up and saw his father standing there looking down at him.

"It'll be okay," his father said.

"I want to see mommy," Tommy said.

"She's over here." His father led Tommy through the blurry atmosphere until a coffin materialized in front of them. "Your mother is in here."

"But I want to see her," Tommy insisted.

His father knelt down to his son's level. "I'm afraid that's not possible."

"Why?"

"Because your mother is horribly disfigured, broken and battered. She is dead Tommy. She's dead Tommy! SHE'S DEAD TOMMY!"

* * *

What the hell? Laura could only watch as Thomas thrashed his head back and forth in his chair. He was mumbling incoherently. *This shouldn't be happening.*

318

* * *

Tommy ran screaming into the blurry fog. His father's yelling retreated in the background. He was alone again. The darkness was all around him, closing in. Tommy kept running; his breathing ragged. A dull light formed in the distance. Tommy moved towards it. The darkness was right behind.

"I'm sorry for your loss, Tommy," a stranger told him.

"Me too," someone else said.

"Me too. Me too. Me too. Me too."

Voices assaulted Tommy from all sides. It was too much to take.

* * *

Thomas was agitated and practically non responsive. Laura tried to soothe him; tell him that nothing could hurt him. He wasn't able to hear her.

* * *

The voices were closer than ever. They were like buzzing insects that he couldn't see. It was too much! A hand grabbed his. Instantly everything went silent.

* * *

Laura was about to invoke the safety phrase when Thomas stopped. He became very still. His eyes rapidly moved beneath his closed eyelids.

* * *

Tommy looked up. His grandfather was eyeing him.

"It'll be okay."

"I want to see, daddy."

"He's over here." His grandfather guided Tommy towards a closed coffin that sat high on a pedestal. "Your father is in here."

"But I want to see him."

His grandfather took a knee and looked in to Tommy's eyes. "I'm afraid that's not possible Tommy."

"Why?"

"You know why."

* * *

Thomas abruptly opened his eyes and saw Laura hovering over him, concerned. He was sweating profusely and his skin was clammy. He looked her square in the eyes.

"What the hell was that?"

"Are you alright?" she quickly asked.

Thomas wiped his forehead. It came away damp.

"Are you okay, Thomas?"

He sat there, stunned, regaining his strength.

"Do you know where you are?"

He looked around. "I'm in your office now. A little while ago I was at my parent's funerals."

Laura grabbed a bottle of water, brought it over to Thomas and handed it to him. He opened it up and drank deeply as she sat down.

"Are you sure you're okay?" she cautiously asked.

320

"I'm getting there. Anything's better than having a nightmare."

"Nightmare?"

"I'll fucking say. Anything's better than having my father scream at me about my dead mother. That fucking never happened. It was horrible. And all the voices that I couldn't get away from. What the hell, Laura?"

"I don't understand, Thomas. I'm sorry. I hadn't regressed you to that memory."

"Memory? My father never spoke to me that way, ever. This wasn't a memory, it was a goddamn nightmare."

It was Laura's turn to be quiet. She sat there, thinking, while Thomas calmed down.

How is this possible? Why was he at his parent's funeral? Those events were five years apart.

Laura had regressed Thomas back to his childhood, to get an idea of his home life. The interaction between his parents was key and Laura needed to experience it. Yet somehow the memory had veered off course, on its own, and ended up with Thomas at their funeral.

Laura spoke up. "Thomas." He looked over at her. "I don't know what to say. Your regression wasn't even in the neighborhood of the funerals."

"Then how?"

"I don't know. It was proceeding just fine when all of a sudden you were just gone; mumbling and unresponsive. I almost had to uses the safe phrase, but you opened your eyes right before I could."

He pondered what she had just told him. "So what you're telling me is that not only did I have a recollection that never existed, it just happened to be a nightmare? On top of that, I snapped out of hypnosis on my own?"

"Do you want to talk about it?"

"Seriously, Laura? You've got to be kidding me."

"I'm sorry, Thomas. I know you're upset. What you just went through couldn't have been easy."

"It fucking sucked, okay!"

"All I'm saying is that it happened for a reason." Thomas glared at Laura. "I know. I know. Just hear me out for a second. With all the memories, experiences and weird shit that has been happening to you in the past month, this moment must have something to do with it. So instead of fighting me on this one, just tell me what happened so we can work through this together."

Thomas was angry and disturbed. His father's words had bitten deep in to him. *But they weren't my father. He never said those things.* He took another drink of water.

"Sorry, Laura. I overreacted."

"I understand, Thomas. Traumatic events, however perceived, spin people up."

"Talk about being spun like a top. I feel exhausted."

Laura waited a few seconds and then asked, "What happened?"

Thomas sat back and tried to shake the images from his head. "I don't know if I can."

"Try," she persisted.

Thomas struggled. "All I have now are images of my father at the funeral. He's telling me my mother is dead. He's yelling at me about it. He's screaming that her body is broken and battered!" Thomas shook. "He won't stop yelling. He won't stop." He started to cry.

"It'll be okay," she said.

His head snapped up immediately and he stared directly at Laura. *No fucking way.* He got up and fled her office.

47
Friday October 14, 1988 11:30 a.m.

"Good morning, Sandbox Enterprises. How can I direct your call?"

"Um, hi. This is Thomas Clark, Bill's friend. Is he around?"

"Of course Mr. Clark. Let me transfer you."

Thomas heard a few clicks and then Bill's familiar voice. "Well well well. Who do we have here? How the fuck are you, Thomas?"

"Happy 31st birthday, Bill."

"Tommy boy. Good to hear from you, and thanks. With everything going on apparently thirty-one snuck up on me this year," Bill replied.

"How's Kim?"

"The wife just gave birth, can you believe that shit? I'm a dad."

"Congrats."

"Course, you'd know these things if you called more often," he razzed.

"Guilty as charged," Thomas acknowledged. "I suck at keeping in touch. It doesn't mean I don't miss you guys."

"We miss you too, brother. Speaking of, let me see if I can track that sonofabitch down. Gimme a sec." Thomas heard the phone being put down and then a few shouts in the distance. A minute later it was picked back up. "He's on his way," Bill said. "Hurry the fuck up!" he yelled.

Click. "Holy shit balls, this had better be good," said Sam as he came on the line.

"Our little brother decided to give me a call on my birthday."

325

"So that's what it takes to get hold of the infamous Thomas Clark these days," Sam said as he chuckled. "How are you?"

"You guys suck the big one," Thomas answered. Sam and Bill started to laugh.

"We just call it like we see it," Bill said.

"Yeah, we almost sent out a search and rescue for you," added Sam.

"Do you guys come up with your own material or what? No wonder I don't call," Thomas joked.

"You'll live," Sam said. "I'm sure Bill appreciates at least someone remembering his birthday."

"You stow that shit, Sam. Kim just made me a daddy; she gets a pass this year."

"Easy there, Ranger," Sam said. "You see what happens to a man when his wife forgets his birthday, Thomas; gets his panties all tied up in a knot." Sam started laughing.

"Sam, you're a dead man," Bill kidded.

"I'll take my chances, Billy." Sam paused. "Anyway. Thomas, what're you up to these days? Mountains still treating you well?"

Thomas always loved the banter that Sam and Bill provided. The eight years they had spent together in the Army, the majority as Rangers, bonded them closer than Thomas would ever know. They were his best friends and he missed them dearly.

"Well, my next book is coming out in a couple of months."

"Let me guess the title on this one," Bill said. "Hmmm, what about 'Thomas does Dallas'?"

"Naw," Sam added. "It's got to be something more artistic like 'The Moon is White'."

Thomas enjoyed their needling. "Do you assholes need a third guess?"

"Aw fuck it, Thomas. What's this one called?" Bill asked.

"The Little Brown Chair."

"No shit," Sam said.

"Quite the mouthful. What about my unborn daughter. Will she like it?" Bill asked.

"She'll have you reading it so many times you'll be cursing my name on a daily basis," Thomas said as he poked fun.

"Will you listen to this fucking guy, Sam. We've got a monster on our hands."

"You'll live, Bill. Besides, this fucking guy is our underwriter, so show Dick some respect."

"Nice, Sam. A little Breakfast Club quotage," Thomas said.

"I do what I can, Thomas," said Sam. "On a serious note, and I'm mostly talking to you Bill, Sandbox is building up very nicely, no pun intended."

"Fuck you too, Sam. But he's right, Thomas; Sandbox is on its way to greatness."

"Just give me the highlights guys," Thomas said.

Sam cleared his throat. "Well roughly three years ago, when Sandbox was founded thanks to you, we've been busy," Sam explained. "We acquired five acres in the Marin headlands for our facility. It's off the beaten path so we're private. We have office space and a training facility that includes an underground firing range and armory. We also have a motor pool."

"Sounds cozy," Thomas commented.

"While we were building up we started with small protection jobs that Bill and I could handle by ourselves. As we neared completion, and our reputation spread, we hired on four additional operators and our secretary. We're gaining momentum here, Thomas. All thanks to you."

Thomas appreciated the comment. "It's the least I could do for you guys. You've always been there for me. To see your dream come to fruition just brings a smile to my face."

"You're going to have to make a trip up here at some point, Thomas," Bill said. "You can't hide forever."

"Bill's right. But knowing you we'll have to come down to the LA area and kidnap your ass because you'll never make it up here."

"Well, the new book is coming out and I might have to make the circuit rounds again. That'll take some time. All depends on how Nick wants to market it."

"Told you," Bill told Sam.

"Let' try another angle. Thomas, what's the name of my little baby girl?" Sam asked.

Oh shit. What was her name? "Amanda?"

"Are you guessing her name or are you telling me?"

"It's Amanda, Sam."

"No shit her name is Amanda, Thomas. The issue is if she only has Bill as her uncle she's going to be pretty fucked up." Thomas laughed.

"Seriously, Sam, you're a dead man," Bill interjected.

Sam continued. "So you'd better get your ass up here one of these days so we actually remember what you look like."

"When you do visit," Bill said, "it'll only be me. Sam will be buried in an unmarked grave by then." They all chuckled.

"I'm sorry I haven't visited. You guys are my best friends. Maybe one of these days I'll figure everything out."

"You do that, Thomas," Sam said. "We'll be here when you're ready."

"What Sam just said, Thomas. Hell, even our mission statement is relevant to your situation."

"And what's that, Bill," Thomas inquired.

Bill turned on his professional voice and said, "SANDBOX Enterprises, becoming anything you need."

"You need anything, Thomas, just give us a holler," Sam added. "We've got to go bro. We have potential clients on hold."

"Time to go pay the bills. See you, Thomas, and thanks for the happy birthday call."

"Bye guys."

The line went dead.

48

Tuesday July 24, 1990 3:30 a.m.

The alarm clock woke Thomas at 3:30 a.m.. He knew he had
to hurry because the drive to Ontario airport was going to take
some time. And he still had to pack, drive down the mountain and
get checked in before his flight took off at 6:15 a.m.. He groaned,
turned off his alarm, rolled out of bed and jumped in the shower.

The session with Laura, the day before, still weighed heavily
on his mind. The raw, unabridged image of his father yelling at
him sent shivers down his back. When Laura had said that
everything would be okay he bolted from her office because
Thomas had felt extremely uncomfortable. As soon as he got
home he ignored his answering machine and unplugged his
phones.

*I was too hard on Laura. I panicked. God, I suck. I'll call her
later.*

Thomas exited the shower and finished prepping for his short
trip as he put things he needed in a carry-on. It was still pitch
black when he armed the code to his house and left in his BMW.
The time was 4:15 a.m..

The drive down CA-330 went by fairly quickly and there was
no one else on the road to slow him down. When he reached the
base of the mountain he turned south on I-210 for a few miles and
then took I-10 west. Twenty-four miles later he arrived at the
airport. Thomas parked in long term, waited for a shuttle, and
eventually got to the United check-in.

"May I help you?" asked the woman behind the counter.

"Good morning. I'm on a flight to San Fran."

"Identification please."

Thomas opened his wallet and handed over his license.

"Are you checking any luggage?"

"No."

"I see. Have your bags left your possession or have you been asked by anyone to carry something for them?"

"No."

"Thank you, Mr. Clark. I see you're booked for a returning flight on Thursday morning at ten-thirty-five. You're sitting in row fifteen F. That's a window seat. Would you like to upgrade to first class for thirty-nine dollars?"

"No, thank you."

"Alrighty, Mr. Clark. Here's your ID and ticket." She handed them both to him.

"Thank you."

"Is there anything else I can do for you?"

"No, thank you very much."

"You're welcome. The security gate is around the corner to the right. You'll find your boarding gate on your ticket. Thank you for flying United."

Thomas turned around and headed for security. The time was 5:34 a.m.. His flight was going to board in twenty minutes.

* * *

The flight from Ontario to SFO International had been routine and Thomas had even managed to lean against the window to get a little shuteye for the hour and fifteen minute flight. San Francisco Airport was notorious for being fogged in and this particular morning was no exception. The good news was that it wasn't too thick so they weren't diverting flights to one specific runway. The flight taxied to the gate and everyone departed. Thomas bee-lined for the Hertz rental car desk and bypassed the majority of the passengers that headed towards baggage claim. The time was 7:42am.

Thomas went through the polite, but long process of obtaining a rental car. Eventually he'd initialed and signed as much as he could stand before heading off to locate the assigned vehicle. He had chosen a Buick Regal, but Thomas missed his 325i already. He followed the appropriate signs, found the floor where the rentals were kept, located the car, inspected it for damages and checked out. He drove off towards Highway 101. The time was 8:03am.

Thomas knew it'd be shorter if he headed north towards San Francisco, across the Bay Bridge and on towards Walnut Creek. But it was Tuesday morning and the work commute was well under way. Thomas headed south on 101. The reverse commute would take more miles but it'd get him to Rossmoor faster. There were plenty of cars on the road but at least he was moving, unlike the northbound lanes that seemed to be standing still.

CA-92 rapidly approached and Thomas merged into the right lane and then banked left to head east onto CA-92. A few miles later it turned into a bridge; one of the four bridges that spanned the Bay. Thomas hadn't seen the ocean for a few years. It was beautiful. Eventually he came across I-880 and exited north. Three miles later he turned on to I-238 which quickly became I-580. He kept traveling east. Nine miles later he turned north onto I-680. The drive was peaceful enough even though here were plenty of cars out heading to work. Thomas didn't envy these people who drove miles and miles every day to a job they probably hated. Fifteen miles later he took the Olympic Blvd exit and turned left. A couple miles later he took another left on Tice Valley Blvd and then down Rossmoor Pkwy. Thomas rolled to a stop at the Visitor's gate. The time was 9:25 a.m..

"How can I help you?" asked the guard.

"Thomas Clark to see Ed Clark."

"The guard typed on his keyboard and smiled. "Go right ahead." The barricade swung up.

"Thanks."

Thomas drove down the familiar streets of Rossmoor. His grandparents had moved here fifteen years ago. *Well, it'll be fifteen years as soon as I turn thirty three on Friday.* The main golf course took up the center of the valley. Tennis courts came in to view. He turned right after the courts and saw a number of people hitting golf balls on the driving range and chuckled. His rental Buick would have fit in just fine here at Rossmoor. He continued past the stop sign, up the hill, and pulled in to his grandparent's driveway.

Thomas put the car in park and stepped out. It had been a long day of travelling already and he stretched his legs.

"Well I'll be."

Thomas turned and saw his grandfather walking towards him from the side of the house.

"Hi grandpa." They hugged.

"The flight was okay?"

"No issues at all."

"Good. Good," said Ed. "Come on in, your grandmother's waiting to see you."

Ed led the way back down the side of the house. Thomas lugged his carry-on and followed behind as Ed closed the door behind him. A delicious smell assaulted his senses.

"Thomas," his grandmother said as she came over, "so good to see you." She gave him a great big hug. "You worry us silly living up there in the mountains all by yourself."

334

"Now dear, now's not the time to get in to that. The boy just arrived and already you're hounding him."

"Oh shush, Ed. Thomas needs a little reality check now and then." Ed grumbled.

Thomas had been lucky growing up with them after his father passed away when he was ten. There was a lot of love in this house but his grandmother also didn't take any nonsense.

"Have you eaten?" she asked.

"I've been up since three-thirty this morning. I hadn't thought about it until you just said something. I'm famished."

"Good. We were just about to sit down for breakfast. Put your things in the guest room and wash your hands."

There was no use arguing with his grandmother so Thomas took his bag down the hall, opened the door to the guest room and walked in. He had visited many times before and had always stayed in this same room. It had a private bath attached to it. Thomas washed his hands then splashed water on his face before he dried himself off with a hand towel. He headed back to the breakfast area. A plate of food waited for him at the table. It contained eggs, mixed with cheese, bacon and toast. Butter was on the table, along with a few selections of jams. Three glasses of orange juice were already on the table. Thomas took a seat.

"This smells delicious, grandma."

"It'd better," she countered. "I cooked it."

"Don't encourage her, Thomas," Ed joked. Thomas smiled.

"I'll come over there and whack you with this spatula, Ed, mark my words."

Claire smiled as she brought over a plate for Ed and herself. She sat down, obviously very pleased with herself.

"Well dig in, Thomas," she offered.

335

Thomas picked up the pepper, doused it over his eggs and put it back on the table. Then he grabbed some butter for his toast and spread it over the two slices to let it sink it. He started in on his eggs and they were outstanding.

Ed spoke up first after a few minutes. "I bet you're wondering why we asked you to come up here."

Thomas finished swallowing the bacon he was chewing on. "The thought had crossed my mind, grandpa."

Thomas caught his grandfather stealing a glance towards Claire. "As it turns out, getting older doesn't always mean things get easier, Thomas. Your grandmother and I are eighty-three."

Thomas was very attentive now. "Is there a health issue?"

"No, Thomas, nothing like that," his grandmother chimed in. "We expect to live for a long time. We just need to plan ahead properly."

Ed continued. "What your grandmother is trying to say is that the paperwork I mentioned on the phone is about our power of attorney. In case something happens to one or both of us we need to make sure we're covered."

"Okay," Thomas said hesitantly.

"We'll be giving you a stack of documents, Thomas. The PoA, our Will, financial information, etc. Basically the whole kit and caboodle."

"It sounds like you've really thought this out," Thomas said.

"Growing old always comes at the most inopportune time," Ed said. They all smiled.

"I don't know if I ever thanked both of you for taking me in."

Claire rose from the table and started to gather the dishes. "Don't you worry about that, Thomas. You're family. Of course we took you in."

"And," Ed started, "we'd do it again in a heartbeat. When we lost our son, and you lost your father, we only wanted to keep you safe."

Ed and Claire shot glances towards each other. Claire took the dishes to the kitchen.

"I know, grandpa. The whole world was so topsy-turvy for me when dad died. There are so many things I don't know about him."

"Such as?" Ed asked.

"Well, the biggest question I have is where did all the money come from?"

Ed sat back in his chair. "That is a good question. I don't have an answer for you."

"What do you mean?"

"I never knew either." Ed took a breath. "Your father set us up financially, like he did for you. Your grandmother and I were completely caught off guard."

"I'll say," Claire said from the kitchen.

"Anyway, after getting over our shock we asked him the same question."

"What'd he say?" Thomas asked.

"Your father looked us square in the eye and said he couldn't tell us."

"What? What does that mean?"

"We immediately thought that it was dirty money," said Ed. "We…well, I...accused him of it. Do you know what your father did?" Thomas shook his head. "Your father smiled at us. He smiled and said 'Pop, it's not illegal and it's not dirty, I just can't talk about it'. And that was it; we never brought the subject up again."

"And you believed him?"

337

"Thomas, he was our son. Of course we believed him."

Claire came back over to the table, sat down and said, "Nobody knows about it, Thomas. We haven't flaunted it and neither have you. Why is that?"

It was Thomas' turn to sit back. "I don't know. I guess I didn't want people hanging around me for the money." He paused. "I just wanted to be left alone."

"Does your remote lifestyle work for you?" his grandmother asked.

He looked at this grandmother. "It used to."

"And now?" Ed asked.

"Now…, now I'm just lonely." Thomas started to tear up.

Claire noticed. "We didn't mean to prod. You've had us worried for years now, living up there all alone, writing your books."

"It's okay, grandma. You're not the only one. Sam and Bill have been riding my ass pretty hard about it. Nick gave me an earful as well. But something has changed."

"Oh?"

Thomas swallowed visibly. "I've been seeing a shrink. A psychiatrist." His grandparents looked at each other and then back at Thomas. "Her name is Dr. Laura Bond. She started helping me out with these nightmares I've been having."

"Nightmares?" said Claire. "Are you alright?"

It's now or never. "Not even close."

Thomas took the next half hour detailing the past month's events. They listened intently and didn't interrupt.

"That's a lot to take in," his grandfather said.

"Are you okay, sweetie?"

338

"I'm getting there, grandma. Laura's really been helping me out." Thomas stopped but then added, "We've started seeing each other."

"Your psychiatrist?" Ed asked.

"I know it sounds completely unethical but we make each other happy."

His grandmother took Thomas' hand in hers. "Sweetie, we only want what's best for you. From what you've told us it's amazing you sound as sane as you do. I'm glad you've met someone special. You've needed someone in your life for a long time now."

"What does she think of all this?" his grandfather queried.

"I'm actually not sure about that. If it scares her she's not showing it. Laura's definitely been very supportive."

"You both are very lucky to have found each other," Claire said. "What are you going to do?"

"I have to keep digging, grandma. These suppressed memories, the blood on the walls, the murders and my nightmares. Sometimes it's just too much, but I don't think it's who I am."

"It's not," his grandmother confirmed. "You were too much of a victim. You'd never become what you hated the most."

"I agree with your grandmother. It doesn't make any sense."

"Thank you. I really needed to hear that."

"Well. Why don't I finish up in the kitchen, then we can head to the lawyer's office in a bit and get that out of the way." They all got up and Thomas helped clean up the remaining items on the kitchen table.

"May I use the phone?" Thomas asked.

"Go ahead and use the one in my den," said Ed.

339

"Thanks." Thomas headed in to the den. He picked up the phone and dialed Laura's home phone. It rang a few times and then picked up.

"Hi. I can't come to the phone right now. Please leave a detailed message after the beep. Have a nice day."

Thomas left his message.

* * *

Thomas drove them to the lawyer's office and all the necessary documents had already been laid out for Thomas' signature. The entire process took less than thirty minutes. The lawyer indicated that a copy of everything would be sent out via Fed-Ex the following day.

* * *

After they returned to his grandparent's house they sat down at the kitchen table and pulled out a set of dominos. While growing up Thomas had the privilege of being included in a variety of games including Liar's dice, Monopoly, Risk, Spite and Malice, Hearts and Dominos. He'd surprised them both with his analytical thinking and intelligence back in the days. And Thomas often won. They spent the afternoon playing game after game, snacking along the way. It was just like old times and they had a grand time.

* * *

Thomas drove out of Rossmoor, with his grandparents, again that evening. They were heading out for his pre-birthday dinner, and he had protested but his grandparents insisted. Thomas swung on to I-24 west towards Orinda. This was familiar territory to him because growing up he'd often driven the CA-24/I-680 route from Orinda to Concord. Lafayette and Walnut Creek were the main cities in between. Sam and Bill had joined him on a number of those trips, post driver's license, to head to the Sun Valley Mall. They liked to walk around the mail, but they typically made the trek out there to go ice skating at the indoor rink.

Thomas took the Orinda exit and banked right towards Szechwan, his favorite Chinese restaurant. It had been years since he'd eaten there but he had fond memories of how good the food was, especially the spring rolls. He hugged right and then took a left on to Orinda Way. About a mile down Thomas parked next to the sixteenth fairway, part of the Orinda Country Club golf course, across the street from the restaurant. They all got out, crossed the street, and headed inside Szechwan.

* * *

When Thomas and his grandparents finally got back to their home it was late. They had spent an exorbitant amount of time chatting away at their table, reliving old memories and the good times they'd had together. It couldn't have been a better night out for all of them.

"I'm definitely ready for bed," his grandmother said.

"I'm off to bed myself," said Thomas. "It's been a long day."

"Don't sleep in too much, Thomas," his grandfather added. "After breakfast prepare for a rematch."

Thomas chuckled. "You got it, grandpa. Goodnight. Love you both."

"Goodnight, sweetie. Love you too."

Thomas retired to the guest room and closed the door. Ed and Claire headed towards the master bedroom and closed their door as well. They had started to prepare for bed when Claire couldn't help but blurt out her own thoughts.

"I'm worried about him."

"You and me both," Ed replied.

"With everything he told us…it's…it's just so unbelievable," she said.

"He's tough. He can take it."

"Ed. He's been through so much."

"He lived through his mother dying. He lived through his father dying. He lived through the bully incident at school. Whatever's eating at him he'll figure out and live through that too."

"But…"

"No," Ed gently urged. "He doesn't need to know."

49

Wednesday July 25, 1990 11:25 a.m.

"Flight ninety-three is now arriving at gate three," the female voice announced over the airport intercom.

Sam double checked the arrival monitor. Gate 3 it was. He was dressed in a black pinstripe business suit accompanied by a red tie. He didn't much care for the feel of the outfit, preferring to wear jeans or fatigues, but the client had specifically requested today's apparel. Sam spoke into the microphone at the end of his left hand. A white wire snaked out of his collar that ended in a small speaker in his left ear. A Glock 17 was in a holster on his right hip, concealed by his suit jacket.

"Bravo Two. Sierra One will be securing the package shortly."

"Roger that, Sierra One. I'll keep circling."

Sam and Bill had a client coming in from Dallas today with a need for moderate security. Mr. Hanson was going to be accompanied by a single bodyguard and had requested a small security detail, and vehicle, at his disposal. Mr. Hanson had indicated that he would need an escort while being transported from the airport, to a meeting, and then back to the airport. He had not given the location of the meeting other than saying it would be in San Francisco. Sam and Bill were used to the secrecy; the less people who knew the details of a plan the better its chances of it actually succeeding.

Five minutes later two well-dressed men approached. They both wore identical suits with red ties. Without saying a word Sam stepped out about ten feet in front of them and started to walk towards the vehicle departure area, rather than the arrivals.

"Bravo Two. Sierra One is inbound. ETA?"

"Forty five seconds, Sierra One," Bill's voice crackled in his ear.

Sam continually scanned the area and slowed his pace by a fraction to match Bill's arrival estimate. The two men behind him matched his pace.

So far so good.

Everything appeared normal and in his line of work that would either translate in to business as usual or oh shit, we're about to be attacked. Sam kept the pace, but he needed to keep his hands free so he walked towards the automatic doors. They opened and all three of them exited as if everything was normal. A large black Suburban approached.

"Five seconds," Sam heard in his ear.

Sam cleared the immediate area quickly with his eyes.

Nominal.

The Suburban pulled up quickly and stopped; its windows tinted black. Sam finally turned around and quickly beckoned to the two men as he opened the rear right door. One man entered and the second quickly followed. Sam jumped in and slammed the door.

"Clear," he said loudly.

The vehicle took off. The locks on the doors engaged.

"Mr. Paige, I'm Mr. Greg Hanson," said the man who sat between his bodyguard and Sam.

"Mr. Hanson, nice to meet you. I'll be with you as soon as we're on the freeway, sir."

He continued to scan the crowd and vehicles that dropped people off for flights. Bill, also dressed in a black suit and red tie, drove the Suburban to one of the many freeway exits and headed north on 101 towards San Francisco. Bill was also armed with a Glock 17. On the seat next to him lay a Heckler & Koch MP5

344

9mm submachine gun. It was covered by a newspaper but was easily obtainable. In the center section, behind the main bench where Bill was driving, the seating had been modified into a hardened armory. It contained two additional MP5's, three Glock 17's and enough magazines to last a sustained encounter. There were also a dozen CS and flash bang grenades.

Sam scanned around them one last time. Attempting a hit, while moving at fast speeds, was not recommended unless there was no other choice but the element of surprise was what every combatant strived for. If an attempt on his client's life was going to happen it'd most likely be on the narrow streets of SF instead of on a freeway. They were clear for the moment. He turned and finally looked at the men who sat next to him.

"Good morning, Mr. Hanson, my name is Sam Paige. My associate driving is Bill Nicholson."

Mr. Hanson extended his right hand out to Sam. He had some slight grey in his hair. Sam placed him in his early fifties. "So far Mr. Paige I'm impressed." Sam shook it firmly and released. "My man," Mr. Hanson said as he motioned to his left, "is my personal bodyguard. His name is John." Sam and John gave each other a curt nod and said nothing.

"Nice to meet you, Mr. Hanson," Sam said. "What can we do for you today?"

"You're aware that I have a meeting in San Francisco."

"Yes."

"The location is a small park by the water. China Basin Park."

"What time is the meeting?"

"Noon," Mr. Hanson replied.

Sam looked down at his watch. It read 11:41. "Bill, we need to move. Take 280 till it dumps us off in the city. A few blocks in take a right on third."

"Roger that," Bill replied without taking his eyes off the road and any impending threats.

Sam scanned the area again and then focused back on his client.

"It's going to be close."

"Understood," Mr. Hanson replied.

Sam continued. "While we have a few minutes, would you please fill me in on your particular needs for today? Be specific."

"I'm meeting an unnamed individual at the park. He set up the meeting. I'm told it's an ideal location due to the wind and water barriers. When we arrive John will accompany me. I need you to provide perimeter security."

"Anything else?" Sam asked.

"No."

"I have a few questions then."

"Go ahead."

"Have you received any threats that would necessitate you hiring our services?"

"Why do you ask?"

"Mr. Hanson, with all due respect, do not be coy with me. Instead of flying in on a private jet you decided to take a commercial airliner, mixing in with a shitload of people in a high security area. This nullified you being out in the open and vulnerable if you had utilized a private jet. Secondly, all of us are dressed the same, as requested. This would indicate the possibility that you will be targeted and want to confuse your enemy. Third, the meeting is taking place at noon. We didn't see each other until 11:31. That's barely enough time, if that, to make it to the destination on time. You knew this, sir. So yes, I believe you are potentially expecting something to go down today."

Mr. Hanson smiled. "Very good, Mr. **Paige**. I see your reputation, and your company, earn the respect it garnishes. You are correct. This meeting is very important to the future of my business in Dallas. I have competitors that desire my latest invention. The meeting could not take place over the phone and has to be completed in person."

"I understand, Mr. Hanson. What can you tell me about the man you're meeting?"

"He will be identically dressed as we are and will have a briefcase for me. I will approach, use a coded phrase to identify him and then retrieve the briefcase. We will then head back to the airport immediately."

Bill called out from the front seat. "Two minutes out from two-eighty."

"Roger that," Sam said. He continued talking to Mr. Hanson. "Any other instructions that you were given?"

"No."

"What about the man you're meeting. What about his security?"

"I have no idea."

"Okay. Thank you, Mr. Hanson."

Sam sat back and brought all the known puzzle pieces together in his head. The location was vulnerable to an ambush and his client would be out in the open for a short amount of time. It was a park and the meeting was set during lunch time, so there would be quite a few people out and about, not to mention dog walkers, baby strollers, etc. *What a mess.* On top of that the area only had a couple of egress points in case they needed to bail. *There's not enough time for a shooter to exit the water.* Sam thought about it more. *If anything, if the threat is real, the target be the briefcase. The briefcase.*

"We're on two-eighty now. Estimating five minutes out," Bill said. The time was 11:54.

"Roger that, Bill."

Sam looked over at John. "Are you carrying?"

"No," John replied. "I couldn't carry on a commercial flight."

Sam retrieved a Glock 17 from the armory in front of them. He ejected the full magazine, which contained seventeen rounds, then re-inserted it and racked a round. Mr. Hanson jumped ever so slightly. Sam turned the weapon sideways and handed it to John who accepted it.

Sam motioned towards their security console. "There's a clip-on holster in the top drawer."

John opened the drawer, retrieved a holster and attached it to his right hip, then holstered the Glock.

"Grab another radio setup from the second drawer. Be quick about it." John complied.

"Bill."

"Yeah, Sam?"

"When we arrive let's make this casual. When I call it you'll stop. John, you will exit the left with Mr. Hanson. I will exit right. Bill, you'll then pull forward ten feet, hold and scan with a purpose."

"Roger that."

"Gentlemen," Sam said, "Let's be professional about this. John, your job is Mr. Hanson. Our job is everybody else. Make your exchange and move back towards the vehicle. Do not run unless instructed to. This is just another day in the park, nothing to worry about."

John finished setting up his radio, microphone and earpiece.

"Radio check," Sam said.

"I've got you," said John.

"Two minutes out," said Bill.

Sam turned to Mr. Hanson and John. "Gentlemen, it's almost go time."

The Suburban exited 280 which quickly turned in to King Street. The traffic light at 4th Street was green and they sailed through it as Bill prepared to take a right on 3rd. The light was red and they had to slow down. *We're now a target.* Sam scanned. Bill turned right on to 3rd and continued over the small bridge. China Basin Park was on the left.

Here we go. "Bill, take a left here and head down to the end."

There were a lot of people in the park. *Crap.* Sam could sense that John was nervous. *Maybe he hasn't seen any action.* They were almost at the end.

"Stop." Bill pulled alongside the curb, placed the vehicle in park and left the engine on. He moved his hand to the MP5, pulled it closer to him, thumbed the safety switch off and made sure it was on single fire mode. "Go."

John and Sam opened their doors and stepped out, scanning everything around them. Some people had looked up and then gone about their business, but no one made an obvious move towards them. Mr. Hanson stepped out, closed the door and started to walk into the park. John stayed about five feet behind him and off to his left.

Sam was still scanning and watched them walk away in his peripheral. *No immediate danger.* He closed his door and walked further down the sidewalk as he kept Mr. Hanson at his nine o'clock. He noticed that his client had suddenly deviated from his path and had diverted to his left. Sam quickly checked out where he was intending to go and noticed a man, in a black suit, who stood under a tree about 100 feet away from him.

Sam brought his hand up and said, "Report."

"We're looking good still," Bill said.

"We have our contact," John replied.

"Brave Two, look lively. Find his backup."

"On it."

Sam continued to walk parallel to Mr. Hanson. He looked around and saw three additional men that seemed out of place, aside from them. There was a muscle bound jock, dressed in exercise clothing, sitting on a bench. A big gym bag was right next to him. He seemed to pay more attention to Sam's client than anything else. There was another man, closer to Sam that wore a leather jacket. He was strolling way too slowly, ahead of Sam, and it was a hot July day. The third was stood close to the man Mr. Hanson was walking towards. *What don't I see?*

Sam raised his left wrist and spoke into his radio. "I have two unknowns. Leather jacket in front of me that is walking is Tango One. The big jock on the bench is Tango Two."

"Acknowledged," came Bill's response.

John turned his head slightly but didn't make a move to talk into the mike in his hand so Sam kept walking. He was thirty feet from leather jacket guy who hadn't noticed Sam yet. Mr. Hanson was twenty feet from the gentleman he was about to meet and had a briefcase at his feet. He picked it up as Mr. Hanson came closer and stopped five feet in front of him. Sam noticed the man behind him look around and then speak into his shirt collar. Immediately both Tangos swiveled their heads and identified Sam.

It's not rocket science guys, I'm wearing a matching suit.

Sam kept his distance and didn't make any overt moves, but his Glock was already primed and ready to go and would be in his hands in a split second. He hoped that wasn't the case, not in this crowd. Mr. Hanson started to speak with his contact. John had stood farther back and was keyed in on the other man's shadow.

Bill had taken the Suburban and crept up, now only ten feet behind Sam.

Sam observed Mr. Hanson shake hands with his contact and the briefcase exchanged hands. Sam scanned the area again. He couldn't make anyone else out that was a potential threat or seemed out of place. *Come on, walk over here.* Mr. Hanson turned towards the Suburban and, as instructed, didn't rush at all. John kept his pace.

"Inbound," came John's voice in his earpiece.

Instead of replying Sam kept his eyes trained on the two men as the contact's shadow talked into his shirt collar again. The Tangos visible relaxed and didn't make any moves. Sam's client was fifty feet away now.

A car horn sounded behind the Suburban. It was loud. Sam didn't take his gaze off his client. Thirty-five feet. *A few more seconds.* The environment hadn't changed. Peripherals weren't ringing his alarm bell. Twenty feet. The horn sounded again and someone yelled, "Move it asshole!"

Sam brought his hand up and said, "Pickup." He moved towards Mr. Hanson and let the Suburban come up and shield him from behind. Ten feet. Sam opened the left rear door. Mr. Hanson, with the briefcase and John, climbed in. Sam stole a look at the angry driver behind him and then got in to the vehicle, closing the door behind him.

"Go."

Bill drove down the street and hung a right. They weren't out of danger by any stretch of the imagination now that his client had his package. John moved to the seat by the right window so Mr. Hanson was positioned in the middle again; protected. Mr. Hanson had a death grip on the briefcase handle. Bill drove the speed limit and took a right on Mission Rock Street and then a left

351

on to 3rd Street. Sam and Bill constantly scanned but nothing out of the ordinary happened. Bill took a right on to Mariposa Street and then took the on-ramp to 280 south.

"Thank you, Mr. Paige," Mr. Hanson said. "That went incredibly smoothly."

"We're not out of it yet. Not until you're back in the airport."

"Of course. Of course."

"John, would you please?"

John knew what Sam meant. He removed the communications gear and weapon, cleared it and handed it to Sam.

"Just dump it all in the 2nd drawer if you don't mind." John complied.

"How're we doing, Bill?"

"Looking good up here. We're almost to one-o-one."

"Roger that," Sam replied. He kept his eyes peeled and said, "When we get to the airport, sir, I will exit and close the door behind me. When I give the signal you will both exit out of the right door and come straight to me." They both nodded.

"Turning south on one-o-one," said Bill.

"Is there anything else you require, Mr. Hanson?"

"Seeing you in action is plenty for me, Mr. Paige. Just get me to safety."

Ten minutes passed before Bill took the exit to the San Francisco Airport.

"Head for Arrivals, Bill."

"But we're departing," Mr. Hanson reminded them.

"I know. Never hurts to mix it up on the fly, Mr. Hanson."

Bill followed the signs and pulled up along the curb next to Continental Airlines. People were outside, waiting for their loved ones to pick them up as Sam looked around and got out. He walked behind the Suburban and made a quick threat assessment on each person he saw. Nothing rang any alarms. He made his way to the doorway, took another glance around, and signaled. John popped the door open and the two men piled out quickly and came towards Sam. Sam turned around and entered the airport, bypassing the luggage retrieval areas and proceeded to walk up the stairs rather than taking the escalators. Behind him he could hear Mr. Hanson mumble something. At the top Sam headed towards ticketing and saw that there was only one other person in line. Sam stood back while he watched Mr. Hanson and John enter the ticket line from a distance. In no time Mr. Hanson had his ticket and was headed towards security.

Sam let Mr. Hanson lead while John shadowed his boss. Sam stayed farther back, his job complete once his client made it through security, which seemed light today. Besides, Sam was armed. He was permitted to carry concealed but it didn't give him permission to carry past airport security.

As Sam continued to scan he didn't let his guard down. Everything seemed normal and no one made a grab for Mr. Hanson or the briefcase he carried. Sam watched as they both made it through security and headed down the walkway.

"We're good. Heading out."

"Give me a few minutes, I just drove past you again."

"Roger that."

Sam started to walk back towards the escalators that would take him down to the baggage claim area and back outside, and had just started down the stairs when he froze.

The briefcase.

Sam immediately turned around and walked quickly towards security, but stopped in the nearest bathroom first.

"I have a hunch," he said into the mike.

"Oh crap," Bill replied. "I'm nowhere near you."

"It's okay. It's probably nothing. Going radio silent. I have to get through security."

"Fuck. Roger that. Be careful."

Sam ripped out the wiring and tossed the radio, mike and earpiece in the trash. He pulled out a few paper towels from the dispenser and wrapped his holster, which contained his Glock, and dumped that in the trash as well.

Wonder when they pick up the trash?

He headed towards security and a few minutes later he looked for the gate on the console. Sam located it and headed that way.

It has to be at the end of the fucking terminal.

He didn't run but people noticed that he was passing everyone. Sam turned the corner and came across gate 31A. His eyes took in the crowd.

Where the fuck are they?

He couldn't locate Mr. Hanson. He hadn't passed them on the way and they couldn't be more than four minutes ahead of him, especially the way he had rushed to the gate. Sam scanned again and picked up on the fact that the men's restroom was close by. He headed towards the door, opened it and headed inside. It was empty. There wasn't any sound at all. Sam was about to leave when he heard a scuffle on the floor. Sam rounded the corner and saw Mr. Hanson on the ground. John was kicking him in the gut repeatedly as Sam rushed him. John caught the movement out of the corner of his eye and swiveled to deflect Sam's incoming blow. Sam didn't have time to think about the situation. His client was down and his attacker was still standing.

Deal with the threat.

John was cornered in the back of the bathrooms. He hadn't anticipated Sam following them through security and his plan had been executed with precision. It couldn't have gone any better.

354

But now he had to deal with this security fuck in front of him or he wouldn't get paid.

John lunged at Sam. Sam saw the strike coming towards his face and had discerned that John held some sort of knife. Sam dodged and backed up. John struck again but Sam countered, quickly bringing both hands across John's, chopping at his exposed hand. The weapon clattered to the floor. John didn't like that and kicked out with his right leg. Sam sidestepped right, putting his left foot behind John's left heel as grabbed John's leg with his left arm. Sam pushed back hard. John had overextended himself and was now off balance. He crashed to the ground on his back, the wind knocked out of him. Sam immediately dropped his knee on John's chest and heard at least one rib crack. He turned his assailant over and applied a sleeper hold on him. John was out within seconds.

Mr. Hanson was partially moving, Sam had noticed.

No time for that yet.

Sam took off one of John's shoes and extracted the laces. He hogtied John and then checked on Mr. Hanson. He was breathing, he was just unconscious.

Probably has some bruised ribs.

Sam didn't move him for fear of a potential neck injury. He stood up, left the bathroom and picked up the first white courtesy phone he saw and explained the situation quickly. Airport security was there within forty-five seconds. Sam showed them his credentials but they still placed him in cuffs. A short while later Mr. Hanson came to and quickly explained that Sam was one of the good guys. The cuffs came off right away.

Bill, on the other hand, had not heard from Sam. Police cars lined up outside and had slowed down traffic coming in to the airport. He made several loops before leaving the Suburban in short term parking, along with his weapon, and ventured into the airport. After identifying himself, and showing his credentials, he learned from a police officer that a man had been attacked in a bathroom but they had a suspect in custody. The SF Police were well aware of SANDBOX and let him through to the scene.

"Do you always cause this much of a scene Sam?" Bill stated as he saw Sam and Mr. Hanson in the hallway by gate 31. A few police officers were around. John had been taken to the hospital.

Sam looked up and smiled at Bill. "Only when the situation calls for it, brother."

Mr. Hanson held his chest but the EMT's indicated it was only severe bruising.

"Are you alright, Mr. Hanson?" Bill asked.

"I'll live."

"What about you, Sam? Heard you put the guy in the hospital."

"Julie is going to kill me, but other than that I'm fine. Our guy wasn't a pro and tried taking me on with a sharp porcelain rod. He was about to cut Mr. Hanson's life short so I had to put him down hard and fast. No sweat."

"Nice," Bill said and gave Sam a pat on the back.

"Yes, thank you again, Mr. Paige," Mr. Hanson said. The briefcase was next to him on the floor, not far from his sight or grasp. "If I may ask, what made you come after me?"

"A couple of loose ends that bothered me," Sam answered.

"I'd like to hear them."

"I never asked you or your bodyguard how long he's been in your employ. He seemed to be doing a decent job but I didn't feel a rapport between you two."

"Nice deduction. He was brought on two weeks ago as a replacement. The other item?"

"The briefcase. You hired us to get you to and from a meeting. The new element was that you would be bringing something back with you."

"Go on," Mr. Hanson said.

Sam continued. "What bothered me was that our services started and stopped outside the security gate. Initially it made sense because we can't carry in the secure part of the airport, but what didn't click is why not use us until you actually board the plane."

"You are correct, Mr. Paige. John set up your services."

"The added element of your briefcase changed the dynamic completely. Wish I had picked up on it earlier."

"I am in your debt," Mr. Hanson said. "Expect a very nice bonus when you send me your bill. In the meantime I have chartered a private jet to take me back to Dallas." He picked up the briefcase.

"Mr. Hanson," Sam said. "We need to escort you to your plane."

Mr. Hanson paused and smiled. "I'd like that very much." He then added, "Please call me Greg."

* * *

It wasn't until later that evening when Sam and Bill arrived back at their Marin office. They called from the airport and let their wives know that everything was fine, after retrieving Sam's radio and handgun from the trash. They pulled into the garage at SANDBOX and started to unload the Suburban. Weapons were removed, made safe and stored in the armory. The electronics gear was tested and inventoried the equi p.m.ent shelves. They retired

357

to the lounge, opened the fridge, pulled out a couple of beers, sat on the couch and drank deeply. Bill was the first one to speak.

"I didn't like how the airport went down this afternoon."

"How so?" Sam asked.

"I was blind out there and you didn't have any backup. As soon as you ditched your radio I had no idea what was going on."

"Any ideas on how to fix that?"

"Well, there are those analog Motorola phone systems out, but they're bulky. I hear there are some new digital versions being tested. I'll have to check on that."

They both drank more of their beer. "We didn't know completely what we were getting in to today and we almost got schooled," Sam sated. "In the future we get the full plan ahead of time, and tweak it as necessary."

"Agreed."

"And to your point, we could have used more people out there today. We should look at having additional teams on standby."

"No argument here, brother." Bill added, "Shit, if Julie thought today was bad then she'd go ape shit over the places we've been."

"What my wife doesn't know won't kill her." Sam smiled. "As Rangers we bled red, white and blue, but at least we have each other to talk to about those days and all the shit that went down."

"Amen, brother, amen."

They toasted each other and drank.

50
Wednesday July 25, 1990 8:15 p.m.

Laura got home later than she had planned that evening. She'd had an appointment with a client that would cry at the drop of a hat; a weeper. They were tough to handle and inevitably took a lot of hand holding and time. Laura pulled into her garage, entered her house, flipped on the kitchen light and noticed her answering machine message indicator was blinking.

Great, what now?

She walked over, put her briefcase down and pressed the playback button.

"Hi Laura, it's Thomas. I'm at my grandparents. Listen, I wanted to apologize for walking out on you. I don't have any excuses. I guess I got scared. Anyway, you mean the world to me; I just wanted to make sure you knew it. I'll call you when I get back in town on Thursday. Bye."

Laura played the message a few times and smiled. She was glad he had called and hadn't liked it when Thomas fled her office, but she hadn't been surprised. His mind had been awash in fresh trauma, whether real or imagined. Laura didn't blame him and had tried calling him that night, but the line kept ringing and Thomas never picked up.

Laura turned and left the kitchen as she illuminated each room on the way to her bedroom. She stripped down, put on pajamas, headed back to the kitchen, and grabbed a bottle of merlot from her wine rack and a glass from the cupboard. After uncorking the merlot she let it breathe while she retrieved some cheese slices from the fridge and dumped some Triscuits on to the plate. Laura nearly filled the wine glass to the brim and then carried her evening treats into the family room.

Laura put the plate on the table and took a substantial sip. She walked back to the kitchen, picked up her briefcase and came back. Inside it were five video tapes, each labeled and dated.

Thomas Clark – July 11, 1990 – 1

Thomas Clark – July 12, 1990 – 2

Thomas Clark – July 14, 1990 – 3

Thomas Clark – July 17, 1990 – 4

Thomas Clark – July 23, 1990 – 5

She pulled them all out, stacked them on the table and moved her briefcase to the floor. Laura stared at those tapes while she drank some more, nibbling on cheese and Triscuits along the way. It was going to be a long night.

* * *

Laura was exhausted. It was nearly midnight. The bottle of merlot was empty, as well as her plate of goodies. She had spent the last three hours going over Thomas' five regression sessions. Her main concern was that he had slipped out of her control and she needed to understand why. She had hoped by watching the session replays they would give her a clue. Session 4 was currently playing and it was her least favorite because she had to use the safe phrase. More to the point, that session had scared the crap out of her.

On the TV Laura listened to herself talk to Thomas.

"Look around again, Thomas. Where are you?"

"HE'S HERE!! OH MY GOD HE FOUND ME!!"

"You're okay, Thomas. He can't hur-"

"CRY TOMMY!!"

Laura couldn't take it anymore and froze the image on the TV of Thomas as he stood up; his eyes ablaze and his teeth caught in a timeless snarl. It wasn't a pleasant image to look at. At that moment Laura wished she hadn't finished off the merlot because she desperately wanted a drink. She got up and headed to the kitchen, but instead of retrieving more wine she opened the fridge and removed a carton of orange juice. Laura poured herself a glass, drank it down and placed the orange juice back in the fridge. She felt wiped out. As she placed the empty glass in the kitchen sink she stood there, unwavering. The tapes had taken their toll on her. That fourth session had been so intense.

But why? What was so different that I lost control?

Something dawned in her mind. She headed back out to the family room, picked up the remote and hit rewind. The static image of Thomas faded as the actions on the television played out in reverse. Laura hit play.

"Look down at your feet. What are you standing on?" Laura heard herself saying.

"White cement. Polished."

"Now where are you?"

"Nowhere." Thomas lifted his head as if he heard something.

"What is it, Thomas?"

"He's here. I know it! I've got to hide. There's nowhere to hide."

"It's okay, Thomas. He can't hurt you." He relaxed back in the chair.

"Look around again, Thomas. Where are you?"

Laura paused the tape. *Bingo.*

51
Thursday July 26, 1990 7:23 a.m.

Thomas woke up later than he had wanted to. His flight back to Ontario left at 10:35 a.m. and he still had to brave the fifty miles of commuter traffic to the airport, return the rental, check-in and get to his gate. He got out of bed quickly and headed to the shower.

* * *

"Please place your chair in the full and upright position. Tray tables must be stowed before landing."

Thomas shifted in his seat and stared out the window as it touched down. The plane landed without incident and Thomas retrieved his car from long term parking. He headed towards home. *Home.* But it didn't feel like home to Thomas anymore.

That morning his grandparents had seen him off. The past two days had been a wonderful visit. They had wished him a happy birthday and told Thomas they loved him. He'd hugged hugged each of them tightly and told them he loved and missed them too. He didn't realize how just much he had really missed his grandparents. They had raised him; been there for him after his father died; became his parents.

Thomas exited to 330 and headed up the mountain towards Running Springs. *Back home. What's that really mean?* Thomas had isolated himself for years now. He'd run away from everyone he knew, and for what? He suddenly hated the idea of being alone anymore and vowed to change it.

Running Springs loomed ahead and Thomas made his way through the small village to his house. He pulled into the garage and turned off the engine but didn't get out of the car. Instead he sat there and let the new feeling cascade over him; feelings of impending change. Except this time, for once, he felt in control.

Getting out of his car Thomas closed the garage door and unlocked the door to his house, disabling the alarm system. He put his carry-on down in the kitchen and saw that his answering machine was blinking. *Be right back.* Thomas walked past the phone and to the front door. He opened it and two fed-ex packages toppled over. *How much crap did the lawyers send?* He picked them up, walked down his driveway, opened his mailbox and pulled the contents out, piling it on top of the fed-ex boxes, and headed back up to his house. Thomas closed the door and put the pile of mail on the kitchen counter and hit play on his answering machine.

"You have one new message…beeeeep……..Thomas, it's Laura. I think I found something. Give me a call as soon as you get in." She sounded excited with a hint of apprehension.

Thomas breathed a sigh of relief. *At least she's talking to me.* Thomas lugged his carry-on to his bedroom and stripped down; tired and hungry. He figured he'd start with a shower, make some lunch and then call Laura back to see what she was talking about.

* * *

After Thomas had chowed down a sandwich he picked up the phone and called Laura. On the second ring it was picked up.

"Hello, Dr. Bond's office."

"Hi. It's Thomas Clark. Is Laura available? I'm returning her call."

"Dr. Bond is currently unavailable, Mr. Clark. Would you like to leave a message?"

"Please ask her to give me a call when she has a moment."

"Good day, Mr. Clark." The phone went dead.

Thomas looked at the dead receiver in his hand. *I never liked her receptionist from day one. What a bitch.* Thomas hung up the phone and headed upstairs to gather his clothes. *Laundry time.*

* * *

His phone rang three hours later. It was 4:43 p.m. and Thomas was folding laundry. He walked over and picked up the kitchen phone.

"Hello?"

"Thomas. I just got your message. How are you?"

"Hi, Laura," he said. "I miss you. Sorry about Monday. I feel like a heel."

"Don't worry about it, Thomas. I miss you too. How was your trip?"

"What a wonderful time I had with my grandparents. I had really missed them. I should have visited a lot sooner; not just for paperwork."

"I'm glad you had a good trip."

"You'll definitely have to meet them at some point. I told them about you."

"You did?" Laura felt her pulse quicken.

"They're excited for me." Thomas added, "I've also come to the conclusion that it's time to get off this mountain."

Laura was stunned. "That's huge. When did that happen?"

"It's been creeping up on me actually. So many things have come to light in the past two weeks that moving is just the next evolution of my change."

"I'm speechless and very happy for you. Wow!"

"Oh, you left a message saying you had found something? I don't understand."

Laura paused and then said, "This is going to sound completely off the wall. I don't even really know where to begin."

"How about the cliff notes version?"

"Okay. I was reviewing the five hypnotic regression sessions I videotaped."

"I'm with you so far," Thomas told her.

"They're not the easiest to watch, and that's coming from a professional."

He could sense she was building up to something. "My head is a messy place to root around in apparently."

"I'd have to agree, Thomas. The fourth session I lost complete control over the regression and you."

"I remember. You had to use the safe phrase."

"Exactly. But looking back over the session I noticed something that seemed odd."

"Okay. I'm on pins and needles here."

"What do these words mean to you?" she asked.

"What words?"

"Cry Tommy." There was a long pause and Thomas hadn't replied. Laura could hear him breathing. "Thomas?" Still nothing, but she heard his breathing was faster. "Thomas?" His breathe was now ragged. "Hello, Thomas?" A loud thump sounded in her ear. *Oh shit, he just dropped the phone.*

"Thomas, don't do anything, I'll be right there," Laura frantically yelled in to the phone.

She hung up, rushed out of her office and headed to her car.

* * *

Thomas looked around. He was in a white room.

Click. *What was that?*

He scanned the completely white environment and didn't see a thing.

Click click.

Thomas was nervous; he doesn't like this.

"Hello, Tommy."

Thomas spun around, was caught off balance and pushed to the ground. He looked up to see the face of Nigel.

"You're dead, Tommy!" Nigel screamed and kicked Thomas in his side. Pain ripped through him but he couldn't scream.

"Awh. Poor Tommy," Nigel mocked as he kicked Thomas over and over, now fetal. Somehow the blows found their mark each and every time. The pain was excruciating.

"You're weak, Tommy!" KICK. "You're pathetic!" KICK. "You're dead!" KICK.

Thomas can't help but to cry. The pain, the pain was more than he can bear. He tried to scream but he couldn't cry out; he had no voice.

KICK. Tears streamed down his face.

"Die, Tommy. Time to die!" KICK.

The white world faded away.

* * *

Laura was frantic.

That was stupid. Why did I try that over the phone?

She was making great time up 330 and was nearly to Running Springs.

You don't know what happened. Calm down. Yeah, right.

Laura's argument with herself had been going on since she'd left her office. She drove into town and headed the two blocks to Thomas' house in record time. She quickly pulled into his driveway, got out of her car, rushed to his front door and tried the knob; it was open. She let herself in and saw Thomas on the ground, thrashing; his face in the worst contortion she'd ever seen. He wasn't making any sounds and the phone lay next to him on the floor.

"THE CHICKEN SAYS CLUCK!!" she screamed.

Thomas started to inhale enormous lungfuls of air, gasping between each huge breath. He was in the fetal position, shaking with tears freely running down his face. Laura lay behind Thomas, pulled him close and started softly talking to him.

"You're safe now, Thomas," she said in a calming voice. "You're going to be okay." She stroked his hair and felt his heart race. "Everything's okay now." Laura kept reassuring him for the next six minutes.

* * *

Thomas opened his eyes and discovered he was on the floor. His eyes hurt. His body ached. Something was touching him.

"It's going to be okay."

Thomas tried to move away and came up short. He was practically debilitated.

"Thomas?"

He tried to speak. "Whooo. Whoo's thhaat?"

"Thomas, it's Laura." She got up from behind him. Thomas rolled on to his back and blinked a number of times. He attempted to focus on the face that hovered over him. "How do you feel? Are you hurt?" she asked, trying to conceal her panic.

368

Thomas groaned. His mind was foggy. "Laaura?"

"That's right. I'm right here." She started to cry. *Hold it together dammit.*

Thomas tried moving again. It was easier this time but he didn't have a lot of energy so he decided to stay still for the moment. "I'm going to catttch myy breath."

"You do that." She cried harder and held his hand tightly. "Take all the time in the world."

* * *

What seemed like an eternity later, Thomas finally was able to sit up on his own accord and saw that Laura hadn't left his side. He had dozed off for a while and during that time she had cried like she'd never cried before. She felt stupid for putting Thomas in danger, again, and berated herself repeatedly. When he did sit up she hugged him fiercely.

"Oh my God, Thomas, I'm so sorry."

He was extremely tired but he regained his senses. He hugged Laura in return and they rocked back and forth.

"Do you mind if we move to the couch?" he asked.

"Of course. Let me help you up."

He got on his knees and stood up. "Thanks. I'm just tired." They headed to the couch and he sank deeply in to it. "I'm thirsty."

"Stay right here, I'll be right back," as she headed back to the kitchen.

"I was actually thinking of running a marathon now," he said. His words came out slower than normal. She came back with a glass of water.

"Here, drink this." She helped him hold the water and he drank half the glass right away. "Easy. Take your time." He continued to sip the water until it was all gone. She took the empty glass and placed it on the coffee table.

He looked at her. "What the hell's going on?"

"I'm so sorry. I fucked up." She had placed all the blame on her shoulders.

"It's not your fault," he countered.

"Yes it is," she said immediately.

"No, Laura, it's not."

"You almost died because of me."

"Listen to me." Thomas looked her directly in the eyes. "I'm alive because of you. Do you hear me? I may not know what the fuck is going on in my head but I'm alive." He smiled at her. "I'm also in love with you. This probably isn't the most romantic time to say that, but I love you."

"I love you too, Thomas," Laura replied. She didn't hesitate. She knew she was in love with him.

"We'll figure this thing out, but right now I've got to lie down and rest. It feels like my chest has been repeatedly kicked in by a mule."

Laura got up from the couch and helped him lay out. As she took off his shoes she noticed he had passed out already.

At least he's breathing normally.

Laura plopped down on the floor. She was tired as well. She lay down on the floor.

I'll just rest my eyes for a second.

Her mind had been racing and she was mentally whipped. She didn't know where to go from here and everything was confusing. As she drifted off she knew one thing was for certain; she knew that they'd face this issue together.

* * *

Three hours later Thomas roused her from the floor. She hadn't moved once she had closed her eyes. She blinked a few times and then yawned.

"Are you hungry?" he asked.

"Starving."

Thomas helped her up. They hugged and held on to each other for what seemed like an eternity.

"I love you, Laura."

"And I love you too, Thomas."

"Whew," he said. "Glad that part was real and not in my head," he joked.

She smiled as they headed off to the kitchen to create a light meal. There was no need to talk about what had happened that afternoon; they knew they'd be talking about it soon enough, one way or another.

They headed to bed around 10:30 p.m. and Thomas fell asleep pretty quickly. Laura lay there for the next hour and a half and just let her mind wander. She needed to help him and was desperately searching for ways to make that happen. Laura looked over at the clock on his bed side table. It read 12:01am. Sleep evaded her.

"Thomas?" she whispered. Nothing.

"Thomas?" she said a little louder.

"Snort. Hmmm," he replied half asleep.

"Happy Birthday."

She fell asleep soon afterwards with her head on his chest.

52
Friday July 27, 1990 6:25 a.m.

"Mr. Peterson."

"Yes, sir?"

"What's the status of Charlie Whiskey?

"Charlie Whiskey has been confirmed. We're awaiting your 'go', sir."

Mr. Glib spun his office chair around slowly, looked out the observation window and examined the empire below him. He was the king of his domain. He smiled and said, "Do it."

"Yes, sir." Mr. Peterson spun on his heels and left his boss to gloat over his accomplishments.

53
Friday July 27, 1990 10:20 a.m.

Thomas opened his eyes and glanced over at his clock; it read 10:20 a.m.. Then he noticed a very enticing smell had wafted about his room, heard movement on the stairs and looked over at his bedroom door just as Laura appeared.

"Oh good, you're awake. Breakfast is almost ready." She walked over to his side of the bed and smiled. Laura was wearing a pair of his shorts and t-shirt. "Happy Birthday."

Thomas returned her smile. "Thanks."

"How are you feeling?"

"A lot better actually." He sat up in bed. "Yesterday I definitely felt like I'd be run over by a train, but now I feel like my normal self. I'm starving though."

"Good. Get out of bed and come downstairs, your birthday breakfast will be ready."

Laura headed back down as Thomas sauntered into his bathroom and took care of business. As he washed his hands he noticed his reflection in the mirror; a haggard man stared back. Today he turned thirty-three. Thomas splashed cold water on his face a few times and in the mirror the water poured down his face. He dried his face with a towel, put on some sweats and a t-shirt and headed downstairs for some breakfast.

"There you are," Laura said. "I was about to send out a search party."

"Ha ha. Very funny."

He sat down as Laura placed a plate with eggs, bacon and some hash browns in front of Thomas.

"Did you want toast?"

"Sounds great; and thank you for breakfast."

"You're welcome."

She placed the bread in the toaster, came back to the table with a plate of her own, and took a seat.

Thomas had dug in to his food immediately. "This is really good," he said between forkfuls.

"I'm glad you like it." The toast popped up and she got up to retrieve it. "Would you like anything on your toast?"

"There's some butter in the fridge door. If you want some jam there should be a jar someplace in the door too."

She opened the fridge and rooted around. "Found it." Laura brought the butter over to the table along with a knife she'd found in the utensil drawer. She put two pieces on his plate.

"Thanks."

She sat down and started to enjoy her breakfast, having woken up earlier and cancelling her appointments for the day. Thomas had been in a deep sleep and she hadn't wanted to disturb him, but her stomach urged her to eat something so she decided to make them breakfast. If he wasn't up by the time she was done she had planned on waking him.

Laura shifted in her chair. "Listen Thomas, I'm sorry about yesterday. I feel horrible for putting you through that. I still don't know what the hell happened."

He put down his fork. "It wasn't your fault. I don't know what's going on or why I have these seizures, episodes or whatever the fuck they are. And yes, they scare the hell out of me, but what I do know is that you're the one who's been helping me."

"I know. But I still feel really bad."

"Don't, okay. You dropped everything and came to my rescue. I should be the one thanking you."

"How do you do it?"

"Do what?"

"I'm still trying to figure out parts of you. You get mentally pulverized and then you make jokes. This shit has to bother you but sometimes you make it seem like it doesn't."

"Just chalk it up to my defense mechanism. I try not to let things get to me. As you know I've had to deal with horrible shit all my life. If I sat down and dwelt on it I'd probably have off'ed myself by now. Life shits on everyone; it's just how you deal with it that makes the real difference." Thomas paused. "I'm just like everybody else. I have good days and bad days. But what makes me different are the experiences I've lived through. What doesn't kill you makes you stronger."

"But you can't be strong all the time, no one can."

"You're right. I've been holding in my emotions for a long time now, hiding in this fucking house for years. And why? I'll tell you why; because I've been afraid. I'm sick of it. I'm my own worst enemy. And then I meet you and I take a chance at life. My heart is on my sleeve when you're around. I don't have to keep my defenses up. It's refreshing. It's opened my eyes to what the world has to offer." Thomas took a breath. "I love you."

Laura took hold of his free hand. A single tear traveled down her face. "I love you too."

Thomas stood up and they hugged each other. "Somehow things are going to be okay. It sounds totally cliché but we have each other."

"I don't even know where to go from here. I'm out of my league," she confessed.

"It's okay," he said with a reassuring tone.

They felt safe in each other's arms.

"I'll clear the table and clean up," she said as she broke the hug.

"I'll help."

"No. Go shower and shave. I'll take care of it," she said and shooed him away.

Thomas smiled and turned and headed back up to his bedroom. He could use a shower, that's for sure.

Laura took the dishes to the sink, along with the pans she used to cook the eggs, bacon and hash browns and cleaned everything. The pile of mail at the end of the counter caught her eye. A fed-ex corner protruded from the bottom of the stack.

* * *

Thomas felt refreshed and clean; the hot water had felt wonderful on his skin. He'd wished Laura had joined him in the shower.

Maybe later.

He shaved and cleaned up. Afterwards he got dressed in his sweats and t-shirt again and headed downstairs. He saw Laura sitting at the table looking at his mail.

Odd.

"Anything interesting?" he asked as he joined her.

Laura looked up. "I saw the fed-ex packages and got curious."

"They're from my grandparent's lawyer."

"One of them seems to be," she said as she pointed to one of the fed-ex packages. "The other one doesn't have any information on it at all." Laura indicated the other fed-ex package. It was thick.

He sat down. "Well that doesn't make any sense. I assumed they were both from the lawyers." He picked up the mystery fed-ex and tore it open. As he pulled out the contents a laminated worker's badge fell out. Laura picked it up while Thomas started to examine the contents.

378

"What's Rising Hope Pharmaceuticals?" she asked as she inspected the badge. "And who's Steve Hodgson?"

Thomas had taken out the thick stack of documents. On the top appeared to be a hand written letter. He put the stack down and picked up the single page letter.

Thomas Clark,

My name is Steve Hodgson. Let me be very clear. You and your family are in grave danger. I've worked for Rising Hope Pharmaceuticals for the past five years before escaping last Sunday. There were eighteen of us working on an undisclosed military funded project. Sixteen of them were killed. Jack Thompson and I, the two senior scientists on the project, were the only two spared. Jack and I attempted to escape. He was shot and killed right in front of my eyes.

"What is it?" Laura asked.

Thomas said, "Give me a sec," and kept reading.

I know that as you're reading this you won't believe a word of it. Why should you? Maybe I'm just a crazy person. To that end I've enclosed as much information that I could smuggle out, combined with news clippings, to paint you the best picture I could. The goal of the project was mind control. It seemed very farfetched at the beginning but as the years progressed we were more and more successful. We used death row inmates as our test subjects. Killers. They were injected with the chemical we'd produced. They were made to do horrible things. You, Thomas Clark, were also injected with this drug.

Thomas' mouth hung open in disbelief.

You were a side project for our boss, a Mr. Glib. For whatever reason he chose you and made you suffer. You were his plaything. From the information I stole from the lab it appears you have been fighting against the process. Our earlier tests indicated that only willing participants, and people with violent backgrounds, accept the changes. It's very hard to explain. Read the information and protect your family.

Steve Hodgson

Thomas dropped the letter.

"What is it?"

He couldn't say anything so he pushed it towards Laura who picked it up and read it herself. Thomas started spreading out the contents that came with the letter. Glancing, as he worked, he came across news clippings of murders, technical documents, and dossiers of four men that were listed only by a first name.

"What the fuck?" Laura said as she finished up Steve's letter.

"I know," he replied.

Laura started helping Thomas organize the pile of information in front of them. She found a fifth dossier. It was labeled 'Thomas Clark'. They both froze as she opened it.

"It just some dates listed," she said. Thomas got up and looked over her shoulder.

June 4, 1990 – Administered
June 12, 1990 – Test run Alpha – Answered. Responsive. Marksman skills tested.
June 23, 1990 – Test run Bravo – Answered. Responsive.
July 3, 1990 – Test run Charlie – Answered. Non-responsive. Nightmares intensifying.
July 5, 1990 – Test run Delta – No answer.
July 15, 1990 – Test run Echo – Female answered. Operation Kilo Lima suspended.
July, 21, 1990 – Operation Charlie Whiskey initiated.

"What the hell does all this mean?" he voiced out loud.

The phone in the kitchen rang and startled them, but Thomas couldn't seem to take his eyes off the dates. The phone rang for the third time. Laura got up and answered it.

"Hello?"

"This is the Walnut Creek Police Department. May I please speak with a Mr. Thomas Clark?"

"What's this concerning?" Laura asked.

"That is a private matter ma'am."

Laura cupped the phone. "Thomas, it's the Walnut Creek PD."

That got his attention. *The Walnut Creek police? Why would they be calling me? Oh shit!* Thomas rushed to the phone.

"Hello? This is Thomas Clark."

"This is Officer Stanley from the Walnut Creek PD. Are you related to Ed and Claire Clark?"

Thomas's mind raced. *Pleaseletthembeokay.*
Pleaseletthembeokay. *Pleaseletthembeokay.* "Yes, they're my
grandparents," he said tentatively.

"Mr. Clark, I'm sorry to inform you that your grandparent's
vehicle was struck head on this morning by a vehicle traveling at
high speed. The man, who hit them, was driving on the wrong side
of the road and alcohol was found in the front seat of the man's
car. I'm sorry, Mr. Clark, but there were no survivors."

Laura witnessed Thomas's body stiffen up. The phone slipped
from his hand as he took a huge breath.

"NOOOOOOOOOOOOOOOOOOOOOOOOOOOOO!!" Thomas
screamed.

He collapsed to the floor. His chest hurt; his vision was
fading; his world collapsed. As Thomas blacked out two words
came to mind. *Not again.*

* * *

There wasn't much Laura could do. She rushed forward as he
fell, but could only partially break his fall and stopped his head
from slamming into the floor. On the fallen phone she could hear
the officer repeating, "Hello. Hello?" before it went quiet.

"Thomas? Thomas? Thomas?"

He was out cold but at least he was breathing relatively
normally. She hadn't heard what the officer had said and could
only assume the worst about his grandparents. She stood up, wet
down some paper towels and used them on his forehead. If he
didn't wake up soon she was going to call 911.

Laura sat there, with Thomas' head in her lap, and stroked his
hair. At this point she didn't know what else to do.

382

Friday July 27, 1990 11:15 a.m.

The black fog lifted. Somebody was close by. *Who is it?* He couldn't make out the face yet.

"Thomas." It was a soothing voice.

His vision started to clear. It was a woman. He looked around and saw that was in a meadow.

"Hello, Thomas." The woman had come closer. He recognized the voice.

He focused. "Mom?"

"Hi sweetie," Betsy said. "It's been a long time."

"Mom? Is it really you?" He took a step forwards.

"It's me, sweetie."

They were within two feet of each other. A warm wind made the tall grass dance back and forth. It also made the trees surrounding the meadow sway.

"I miss you." Thomas hugged his mother as only a little boy could. "I miss you, mom."

Betsy returned the hug to her son; her boy that had grown up. "I miss you too, Thomas."

They broke the hug. The grass played around their legs; the sun warm on their faces.

"Where are we?" Thomas asked. It felt like a dream.

"You've been here before. Do you remember?"

He looked around. It did seem familiar and inviting. Although he didn't like the look of the dark trees in the distance. "Maybe."

"I don't expect you to remember. You're not really supposed to. But we had many conversations here when you were younger."

Thomas nodded his head.

"I don't have a lot of time, Thomas. You need to make a choice."

"A choice? I don't understand."

"You can either stay here with me or walk home through the woods." Betsy pointed towards the dark trees in the distance.

"Why would I want to leave?"

His mother touched his cheek with the back of her hand. "My sweet boy. It's not time for you to be here. Laura loves you. You have much more to offer the world."

"Where's Laura?"

"She's beyond the trees."

"I don't like the trees," he replied.

"She needs you and you need her. You love each other."

He looked at the trees in the distance and then back at his mother. "I don't want to lose you."

Betsy smiled and said, "You never have, Thomas. I'm always with you. Now go. I'll see you when you're ready. I love you."

"I love you too."

They hugged again, deep and mothering. She let her son go as he walked slowly towards the trees.

* * *

Friday July 27, 1990 11:21 a.m.

"Thomas." A pleasant voice; a caring voice. He opened his eyes, stared up at a blurry figure and blinked a few times.

"Thomas? Are you okay?" Laura came in to focus. His head was in her lap.

"I….I don't know."

384

"See if you can sit up."

He braced himself, managed a sitting position and looked around. He was in his kitchen and, like a freight train, it all came back to him.

Grandparents. Dead. Drunk driver. Birthday.

* * *

Laura had called out Thomas' name every ten seconds or so while she stroked his hair. He appeared to be asleep but that didn't seem plausible based on his collapse that had occurred a few minutes prior. His mouth moved ever so slightly, but no words were articulated. Her five minute deadline she had given herself was rapidly approaching. He continued to move his mouth and then suddenly stopped.

"Thomas." Laura called his name very softly.

He opened his eyes and blinked at her.

* * *

Tears ran down Thomas' face and into his lap. He sobbed as Laura sat there with him, held his hand and comforted him. His grief ran deep. Fifteen minutes later the initial wave of shock had subsided.

"Your grandparents?" she asked lightly.

Thomas nodded.

"What happened?"

He shook his head as if he was trying to forget and said, "They were hit by a drunk driver head on this morning. Nobody survived." More tears filled his red eyes but didn't spill over.

"I'm so sorry." Laura squeezed his hand.

There was only so much that could be said at moments like this. *He's suffering again. His fifth birthday with his mother, and now his grandparents on his birthday; in the same manner. Suffering.*

Laura stood up. "Thomas, get up."

He looked at her with confusion. "What?"

"Get up. Something's not right."

"What do you mean?" he said as he slowly got to his feet.

"There's a pattern," she told him as she hunched over the table's documents.

"Pattern?"

"Your suffering is the pattern."

"My suffering?" He stood next to her now.

She looked at him. "Let me run this by you. For the past two months everything's gone to hell. Your nightmares are horrific. You wake up with blood on your walls; the axe in the garden. Suddenly you think you've killed people. The pattern is that you've been suffering."

He stood there and took everything Laura said in. "But why?"

"Exactly," she said. "I'm sorry about your grandparents, but right now we need to go through what Steve sent you and try to figure this out. He could be absolutely right that you're in grave danger. We need help."

Thomas couldn't believe what he was hearing but it made sense; he was being targeted. He kissed Laura, picked the phone off the floor and dialed.

"Hello. Sandbox Enterprises, how can I help you?"

* * *

"We'll be there as soon as we can, Thomas."

Sam hung up the phone. Bill had just walked in to Sam's office.

"I heard Thomas called," Bill said.

"Yeah, I just got off the phone with him and we have to move now," Sam said with urgency.

Bill didn't argue. "Where are we going?"

"We're headed south, to the mountains, and pack heavy. I'll fill you in on the road."

"Roger that." Bill rushed off.

They were on the road within ten minutes. They crossed the San Rafael/Richmond Bridge, which turned in to 580, and then south for the long haul on to I-5. They chose to ignore the posted speeding limits.

54

Friday July 27, 1990 9:15 p.m.

Laura and Thomas had been at it all day, piecing together the clues. They glanced up towards the front window when they heard a vehicle in the driveway.

"I hope that's them," Thomas said and headed to the front door.

Two doors slammed outside and he opened the front door.

"There's our boy," Sam said as he walked towards the front door. Bill was right behind him.

"Hey guys." Thomas gave each of them a hug and invited them inside, closing the front door behind them. The trio entered into the family room and stopped as they encountered Laura. Sam immediately stepped forward and extended his right hand.

"You must be Laura. I'm Sam. This mutt behind me is Bill." Bill waved hello and they all shook hands.

Thomas walked over to Laura and stood by her. "Thomas has told me so much about you two. I can't thank you enough for coming down here on a moment's notice."

Bill spoke up. "It's the least we can do. He's our brother. And Thomas, I heard what happened to your folks, I mean your grandparents. I'm sorry."

"Me too," Sam added. "Me too."

He could only nod. "Thanks guys."

"And not to forget tradition, even on a shitty day like this…," Bill stuttered. "I mean, it's not a shitty day….it's just something bad happened….awh fuck. Way to go me. Happy birthday Thomas. I officially suck."

"Way to go dick," Sam said and hit Bill in the shoulder. "But he's right. Happy birthday, for tradition sake." Sam took a different tone. "Now Bill and I don't know what's entirely going on, but we can see you have a shitload of Intel on the table there. We've been driving like madmen and need to unpack, refresh and get some food in us. Afterwards I need to call Julie, and Bill needs to talk to Kim, or we're both up shit creek."

Laura took everything in. These were the two boys that Thomas grew up with, played in the sandbox and were terrorized by that bully Nigel. *Score another point for childhood trauma directly affecting life choices.* She liked them both immediately.

"Thomas," she said. "Why don't I start cooking something up for everybody while you help them get situated?"

"Good idea," he replied.

Everyone moved with purpose.

*   *   *

Thomas, Bill and Sam had headed outside to unload the Suburban. They removed a number of duffel bags and equi p.m.ent crates and stacked them against the wall by the guest room doorway. The bags contained clothes, tactical gear and vests while the crates contained arms and munitions. The two operators didn't know what to expect so they'd over compensated.

Laura started on dinner. She filled a large pot with hot water and placed it on the gas range. The spaghetti was on the counter waiting to be added as soon as it started boiling. She had found a jar of Prego and she placed this on the counter as well, knowing she could heat that up quickly in a saucepan later on. She then worked on prepping salad.

"I haven't used this room in years but you're more than welcome to it," Thomas said as he opened the guest bedroom door.

"Bill," Sam said, "Go ahead and take the guest shower. I'm sure Thomas won't mind if I use his."

"Wilco," Bill replied. "Towels, Thomas?"

"As far as I know there are some in there."

Bill entered the room and closed the door behind him.

"Up the stairs, Sam," Thomas said.

"Be back in a bit, bud." Sam bounded up the stairs and disappeared.

Thomas walked into the kitchen and Laura stopped what she was doing.

"I like them."

"That makes two of us."

Thomas was worn out. It had been a grueling day and so much had happened. The fact that something, outside of his control, was playing him didn't sit right with him. He was really glad his two best friends were here, and loaded for bear.

Laura stopped working on the salad and hugged Thomas. They had spent the afternoon pouring over the files that had arrived in the fed-ex package. The fact that they could focus on the information was a godsend and she was very glad for the distraction. Not necessarily for her, but definitely for him. Besides, the data they were combing through was incredibly interesting and practically impossible to believe at the same time.

"I love you. Thank you a million times over." Thomas gently kissed her forehead.

"We're going to get through this, whatever it is."

"It's a lot to take at face value. I don't know what to believe."

The water started to boil so she added the spaghetti. "I tell you what. Let's get some food in everybody first, then we can get their opinion on what we've discovered. In the meantime, could you get us both a beer? I think we deserve it."

* * *

"Thank you," Sam said as Laura handed him a plate of spaghetti topped with hot Prego.

"You're welcome." Bill and Sam sat on the couch while Thomas and Laura had pulled chairs up to the coffee table. "Would either of you like something to drink?" she asked.

"I wouldn't mind a one of those beers you have," Bill said.

"I'll take one too please," Sam added. "Thank you."

"I'll get them." Thomas retrieved them and came back.

"Thanks, brother."

All four of them worked on their dinner without saying much of anything. The anticipation, of the discussion they were going to have, continued to mount. Sam had received a call from Thomas letting him know that his grandparents had just been killed, that there was a potential conspiracy in the works and that he needed their help immediately. Sam and Bill had naturally dropped everything to help out their friend. They had been on the road for eight hours and now needed to know what was going on.

As they finished eating they individually took their dishes to the sink. They'd deal with them later.

"Okay Thomas, break it down," Sam said.

They huddled around the table; information was everywhere.

Thomas took a deep breath and began. "Two months ago I started to have nightmares. I told you about them. Flashbacks to Wagner Ranch and our common bully, Nigel."

"Fucking hate that guy," Bill said under his breath.

"So a month goes by, and I'm on edge. I'm not able to concentrate on writing or much of anything. At the beginning of

392

this month I wake up from another nightmare and discover I have blood all over my hands, my window and my walls."

"What the hell?" Sam exclaimed.

"And it's not just smeared on the wall; there's a message written in blood. It says 'Make me'."

"That's pretty creepy," Sam said.

"So then I see a newscast that mentions some guy that got axed to death, and in my mind I'm automatically thinking it's me. That's the same day I start seeing Laura professionally. The next day I dig up a bloody axe in the garden."

"An axe, in the garden outside?" Bill asked.

"The very same. I fucking lose it. I think I'm definitely the murderer. I bring the axe to Laura and she initially freaks out. I think it's still there."

"I still have it at the office," Laura confirmed.

"So then a third guy winds up dead the following day, and they're all in Laura's neighborhood. Then there's a fourth killing; a woman, who is killed right in front of her young son. Since then there haven't been any other murders reported."

"You? A killer? Not likely," Bill said.

"What else?" Sam inquired.

Thomas passed the torch to Laura. "I started Thomas on regression hypnosis. It has produced some bizarre behavior. He's been experiencing things that should not be happening."

"Such as?" Sam queried.

"I've lost control of him in the past two sessions for starters. He thrashes around like he's being beaten. I have video tapes of the sessions." Laura paused. "But that's not the most interesting thing. Thomas apparently is susceptible to a key phrase."

"I don't understand," Sam said.

393

"I reviewed the video tapes when I lost control of him. I thought I'd found something so I called Thomas and tested my theory."

Sam looked at his friend and said, "What is she talking about?"

"I remember answering the phone and talking with Laura. The next thing I know is that Nigel is kicking the living shit out of me and I can't fight back. I think I was close to dying if Laura hadn't saved me."

Sam shook his head. "Nigel was beating on you? This is all too farfetched. I love you bro but this is too much."

"I was right there with you, Sam. I was right there with you until we opened this package of information." Thomas indicated the papers all over the table. "Take a look at this letter." Thomas handed Steve Hodgson's letter to Sam and Bill looked over his shoulder as they both read it.

After a minute Sam slowly put the letter down on the table. He looked around at all the Intel and his face went pale. His eyes refocused on Thomas.

"I now understand why you called. Now make us believers."

55

Saturday July 28, 1990 7:45 a.m.

"Ding dong."

Thomas slowly opened his eyes, peered around and realized he was on the couch. Laura spooned him from behind. Sam and Bill had kept at the data while they took a break, although they must have passed out at some point. It had been well past midnight.

"Ding dong."

Goddamn doorbell.

Thomas got up. Laura stirred but didn't wake up. Thomas walked towards the door and noticed the guest room door was closed.

Don't worry, I'll get it. Sleep tight you bastards.

As he opened the door it was violently kicked in with tremendous force which sent Thomas sprawling to the floor. A large man walked through the entry way, dressed in black clothing and carried an axe in his right hand.

Thomas, now on his back, quickly scrambled backwards into the family room, with his hands and feet, as the large man bore down on him; his eyes were fixated on his prey. He reached down and grabbed Thomas by the throat with his left hand.

"Stop it," Thomas croaked.

"GET OFF HIM!" Laura screamed as a beer bottle sailed by the man's head and exploded on the wall beside them. Thomas's attacker didn't blink as he raised the axe above his head. Suddenly a blur hit the attacker from the left, which made him drop Thomas. Strong hands then pulled Thomas towards the stairs.

Laura was screaming. Sam left Thomas and headed back to the fight. Bill had tackled the intruder, now face down on the carpet and had both of his arms wrapped around the man's chest.

Bill repeatedly kneed the attacker's side but the axe remained in his hand.

No time for finesse. Sam grabbed the man's hand, with both of his, and violently twisted. The wrist snapped and the axe fell free. Sam kicked it towards the front door as the intruder rotated his body to the left and trapped Bill underneath him. He swung his left arm around, and his fist caught Sam in the face, who staggered back. The momentum gave Bill the opportunity to quickly bind his right arm around the man's neck and tightened his grip. Sam recovered and held the man's left arm inert as Bill applied the choke. The attacker was strong and kept fighting, but the two Rangers had already won.

Thomas and Laura had barely had time to react because the encounter was over almost as fast as it had begun. Thomas stood up and went over to Laura. "You okay?"

"Fine....I'm fine." She was shaking.

Sam pulled Bill out from underneath the unconscious man and helped him up.

"You good, Sam?" Bill asked.

"Fucker punches like a pussy," Sam replied. "I'm good. Nice choker."

"An oldie but goodie. Let's tie this fucker up."

"Duct tape, Thomas," Sam barked.

"On it." Thomas disappeared into the garage, returned with a roll that Bill took it from him and secured their attacker.

"Well, if I had any doubts left from all the coincidences you showed me last night, they're certainly gone now. This guy wanted to kill you. You okay?" Sam asked.

"Yeah. I think we're good. Thanks you guys." Thomas paused. "Fuck me."

"What?" Laura asked.

"I've seen this guy before." Thomas turned towards the table, rustled through the four dossiers, pulled one out and opened it. "Here...this is the same guy."

Thomas handed it over to Sam who looked down at the picture and then at the man tied up on the floor.

Holy shit. "File says his name is Chris. No last name. Nothing else. Death row inmate out of San Quentin. According to this he's only been in the program for a month."

"Fucking RHP is sending out assassin's bro," Bill said. "Look at him. He never said a fucking word the entire time. I was wailing on his ribs and you broke his wrist. Not a goddamn peep."

Sam looked around the room. "Thomas. Call the police and report a break-in. Get them over here now. Laura, gather all the Intel. Bill, you and I will load up the truck. We're not safe here."

* * *

Sam and Bill had just finished loading the gear in the Suburban when two police cars pulled up and four officers got out. Thomas met them in the driveway and led them inside. They witnessed the busted front door; the axe; the broken glass from the bottle; and the duct taped intruder with a swelled wrist that lay on the family room rug, still unconscious. They handcuffed him, carried him outside and placed him in the back of one of the cruisers.

"Mr. Clark. It's going to be awhile before our crime guys can make it up the mountain to take pictures. I'm going to have to cordon off your house. Do you have a place you can go?"

"We can head to a motel," Thomas told the officer. "We'll need to pack though."

The officer took a long look at the house and the man who had regained consciousness in the back of the squad car. "Tell you what. I don't like the look of the guy who we have in custody. He gives me the fucking chills. I'll be back in an hour. Pack and get out of here but leave everything the way it is."

The officer turned and motioned for the other three officers that they were leaving. The two squad cars pulled out and took off.

"Well, well, well," Bill said. "It looks like celebrity status has its perks after all."

Everyone headed back inside.

"What else do we need?" Laura asked.

"Pack lightly; just the essentials," Sam said. "We can buy what we need later."

The phone suddenly rang. Thomas walked towards it and picked it up on the second ring.

"Hello?"

"How'd you like my guest, Thomas?" The voice was not friendly.

"What? Who is this?" He motioned everyone over with his free hand.

"You're lucky you had your friends over," the voice rasped. "You and your girlfriend would be gutted if it wasn't for them." Laura. Sam and Bill had heard that last statement.

Thomas swallowed. "Who are you? What do you want?"

"You will suffer before you and your friends die." The line went dead.

They all hung on those last words for a few seconds before they snapped out of it.

Sam spoke up first. "Thomas. Laura. Pack quickly." He turned to Bill and motioned for him to follow him outside. Once on the driveway Sam said, "Once again something just doesn't feel right. Whoever that was knew you and I were here. Let's do a quick search of the house." They headed back inside and started in.

* * *

Thomas and Laura headed upstairs. She didn't have a change of clothes since she had come directly from her office.

"This is some pretty fucked up shit, Laura. You could have died today and it would have been my fault."

"You haven't done anything wrong. You're the victim here, Thomas. Let's pack up, get the hell out of there and then we can figure this shit out. K?"

"Sorry. You're right. All I see is that axe over my head. Thank god Sam and Bill were here."

"No shit. Told you I liked them."

Thomas turned and smiled at Laura who was already grinning.

* * *

They came back downstairs with a duffel bag and Laura took the refilled fed-ex package and dumped it in the bag as well. Something caught Thomas' eye and he stopped.

"What?" she asked.

"Look."

He pointed at the phone and she saw that it had been taken apart. After that they headed outside.

"What'd you guys do to my phone?"

Sam and Bill stood in front of the Suburban. In Bill's hand he held a few bits of wire and an electronic looking widget. "Here's your phone," he said and then dropped the widget on the ground and crushed it under his heel.

"Get in the car, we're leaving," Sam told them.

"One last thing. I'll be right back." Thomas ran back in the house. He came back with two full black trash bags.

"What's in those?" asked Sam.

"Bloody bedding."

"Oh goodie, this shit keeps getting better and better. Put it in the back."

Bill got in the driver's seat of the Suburban while the rest of them jumped in the back. Bill started the vehicle and drove down the street.

Sam turned to Thomas. "That was a listening device which means your phone was bugged. Our assumption is that the rest of your house, and probably your car, are too."

"You're infested, brother," Bill said from the front seat.

Thomas believed them because there was no reason not to. With all the shit he'd seen and experienced in the past month the news that his private life hadn't been private came as no shock to him at all.

Bill headed down the mountain into San Bernardino. They needed a new safe house and they needed a plan.

* * *

"You will suffer before you and your friends die, Thomas."

Mr. Glib hung up the phone. He chuckled to himself. *That should get them motivated.*

400

Saturday July 28, 1990 10:05 a.m.

The black Suburban made its way west on I-10, as the four occupants inside silently relived the attack just a few hours ago. They were tired from the night before from tirelessly pouring through the information Mr. Hodgson had supplied them. But driving around wasn't going to cut it; they needed a plan.

"I don't mean to sound whiny but I could use some food and rest," Laura announced.

"You're not the only one," Thomas added.

"You're right," Sam said. "We need to stay alert. Bill, find us a fast food place and then we'll locate a motel."

"Roger that."

* * *

Sam checked them into a Motel-6 under his name and came back with two different room keys, 13 and 14 next to each other. He handed one to Thomas and kept the other one for Bill and himself. Once inside they opened the interior adjoining room doors, left everything in the vehicle and walked across the street to McDonald's. Breakfast had just ended at 10:30 and it was time for the lunch menu. They ordered and then sat down at a table in the back, away from everyone else. They were beat.

"Thanks again for saving our ass," Thomas said gratefully.

"Yes," Laura said. "Thank you very much."

"What can we say, we love this sonofabitch," Bill joked.

"Thomas, you definitely have us wrapped up in some weird shit here," Sam said. "I'm just glad we were there to help. That guy definitely wanted you dead." The weight of those words hung over the table.

"I don't know who the man on the phone was," Laura said, "but he's not going to stop, is he?" She looked around the table for reactions.

"I wouldn't count on it," Sam replied.

"Order two-o-four?" uttered the attendant that had taken their order.

"I'll get it." Bill got up and headed over to retrieve their meal.

Sam continued. "Let's just eat and regain some strength. Afterwards we'll head back to the motel, take some showers, freshen up and then figure out what the right course of action is, okay?"

Bill came back with their food, put the tray down and each of them took their respected burger and drink. The fries were dumped out on the tray so they could all partake in them. For whatever reason their food tasted exceptional.

* * *

After eating they crossed back over the street, opened their motel doors and offloaded a couple of the duffel bags in Sam and Bill's room. Thomas took the only bag he had from the Suburban and brought it inside. They all gathered in Thomas' room.

"I'd love to take a shower and change in to something else, but I don't have anything."

"Easily rectified," Sam said. "Laura and I will go out and pick up some new clothes. I think I saw a GAP down the block. Thomas, is that okay with you?"

"I should go."

"The less exposure the better at this point. Take a shower while we're gone. We'll be back in twenty minutes."

Laura gave Thomas a hug and kiss. "I'll be right back."

She turned and walked out the front door, got in the Suburban with Sam and drove out of the parking lot. Bill closed the door and the curtains.

"She'll be fine, brother."

Thomas said, "I put her in harm's way, Bill. This is my fault."

Bill put his right hand on Thomas' shoulder. "That's bullshit and you know it. Whatever the fuck's going on it's not your fault. I barely understand what's happening. What I do know is that my best friend needs my help." He took his hand away. "Now, before I get all teary eyed, go take a shower before they get back, fucker."

Thomas smiled. "You sure have a way with words bro."

Bill smiled back. "Yeah, I'm a regular Shakespeare shithead."

*　*　*

Sam and Laura returned twenty-two minutes later. She had picked up underwear, tennis shoes, two short sleeve t-shirts, one long sleeve shirt, a pair of jeans and a light jacket. By that time Thomas had finished his shower and had changed into new clothes from his bag. Laura kissed him on her way to the bathroom and closed the door behind her.

"Thanks for taking her, Sam."

"My pleasure." Sam walked into his room, Thomas followed and Sam motioned towards the table where Bill was already sitting. "Let's go over what we have."

Thomas retrieved the fed-ex package, pulled out the contents and spread it out on the table. Bill and Sam started pawing through it.

"Wait. Check this out," said Bill a few minutes later.

"What'd ya find?" Sam asked. Bill placed the written note from Steve Hodgson in front of them. Sam gave him a strange look. "So?"

"Turn it over."

Thomas reached out and flipped the piece of paper over. It appeared to be a crude drawing of a building. The perimeter, parking lot, guard shack and entrance to the building were all marked accordingly. There was an X in the guard shack and two additional X's just inside the entrance, off to the left. A dotted line ran from the building's entrance, around to the left and stopped at a wall where the letter E was marked. An address was scrawled on the bottom of the paper.

"Nice find, Bill," said Sam as he lay out the map. "It's obviously not to scale but this gives us a target."

"A target?" Thomas asked.

Sam sat down. "Laura said it earlier. This isn't going to stop and I think you know that. Bill and I just got here and we've already come to that conclusion."

"Yeah brother, this fucker thrives on your suffering. Check this out as well." Bill put the dossier that had Thomas Clark written on the tab, in front of them. "This is you, bro." He opened it up. "Look at these dates. They have something to do with you."

June 4, 1990 – Administered

June 12, 1990 – Test run Alpha – Answered. Responsive. Marksman skills tested.

June 23, 1990 – Test run Bravo – Answered. Responsive.

July 3, 1990 – Test run Charlie – Answered. Non-responsive. Nightmares intensifying.

July 5, 1990 – Test run Delta – No answer.

July 15, 1990 – Test run Echo – Female answered. Operation Kilo Lima suspended.

July, 21, 1990 – Operation Charlie Whiskey initiated.

All three of them looked at the dates listed.

Bill continued, "Look at the July third listing. It specifically talks about your nightmares. What can you tell us about that date?"

Thomas thought for a couple of seconds. "I think that was the night before I woke up with the blood on my hands."

"What about the one on the fifteenth?"

Thomas read the line out loud. "Test run Echo. Female answered. Operation Kilo Lima suspended. What's Kilo Lima?"

"That's from the military alphabet," Sam said. "It stands for KL, but who knows what KL actually means."

"What about the last one?" Bill asked.

"Operation Charlie Whiskey initiated," Thomas read. "That'd be CW?"

"Correct," Sam said. "Does it mean anything to you?"

Thomas shook his head. "Not a thing guys."

"Oh fuck me," Bill exclaimed.

"What?" Sam said.

Bill looked around at Sam and Thomas, clearly agitated and apprehensive.

"Out with it, Bill."

Bill looked slowly up at his friends. "Charlie Whiskey might stand for.....Car Wreck." Bill hesitated. "It's just a guess, but your grandparent's, Thomas. A coincidence?"

Thomas went pale.

"There are no coincidences in our line of work," Sam said. "You still with us, Thomas?"

"Yeah, I'm just shell shocked. What if Bill's right?"

"Then we have one nasty motherfucker on our hands."

"Going with Bill's assumption, for the time being, it's possible that the Lima, from the fifteenth, might stand for Laura."

Bill caught on. "You're right. Kilo Laura." Sam and Bill looked at each other and spoke in stereo, "Kill Laura."

"Who wants to kill me?" Laura asked behind them.

"It's possible, Laura, that the timeline in Thomas' dossier has a mission listed to kill you. Do you remember anything about the fifteenth?"

Laura thought for a minute and said, "Thomas, isn't that the night we first....um."

Sam and Bill looked at each other. "We get it," he said. "Do you remember talking on the phone?"

"I do," she replied. "One of you guys called and said "Hi Tommy" but then it was disconnected. I thought you'd call back."

Sam looked at Bill and said, "Did you call?"

"Not me. You?" Bill asked.

"Can't say that I did."

Laura was stumped. "Well if neither of you called then...." Laura trailed off and then said, "Holy shit."

"Explain," Sam said.

"Remember when I said that Thomas has a trigger...,well, I just figured it out. The caller didn't say 'Hi Tommy'. They were using his trigger and I just assumed they had said 'Hi Tommy'. Goddammit."

"What's the trigger?" Bill asked.

"Don't even go there," Laura said firmly.

"Sorry."

"We don't have a choice," Sam said as he back control of the conversation. "We need to take this guy out and soon." He looked around at everyone. "Whoever this Mr. Glib is, he's continued to come at you, Thomas. He's fucked with your head. He's fucked with your heart. He's tormenting you. He has to be removed." Sam's eyes were on fire.

Thomas was tired of the abuse. All the family he had left was in this motel room with him. *How long until they get targeted and killed?* Thomas was done being the victim.

"What do you need me to do?" he asked.

Sam and Bill looked at each other. "We're going to need another car, Sam," Bill said.

"I agree. Tonight the three of us will recon this place," Sam said as he pointed at the hand drawn map.

"There are four of us," Laura reminded them.

Sam paused. "This could be dangerous, Laura, for one thing. Secondly, this isn't your fight."

She walked over to Sam and poked him and plated a finger in his chest. "Don't give me that crap. I'm knee deep in this shit. I'm so deep I can fucking taste it so you can take your macho, military bullshit and shove it right up your ass. You're not doing this without me." Laura didn't budge and Thomas's mouth fell open. Sam was stunned.

Bill broke the ice. "Can we keep her? I like her." And just like that the tension subsided.

Sam was used to giving the orders, and his wife, Julie, had dressed him down more than a few times during their marriage. It had stopped him short then, just as Laura had done now.

"Okay, okay," Sam said.

"The phone's ringing, Sam," Bill said, "It's your balls, they want to come home."

Everyone started to laugh.

"Fuck you very much," Sam said. He was smiling.

Laura moved next to Thomas. "Who are you?" Thomas asked her jokingly.

"Sorry, Sam," she said.

"Hell no, Laura, you're right. Tactically we need you. I don't like putting you in danger but you already made that call."

Laura looked at Thomas and said, "I'm in. Tell me what you need me to do."

He whispered in her ear, "I love you."

She smiled and replied, "You'd better."

<u>57</u>
Sunday July 29, 1990 1:33 a.m.

The four of them left the motel at 1:33am wearing dark tops, jeans and tennis shoes. Before they stepped out they put on their earpieces and microphones. Sam and Thomas climbed into the Suburban while Bill and Laura took the Jeep Cherokee rental.

"Testing," Sam's voice broadcast in to each of their ears. "One, Two, Three. Testing."

They all responded and quickly verified that communications were up and running. The two vehicles pulled out of the motel's parking lot and headed towards RHP.

* * *

After Laura had put her foot down they'd finalized their plan fairly quickly. Based on the intelligence they'd reconnoiter RHP early the next morning in an effort to look for weaknesses in their security and potential penetration based on those observations. Two teams would be needed so Sam and Bill decided to leave to rent another car. Before they left Sam extracted two Glock 17's, and four extra magazines, from their car armory. Sam and Bill quickly showed Thomas and Laura the basics of the weapon. In ten minutes they were both relatively proficient with loading, clearing, stance, trigger pull and making their weapons safe.

"Thank you guys," Thomas said.

"You seem to naturally know how to handle that Glock, Thomas," Sam said.

"I don't know, Sam; my dossier did mention something about shooting. It's creeping me out a little."

"We'll be back in a bit," Bill injected. "Make sure not to point that at anything you don't want to kill."

Sam and Bill closed the motel door behind them and left in the Suburban.

Laura put her Glock down on the bed and sat down. "They've really changed haven't they?"

"What do you mean?"

"Well," she started, "you all went through some serious shit as a kid. Now look at them. They wouldn't take shit from anybody."

"Yeah. I might have been the only one that stayed the same."

"Oh, I didn't mean anything by it, Thomas. I'm sorry."

"I didn't take it as a slight." He smiled at Laura to reassure her. "Most of the time I felt like I was barely keeping my head above water." He sat down on the bed too and placed his Glock next to him. "My mother was killed when I was five and no kid should have to go through that. I was bullied to hell and back and almost died. Then I lost my dad. I'm not sure I've ever recovered from all that. Sure, I can put on a smile and make people believe I'm okay, but inside I'm screaming. Some of it's real I'm sure, but some of it is my own hell I've kept alive. It's hard to explain." Laura put her hand over Thomas'. "Maybe I think that if I'm not suffering then life treat me differently."

"I don't understand."

"I guess what I mean is, I'm used to suffering. If it stopped I'm not sure I'd be used to it. Is that weird?" he asked.

"You're not alone. The world is full of misery. For a good portion of your life you experienced it. It's not unusual that you got accustomed to it."

"I'm not sure I want it anymore. I want something different. I NEED something different. I may be a decade too late in learning

410

that lesson, but with you in my life all I can see is happiness ahead of us."

"Aww," Laura said.

A loud rapping on the door startled them and they grabbed their Glock's and looked at each other. Their eyes spoke louder than words. *What do we do?* The rapping came louder this time. Thomas and Laura didn't make a sound as she moved to the bathroom doorway and he stood behind the door. They had both hands on their handguns with the muzzles pointed at the ground, fingers off their triggers, as instructed.

A key scrape sounded in the door and a moment later it started to open.

"Housekeeping," an accented female voice announced.

Laura stepped out in to the room and headed towards the door as it opened in front of Thomas. "We're fine."

The housekeeper jumped a little. "Ai! Lo siento." She backed out of the doorway and closed the door behind her.

Thomas exhaled unaware that he'd been holding his breath. Laura smiled and pulled out her Glock from the small of her back. She sat back down on the bed and placed her weapon beside her.

"Nice, Laura."

"Could have been worse. We're in a different world now with new rules."

"No shit. Time to become fast learners."

* * *

Sam and Bill returned a little while later sporting a Jeep Cherokee and gathered the four of them together.

"Okay. Bill and I have run it down. We'll break in to two teams and head over to RHP later tonight. We'll be in communication."

"How?" Thomas asked.

Bill pulled out the radios from a bag and said, "With these. The miniature microphone goes down your arm and clips onto your sleeve. There's an earpiece."

"Ahh, secret service style."

"Exactly," Sam said. "We'll observe and report back to each other. It's not exactly exciting work but we need to assume that the situation can become dangerous at any moment. So, try and get some sleep now. We'll have a late dinner, some takeout or something, that we'll eat here. We'll get ready around 1am and go from there. Questions?"

Laura and Thomas looked at each other and then back at Sam. The situation was becoming even more real.

"I think we're good for now," Thomas said. "Thanks."

"We'll be right next door then. And seriously, get some sleep." Sam winked at them and then closed the adjoining door.

Laura motioned towards the bed. "Shall we?"

They stripped down to their underwear and climbed into bed. The events of the day, combined with the upcoming evening had left them exhausted. They kissed and then Laura snuggled in and placed her head on his chest. They were out in minutes.

* * *

Sunday July 29, 1990 2:02 a.m.

"We're getting close," Sam's voice announced through the radio. "Bill, Thomas and I will take the front. Head around back and give me a sitrep every ten minutes."

"Roger that," came Bill's reply.

"Sitrep?" Thomas asked, who sat next to Sam.

"Situation Report," Sam stated matter-of-factly.

The night was slightly illuminated by the half moon and would give them at least some cover. Sam cut the lights, slowly pulled over to the curb and cut the engine. He and Thomas could see the front gate from where they had parked. Sam scanned the area and observed that the guard shack was manned by a single officer. He then pulled out a pair of binoculars and inspected the RHP facility closer.

Bill's voice crackled over the radio. "We're in place. Nothing to report yet."

"Roger," Sam replied.

Sam put the binoculars down. "They've got the perimeter covered by the roof cameras. The floodlights surrounding the facility overlap each other. That's a lot of exposure."

Thomas sat quietly and watched his friend work. *He's really in his element. I wonder what he's done.* "Hey, Sam."

"Yeah?" He was using the binoculars again.

"What was it like?"

"What was what like?" Sam replied.

Thomas readjusted in his seat. "You've never talked about what you've been though in the military; your years as a Ranger."

"Those were some of the best years of my life," Sam said. "The camaraderie is something I can't describe. Knowing that the

413

man next to you has your back and you have his. That bond is eternal."

"I was actually talking about what IT is like?"

Sam lowered the binoculars and glanced over at Thomas. "I know what you meant. I don't go around talking about the places I've been or the bad guys that are no longer breathing. And you should know better than to ask." He sighed and pointed at the facility. "Who knows what we're going to find in there. We're pretty blind right now. The Intel we have is less than stellar."

"Sorry." Thomas looked away.

Sam brought the binoculars back up. "Forget it, but I see where you're coming from though. Revenge, right? I don't blame you. If this fucker is responsible for the myriad of shit he's put you through then he needs to be taken out." Then he thought for a few seconds. "But now I get it….you're wondering if given the chance you're capable of actually pulling the proverbial trigger."

"Something like that."

"More like exactly like that. Besides, we have the backup plan in place with Laura. Whatever we find in there will be dealt with one way or another."

"You guys are used to this. I'm just a writer."

"It's okay to be nervous," Sam replied. "Just breath. Compartmentalize."

"Compartmentalize?"

Sam kept his eyes forward, alert. "Keep your important thoughts on the top of the list and let the fear and the doubts trickle to the bottom."

"I don't understand."

"Okay. Does the fact that you've been injected with a brain washing drug, forced to endure nightmare after nightmare, led to believe you're a murderer and just lost your grandparents, piss you off?"

Thomas exploded from his seat. "You ASSHOLE! Why would you say that?"

Sam remained calm and collected. "I'll take that as a yes. Keep all that shit on the top of your list, Thomas, it's the reason we're all here tonight. Take that fear and doubt and shove it way down, it doesn't belong in your head."

Thomas was furious. Sam had just run down a synopsis of the past two months and it didn't feel good.

Crackle. "Sam, no movement back here," Bill said.

"What do you see?" Sam asked.

"Perimeter chain link fence with barb wire; cameras on the building corners; four parked vehicles illuminated by multiple floodlights; and a set of double doors marked Emergency Exit Only."

"Roger that. We're very similar on this end. One guard in the shack; cameras and floodlights. I can't see in to the building's entrance, the windows are tinted."

"Roger. Talk to you in ten."

"So when did this leadership quality kick in?" Thomas asked.

"What are you talking about?"

"It's pretty obvious. You're the one running the show. I thought you both ran SANDBOX?"

"We do. We're equal partners, not excluding you of course." Sam took his time. "Bill and I have worked together for years. You knew us as kids and we've changed and grown quite a bit since our High School days."

"I can tell."

"Anyway," Sam continued, "when Bill and I work together we rely on each other, and our team, for different strengths. Bill's

415

very confident of me taking the lead in a situation. He'd rather have my back and that's not an issue with me. I rely on him to do just that."

"I've definitely got some catching up to do, after this, with you guys. I feel like I'm years behind knowing what's going on."

"We know, and now you know why we've been badgering you to come out and play." They both smiled.

"Now, if you don't mind, would you kindly step out and remove our license plates?"

"You got it."

* * *

"Roger. Talk to you in ten," Bill said.

"Is this supposed to be this exciting?" Laura joked.

"Recon is recon. All data is valuable. But yeah, this shit is about as exciting as watching grass grow. It's tough to stay alert for long periods of time when nothing is going on, but it's part of the job. You lose your concentration and that's when you're dead."

"I understand." Laura sat there looking at their target building in the distance. "Can I ask you a personal question?"

"Go for it."

"Why did you and Sam leave the military?"

"You like the loaded questions, don't you, Laura?" Bill kept his eyes peeled as he answered. "Our re-ups were around the corner and it was either put in another four years of third-world countries or leave with what we'd learned and do our own thing. We'd talked about starting our own business but it was really more of a pipe dream."

"What happened?"

"Funny you should ask. We met our wives. Well, our future wives at the time."

"Oh?"

"Yeah. We'd come back from....well, that's not important. Sam and I were on leave and decided to come back home. We were out drinking at a bar in Walnut Creek when we met them."

"You met your wife in a bar?"

Bill looked over at her. "Told you it was funny." He then went back to looking at the building. "Anyway, we met Julie and Kim out at a bar. Turns out there were sisters."

"Come on, you're making this up."

Bill chuckled. "I swear you can't make this shit up. Anyway, they apparently were in to soldiers. Things between us progressed normally after that but they didn't like us being away and were all for us creating a business at home. There's still danger, mind you, but Sam and I have full control over the situations we put ourselves in to now."

"I get it," Laura said. "You're a softy."

"Hey now!"

"Don't worry. Your secret is safe with me." It was Laura's turn to chuckle.

"Anyway, Thomas really came through for us, financially speaking, and the rest is history."

Laura mulled over what Bill had just told her. "Any children?"

"I have a baby girl. Her name is Sarah. She just turned two."

"And Sam?"

"A two year old girl as well. Amanda."

"I can't wait to meet your family."

Outside the darkness enveloped their car. Nothing moved; everything remained static.

"How's our boy doing?" Bill asked.

"Thomas? He's been through more shit than I can shake a stick at."

"He's a tough bastard, but he also wears his heart on his sleeve."

"You can say that again," Laura replied. "I understand why he has been hiding away from everything and everyone for so long."

"Well, I can tell you one thing…., we miss that bastard."

"There's that soft side again. Careful, you're making a habit of it." Laura smiled.

"You're lucky I like you and Thomas, Laura. You two fuckers are made for each other. If we get through this thing just promise me one thing."

"What's that?"

He looked at her. "Take care of him for me; for us. I see the way he looks at you."

* * *

Sunday July 29, 1990 4:00 a.m.

A phone started to ring deep within RHP. On the third ring it was picked up.

"Sir, we have intruders on the perimeter."

Mr. Glib swiveled in his office chair. It was deathly quiet. "Give them a reason to enter."

"Yes, sir." The line went dead.

* * *

"Bill," Sam said, "make your way to us. I think we're ready."

Crackle. "Roger that. On our way."

When Bill and Laura arrived they exited their rental and joined Sam and Thomas inside the Suburban.

"No change for hours," Sam informed them. "It's the perfect time to hit them."

"Why's that?" Laura asked.

Sam turned address her. "It's early morning. The guards are potentially at the end of their shift and we haven't seen any patrols. Instead they've been relying on their video cameras to be their eyes. This works in our favor."

"How so?" she pressed.

"If this is supposed to be a covert facility, or at least part of it is, then having too much obvious security prompts too many questions. I'm hoping for minimum resistance at this hour because it's Sunday and well before anyone should be arriving to work."

"We've danced this dance before, Laura, don't sweat it," Bill said.

"Laura, the three of us are going to breach this facility. You're our backup." Sam pulled one of their SANDBOX business cards out of a drawer on the dash, wrote on the back of it and handed it to her. "There's a name and a number. If we're not out of there in forty-five minutes you need to call him."

"What do I say?" she asked.

"Tell him exactly what's going on. You've got a crap load of evidence too."

"Okay."

"We'll stay on comms as long as possible, but I can't guarantee that when we go underground the signal will be able to reach you."

She leaned forward, embraced and kissed Thomas. "Be careful." She opened the door, got out and then got in to the driver's seat of the Cherokee. The loaded Glock 17 was on the seat next to her just in case.

Sam focused back on Thomas. "Okay, this is what's going to happen. I'm going to sneak around and flank the exterior guard. Once he's down I'll pop the gate and Bill will drive up, get me, and we'll make a bee-line for the front door. When you exit stay behind the vehicle and watch our six. If you see anything you yell into your mike. Bill and I will neutralize the lobby guards."

"What' ya think, Sam, flash bangs?" Bill said

"As far as we know they're not part of the bigger picture here and are probably just rent-a-cops. Blind and gag," Sam nodded. "Thomas, you have the access badge that Steve sent you?"

Thomas reached in to his pocket and pulled it out. "Yup."

"Do you think it'll still work?" Bill asked. "Wouldn't they have deactivated the access by now?"

"That's a damn good point," Sam said. "If it doesn't work then plan B will be to grab an access card from one of the guards. If that doesn't work then we'll have to abort."

"Roger that."

"One we're inside and the explosions go off, Thomas, follow us in. I won't put you in direct danger."

Thomas nodded but his fingers were clammy and his stomach was doing somersaults.

"You okay?" Sam asked him.

"Jittery."

"That's normal, brother," Bill said. "The adrenaline will hit soon enough. Just remember to breath."

"Questions?" Sam asked his friend.

"Do I shit my shorts now or later?" Thomas joked.

"That's the spirit," Bill said.

Sam and Bill put on tactical vests, pulled out two flash bangs each and put them in their pouches. Sam thought about taking the MP5 for his sneak around but decided against it. He loaded up on handgun magazines. Bill removed an MP5 and placed it on his lap. He secured four additional submachine gun and six handgun mags. Thomas watched all this with this mouth open.

Holy shit, this is really happening. Thomas was shaking.

"Easy, Thomas," Sam said. "Drink some water, then step outside and piss in the bushes."

Thomas picked up a bottle of water, drank deeply then opened the front right door of the Suburban and stepped out. He looked over at Laura who sat in the Cherokee parked behind them and gave her a half smile, and then sauntered into the bushes to relieve his nervous tension.

"Alright Bill, I'm heading out. Give me five minutes to work my way around." Sam pulled a black baklava over his head.

"You got it. Be careful."

"Always." Sam stepped out, closed the door quietly and slipped into the night, working his way left to come in on the guard shack from behind. Bill took over the driver's seat. Thomas was done and sat back in the passenger seat. He closed the door softly.

"I'm not used to the weight of the gun on my belt," he said.

"Don't worry about it," Bill said. "Get ready and stay alert. Put this on." Bill handed a baklava to Thomas and then put one on. They didn't want the cameras identifying them.

Bill scanned the area with the binoculars. "No change," he said into his mike. He received a double click in his ear as the reply.

"Wait. What's this?" Bill said out loud to no one in particular.

At the guard shack the man inside moved and the facility's front gate gate swung open. The guard stepped out, briskly walked towards the front entrance, opened the doors and disappeared inside.

"Fuck. We're going now," Bill said to Thomas. He started the Suburban. In to his mike he said, "Meet you at the gate in ten seconds." Bill drove forward quickly and scanned the entire area. As he approached the open gate Sam ran at them from off to the left and jumped in. Bill drove up to the front of the building, cut the engine, and jumped out. He had his MP5 up and ready. Sam and Bill headed towards the front doors. Thomas climbed out the right door, pulled out his Glock and held it down in the ready position.

"Trap?" Bill asked.

"Maybe, but we don't have any time to second guess. We were seen on the cameras for sure. Let's go!"

Sam switched his Glock to his left hand, pulled out a flash bang, disengaged the pin, but kept a solid grip on the spoon. Bill opened the front door and Sam tossed the grenade inside. They turned around, covered one ear with their free hand, pressed their other ear into their shoulders and closed their eyes. Moments later they heard the muffled explosion and the tinted windows glowed brightly.

"GO!" Sam commanded.

They entered the lobby and the doors closed behind them. When they entered Sam immediately moved left, his weapon extended, while Bill moved straight ahead. Sam encountered a closed door with the word SECURITY and kicked it in. Bill, his submachine gun at the ready, didn't encounter any resistance in the lobby and turned towards the security counter just as Sam broke the door in.

"CRAAACK!"

The stunned guard, behind the door, flew backwards and hit the far wall, his gun clattering to the ground. He recovered and focused his eyes on Sam, obviously unaffected by the grenade's flash.

"On the ground!" Sam yelled. The guard rushed him.

Bill approached the counter that separated the desk from the lobby. Two guards were standing, handguns extended, but clearly blinded and deaf having caught the full effect of the blast. Bill jumped the counter.

Sam sidestepped the guard and brought his right knee up sharply into the man's stomach.

Bill slung his weapon, grabbed both of the guard's handguns and twisted them upwards in their hands. They two men cried out and released their grips rather than risk broken fingers.

Sam lowered the defeated man to the floor and restrained him.

Bill pushed both men to the floor, which were in no condition to resist, and restrained them as well.

"CLEAR!" Sam yelled.

"CLEAR!" Bill yelled.

*　*　*

Thomas watched them, wasn't prepared the flashbang and was now temporarily blinded. *Fuck.* He ducked down but didn't hear anything but the distinctive hum of the powerful overhead floodlights. Thirty seconds later he had retained most of his eyesight.

Thomas spoke in to his mike. "Guys?"

"Clear," Bill said. "Come on in, Thomas. Laura, so far so good."

Thomas stood up and looked around. Nothing had changed other than the gate by the guard shack was still wide open. With his Glock ready he sidestepped from the Suburban to the front doors, glanced around one more time, pulled the door open and slipped inside.

A large burn mark scarred the white floor where the flashbang had exploded. Thomas didn't see anyone at the guard desk.

"Over here."

He swiveled to the left, gun down, and saw Sam. The doorway that led behind the guard counter was open, and three men were on the ground, their hands and feet were bound with plastic cuff ties. Duct tape had been placed over their mouths. They appeared unharmed but dazed.

"Let's go," Sam said.

The three of them, weapons ready, quickly headed around the exterior of the guard desk and down the hall. The map that Steve had provided had been correct; the lone elevator was right where it said it would be. Thomas pulled out Steve's ID badge.

"Now or never," Bill said.

He slung the MP5 over his back, drew his Glock and pointed it at the closed elevator doors. Thomas used the ID badge on the raised pad that was on the wall. Nothing happened.

"Try it again," Sam said.

Thomas placed it on the raised pad again and held it there. The light blinked green and they heard the elevator move.

"Well fuck me, it worked," Bill said.

Thomas moved against the wall and watched the hallway where they'd come from. It was still clear and deathly silent. Bill and Sam had taken up forty five degree angles that faced the elevator. If any opposition appeared they had it covered. The sound of the elevator stopped and the doors slid open quietly. Sam and Bill braced themselves but it was empty.

"Go."

"Laura, we're entering. Comms will probably be non-existent after this. Give us thirty minutes."

The doors to the elevator closed behind them and Thomas placed the badge on the pad until it blinked green. The elevator descended.

"Good luck," Laura said as her earpiece went dead.

* * *

Between the three of them Thomas' heart was racing. *How can anyone get any air through this hood?*

"Just breathe, brother," said Bill.

The elevator continued downward. Sam and Bill stood, angled, ready to clear the room the moment the doors opened. Their descent slowed.

"Here we go," Sam said.

The doors opened and time seemed to stand still. Thomas watched as his best friends exited the confined space, handguns up, and entered the next room with purpose. The only illumination came from the elevator. Sam and Bill flanked the elevator doors, pulled out small flashlights and scanned the room. It was ten by ten and incased in what appeared to be glass; their lights reflected back on them. There was a door on the far wall opposite the elevator.

425

"Clear," they both whispered.

Thomas stepped out of the elevator and inspected the room. Above the door he could barely make out a monitor. The elevator doors behind him slid shut.

"Scan the badge, Thomas," Sam instructed.

Thomas held up the ID badge to the raised panel. Nothing happened. He tried again. No response.

"It's not working," Thomas replied.

"I don't like this," Bill said.

The lights in the ceiling started to flicker and then the glass encased entryway filled with light, as did the rest of the underground laboratory. A huge open space opened right outside the closed door in front of them and they saw what appeared to be a large office that overlooked that large open space.

"Holy shit, look at the size of this place," Bill exclaimed.

Sam scanned but didn't discern any movement. He didn't like it either. "Try that door."

Bill placed his hand on the handle and pulled. It didn't budge. "No go, brother."

The monitor above the door powered on and caught their attention. An image of a man appeared on screen.

"No fucking way," Bill said.

"Hello you little shits. You fell right in to my trap."

On screen the three of them stared into the eyes of an older Nigel Clemmings. The last thing they heard was the sound of gas venting out of the ceiling.

58
Sunday July 29, 1990 5:58 a.m.

THUMP!

"OOOOWWW!" Thomas screamed.

It was dark. He was blind. Intense pain rippled through him again. THUMP!

"FFUUUUCCKKKIINNNGGG HELLLL!" he cried out in anguish.

Someone moved around him; shoes on the floor. THUMP!

"OOOOUUUCCCCHHHH. STTTOPPP ITT!"

The pain was too much. Suddenly there was light as his blindfold was removed. He blinked furiously and tried to look around. *I can't move.* A hazy figure walked over to him. Thomas blinked a few more times before he was able to focus.

"So glad I could hear you cry out again....Tommy."

Nigel stood over him, definitely older.

"Welcome back, Tommy. As you can see, or maybe you can't, you and your cohorts are now at my mercy."

Thomas shifted his head around and realized that he was strapped to a table. Sam was on his left and Bill was on his right, both still unconscious.

"Oh, don't you worry about them, Tommy. They'll be awake in no time."

He struggled to move but the leather restraints had him firmly secured. He struggled to comprehend what was happening. His stomach hurt. *Is this a dream?* Bill and Sam started to stir.

"Oh good, Sammy and Billy are going to join our party," Nigel said, obviously pleased with himself. He backed off.

"What's....what's going on?" Sam murmured. The gas was wearing off.

427

"Ow…, my head," Bill said.

Thomas looked at Sam and then checked out Bill. "Sam! Bill!" They opened their eyes and started blinked as Thomas had done. "Sam! Bill! Are you guys okay?"

"Thomas?" asked Sam as he emerged from the fog.

"I'm here."

"What the fuck," Bill said off to the left.

"Hey, Bill, you okay?"

Bill flexed and remained stationary. He tried to move again and was denied. "What the fuck! I can't move!"

"Neither can I," Sam said. "What the hell?"

"Are you guys alright?" Thomas asked.

"Just fucking peachy," Bill said irritably.

"Ditto," Sam said.

"Well, looks like all of my guests have arrived."

"I know that fucking voice," Bill said through clenched lips.

Nigel walked over and slowly gawked over his captured prizes. "I would hope so, Billy."

Bill strained his neck to look at Nigel. "Fucking Nigel. You piece of shit. You're still alive?"

"Indeed," Nigel said as he took his time, clearly enjoying the moment.

"Release us," Sam commanded.

Nigel sauntered over to Sam's table and peered down. "Now what fun would that be, Sammy? Here I've gone to all this trouble and you don't want to play anymore?"

"Fuck you!" he yelled and continued to struggle against his bonds.

"That's better," Nigel said, smiled and walked back over to Thomas.

"What the fuck, Nigel?" Bill asked. He was getting nowhere with his restraints either.

"Oh how much fun this is going to be," Nigel said. He had quite the smile on his face. "Where to begin? Where to begin? Ah yes." He began pacing the room as he talked. "I see that your informant, Steve Hodgson, was nice enough to send you that packet of breadcrumbs he stole from me."

"His letter said he was lucky to escape with his life," Thomas said.

"Yes, about that," Nigel replied. "I knew he was planning an escape. I mean, I did order his sixteen fellow scientists to be killed. His paranoia was well founded."

"You sick fucker," Bill said.

Nigel smiled and continued. "All I did was make it easier for him; although I have to say I was relatively impressed with his ingenuity. Do you know he concocted a variant of CS gas to procure his escape? It was brilliant and I loved every second of it! Anyway, his accomplice didn't fare so well, as intended. Poor Jack Thompson, shot in the back. It almost brings a tear to my eye." Nigel made a sad face and then laughed.

"You've always been one twisted fuck," Sam said.

"Now now, Sammy, don't spoil the game. I wouldn't want to remove a player too soon." Nigel extended his right arm and pointed a gun at Sam's head. It was one of their Glock 17's. "Very nice choice, Sammy. I absolutely love this model. Now say you're sorry!"

Sam looked at Nigel with contempt. "Fuck you psycho."

Nigel lowered his arm and forgot about Sam as he paced. "Anyway, where was I? So Steve got away and sent you information on my little project here."

"He's out of your reach now, Nigel," Thomas said confidently.

Nigel's smile grew even larger. "On the contrary, my dear Tommy, Steve is nothing more than fish food. He played his small role, warning you, but that's as far as I wanted him to go."

Collectively Thomas, Sam and Bill still struggled to free themselves, but it was a losing battle. Nigel continued to walk around the room, very pleased.

"Do you know how fucking rough it was growing up?" Nigel practically growled. His entire demeanor shifted. "Nigel, shut the fuck up. Nigel, you're a disgrace. Nigel, I can't believe you got whooped on. Nigel, stop crying you faggot. Nigel, you'll never be a man." He stopped pacing as the memories flooded through him like hot daggers. He pointed at Thomas. "You had NO idea what it was like, Tommy!!" Nigel pulled the Glock out of his pants and shoved it in Thomas' face. "I should just end your suffering right now!!"

"DOOOONNN'T!!" Sam and Bill cried out in unison.

Thomas only saw the end of the barrel and his eyes fixated on it; the low light in the room only allowed him a small glimpse up the dark barrel. The bullet was coming. Nigel was going to kill him.

"You're right. You're absolutely right. Tommy needs to suffer. What was I thinking? Sheesh. That was close." Nigel lowered the weapon and tucked it back in the front of his pants. "Sorry about that, Tommy, I almost ruined the game." He started moving around again. "The horrors that were introduced in that household….my father was a madman! You know NOTHING of suffering, Tommy!"

The three of them remained silent as Nigel ranted. There wasn't much they could do at the moment.

430

Nigel continued. "The atrocities he was responsible for. I hated that sonofabitch. I hated you, Tommy! YOU are the one responsible!"

"What the fuck did I do?" Thomas asked.

Nigel quickly bore down on him and stopped when we was two inches away from Thomas' face. His breath was rancid and hot. "You killed him."

"I what? What the hell are you talking about?"

"Don't pretend, Tommy." Nigel stepped back. "There's no need to pretend anymore. You killed him."

Thomas struggled. Sam and Bill didn't know what was going on and could only listen. "What the fuck, Nigel! I didn't kill anyone!"

Nigel stood there, calmly. "Oh, but you did, Tommy. You killed my brother. You killed Nigel." The words hung out there. The room was silent.

Thomas spoke up. "You're not making any sense. I have no fucking idea what you're talking about. You're standing right there. You're Nigel you fucking lunatic!"

"Oh, poor Tommy. Raise your hand if you're confused. Anyone? No?" Nigel smiled and approached Thomas once more. "I really should have been upfront with you from the beginning. I apologize. My real name is Eternal Glib and I'm very happy to meet you."

"You're a fucking creep job!" Thomas screamed. "Back off!"

"Bullshit, Nigel," Sam said. "Aside from having us strapped down you feel the need to feed us this line of bullshit?"

Mr. Glib continued. "I run this project at RHP. This place, all of it, is mine."

"Who cares Nigel...we don't give a shit," Sam said.

"How about this then, Sam…my twin brother's name was Nigel Clemmings." He paused.

"Twin?" Bill said. Sam and Thomas stole a glance at each other.

"My real name is Albert Clemmings. Nigel was my identical twin."

Albert backed away and no one said a word. Each of their minds tried to process this new information.

"Bullshit," Bill said.

Albert stole Bill a glance. "Oh really." He looked back at Thomas. "Not that it's of great importance. In reality my name is still just a pseudonym. Eternal Glib, is actually an anagram." Albert waited for a few seconds. "Anyone? Anyone at all? No? Well then I'll tell you. When rearranged it spells out Albert Nigel. Isn't that the cutest?"

"You're insane," Sam said.

Albert ignored the comment. "Tommy here decided to rid the world of Nigel that one night. You remember that particular Christmas, don't you, Tommy?"

Thomas struggled. "I don't know what you're talking about."

"Oh sure you do. That was the Christmas you came in to my house and killed Nigel. You must remember that?"

"I never killed anyone!!" Thomas screamed.

"Leave him alone," Sam threatened, "or so help me…"

"Shut up, Sammy, or do you want the gun to your head again?" Albert said coolly. He turned back to Thomas. "I don't see how you can forget such an event, Tommy. But then again, you've forgotten so much about your past, haven't you?" Albert's smile was vicious. "Maybe we should ask your girlfriend, Laura."

"DON'T YOU FUCKING TOUCH HER! I'LL KILL YOU MOTHERFUCKER!" Thomas breathe was ragged.

432

"There it is. We all knew it was inside you, Tommy," Albert replied. "But back to you killing Nigel."

"I don't care if he's your brother or if you're Nigel. He was a fucking prick. If he's dead I'm not going to shed any tears, but I didn't come in to your house, let alone kill him."

Albert walked around the room and finally said, "Are you sure?"

"Of course I'm sure," Thomas replied.

Albert reached down and picked something up. "Then what can you tell me about this?"

All three of them strained to look at what Albert was holding. It looked like a big stick. Albert came closer and held up a baseball bat. The upper part of it was covered in a rustic red.

"Do you remember now, Tommy?" He drew closer. "This is the bat you used to kill my brother with. That's his blood." Albert extended the bat over Thomas who had no other choice but to look at it.

"No, I didn't do it."

Albert moved his hands and exposed five letters on the side of the bat. They spelled out 'TOMMY'.

59

Monday October 16, 1967 7:39 p.m.

The front door opened to the Clemmings residence, Nigel stepped inside and he closed it behind him. He still felt woozy from his head wound. On the bus ride home he had sat in his standard seat in the very back where the other kids knew to give him a wide berth. On this particular day it was probably the calmest drive home the bus driver had ever experienced.

That fucking Sammy. Man, I hate him.

Nigel headed down the hallway to his bedroom and dropped off his backpack. He walked across the hall and went into the bathroom. He looked in the mirror and saw the damage the rock had done.

Fuck. No way the old man is going to miss this.

He put a baseball cap on, winced, and checked out his reflection.

Better.

Nigel left the bathroom, headed back down the hallway and passed a few family pictures along the way. They each were of himself and his father from various moments in their life. At one time Nigel had mistakenly asked his father why Albert was never in a one of them. His father had answered, "You both look the fucking same, I don't need two fucking photographs."

Nigel turned left into the kitchen, opened the fridge, took out two root beers, unlocked the door to the basement, turned on the light which illuminated the darkness and headed down the steps. He stopped at the bottom. The air was stale and stank of urine.

"Come on out, Alfart."

"My name is Albert," a voice said from underneath the stairs.

"Nigel turned around. Whatever, Alfart. Do you want a soda or not?" Nigel raised the root beer in his hand and swung it back and forth.

"Gimme!" Albert came out and reached for the soda. Nigel dropped it and the can split open when it struck the concrete floor, spewing carbonated root beer everywhere. Albert scrambled to open the can and drink whatever contents were left.

"Nice catch, Alfart."

Nigel laughed and opened his own pristine soda. He drank deeply and belched. He sat down on the stairs. Albert had soda all over his dirty bare feet and torn blue pajamas. He sucked down what little root beer he could and grinned.

"What do you say, Alfart?"

"Thank you, Nigel."

"You'd better fucking believe you're thankful. Speaking of, here's my homework. Get busy on it." Nigel dropped his backpack on the floor next to his brother.

The basement was where their father kept Albert locked away, day after day. Harold Clemmings ruled the house with an iron fist that served only his needs. His wife Susan had died while given birth to the two boys. Nigel had been born first and Albert had gotten wedged in her birth canal and that complication had caused her to bleed internally. The doctor didn't catch the problem in time and his wife never saw their identical twin babies before she died right there on the table. Harold, in his ultimate wisdom, had blamed Albert for her death, and had punished him since the beginning and had kept Albert locked away, out of sight, from everyone for his entire life. He's never gone to school nor had any friends. When asked if he had any children Harold would only talk about Nigel. To him, he only had one son.

The three Clemmings had just moved to Orinda and rented a house off of Camino Sobrante. Harold had currently found work as a garbage man, which made the time he got home every day somewhat unpredictable.

"Why are you wearing a baseball hat, Nigel?"

"Shut the fuck up and mind your own business," Nigel snapped back. "You're lucky I brought you a soda, you runt."

Albert took Nigel's backpack and retreated backwards to his stained mattress which lay on bare concrete. He sat on it and finished up his root beer. A dirty comforter lay halfway off the mattress. A few textbooks were piled next to the makeshift bed, apparently meant to keep Albert busy during his long days of confinement. A paint can was in the corner with a mostly used spool of toilet paper sitting next to it. That was Albert's bathroom.

"What happened at school today?"

Nigel sat down on the stairs and started ranting. "Fucking Tommy and Sammy. They were out in the field playing with a baseball bat. I snuck up on them and took it. I was about to bash that little fucker when Sammy hit me in the head with a rock. Fucker hurt."

Albert got up from his bed. "Let me see."

"Sit your ass back down." Albert complied. "I'm going to get those sons of bitches."

"Is it fun?"

"Is what fun?"

"Beating on other kids?"

"It's the best thing in the world," Nigel replied quickly.

"In the world?"

"Better fucking believe it, Alfart."

The front door opened upstairs. Nigel heard it and raced up the basement stairs, closed and locked the door behind him. He opened the fridge.

The front door closed. "Where's my beer? Get me a fucking beer you worthless piece of shit."

Nigel had a beer in his hand already and knew the drill. He closed the fridge and headed towards the front door with it extended.

Harold saw him said, "About fucking time you moron." He snatched the beer out of his hands and opened it. He emptied half of it. "What the fuck are you wearing a baseball hat for?"

Nigel didn't answer.

"Are you fucking deaf? Answer me!"

Nigel backed up slowly as his father advanced. The smell of the garbage dump filled Nigel's nostrils and he gagged. Harold knocked the hat off his son's head and the swelled bloody bump stared back at his father.

"What's this tough guy?" his father asked as he pointed to the injury.

"Nothing."

"Nothing? I don't think it's nothing. It's fucking something alright." He grabbed Nigel's right shoulder with his free left hand, finished off the beer with his right, squished the can and dropped in on the floor. "Looks like you need another lesson in toughness."

Nigel tried to break free but his father's strong grip kept him right where he was. Harold backhanded Nigel across the face which sent him flying across the living room floor.

"Owwwwww," Nigel cried out.

His father came at him. "Did you just say ouch? I don't fucking think so." Harold slapped him again

438

"Owww!!"

"Try it again you spineless wimp!"

He hit Nigel again and again.

At the top of the basement stairs Albert had his ear plastered to the bottom of the door. There was a gap there and he listened as his brother got the shit beat out of him. He knew that six or so beers later the basement door would open and it'd be his turn.

Albert walked towards Thomas and pushed the bat near his face.

"So what I hear you saying is that you didn't kill Nigel, is that right Tommy?" he sneered.

"That's right." Thomas was panicking. *What the fuck. How did this psycho have my childhood bat?*

"Surprisingly, Tommy, I don't believe you. How the fuck else could I have your bat?" Albert walked away and put the bat down. "Let me fill you in on what's been keeping me busy for all these years." He looked around at his three prisoners. "Who's ready for a story? Pay attention now. Oh wait, you don't have a choice." He laughed while they remained silent.

"My father beat us mercilessly, day after day, when he wasn't passed out drunk. I was kept in basement after basement as we moved from state to state. I was the secret Nigel and my father kept; the dark secret that my brother would never breathe a word about to anybody. When our father was working, and out of the house, Nigel would sneak down stairs. Sometimes he'd treat me nicely, talk and even play with me; teach me things or bring me books. Most of the time, however, he'd emulate what our father did. In essence I got the brunt of the beatings in our family."

"Boohoo," Bill said.

Albert quickly walked over to Bill and punched him in the mouth and split his lip. "Watch your mouth. Billy." He walked away.

"Our father didn't care about either of us, especially me. When he'd visit me in the basement he'd constantly remind me that I was the reason his wife died. There was a complication at

441

birth after Nigel was born. I twisted inside my mother. She bled out." Albert kept pacing the room, talking out loud. "After you came into our house that Christmas night everything changed."

"I've never been to your house!" Thomas yelled. "Listen to me dammit!"

Albert ignored him, lost in the story. "Our father had gone off the deep end that day, drinking, and had passed out on the couch. That was probably our Christmas present; no beatings. Nigel had unlocked the door to the basement that night and I finally was able to go outside. The air was so fresh and it tasted delicious." Albert almost smiled as he recalled the memory. "But then later that night you came by, with your bat, and you beat my brother into nothing!" Albert screamed. "I heard it all!"

What the fuck? What the fuck? What do I do? We're so fucked. Thomas continued to panic.

"So, as you can imagine, when my drunken ass father woke up the next morning, and found the bloody remains of my brother, he did the only thing he could do. That's right, you guessed it. He buried Nigel in the backyard and we moved out two days later. Fucking cold, don't you think?" Albert looked around the room at his audience who only stared back at him. He continued. "For years, after we moved away, I dreamed of revenge. That's all I wanted. I eventually ran away and started my own life. Goddamn amazing what you can do when you put your mind to it." Albert walked back over to Thomas. "So you see, Tommy, you've been a killer from the very beginning."

"Leave him alone," Sam said. Albert glanced over at Sam.

"I didn't do it," Thomas replied as he got Albert's attention again.

"You're not so sure anymore, are you, Tommy? All those hours of hypnotic regression with your girlfriend. All those repressed memories in your head. You know you killed Nigel, don't you?" Albert taunted him.

"How do you know about the regressions?" Thomas asked.

"You really want me to spell it out for you? Anyone care to jump in here for me?"

"Thomas, he probably bugged her office just like your house," Bill said.

"Dingdingding. We have a winner. Thank you, Billy. Now, that wasn't so hard, was it, Tommy? I've been listening to your progress for the last two months."

"My progress?"

"Oh right. Well, maybe my progress of you is a better description." Albert walked away and paced again. "I've developed a chemical compound that allows me to control anyone who's been injected with it. It took a long time to perfect really. The military underwrote the entire project, which was very nice of them I must add. Of course, like the scientists that worked for me, the military contacts that knew about this project are dead. Too bad really. I was rather fond of General Michaels." Albert paused and came back over to Thomas. "Anyway, back to my point. I had you injected on June fourth. Trust me when I say that your nightmares started shortly thereafter."

"You sonofabitch." Thomas fought against his restraints and then collapsed.

"Oh, but Thomas, they were so much fun to listen to. There's nothing like creating memories, in your head, of you being beaten by Nigel. You have no idea how much fun it was for me!"

"You sick bastard," Sam said.

Albert continued. "I sent you out on two initial missions, Tommy. Do you remember? No, of course you don't. The drug worked perfectly."

"What did you do to me?"

"Oh relax. Those two missions didn't have you killing anyone. They were tests. The bottom line is that I had you leave your house and run around the neighborhood for a while, tire you out so you'd wake up exhausted the next day. The best part was that I had real people killed on those nights just to mess with your head. It was fantastic fun. Actually, come to think of it, you really seemed to enjoy shooting a gun during my first test."

"Why? For what purpose?"

"Isn't it obvious?" Albert said. "The third mission was about sending you out to kill."

"The blood on my hands."

"That's right. You do remember. I even had an axe buried in your garden. You about shit yourself that day." Albert was very pleased with himself. "Ahh, good memories." He smiled. "Of course, the news report did say the axe was left at the scene. Guess you missed out on that little detail, Tommy."

"But I didn't do it."

"Alas, you're correct on that note Tommy. When I called you that evening and, how do I say, activated you there was a problem. You didn't obey my order to kill."

"I knew I fucking didn't kill anyone."

"I was gravely disappointed and so I set you up with the blood and the writing on the wall instead. You freaked out, as intended." Albert walked over towards Bill. "What I didn't take in to account was that it would motivate you to get your head examined. A small oversight, but you're still here, trapped, in my endgame."

"Fuck you psycho," Bill said. "It's not over yet."

"Oh poor, Billy. Please, continue to struggle, it amuses me."

"Fuck you." Albert grinned.

444

"As it turned out, during my research of the chemical agent, it only really worked on people that were prone to violence. My test subjects were Death Row inmates from around the country. As you may imagine they were of the violent persuasion. Tommy here," as he slapped Thomas on the shoulder, "was hardly made of the same material. Your brain refused to obey the order to kill. Believe me when I tell you how much that really pissed me off."

"Too bad fucktard," Thomas said somewhat relieved.

"But your suffering, young Tommy, was to continue and continue it did. If I couldn't make you kill then I'd make you think you had killed. It was just as much fun, trust me. To have you think that innocent blood was on your hands. That you had axed someone to death without even knowing it, well, that was a thing of beauty."

"You're sick." Thomas spat on Albert.

Albert wiped his face off and smiled. "How's your mother, Tommy? She still dead and twisted in that car wreck?"

"Fuck you! Fuck you!" Thomas cried out.

"Or how about your dead father? Another Christmas miracle. You miss him too?"

"FUCK YOU!!"

"Shut the fuck up!" Sam warned.

"You're a dead man," Bill added. "You're a fucking dead man."

"I'll tell you a little secret." Albert leaned in closer to Thomas. "I killed your grandparents."

Thomas was crying now, struggling in vain to get free, beyond panic. This was too much; too much all at once.

"Easy, Thomas," Sam said. "Don't let him get in your head."

Albert walked away, leaned against the wall and took it all in. The waves of suffering, which emanated out of Thomas, he drank it in deeply.

"Breathe Thomas, breathe," Bill said.

"I...I...I can't breathe," Thomas whispered.

"Get him some air damnit!" Sam yelled at Albert.

"Oh shut up, will you. He'll be fine in a few minutes. Panic attacks are always so much fun to enjoy."

I have to get myself under control. Thomas concentrated on the white ceiling and forced himself to relax. *Breathe Thomas. Easy.* More air flowed into his lungs and his heartbeat slowed.

"Well, wasn't that fun," Albert said. "Playtime is over I'm afraid." He walked back over by Thomas. "I have another story for you, Tommy."

"I don't want to hear it."

"Maybe not but you have little choice. Let's travel back to that fateful Christmas again, shall we.

"Fuck you already."

"Our father had passed out on the couch, that drunken shithead. You remember that part I'm sure. There were some legal papers on the table. Something to do with being sued; I don't know. Anyway, it was well past bedtime and I was still awake and in Nigel's room, having tasted my freedom for the first time in years. Nigel had fallen asleep and I was playing with his toys because I didn't have any of my own, mind you. I heard the front door open and scrambled into Nigel's closet as quietly as I could and hid. I heard someone walking around the house and eventually come down the hall. The only light that was on in the room was a little nightlight because I was afraid my father would wake up and investigate if he saw the actual room light. Anyway, this man pushed the door open with a bat in his hands. He walked over to Nigel and just stared at him for the longest time. He eventually raised the bat over his head. But he just stood there, like a statue, and then lowered the bat. It slipped from his fingers, rolled on the floor and he fled our house."

"No," Thomas said.

"Actually, yes Tommy. I came out of hiding and stared at that bat. It's the same one I have with me today. It's your bat." Albert paused. "Your father was going to kill Nigel."

Thomas' mind raced. *It's not possible. He's lying.* "You're full of shit."

"Maybe I am, maybe I'm not. However, the next part I'm pretty certain of."

"What are you talking about?" Sam asked.

"Oh, the story gets better, don't you worry." He started pacing the room again. "I came up with a plan at that moment. It just came to me. Fancy that. I had touched my freedom and now knowing what that tasted like I wanted more. I didn't want to live in the basement anymore, beat on like a useless piece of meat, so I decided that that part of my life was over. So I did what came naturally to me, Tommy, what had been taught to me for years, by the hands of my father and by my twin brother Nigel. I took your bat and felt the endless rage flow through me. I took your bat, swung it high and cracked my brother's skull wide open." Albert grinned as he thought back on the event.

"What the fuck?" Bill said.

"You? You killed Nigel?" Thomas asked.

"Sorry to have misled you, Tommy. If it's any consolation your suffering pleased me greatly."

"You sick fuck," Sam said.

Albert continued his story. "But I digress. I continued to beat Nigel with all my strength, over and over again. His blood and brains were everywhere."

"You're sick."

"After I was done I felt liberated. It was the most amazing feeling. Euphoric is the closest word I think. My brother was just a pile of guts, blood and broken bones. He wasn't a threat to me anymore. I had freed myself. I thought about doing the same thing to my father, trust me, but I had something better planned, oh yes I did. You know what I did then. Tommy? Do you?"

"Dropped dead?"

"I took a shower. It was spiritual. I was reborn. Afterwards I dressed in my brother's clothes and packed some of them in a large backpack. I took all the money I could find in my father's room and I left that life behind. I had but one more stop along the way. You'll never guess where." Albert was ecstatic.

"To the mental hospital?" Bill quipped.

Albert leaned over Thomas. "I went to your house, Tommy."

"Like hell you did you fucking liar," Thomas snapped back.

"The house my father had rented on Camino Sobrante wasn't that far away from your house. I just climbed the fence and walked on the country club's golf course."

"You didn't know where I lived," Thomas countered.

"Personally I'd never been there, you're right. But Nigel knew where each of you lived. How sick is that?"

"You're lying and I know it," Thomas said.

"Then you might want to cover your ears for this next part." Albert looked at Thomas. "No? You're not going to cover your ears?" Thomas struggled against his bonds. "Okay, remember that I gave you fair warning." He started up his pace again. "When I got there your garage door was up. I thought that was strange but maybe your father forgot about that in his rush NOT to kill my brother. The alarm light was green so I was two for two. Let's just call it another sign of my new found freedom. I took off my backpack and left it by the garage door."

"Bullshit. Bullshit," Thomas mumbled.

"I opened the door, stepped inside, and closed it. Your house was pretty dark and quiet. I crept down the few stairs to your eating area."

"It's all bullshit. You weren't there."

"I tip toed, bat in hand, through your family room. There were so many Christmas decorations, too many if you ask me, and there was a light emanating from the hallway. You remember your house right? Let me know if I make any mistakes."

Thomas struggled.

"I stuck my head in the hallway and looked left. It looked like a master bedroom. I slowly inched my way down that hallway. The light was coming from your dad's study, wasn't it, Thomas?"

"There's no way you know this shit. No fucking way."

"I peeked again and saw the same man who had stood over my brother. His back was to me. He was sitting at a desk, writing something. I silently crept into the walk-in closet and waited. I'll freely admit to you, Tommy, my heart was racing and I needed to pee really badly. Strange, huh? Anyway, as I stood there waiting I heard a clank and then something spin. The man, your father, walked right past me heading towards the bathroom, I guess. I stepped out behind him and wacked him across the back of his head with your bat."

Thomas shuddered. Bill and Sam were helpless, not only within their bonds but listening to this madman's rant.

"Your father collapsed like a sack of potatoes with barely a grunt. He took it like a champ." Albert stopped like he had remembered something else. "But I was curious, Tommy. I was curious what that sound had been. So I turned around and went into your father's study. At first all I saw was the desk that he'd sat at. I tried opening and closing the drawers but they didn't make the same sound. So I turned around I saw the massive safe along the wall. You know what I did then? Do you? I reached out and spun the dial. What a delightful sound Tommy. I must have spun that thing two dozen times before I looked up. Do you know what I saw?"

Thomas was helpless. This man kept entering his brain, fucking with him. He was suffering.

"I saw the most beautiful thing ever. It was a gun. A shotgun to be precise, wasn't it, Thomas? I moved your father's chair and, while standing on it, managed to reach the shotgun and pulled it off the wall. Now, I won't bullshit you here, Tommy, I'd never held a weapon before in my life, let alone seen one. But I'd heard about them from Nigel and it looked simple enough. I figured out that you put your hand here," Albert mimicked the motion, "and your other hand farther up to hold it up. Something seemed loose. I examined it more closely and then pulled and pushed on it. What a beautiful sound that made. *Crack-Crack*. Just music to my ears." Albert stopped pacing and came over to Thomas again. "Do you know what I did then, Tommy?"

Thomas had his eyes closed. He was sweating and breathing heavily again.

"I walked back in to your father's bedroom. I put the shotgun and the bat down. Your father was still unconscious. I dragged him over to the side of the bed and propped him up against it and the nightstand. Nigel and I were big kids so you know what I'm telling you is true. I picked up the shotgun and placed the barrel under your father's jaw."

450

Thomas could barely hear Albert now. He was heading down a long, dark tunnel in his head.

"I placed his right hand on the trigger. Do you know what I did then, Tommy? Do you? Does it keep you awake at night?" Albert smiled over Thomas. "I pulled the trigger with his finger, Tommy, but I wasn't ready for the sound. It was the loudest sound I'd ever heard. I was deaf. I was deaf and bits of your father were all over. It was glorious." Albert had the most evil sneer on his face that Sam or Bill had ever seen in their lifetime.

Thomas's body exploded off the gurney, but was held fast. "I'LL KILL YOU MOTHERFUCKER!! I'LL FUCKING KILL YOU!!"

"THAT'S THE SPIRIT!!" Albert yelled.

He pulled out a needle and stuck Thomas in the neck.

61

Tuesday December 26, 1967 1:32 a.m.

BLAM!

Tommy woke up suddenly.

What was that?

He looked around his darkened room. Nothing had fallen. He climbed out of bed and headed down the hall towards the eating area. Tommy heard some rustling in the garage and then it was quiet.

"Dad?" he called out softly. Nothing. Quiet.

Tommy walked through the family room towards the soft glow of the alarm panel. The green light was on.

Weird. Why isn't it red?

Tommy stopped and stared at it for a few seconds, then noticed that the light was on in his father's room.

"Dad?"

What is that smell?

A lingering scent filled Tommy's nose.

Firecrackers?

Tommy walked down the short hallway and pushed open the door to his father's room. His father was sitting on the ground beside the bed.

"Dad?"

Tommy froze. The face....most of his father's face was gone. Blood and brain matter were everywhere. An empty eye socket stared back at him.

Tommy collapsed at his father's dead feet.

* * *

Tommy woke up with a start. Noise. Loud noises were all around him. He was confused. It was like he hadn't woke up completely yet and things were happening all around him that frightened him.

What's going on?

"Get the kid out of here!"

"Someone grab the kid."

Tommy's eyes were just beginning to focus when two strong hands came down and plucked him out of bed. He was carried through his house and out the door into an awaiting police car. The door was slammed behind him and it started to pull away from the curb. Tommy was coming out of his trance and saw an ambulance parked in his driveway along with a couple of other police cruisers. He didn't know what to do. The excitement caught up with him and he started to cry.

62
Sunday July 29, 1990 6:34 a.m.

"What the fuck did you just stick him with!?" Sam bellowed.

"Let me out of here!" Bill screamed. "I'll kill you myself!"

Thomas' neck was on fire. He looked up in to the grinning face of the man who had killed his father.

"Oh, so now you remember," Albert cackled.

Thomas felt bold, strong and impervious. He looked straight in to Albert's eyes and said, "Release me so I can kill you."

Albert was delighted. "Finally!"

He unclasped Thomas' legs first, the strap over his chest, his right hand and then backed away. Thomas immediately used his free hand to undo the leather strap that pinned his left hand to the table and was free.

"Get him, Thomas!" Bill yelled.

He got up off the table and advanced on Albert, his hands shaped in claws, face drawn back in a snarl. Thomas was out for blood.

"Oh dear," Albert mocked. "Whatever do I do now?"

"You're dead, Albert!" Thomas promised.

"Can a condemned man at least have his last words?" Albert said as he backed away. "Yes? No? Tell you what, I'll just go ahead with my speech then." Albert cleared his throat and said, "Cry Tommy."

* * *

Sam and Bill watched as Thomas progressed towards Albert. They had never seen their friend with such bloodlust in his eyes. The taunting that he'd put their friend through; telling him that he

455

was responsible for his grandparent's death, and now even his
father's death. Their friend was long gone in a haze of revenge.
Whatever Albert had injected into Thomas seemed to have pushed
him way over the edge as Bill and Sam continued to struggle
against their leather restraints.

Albert backed away and said, "Can a condemned man at least
have his last words?" Albert was clearly unafraid as he smiled.
"Yes? No? Tell you what, I'll just go ahead with my speech
then." They heard Albert clear his throat and then say, "Cry
Tommy."

Sam and Bill saw Thomas stiffen and freeze. His face relaxed;
the snarl gone as his arms dropped to their sides. His entire body
remained stiff, but he was no longer a threat. Albert approached
Thomas.

"Well boys," Albert said as he looked over at his remaining
two prisoners, "how do you like my creation?"

"What have you done to him?" Sam questioned.

"When I get out of these restraints you're going to pay for
what you've done to him," Bill promised.

Albert was deliriously happy. "You have no idea how happy I
am right now. Billy. Sammy. I'd like to introduce you to,
Tommy. He's the last thing you're going to see before you die."

Sam started to shout. "Thomas! Wake up, Thomas!"

"Oh, he can't hear you, Sammy boy, he's off in his own world,
having a nightmare. It was fun implanting those beatings in his
head. Oh, how he must be suffering. What fun!"

"You sick fuck!" Bill hollered.

Albert looked at them. "It's too bad really. All good things
must come to an end at some point." He walked away and
retrieved the bat. "Tommy." Thomas turned to face Albert.

456

"Take this bat and smash those two into oblivion." Albert handed Thomas the bat who took it without hesitation.

"Don't listen to him, Thomas!" Sam screamed. "Snap out of it!"

"Stop it, Thomas. Don't let it end like this!"

Albert grinned madly and clapped his hands together in anticipation. "Do it."

Thomas calmly walked over to Sam and looked down at him without any expression on his face whatsoever. His friend couldn't believe what was happening.

Not like this. "WAKE THE FUCK UP!!"

Thomas slowly raised his old, bloodied bat. Sam's eyes widened in fear; he knew this could be the end.

"COME ON, THOMAS. STOP IT!!" Bill yelled from the other table.

The bat slipped from Thomas's hands and clattered to the floor, who then fell to his knees.

"Nooo!" Albert cried out. "Get the fuck up. Finish them!"

Thomas didn't move. His head was lowered; shoulders slumped over. Albert came over to him and smacked his head with his hand. "Get up and kill them!" He hit him again and still didn't get a reaction. Albert then grabbed Thomas by both shoulders, twisted him around, picked up the bat himself and thrust it at Thomas. "Take this bat and you will kill them, Tommy. You will do as I command. You will worship the ground that I walk on."

Thomas stirred. He tilted his head up and saw the bat offered to him.

"Good, Tommy. Now take it and finish them off," Albert commanded.

Thomas grabbed the middle of the bat with his left hand, while Albert tightly gripped the bat with both of his, and looked into Albert's face.

"Do it, Tommy. Do it!" Albert was beyond himself with anticipation.

Thomas smiled and sharply pulled the bat towards him. Albert crashed into him and they sprawled to the floor. Albert bounded up with the bat in his hand.

"What the fuck are you doing? Kill them with this bat goddammit!" He was frothing at the mouth.

Thomas slowly stood up. "I'd rather use this," and raised his right arm.

Albert tracked Thomas' arm and realization set in. "MR. PETERSON!"

Thomas promptly discharged three rounds into Albert's chest and the sound deafened everyone in the enclosed room. The bat slipped from Albert's hands and joined the expended brass casings on the floor. A red spot spread on the front of Albert's chest and he gasped; his eyes wide.

"No…fair…" He collapsed to the floor.

The door to the room burst open and two large men bee-lined for Thomas. Thomas, with his right arm still extended, adjusted his aim slightly and expertly squeezed off six more rounds. Both men united Albert.

"Holy fucking shit," Bill exclaimed.

Thomas dropped the Glock and it clattered to the floor as a third man entered the room.

"George?" Thomas questioned.

* * *

458

George Miles slowly stepped through the laboratory door. He looked around at the three bodies on the floor and then at the two men still strapped to tables. He walked over and stood over the body of Albert.

"George?"

"It's me, Tom."

"George, I don't understand. What are you doing here?" Thomas was confused. Sam and Bill didn't know what was going on either.

"I came by to tell you that you're going to be just fine."

Thomas shook his head. "Where did you come from? What's happening?"

George walked over to Thomas and smiled and Thomas returned it. "Everything's going to be just fine now son." George put his right hand on Thomas' shoulder. "Close your eyes, Tom." Thomas felt very comfortable, but he wasn't afraid so he closed his eyes.

"Go ahead and open them now."

Thomas heard a different voice; familiar. He opened his eyes wide. Michael, his father, stood before him.

How is this possible? "Dad?"

"It's me, son." They embraced fiercely.

"Oh my god, dad, it's really you! I've missed you so much!" Huge tears ran down his face. He sobbed into his father's shoulder.

"Everything's going to be okay now, son. I've missed you too."

* * *

"Thomas! Thomas! TOMMY!!" Sam continue to yell.

Thomas blinked and found that he was standing up, hugging himself and crying heavily.

"Thomas?" Sam asked. "Can you hear me?"

"Hey brother…earth to Thomas." Bill chimed in.

He looked around at both of his best friends. "Hey. What's going on?"

"Holy shit balls. About damn time bro. Get me out of this shit." Bill was adamant.

Thomas slowly went over and released his straps, then repeated the process with Sam. The two groaned as they sat up and rubbed their wrists, which were raw from their struggles.

"Who were you talking to, Thomas?"

Thomas sat down on the edge of the table as Bill picked up the fallen Glock and checked the condition of the three bodies on the floor. He wiped away his tears, looked Sam in the eyes and gently answered, "My father. As strange as that sounds, Sam, I was talking with my father."

Bill had finished and discovered that all three were dead. "Impressive, Thomas. I guess we know you have it in you now." To Sam he said, "The room's clear."

"I'm not a killer, Bill. The situation called for me to act. I acted."

Sam patted him on the back. "Works for me. Thanks for saving our asses."

"What the man said, brother. Thanks."

Sam took charge. "We're not out of danger yet. Bill, lead the way."

"Roger that. Taking point."

Staying together they quickly cleared the rest of the lab. It was empty so they made their way back to Albert's office.

"Bill, tell me it worked," Sam said.

"Oh shit, I totally forgot." Bill reached into his boot and withdrew a Dictaphone and rewound the tape.

"What the hell?" Thomas probed.

"Aside from the shit that went on in this facility, and the information that Steve sent you, we decided to get creative. I hope it paid off," Sam told him.

The rewind button clicked off so Bill pressed play. There was a lot of static and then they heard Bill's voice.

"Holy shit, look at the size of this place."

"Try that door."

"No go, brother."

"No fucking way."

"Hello you little shits. You fell right in to my trap."

Bill clicked the Stop button. Sam picked up Albert's phone and dialed a number.

"F.B.I. Riverside Field Office. How can I direct your call?"

"I believe Agent Johnson is waiting for my phone call."

63
Sunday July 29, 1990 7:33 a.m.

It didn't take long for the F.B.I. to arrive in force. Laura had instructions to take all the evidence to the field office if they hadn't returned in thirty minutes. She hated driving away but she knew she might be their last hope of defense to get them back alive.

During the past five years of building, and running SANDBOX, Sam and Bill had acquired a number of contacts. An Agent Johnson, who headed up the San Francisco branch, had hired SANDBOX to train a group of his men on CQB firearms and tactics. Johnson had been genuinely impressed, had given Sam his personal number and had told them to call him if they ever required the help of the F.B.I..

The elevator doors finally opened thirty-five minutes after Sam placed the call. The three of them stood there, with their hands over their heads, as five armored assaulters leveled their weapons at them.

"Stand down," came a shout from the elevator. "They're okay. Clear the building."

The tactical group headed out to start their sweep. Sam, Bill and Thomas lowered their arms as Agent Johnson appeared out of the elevator.

"Nice place you have here, Sam," he said as he extended his hand.

"Only the best in secret laboratories." Sam shook his hand.

"I was skeptic when you had Ms. Bond contact me. But when she used your name and gave me the highlights I dropped everything to head here. The LA office is going to kill me on jurisdiction, but we're all supposed to be friends, right?"

"Where's Laura?" Thomas asked.

"Who are you?" Agent Johnson asked.

"Thomas Clark."

Agent Johnson smiled. "Very nice to meet you, Thomas. Laura's in the lobby upstairs. We'll need statements from all of you before you leave but after that you're free to go. Good to see you two again." Agent Johnson stepped past them and barked into his radio. "Three coming up. I need more men down here ASAP."

The three of them, along with another agent, took the elevator back up to the lobby where another group of agents filled the elevator to head back down. Laura saw them and ran over.

"I was so worried."

Thomas pulled her in close. "I never want to let you go again."

"Me either," she replied.

"It's over, Laura. It's finally over."

Sam and Bill stood close by and took it in. They had almost lost their lives but they'd both do it again in a heartbeat to help Thomas out.

The two new lovers pulled back and smiled at each other.

Bill finally spoke up. "We're okay too, Laura," he joked.

Laura let Thomas go and hugged Sam and Bill tightly. "Words don't express how I feel. Thank you so much."

"Your boy here was the one that saved us," Bill informed her. "Imagine that."

"Shut up, shitbird," Thomas said and everyone smiled.

* * *

464

Sunday July 29, 1990 2:50 p.m.

They pulled into the Motel-6 parking lot, got out, stretched and yawned. Making their statements had taken a long time. The good news is that they had been able to retrieve all their gear and no charges were being pressed.

"Kim is going to kill me. I'm heading inside to call her." Bill opened the door to their room and closed it behind him.

"Thank you, Sam…," Thomas said, "for everything."

"Anytime. I don't understand half the shit that went down quite honestly. What I do know is that when push came to shove you shoved back. We wouldn't be here having this conversation if you hadn't. Thank you."

Thomas didn't know what to say.

Sam changed topics. "So what are your plans now?"

Thomas looked over and Laura. She smiled and so did he. He turned his head back to Sam.

"How would you two like to have new neighbors?"

64

Friday August 3, 1990 1:15 p.m.

Laura and Thomas had just arrived at Oakmont Cemetery and the weather could not have been nicer. They parked and got out of their rental. The funeral for his grandparents would start in fifteen minutes. It had only been a few days since their adventure in San Bernardino but they had already started packing up their houses in preparation for the move. Aside from the funeral they wanted to take some time and look for a house to purchase.

They saw that Sam and Bill, along with Julie and Kim, had already arrived, each holding their daughters, Amanda and Sarah. There were quite a few unfamiliar and older faces; Thomas assumed they were friends of his grandparents. They walked over and joined the group.

"Good to see you two again," Thomas said to Sam and Bill. "Hi, Julie. Hi, Kim."

"Sorry for your loss, Thomas," Julie said.

"Me too," added Kim. "If there's anything we can do please let us know."

"Thank you." He stepped back. "I'd like you to meet Dr. Laura Bond."

"Call me Laura."

"We've heard all about you, Laura," Julie said. "The boys have done nothing but rave about you since they got back."

"Lies," poked Bill. "I think they're just secretly thrilled that Thomas is coming down off the mountain, and has found a woman no less."

"Take it easy," Sam cautioned. "We're at a funeral."

"It's okay, Sam, really," Thomas said. "I'm going to go thank everyone else who showed up. Excuse me."

Thomas left Laura in their very capable hands and worked his way through the crowd, thanking each and every one of them for attending. Thomas couldn't have felt any younger.

Two hearths drove up and even though he hadn't been through this in twenty three years it still brought a lump to his throat. He wasn't a child anymore. Everything around him seemed smaller, even the gravestones. The two caskets were removed, with dignity, and placed on the pedestals as he'd remembered. Laura walked up and gently put a reassuring arm around him. He glanced over and gently smiled at her. He was a lucky man.

The ceremony had been beautiful and Thomas let silent tears fall down his cheeks as he remembered all the good times he'd had growing up with them. People started milling around and Thomas took this moment to walk up to the caskets. He put one hand on each. He missed them.

"Hi grandpa. Hi grandma. I miss you both so much." Thomas paused. "I'm sorry for what happened but the man who was responsible has paid the price. I can't tell you how much it meant to me that we were able to spend some time together, just like the old days." He smiled as he spoke. "You were always there for me and I love you both." Thomas kissed each casket, stepped back a few feet away and knelt down at his parent's gravestone.

"Hi mom, dad. You'd think this would be easy for me but it isn't. I don't even know where to begin. I miss you both. Life was never the same after....well, you know. Thanks for looking after me." He took a breath. "I'm still trying to piece all of it together." He looked around to make sure he was alone. "You'd love Laura. She's a sweetheart. Just between you and me I'm going to ask her to marry me." Thomas kissed his fingers, pressed them on the gravestone and stood up.

468

"Excuse me," a man said off to his right.

"Yes?"

"Are you, Thomas Clark?"

"I am."

"I'm sorry to intrude on you, Mr. Clark. I'm Mr. Davenport, your grandparent's attorney," he said as he extended his hand.

Thomas shook it. "Nice to meet you, Mr. Davenport. What can I do for you?"

"I trust you received the power of attorney, the will and other documents I sent you?"

"Yes, of course, Mr. Davenport. I'm sorry. I haven't had a chance to look through anything yet. We're in the process of moving here."

"No no. My apologies, Mr. Clark. Take your time. I'm actually here today as requested by your grandfather's addendum clause."

"Excuse me?"

"It states that in the event of his death my firm is to deliver this package to you." Mr. Davenport pulled a small jewelry box from his pocket and handed it over. "Please, take it, Mr. Clark."

"What is it?"

"That sir, I do not know. Of course, when you do have a chance to look over the documents, after you've relocated, please give me a call. Good day, Mr. Clark."

Before Thomas could say anything else the man turned and left.

"Who was that honey?" Laura asked behind him.

"My grandfather's lawyer apparently. A little strange but I liked him. He said my grandfather wanted me to have this." Thomas held up the jewelry box.

"What's in it?"

Thomas didn't answer. *Good question.* He unclasped the hinged lock and gently pried it open. Inside there was a small piece of typewritten paper. It had the words 'Bank of America – Orinda branch' printed on it. The wind kicked up for a second and blew the small slip of paper out of the box. It had been hiding a key; a safe deposit box key.

*   *   *

"May I help you, sir?"

"I'd like access to a safe deposit box please," Thomas replied.

"Certainly, sir. Box number please?"

"I don't know. I only have the key."

"That is highly irregular sir. What's your name?

"Thomas Clark."

The man looked through the records in front of him. "Mr. Clark. Do you know an Ed Clark?"

"Yes, he was my grandfather. We were just at his funeral."

"My condolences, Mr. Clark. Our records show that a Mr. Ed Clark rented out a safe deposit box for a life term."

"What does that mean?"

"Quite frankly, Mr. Clark, it means that as soon as you access that box our contract with your grandfather is terminated. In layman's terms it means you need to remove all the contents as soon as you access it. The box was paid for well in advance so there's no rush whatsoever."

Thomas and Laura looked at each other. "What' ya think?"

"My curiosity is piqued, that's for sure."

"Mine too." Thomas turned back to the bank agent. "We'll access it today, thank you."

"Very well, Mr. Clark. Please sign here." Thomas did. "Come around the side and follow me please." The man led them in to the safe deposit vault, located the particular box and inserted a key. "Your key please, sir." Thomas handed it over. The man unlocked the door and pulled out a long box with a single lid and handed it to Thomas. "I'm going to keep your key, Mr. Clark. If you would like to rent the box yourself please feel free to let me know. Feel free to view the contents in an adjoining room."

Thomas and Laura were ushered in to a small room and the door was closed behind them. They looked at each other in anticipation.

What could possibly be in this box?

Thomas lifted up the hinge and they both peered inside to discover two envelopes. The one on top was addressed to Thomas and was in his father's handwriting. It was sealed. The second envelope also was addressed to Thomas, but this one was in his grandfather's handwriting. There was nothing else in the safe deposit box.

Laura took them from Thomas and examined them. "The sealed envelope is old, Thomas, but the second one is much more recent." She handed them back. "Are you going to open them?"

"I'm not sure. I'm kind of afraid of what they'll say. But if I do it certainly won't be in this bank. Come on, let's get out of here."

They left the empty deposit box and made their way towards the exit.

* * *

Thomas drove them a few blocks up to the park at the Community Center where they sat down at a picnic table on a

471

small knoll which overlooked the park. Thomas was wary of the contents of the two envelopes and knew they contained voices from the past.

Laura took his hand and smiled. "It's going to be fine," she said reassuringly.

He opened the one from his father. It contained a handwritten letter.

My dearest Tommy,

Today is Christmas and I just watched you ride away on your new bicycle. Today is also the day of painful truths, for me and for you. I can only tell you, Tommy, how very sorry I am for how blind I've been. I had no idea what Nigel had been doing to you and your friends since school began this year. It sickens me to the core. After tonight Nigel will no longer be a threat to you, or anyone else. I can't predict what's going to happen to me but I want you to know that I did it for you. I love you so much, Tommy. You were the best thing to happen to your mother and me. When she was killed we both lost a huge part of who we were. I know we both miss her terribly.

Your grandfather is going to have something special for you when you turn eighteen. I can't tell you what that is right now. What I will tell you is that you're going to have a lot of questions. I can't answer too many of those either. I work for a company that I can never tell you about. I specialized in acquisitions and investments making sure our family never lived above our means. I know this doesn't make any sense right now, Tommy, I'm sorry.

I'm sorry for leaving you. I can't deal with the fact that you live your life with fear and suffering. It's not fair.

I love you very much, Tommy.

Your father, Michael

A single tear silently crept down Thomas' face and dripped onto his father's letter. He handed it to Laura who read through it.

"I'm sorry," she said.

"Me too. He was going to kill Nigel for me. He wanted to stop my suffering."

"He was."

He caught her eye. "Yeah, but he couldn't bring himself to do it at the end. He knew he needed to be around for me rather than spending it in a prison." Thomas shook his head. "Fucking Albert."

Laura rubbed his hand from the other side of the table.

"My father had a whole other world that I didn't know anything about. Hell, I still don't know. I'm even more confused now."

473

"Kind of sounds like he was a spy."

"Who knows. It doesn't matter. What I do know is that I miss him."

Thomas folded up the letter and tucked it back in the envelope, then picked up the one from his grandfather. Inside was a typewritten letter, a folded piece of newspaper and a key.

Thomas,

By now you must be aware of how your father died. I never saw it coming, him taking his own life. It shocked us all. That morning after Christmas, when you woke up in the hospital, you didn't fully remember what had happened. I didn't have the heart to tell you and led you to believe he died in his sleep. Please forgive me for hiding such an awful truth from you, but I thought it was for the best.

You never wanted to go back to that house; at least you never asked to go back. Your grandmother and I never sold it either. The deed is under your name and the key to it is enclosed. After your father died his company came and sanitized the house. We didn't ask any questions. It's been sealed since then, Thomas. Only one thing remains in that house, Thomas. They left your father's safe in his

474

study. I'm not privy to its contents but you'll find the combination to it at the bottom of this letter.

I'm sorry for your loss as a son as I'll always be sorry for my loss as a father. Your grandmother and I love you very much.

Ed Clark

45-13-54-16-33

P.S. – I've enclosed a news clipping I thought you'd be interested in.

"Oh my god," Thomas said.

"What? What is it?"

Thomas handed her the letter. "All those years I thought my father died in his sleep. The worst part is that all these years my grandfather thinks his son killed himself. He thought that till the day he died." Thomas looked off at the horizon.

Laura read the letter as well, picked up the news clipping Thomas had forgotten about, unfolded and read it.

"Thomas. You have to look at this."

Early Tuesday morning, December 26, acting on an anonymous tip, police arrested Harold Clemmings, age 40 in his Orinda house located just off Camino Sobrante. Inside they found the bloody and battered remains of his son Nigel Clemmings, age 11. Harold immediately proclaimed his innocence but there were no signs of forced entry.

Only he and his only son lived there. A further search of the house led police to the basement where they discovered horrid living conditions. Apparently Harold Clemmings kept his son locked in the basement with minimal sanitary outlets and food. He's being held without bail and due to the severity of this crime will most likely face life in prison without the possibility of parole.

"What a neat little Christmas present Albert managed to get himself," Thomas said.

They both sat there, quietly, for a few minutes just enjoying the view but Thomas eventually stirred.

"Shall we?"

"Where are we going?" Laura asked.

"I thought maybe you'd like to see where I grew up."

* * *

The key fit in to the lock and made a snap as it was disengaged. They pushed the door open with some force, stepped inside and closed it behind them. Two decades of useless brochures, Sears catalogs, magazines, leaflets and Ed McMahon Publishers Clearing House prize envelopes had created a huge pile that had blocked the door, along with a thick layer of dust that coated the empty wood floors. In the living room the floor was wrought with leaves, having gained access from the chimney flue that had apparently blown open a number of years prior.

Thomas led Laura through the empty dining room and into the kitchen. Their footsteps echoed off the bare floors and walls. He opened a few cupboards and saw that they were all empty.

476

"It's strange being here."

"I can imagine," Laura replied.

He turned and slowly walked into the eating area. The family room was on his right, barren, and the laundry room, pantry and garage access were off to his left, but he headed for his old room down the hall instead. The carpet had long ago given up on looking fresh as years of sunlight beating down through the windows had significantly weathered it. Thomas pushed open the door to his room and entered with Laura right behind him. It was empty, like all the other rooms, but that didn't bother Thomas. He smiled as he envisioned exactly what it had looked like when he was a child. His bed was there, his desk, his little chair and all his toys in their nooks and crannies. To some degree he never wanted to leave this room again. For a while, at least, it had been a factory of pure happiness and joy.

"You okay?" Laura asked.

Thomas continued to look around and look at things that she didn't see. "It's hard to believe that we start out so innocent." Thomas paused. "And then how quickly it can be taken away."

She put her arm around his waist and he looked down at her.

"Is it time?" she asked.

"Yeah, it's time."

Thomas took her hand and led her back down the hall, through the eating and family rooms. The alarm panel in the hallway was dark because there was no electricity flowing to the house. The door to his parent's room was closed.

Laura squeezed his hand. "You can do this."

Thomas exhaled, opened it and stepped inside. His parent's room was also empty. The bed, dressers and mirror were all gone. Thomas looked down at exactly where he'd stood that fateful night, but there was no indication of foul play anymore. There was nothing left to show that his father had been murdered in this very room.

"Is this the place?" Laura gently asked.

Thomas only nodded in return. After lingering for a few seconds more he purposefully and reverently walked around where his father had lain and headed towards the study. The large desk he'd seen his father work at was missing and the room looked bigger than he'd remembered. He turned around and saw the massive safe standing exactly where it had always been. Two ominous hooks were also attached to the wall above the safe, now empty.

"You weren't kidding, this safe is a monster."

"I can still hear my father's voice telling me never to touch it."

Thomas pulled out his grandfather's letter and dialed in the combination. His hands shook a little. When he was done he hesitated and then turned the handle. The safe begrudgingly unlocked and he pulled. It swung open, squeaking ever so slightly. Laura tried to peer over his shoulder to see what treasure lay inside but it was completely empty except for a single white envelope that sat alone on one of the shelves. He carefully retrieved it.

"What is it?"

"It's another envelope, just as old, with my father's handwriting."

"Anything else?

Thomas took another look around the safe. "Nothing."

Thomas opened it and removed two pieces of paper.

My dearest Tommy,

I don't expect you to ever read this letter. I think I'm just writing to get my feelings out. I had written you another letter, which I gave to your grandfather earlier, and I'm going to get that back so I can burn it along with this one. But I needed to write so I could thank you. You gave me the strength I needed tonight. I almost did it. I was there and I almost did it. I almost became the monster I was trying to save you from. Please forgive me. We'll find another way. You give me strength, Tommy. I love you.

    Dad

The letter slipped from Thomas's hand and fluttered to the floor as his knees weakened. He sat down before he collapsed.

"Are you alright?" Laura hovered over him.

"I'll need a moment."

She saw the loose letter. "May I?" Thomas nodded.

As Laura started reading it he noticed he had the second piece of paper still in his hand. He looked at it. The title confused him.

Transcript of Tommy Clark, son of Michael Clark
Monday December 11, 1967 12:23 p.m.
John Muir Hospital

"Hi mommy." (TC)
 "I miss you mommy." (TC)
"I'm always good." (TC)

"Who are you talking to son?" (MC)

"I ate all my food today. I'm part of the clean your plate club!" (TC)

"Don't go mommy. Don't go!" (TC)

"Come back!" (TC)

"Tommy, what's wrong?" (MC)

"Mommy, come back!" (TC)

"Nurse! Nurse!" (MC)

"I love you too mommy." (TC)

Old memories tickled Thomas' memory, taunting him. He was in the hospital. He had almost died.

"Thomas? Thomas?" Laura was shaking him.

He looked at her, confused.

"Where were you right now?"

"I....I was at the hospital. I was talking with my mother." He handed her the transcript.

"I don't see her talking, Thomas." Laura looked at the date. "Wait. This is five years after..."

"I know," Thomas interrupted. "Five years after she was dead. But I remember the conversation now."

"Hi mommy." (TC)

"Hello sweetheart."

"I miss you mommy." (TC)

"I miss you too. Have you been a good boy?"

"I'm always good." (TC)

"Who are you talking to son?" (MC)

"I ate all my food today. I'm part of the clean your plate club!" (TC)

"I'm so proud of you honey. I have to go now Tommy."

"Don't go mommy. Don't go!" (TC)

"I'll see you again, don't you worry. Remember, everything will be just fine."

"Come back!" (TC)

"Tommy, what's wrong?" (MC)

"I love you."

"Mommy, come back!" (TC)

"Nurse! Nurse!" (MC)

"I love you too mommy." (TC)

Thomas looked at Laura and there were tears running down his face. "I miss them both so much." She pulled him in close and comforted him as best as she could.

"It's going to be okay. Your parents loved you very much and I love you very much."

He squeezed her. "I love you too, Laura." He wiped his face. "I'm okay. I'm good now." Thomas stood up.

"What do you want to do now?" she asked.

He took another long look around his father's study and then back at her. "I can't change the past but I can control my future. Tomorrow is a brand new day. It's time to sell this house and move on. Tomorrow we'll find our new house, and plan our future."

65
Wednesday August 8, 1990

Before they left the Bay Area Laura and Thomas had found a lovely four bedroom house in Tiburon. As it turned out their new house was only a few miles away from Sam and Bill's. The sellers were apparently fans of Thomas' books and agreed to let them move in prior to escrow.

Upon returning to SoCal they had descended upon Thomas' house and, in two days, had packed his entire house. The moving van had arrived that morning, loaded up and was currently traveling north. The realtor Thomas was there when the van pulled away.

"Mr. James, thanks for coming by this morning," Thomas said. "This is Dr. Laura Bond."

"Very nice to meet you, Laura," he said as he shook her hand. Mr. James turned to Thomas. "I'll handle all the details, Thomas. You had quite a run up here. Our little town is going to miss you."

Thomas looked around slowly at the outside of his house and then handed his house keys to Mr. James. "Thank you." Thomas looked at Laura and said, "But it's time to move on to something better."

*   *   *

That night, at Laura's house, after a few hours of initial packing, the doorbell rang.

"I'll get it," Thomas called out.

He headed to the front door, opened it and paid for the Domino's pizza. He closed the door, took it over to the couch and placed it on the table.

483

"What can I get you to drink?"

"A beer sounds perfect right about now," Laura called from the back.

Thomas pulled two Coronas from the fridge, opened them and sat them down on the table as well. He opened the pizza box and the fresh, hot smell wafted up. He unpackaged some birthday candles he had seen in one of the kitchen drawers and positioned six of them in the pizza. He struck a match and lit them.

"What is that delicious smell?" she asked as she entered the room, clearly exhausted.

As she eyed the pizza, and the lit candles, Thomas turned to her and started to sing, "Happy Birthday to you. Happy Birthday to you. Happy Birthday to Laurrrraaaa. Happy Birthday day tooooo yooooouuuuu."

She had a big grin on her face and came over. Thomas gave her a huge birthday hug.

"I love you," he said. "Bet you thought I'd forgot?"

"I had my doubts," she replied, "but I also thought you were being extra sneaky today."

He handed her a beer. "With everything going on I haven't had time to buy you a present. I'll make it up to you," he promised.

She took a long swig and put it down. "With everything that's happened we're lucky to be standing here with each other sweetie. Thank you for my birthday cak..er...pizza." She smiled and moved in close to Thomas. "As for making it up to me....you can start right now."

* * *

Monday August 13, 1990

Thomas and Laura were beat from packing for the past week and their second moving van left San Bernardino, heading north Friday afternoon and would arrive at the house on Sunday. They made a final sweep of her house and then got in her Volvo. For the next seven hours they travelled north, taking turns, and it was dark when they crossed the San Rafael Bridge and made their way into Tiburon.

That weekend they relaxed and spent time with Bill and Sam's family, getting to know each other and play with the two girls. Laura couldn't be happier with Thomas. She had taken a risk and everything had worked out. She also noticed that he was very happy to be around his best friends again, not that it would have been easy to hide. His face glowed.

On Sunday, as the moving vans arrived, Sam and Bill helped them move two houses worth of boxes and furniture into their new one. It went relatively quickly and that evening Thomas took everyone out to dinner at a local restaurant for a great time. They came home pooped, but very happy. Laura dug some bed sheets out of a box while Thomas unceremoniously dumped a mattress on the floor that had been leaning against a wall. They washed up, made the bed, and climbed in, snuggling close against each other.

"I love you, Laura," Thomas said a few minutes later.

Laura turned and looked at him, smiling. "I love you too."

"I know things seem to be moving pretty quickly but I want you to know that I trust you. What we have makes me feel really good inside. Thanks for taking a risk on me."

She caressed his face. "I should be the one thanking you. We ended up saving each other." She kissed him deeply.

Thomas broke the kiss and sat up.

485

"What is it?" Laura asked.

"I have something else to tell you and I'm not sure you're going to like it."

She sat up and looked at him. He was nervous. *Uh oh. What could he possibly be hiding?*

"Laura."

"Yes?"

"Will you marry me?" Thomas smiled.

Laura beat on his chest with her fists. "You bastard! You had me going." She laughed. "And yes, yes you silly man, I'll marry you."

*   *   *

Sunday October 14, 1990

"Happy Birthday, bro," Thomas said as Bill opened the front door to let them in.

"Happy Birthday," Laura said and gave Bill a hug.

"I should have birthdays more often," he said as he returned the hug, "I could get used to this."

"Hey now, get off of my fiancé," Thomas joked.

Bill let her go and pulled Thomas in for a bear hug. "Good to see you too, bro."

"Thanks for the invite."

"Like you could help yourself. You know you can't resist any party that I host," Bill said as he smiled.

"Where can I put the wine?" Laura asked.

Bill pointed to the kitchen. "The other hens are in there," he jested.

Laura hit him on the shoulder on her way by.

"Ouch," he feigned then looked at Thomas. "She's a keeper, bro. What can I get you to drink?"

"A beer's good."

"One beer coming right up. I'll meet you in the living room."

Bill walked off to the kitchen. Thomas headed around the corner and saw Sam and Nick talking on the couch. They looked up.

"Hey, good to see you," Sam said

"Hey, Thomas," Nick said.

"Well holy shit. Nick, I didn't know you were going to be here." Thomas walked over and shook his hand before sitting down.

"If they had told me you were going to be here I wouldn't have come." Nick smiled.

"Yeah, yeah, fuck you too," Thomas replied. "Is Susan here?"

"In the kitchen with little Lisa. Sam and Bill's girls are loving her to death."

"Cute."

"Speaking of cute, Thomas, you really powered through your new book. My people can't get enough of it. How the hell did you get it done so quickly?"

Thomas had stopped working on 'The Haunted Trees'. Since the move he'd started a new book called 'Make Me'. It was about bullies and how they don't have any real power over you.

Thomas glanced over at Sam and then turned back to Nick. "Let's just say that I had some inspiration. I'm happy to hear that they like it."

"I'm telling you, Thomas, they want more, but we'll talk business later."

Bill walked in with a beer, gave it to Thomas and sat down. "Did you tell him?"

Sam spoke up, "I haven't had a chance. Mr. Agent man over here just keeps yapping away." Nick held up his beer in a mock toast as he gave Sam the bird with his other hand. They all chuckled.

"What's up, Sam?" Thomas asked.

"Well, thanks to your shenanigans SANDBOX now has overseas contracts. We're sending some of our people to the Gulf as security liaisons."

"That's great," Thomas said.

"You're damn right it is," Bill added. "This will only allow us to grow the business since it gives us global opportunities."

"Well, a toast then," Thomas said, "to everyone's success."

They all raised their bottles and drank deeply.

* * *

Bill pointed to the kitchen. "The other hens are in there."

Laura hit Bill on the shoulder and headed towards the kitchen with the white wine they'd brought. Julie and Kim, along with their daughters Amanda and Sarah, were talking to a third woman who held a baby. Laura recognized her and suppressed a smile.

"Hey Julie. Hey Kim." They hugged.

"So good to see you," Kim said. "Have you met Susan, Nick's wife?"

Susan turned a little white. "Hello, Susan," Laura said.

"Hi Dr. Bond...I mean...Laura," Susan replied, a little nervous.

"Oh," Kim said looking at both of them, "you know each other?"

Susan pleaded to Laura with her eyes.

"In a manner of speaking," Laura said smiling. "Here's some wine," she said deflecting.

"Thanks Laura," Julie said. "Let me pour you a glass of what we're working on."

"Hello girls," Laura said as she bent down and hugged Amanda and Sarah who had attached themselves to her legs. "Wow, they're getting big."

"Every day it's something new," Kim said. "How's the new house?"

"We're contemplating a little remodeling of the master bedroom, but aside from that we couldn't be happier." Laura stood up.

"And your practice?" Julie asked as she handed over a glass of wine.

"Thanks, but I can't drink."

"You're not..." insinuated Julie.

"I am!" Laura excitedly confirmed.

"Oh my god. Come here!" Kim said as they hugged. "Congratulations!"

"That is fantastic news, Laura." Julie came around and hugged Laura as well. "I'm so excited for you two. Any indication of what it's going to be."

"Congratulations," Susan added.

"The doctor said it's too early to tell but my gut says it's going to be a girl."

"If it is it'll drive all the men crazy. We'll have our own little three musketeers that will look out for each other. This is so exciting!" Kim said.

"Thanks. You guys are the best. As for my practice I'm close to finding an office. I thought about San Francisco but I've been getting used to Marin and it's been growing on me. But now with the baby on the way I'm going to hold off for at least a year."

"Good for you. Marin is beautiful," Julie commented.

"We're really happy here too," said Kim.

"Oh, this is going to be so much fun!" said Julie. "Do the boys know?"

"Not unless Thomas has said something. We might as well go surprise them." Laura smiled.

* * *

"Well, a toast then," Thomas said, "to everyone's success."

Laura, Kim, Julie and Susan walked into the room followed by Amanda and Sarah. They all sat down and the two little girls climbed on their mother's lap. Lisa was asleep in Susan's arms as she and Nick exchanged nervous glances. Laura caught this.

"Don't worry, Nick. Your secret is safe with me." Laura grinned.

"What are you talking about," Bill asked.

"Laura is pregnant," Susan blurted out.

"With Nick's baby?".

"Nick, I had no idea. You sonofabitch," Thomas joked. "Actually, the baby is mine. We didn't want to tell anyone till we were a few months in."

"Way to go, Thomas," Bill said.

"Nicely done," Sam added. "Congratulations."

Nick looked relieved and said, "That's fantastic, Thomas."

"Thanks everyone. We couldn't be happier. Here's to family and friends." Thomas raised his bottle high.

"Here, here," came the unanimous reply.

* * *

Later that evening, after the birthday dinner and festivities, Thomas and Laura watched as Kim tucked Sarah and Amanda into bed.

"What bed time story would you like?" Kim asked them.

They both pointed to 'The Little Brown Chair."

Kim looked over at Thomas. "It's their favorite. Would you mind?"

Laura squeezed Thomas' hand. "Sure, I'd love to," he said and took the familiar, and well used book from Kim's hands. He sat down on the edge of the bed and the two girls couldn't wait. Kim joined Laura at the doorway just as Julie approached. Thomas opened the book and began reading about the amazing adventures of the Little Brown Chair."

www.ingramcontent.com/pod-product-compliance
Lightning Source LLC
Chambersburg PA
CBHW071630260626
47170CB00001B/42